THE HINDMOST

Also by William Paul:
SEASONS OF REVENGE
MUMMY'S BOY

THE HINDMOST

William Paul

Macdonald

A Macdonald Book

Copyright © William Paul 1988

First published in Great Britain in 1988
by Macdonald & Co (Publishers) Ltd
London & Sydney

All characters in this publication are fictitious and any resemblance to real persons, living or dead, is purely coincidental.

All rights reserved
No part of this publication may be reproduced, stored in a retrieval system, or transmitted, in any form or by any means without the prior permission in writing of the publishers, nor be otherwise circulated in any form of binding or cover other than that in which it is published and without a similar condition including this condition being imposed on the subsequent purchaser.

Paul, William, *1955–*
The hindmost.
I. Title
823'.914 [F] PR6066.A883/

ISBN 0-356-15036-4

Typeset by Leaper & Gard Limited, Bristol
Printed in Great Britain by Redwood Burn Ltd
Bound at the Dorstel Press

Macdonald & Co (Publishers) Ltd
Greater London House
Hampstead Road
London NW1 7QX

A member of Pergamon MCC Publishing Corporation plc

For Mum and Dad

Know ye not that they which
run in a race run all, but one
receiveth the prize? So run,
that ye may obtain.

Epistle to the Corinthians 9:24

The mud was twelve inches deep in the narrow channel cut into the side of the steep embankment which carried the autobahn the last few kilometres towards the border beyond the West German town of Herleshausen. Water seeped into the low-lying patch of ground round the entrance, keeping it permanently wet even in the height of summer. The hooves of the dairy herd which regularly occupied the field it was part of had churned the mud into a glutinous morass of peaks and troughs. The weak moonlight that escaped from behind the sky's ragged covering of cloud lay unevenly across its surface, creating a static pattern of silver and black like the reflection of a frozen sea.

The open channel was barely four feet wide and lined by smooth concrete walls, running with damp, that followed exactly the slope of the embankment. After ten feet it became a tunnel stretching several yards underground in a straight line. The tunnel was high enough for a man to walk into it and ended with a barred gate across its width immediately in front of a solid steel door. Both gate and door were secured by two separate locks; one combination and one conventional. On the top left-hand corner of the door, just above the bulge of the hinge, a rectangular strip of much newer and much shinier steel had been riveted. On it was etched a stylized drawing of a pair of bull's horns and the word Minotaur followed by the figure thirteen in Roman numerals. The tunnel was pitch black but every now and then enough moonlight escaped from behind the clouds to penetrate as far as the door and make the strip of steel glow faintly, like the eye of an animal looking out of the darkness.

Hugh Divers could see the occasional blink of light from whcrc hc was forty yards away, seated on the stony bottom of a drainage ditch with his back propped against the corner post of the fence that marked the northern boundary of the field. Most of the time he concentrated on the wide, grassy plateau area directly in front of him where the two dozen cows were now grazing peacefully, their fat carcases and heavy udders dimly silhouetted against the dirty grey sky. But whenever the name tag on the chamber door flashed he would shift his gaze to the channel entrance on his left and nod confidently as though it was some agreed signal and he and it were old friends waiting together with a common purpose. The name tag was new. It had not been there when he had had the responsibility of depositing the Minotaur behind the door. Nothing else had changed though. The locks were the same. The system was the same. And the mud, of course.

Divers had been sitting in the same place for two hours since arriving at midnight. It had taken him more than twenty minutes to reach the spot by walking cross country from where he had left Gudrun and the car in a lay-by on a secluded back road. It was a cold night but he was well clothed beneath his British army combat uniform with the bright major's pips on the epaulettes. He was unarmed, and his face was blackened. Fingerless gloves kept his hands warm. Reaching up he scratched the coarse stubble on his chin. He could have chosen any site from one to thirty-eight. He had chosen thirteen because he knew it well. The choice of any site was a gamble. If an officer had appeared he would have melted anonymously into the background and waited another two weeks for another opportunity. But no officer had come, and it was probably too late for one to do so now. Divers was on his own in the field, just him and the herd of cows. The number thirteen, he thought, is unlucky for some.

He lifted his eyes to watch a coach speed past the screen of young trees covering the top half of the embankment. Its windows blazed a flickering trail of yellow light, leaving a smeared impression on his dark-accustomed eyes that quickly faded with the sound of the engine. The traffic was few and far between. That had been the first vehicle for at least ten minutes. The restless silence of the night settled around him once more and he turned his attention to the elevated plateau a quarter of a mile away. The cows had all drifted across to one corner, following some communal instinct. He imagined he could hear the sound of their teeth tearing mouthfuls of the lush grass out of the ground. They would be ready for milking soon, probably at dawn, around five. Their milk would be warm. As a boy, Divers had once been taken to a farm and shown how to milk a cow by hand. It had surprised him that the milk had come out warm and foaming. Somehow, he had assumed it would be as cold as the stuff in the glass bottles he had used to deliver to hundreds of doorsteps every morning before going to school. It was hard work milking a cow, he remembered, rubbing his hands together. Sore on the wrists.

He saw the helicopter moments before he heard it. A movement on the horizon made him look up. At first he thought it was just a loose scrap of cloud but then the distant wop-wop noise of the rotor blades reached him, and the movement rapidly resolved itself into the awkward shape of a Puma troop-carrying helicopter. It came in low and fast from the west, the noise of the blades advancing well ahead of it. Its approach sent the herd of cows stampeding down the hill towards the safety of the opposite end of the field.

Divers did not move but the adrenalin began to flow in his blood and his whole body stiffened and tensed. He could feel the vibration caused by the cattle's hooves shaking the ground all around him as they passed. The outer fringe of the down draught was cold against his cheeks and nose. It tugged at his hair. The black-painted Puma hovered for a few seconds, turning broadside on as the undercarriage was lowered, then it bumped down. As it touched one man jumped out and turned to help another who was carrying a square, bulky back-pack. They ran, doubled over, in the direction of the autobahn, straightening up as soon as they were out from under the spinning circle of the blades. The helicopter was already rising from the landing zone. It retracted its wheels, rotated through one hundred and eighty degrees, and flew off to the north.

Divers watched it go. He had jumped from a Puma, probably that very machine, with a Minotaur pack on his back many times. He had landed in this field and in many others along the border. He had caged the beast in the chamber and then waited patiently to be picked up again to return to the Paderborn base with the seven other Minotaur teams covering their sector. It was a simple exercise once you had done it a few times. The most exciting thing about it was the helicopter flight.

The two soldiers were trotting unhurriedly in single file along the foot of the embankment down the hill towards the chamber entrance. They stopped at the edge of the apron of mud and turned to face each other. Divers smiled. He could see that they were complaining to each other about the mud, although the words were inaudible. He had done it himself at this place. He had made a formal complaint about the state of the ground to his superior officers but nothing had ever been done.

A car passed by on the autobahn above the soldiers and they crouched down instinctively. The headlights poking through the trees briefly swept over their faces, outlining the features. Divers saw that one was a young boy, maybe nineteen years old, baby faced with large eyes and the tips of his ears squashed down by the rim of his beret. The other one was not much older but he was more heavily built and looked more mature, more manly in appearance. He had the Minotaur pack which he unclipped from the shoulder harness, lowered to the ground and began fiddling with the canvas covering. The young boy took his companion's Bullpup rifle and balanced it against his own so that they stood up with the stubby barrels off the ground out of the dirt. Then he went to the edge of the mud and took a long, tentative step out into it. Divers heard him swear loudly as his foot sank in and his leg disappeared up to the calf. The boy brought his other leg over and began to wade slowly through the heavy mud into the channel itself. He held his arms out to either side for balance and his fingertips brushed along the dripping concrete walls. His outline faded as he was swallowed by the darkness of the tunnel.

Divers waited. He knew when he would make his move. Without looking down he gripped the lanyard hanging round his neck and worked his fingers along it until they found the whistle at its end. He raised it to his mouth and held it there in readiness.

There was a distant metallic clunk as the gate was swung

back against the wall. A few moments later another noise followed it, this time of metal grating on metal; the chamber door swinging open. Thirteen, Divers thought as he got to his knees, is unlucky for some. He could see that a faint glow was now coming from inside the tunnel. The young soldier emerged into the outer channel, walking stiffly, his progress marked by the sucking, squelching sound of each footstep. Divers stood up and began walking towards the embankment. He took a deep breath, placed the whistle between his lips, and blew a long, piercing blast that ripped through the night air. The cows that had been quietly moving back across the field turned and ran again.

The two soldiers froze, startled by the sudden loud noise. Then they tried to go for the guns. The boy standing in the mud tried to move too quickly and his feet could not follow him. He toppled onto his face. The other soldier's hand was within inches of his rifle when it stopped as if skewered on the shrill sharpness of the whistle's second blast.

Divers stopped ten feet away and folded his arms over his chest. 'As you were, soldiers,' he said aggressively. 'I'm here to tell you what you're doing wrong.'

The boy in the mud struggled to his feet and stood to attention, uncertain whether he should move across onto firm ground without a clear order to do so. The older soldier slowly straightened from his half-crouching position. His adam's apple bobbed up and down in his throat as he swallowed the saliva that had suddenly collected there. The boy finally made up his mind that he ought to extricate himself from the mud and struggled free. He tried to brush the mess off his combat jacket but only succeeded in making it worse. Some mud got in his eye and he tried to wipe it away with a sodden sleeve. The two of them stood shoulder to shoulder in front of the Minotaur pack like a couple of naughty schoolboys about to learn what punishment they must suffer for their bad behaviour.

'I said as you were, soldiers,' Divers repeated. 'That means at ease.'

Two pairs of eyes stared resolutely over his head. Both soldiers relaxed slightly and stood with their legs apart and their hands clasped behind their backs. A cow lowed mournfully and another answered. The herd's curiosity overcame its fear and the beasts gradually came closer to the source of activity in their field. Divers walked round behind the two soldiers who continued to stare straight ahead.

'Do you know who I am?' he asked.

Neither of them offered an answer. Divers went up behind the young boy so that his lips were only inches from his ear. A rash of spots ran from his neck over his chin and onto his cheek. 'Do you know who I am?' he asked again.

'Field supervision officer, Sir,' the boy replied loudly.

Divers stepped back. 'That's right and it's obvious you didn't expect to meet me tonight, did you? I'm the nasty major who checks up on you when you're let loose to see that you don't just curl up in a ball and go to sleep, or that you don't flog off our friend here on the black market.'

He touched the Minotaur with his toe. The camouflaged canvas was half off and he could see the bull's-horns symbol stencilled in luminous red paint on the metal side. A break in the clouds passed in front of the moon and every shadow seemed to move six inches to the right.

'I observed you as you left the chopper and crossed the open ground to the chamber entrance. If I was an innocent member of the public I might well have gained the impression that the two of you were going on a picnic, or that you were looking for flowers to make daisy chains.' Divers bent down and picked up one of the rifles, letting the other one fall over. 'Tell me. Is that what you are here for?'

'No sir,' they answered together.

'No. Have we so soon forgotten our training? Do we stroll down to cage the beast in the same way we would walk down the street to post our football pools coupon, or a letter to our loved ones back home?'

'No sir,'

'No. That is correct,' Divers said, walking back round to the front. 'We act as if war was declared five minutes ago.' His voice began to rise. 'We are on our guard every second we are out here. We act with speed and urgency at all times. Every sense should be straining to detect the enemy. We should be watchful and alert. One thing we most certainly do not do is dump our weapons on the ground because they are too heavy for our delicate hands.'

'No sir,'

'No sir. You're bloody right sir,' Divers shouted. 'Tell me men, just what would you do if the Red Army hordes came over the brow of that hill at this very moment.'

There was no reply.

'Well? What?'

'Defend ourselves,' the young boy said.

Divers thrust the rifle into his hands, knocking the boy off balance so that he had to take a step backwards to steady himself. 'With this.' Divers almost screamed. 'You would defend yourself with this.'

'Yes sir,' he snapped back.

'Tell me what is wrong with that rifle,' Divers said more quietly.

The boy looked down at the gun in his hands, confused. The other soldier continued to stare directly ahead. The air suddenly became laced with tiny drops of rain. The boy looked up, his eyes blank with incomprehension. He shook his head dumbly.

Divers sighed theatrically and took the rifle from him. 'The safety catch is on,' he said slowly, spacing the words out. 'On active service you should always be prepared to go into instant action. In a confrontation situation it would be easy to forget to take off the safety catch and any Commie with his finger on the trigger would have the advantage, wouldn't he?'

'Yes sir.'

'And we never put our rifle down. We have it in our hands or on the carrying strap at all times. It is part of our bodies. Without it we bleed. What happens?'

'We bleed sir,' they said together.

Divers thumbed off the safety catch and went round behind the two soldiers again. 'We have been very careless tonight, haven't we?' he said.

'Yes sir.'

'Shall I tell you what becomes of people who get too careless?' he said, placing the rifle butt against his own shoulder and the muzzle a few inches from the nape of the young boy's neck. 'Well, would you like to know?'

'Yes sir.'

'They die soldier. They die.'

Divers squeezed the trigger and felt the mild recoil push into his shoulder. The crack of the shot hardly seemed to make any sound at all. The boy jerked forward as though he had been thumped in the back. His hands went up to his throat as he sank to his knees, gargling on the blood pouring from the exit wound torn in the front of his neck. The other soldier turned his head, his face white with shock. Divers swung the rifle, sighting along the barrel, and fired a second time. The bullet caught its target right between the eyes. He jerked into the air as though his feet had been kicked out from under him and landed on his back, dead before he hit the ground.

Divers walked round and looked down on the young boy, staring back into the huge, wondering eyes. He was on his side, lying in the foetal position. It took less than a minute for him to die. His hands at his throat could not staunch the flow of blood, black in the moonlight, as it poured out of him. He could not stop the life leaving him. His eyes blinked and then closed. The night seemed to grow darker. The rain started to fall more persistently.

With both members of the Minotaur team dead, Divers began to work with controlled haste. First he picked up the young boy in his arms and waded into the mud. It was hard going in the mire, but Divers knew that the best way to move was to high-step like a prancing horse, taking long strides. The boy was not very heavy but it was awkward to manoeuvre him along the narrow channel and into the tunnel. The chamber gate and door were both standing open as Divers had expected. The interior of the chamber was illuminated by a faint white light. He lifted the body onto the waist-high ledge and pushed it as far back as it would go, jamming it against the panel of electronic equipment at the rear. He went back to get the other body, picking it up in the same manner but then shifting it onto his shoulder because it was much heavier. It took him longer to reach the chamber with the second one. He stumbled in the mud at the entrance to the channel and struck the side of his head against the concrete wall. He was stunned for a few seconds and remained where he was resting against the wall with the rain falling on his hair. Blood trickled down over his cheek and into the corner of his mouth, warm and salty. He liked the taste of it on his tongue.

The two bodies fitted into the chamber snugly. He swung the steel door shut which locked itself automatically, and spun the combination numbers at random. Then he closed the gate and did the same. When he came out of the channel the dairy herd was ranged round the muddy patch watching him curiously. One turned away as he emerged and kicked its hind legs in the air. The rest did not move. They just stood there, their jaws working continuously.

Divers replaced the canvas covering on the Minotaur and stuffed the two rifles down the side. He hoisted the pack onto his back and set out across the field. Some of the cows started to follow him.

It had taken him twenty minutes to get from his car to the chamber site. Jogging, it took him only ten minutes to get back. The white Audi with rust bubbles on the wings and sills was parked well off the road. A few early Autumn leaves had fallen onto its roof. The person in the driver's seat stirred as he opened the boot and put in the Minotaur pack and the rifles. He stripped off the camouflage jacket and the rest of the badly blood-stained uniform and his boots and threw them in as well. He rubbed his hair dry with an old towel and pulled on a new pair of shoes and a quilted anorak before going round and getting into the passenger's seat.

The driver was a woman with short blonde-streaked hair and a sharp nose like a bird's beak. She fidgeted nervously as Divers settled into the seat beside her. She was clutching the steering wheel too tightly.

'Did you get it?' she asked, speaking first in German then repeating herself in English.

'Like taking sweeties from a bairn,' he replied.

'Really?'

He grinned in the darkness of the car. 'If you're a good girl I'll let you see it when we get home.'

'You're bleeding,' she whispered urgently.

He put his fingers to the side of his face and felt the crusty trail of dried blood over his skin. He took a tissue from a box on the dashboard, spat on it and began to wipe at the blood. 'If you think this is bleeding you should see the other two,' he said, laughing loudly. 'Come on Gudrun. Take me home.'

She started the engine and the car pulled out from the shelter of the trees onto the empty road. A single sweep of the windscreen wipers cleared the glass of the scattered collection of raindrops. Immediately new pinpoints of rain began to appear. The helicopter would be back at the field in about half an hour, Divers thought. What would happen then was anyone's guess. To the best of his knowledge they had never lost a Minotaur team before. He laughed again and saw Gudrun glance sideways at him. She was uncertain at first then she too began to laugh.

The house on the outskirts of Calais was a large modern one with a gently curving, smoked-glass sun porch running the entire length of one side. It stood in more than an acre of its own grounds, completely surrounded by a ten-foot-high wall which was broken only by the solid wooden driveway gates and the small wooden door alongside set into the actual stonework. Joe MacDonald had first seen the house through the crack where the gates joined in the middle. It looked a likely prospect so he followed the perimeter wall round until he found a suitable tree that offered him a leg-up onto the top. He sat there for a while, hidden among the leaves of an overhanging branch, watching for any sign of life while the morning sun grew steadily warmer. Birds and insects were the only things that moved in the secluded garden. The black shutters on the house windows remained firmly closed. There was no one at home.

The ferry from Dover had dumped its load in a near-deserted Calais at three in the morning, having been delayed at its home port for several hours by industrial action among the crew. The tourist season was still at its peak so the ferry was packed with crowds of impatient, grumbling people. MacDonald stayed out on deck, claiming a place to lay out his sleeping bag among the dozens of others which formed a long row along the rail. Most of his companions were younger than him and MacDonald enjoyed chatting up the fresh-faced teenagers on either side. There was only one girl on view he really fancied but she had a sullen boyfriend who kept her well out of harm's way. MacDonald saw only one person in the row who was older than him; a tall, grey-haired man with unhealthily thin arms and legs who spoke to no one and found his own private little corner under a lifeboat to sleep in. When the ferry finally got under way. MacDonald lay on his back with his hands clasped behind his head feeling the vibration of the engines through the hard deck and looking up at the patterns of stars slipping past.

The last of his money had gone on the ferry ticket. He had hitch-hiked south with almost two thousand pounds to play with after being laid off from his job at the oil-rig repair yard at Ardersier, near Inverness. It was what he had managed to accumulate over three months of non-stop, seven-days-a-week work and it was supposed to finance a long holiday on familiar ground in Europe. Instead, he had blown everything but a pocketful of change on an unplanned, ten-day binge in London which began in the best hotels with the most expensive women and ended sharing bottles of cheap wine with the derelicts down by the banks of the Thames. It had been a choice between another few bottles or the ferry ticket. MacDonald had given himself a shake and bought the ticket. He did, after all, have somewhere to go in Europe, a destination to travel towards. There was nothing for him back home.

The soulless harbour at Calais in the half-light before the dawn had seemed to him extraordinarily welcoming. He could see no real reason for the mood of sudden optimism but he was prepared to enjoy it while it lasted. When he stepped ashore in France among yawning, sleepy-eyed crowds he did not wait for the lorries and cars to come off so that he could hitch a lift, but wandered off into the town on the look-out for an opportunity to do a spot of breaking and entering. If he could restore his finances he would feel even better.

MacDonald threw down the nylon holdall containing all his possessions and jumped from the top of the wall after it, then threaded his way through a fringe of bushes to the edge of the main lawn. It ran right up to the front of the house except for the last five or six yards where the driveway flattened out to give cars a turning space. There was a blue burglar alarm box above and to the side of the front door. He went round the house checking all the ground-floor windows and the porch for possible entry points. Guessing that all the glass would be wired to set the alarm off if it was broken, he thought about smashing one of the windows anyway and going straight in to turn the system off inside. A few minutes of ringing would be unlikely to attract any attention, but there was always the possibility that a place like this was linked to the local police station. If the house was owned by a local celebrity or rich businessman the gendarmes would come running hot-foot.

He found what he wanted at the garage which was attached to the rear of the house. A window in its side wall had been broken and boarded up with a single panel of plywood. It gave easily as he punched each of the four corners to knock the nails out. It was awkward for him to get his body through the relatively small space. Eventually he had to climb through head first and roll over onto his shoulder and back on the dusty floor inside.

It was a huge garage with room for at least three cars but containing only one, a small Renault hatchback. The pale sunshine streaming through the gap where the window had been boarded up shone on its red bonnet like a spotlight. It was cold and gloomy inside the garage. Particles of dust floated in the square shaft of light. MacDonald hurried across the floor and went up the two steps to the interior door which connected with the house. He tried the handle but it was locked. Swearing under his breath he stood back to kick it, reasoning that the chances were that an interior door would not be linked into the alarm system. If he was wrong, he was ready to run. It took half a dozen hard kicks before it finally gave way. No bells started clamouring. MacDonald smiled, pleased with his luck. He was in.

The garage connected directly to the kitchen. It was spotlessly clean. He could see his reflection disappearing downwards into the shiny floor. He went out into the hall, keeping to the edge of the carpet. If the alarm system used pressure pads they would almost certainly be behind doors and below windows, so he moved about carefully. The electronic control centre for the system was in the most obvious place, a cupboard in the vestibule behind the front door. Small red bulbs glowed at a variety of positions around a schematic diagram of the house, showing where the triggering devices were located. He could not turn off the control centre without the appropriate key but at least he could see what parts of the house to avoid. A few minutes later he realized he did not even have to bother with that. The electricity meter and the mains switch were in a separate cupboard on the opposite side of the vestibule. He threw the switch and all the little red bulbs died together.

MacDonald searched the place systematically, beginning downstairs. He tried to make as little mess as possible because framed photographs in the living room showed a pleasant, middle-aged couple and their adult son and daughter. He liked them without knowing who they were or what they did. It was clear from the quality of the furnishings that they had plenty of money to spread around. They would not miss the tiny bit he hoped to spread around for them. He found it in the downstairs study in the top right-hand drawer of an antique desk. It was a thick pile of crisp, new one-hundred-franc notes. He did not know what the exchange rate was but knew the notes amounted to a fair sum of money. It was certainly enough to keep him going for a while.

Upstairs in one of the small bedrooms there was an old wine bottle full of five-franc coins. He unzipped his bag and emptied the coins into it. In the largest bedroom overlooking the front garden he found a set of car keys on a bedside table. The leather fob had a Renault symbol on it. His luck was holding. They had to be the keys for the car in the garage. That would do him nicely.

He washed and shaved in the bathroom before going downstairs to look for food in the kitchen. All he could find was some hard cheese and some canned peaches, but it filled a hole. Going into the garage he released the lock on the up-and-over door, and was momentarily blinded by the flood of dazzling sunshine as the counterweights swung it open. Blinking to clear his eyes he climbed into the car. The engine started smoothly. There was virtually a full tank of petrol. A paperback road map of France was in the glove compartment. He checked the best route to Paris, deciding that he would abandon the car there, probably before anybody knew he had taken it.

He drove out of the garage and closed the door behind him, and then down to the main gates, where he got out and pushed back the bolts to drag them open. He parked just outside and went back to close the gates again. Quite a number of cars passed as he moved unhurriedly, but none took any notice of him. Taking his time he adjusted the rear-view and the door mirrors, and then started driving away. There was a floating compass attached by a sucker to the dashboard. It showed that the car was travelling south-east.

The heavy metal gate swung open easily on its well-oiled hinges once it had gained momentum. It crashed against the low wall and vibrated strongly until the farmer clipped on the hook to hold it steady. The noisy clatter of the hooves of his herd of cows on the concrete floor of the farmyard was gradually silenced as they moved through the gateway onto the soft ground of the fields. The farmer had a thin stick in his hand. As the last cow went past him, its empty, shrunken udder swinging from side to side, he gave its rump a hard smack. The beast lowed loudly in protest and broke into a shambling trot for a few yards before being stopped as it barged into the backsides of the others in front of it.

The farmer was angry. The herd's milk yield was down again, as it was every time the army helicopters used his field as a landing pad and had the cattle stampeding all over the place. And it always took several days for the low yield to climb to something approaching normal. Then the damned helicopters would be back again to restart the whole process. He told them that if they would only inform him of when they wanted to use the field for an exercise he would move his cows out, but they said that wasn't possible for security reasons. He was reluctant to abandon the field altogether because it was the best grazing land he owned and the compensation he received for the land-mine storage chamber they had built into the embankment was hardly enough to make up for its loss. So kept using the field in normal rotation with his others and kept filing formal complaints every time a helicopter landed. He had negotiated his own personal compensation deal with the army and the agreement was due to be renewed at the end of the year. Every time he complained he reckoned he improved his bargaining position. There would be another complaint sent in tonight, not only about the effect of the helicopter on his cows but also about the fact that he could not use his field because of the soldiers swarming all over it. He could see them in the distance lined up beside the embankment. They must have lost something last night, he thought. Serves the bloody fools right.

He watched as a car came up his driveway and parked beside the farmhouse. He stayed where he was, tipping his fur hat further back on the crown of his head as the driver got out and opened the door for the man in the back seat. The farmer recognized a senior officer by the amount of gold thread on his cap and shoulders. Slipping his thumbs into the braces of his lederhosen he waited sullenly as the officer approached him. The herd of cows stood a few yards to his side, also watching.

'Herr Kessler, I believe you speak English. My name is Brigadier Daniel Evans.' He tapped the side of his beret with his baton in a casual salute.

The farmer carefully examined Evans and then nodded slowly. This was a very high-ranking officer. Dry mud was caked on his boots and on his trousers up to the knee. Something very serious must have happened, Kessler reasoned, for an officer to get himself into a state like that.

'I would just like to ask you a few questions, Herr Kessler,' Evans said. 'Routine stuff. It's all routine.'

Kessler shrugged submissively and leaned against the wall. 'What do you want to know? All I know is that my cows give fewer milk this morning because of the helicopters.' He nodded towards the ragged semi-circle of cows that stood looking at Evans through large, disinterested eyes.

'Quite,' Evans said. 'Did you see the helicopter land in your field down by the autobahn earlier this morning by any chance?'

'No.'

'Did you hear it?'

'I no longer hear it.'

'I see. Can I ask when you brought your herd in for milking.'

'It was about six.'

'Did you notice anything unusual in the field at that time?'

Kessler pursed his lips and shook his head. 'Nothing,' he said.

'What about last night?' Was there anything out of the ordinary last night?'

'Nothing. It was ordinary like any other night.'

'In the last few days have you seen any strangers hanging about your land or around the farm?'

'No one.'

Evans sighed with frustration. He slapped the baton against his thigh and turned his back on the farmer. In the distance he could see the line of the autobahn on the embankment and the dark slash of the Minotaur chamber entrance cut into its side, the apron of mud in front of it hanging out like a tongue. Two dozen soldiers were inching their way across the field, looking for the minutest scrap of evidence. They had already found one of the fatal bullets and it was unlikely there was anything else. A professional job, the platoon commander had said. Our boys were taken out clinically. No sign of a struggle. A very professional job.

The sight of the bodies crammed into the chamber itself had disturbed Evans. The ghostly interior light was all but obscured by their bulk and in the torchlight he had seen them one on top of the other in an untidy embrace. Two hands lay nearest the door, fingers entwined. A young face cushioned against a combat uniform sleeve stared out. The eyes were half closed, the mouth slightly open. The chin was unshaven. At least he had thought it was. When he looked closer he could see that it was actually a film of dried blood. The boy probably hadn't even started shaving.

And the piece of kit was gone, of course. Evans ran his hand over his face. He had known the fact for the last three hours but still could not appreciate it fully. The Minotaur was gone. Whoever had taken it had killed the two soldiers with their own weapons. A very professional job. Evans did not want to believe that it had happened. The sun broke through. He could feel it warm on his face and hands. It was going to be another hot day.

Kessler came up behind him. 'What is it that is going on?' he asked.

Evans turned to face him. This time he was smiling. 'It is

not a serious matter, Herr Kessler, I assure you. Do you have any workers on your farm?'

'I have two men, but they live further away. They would not see anything.'

'Are they here? I must speak with them anyway.'

'One has taken my tractor for repair, the other is somewhere around. I will find him but tell me, if this is not serious, why all the soldiers? Has war broken out?'

Evans laughed politely. If the incident was to be hushed up he would have to provide some kind of rational explanation for all the activity. The farmer looked the kind who would spread news around among his friends. It would be better to influence his version straight away. Evans put a confidential arm on his shoulder.

'To tell you the truth, Herr Kessler, a couple of our lads have decided to take an undeserved holiday.'

Kessler frowned. 'Then why all the searching of the fields? Do you expect to find them in the grass?'

Evans laughed again. 'No, no. They have smashed up some military equipment. Out of spite, you understand? Spite. It was their parting shot.'

'Ah, I see.' Kessler's weather-beaten face cracked in a huge smile, 'They are thumbing their nose at you.'

'That is it exactly,' Evans said. 'But we will catch them. Don't worry.'

Kessler's mood changed abruptly. 'I hope that none of this stuff they break up is eaten by my cows,' he said seriously, looking over at the row of bovine faces solemnly chewing the cud. 'Is it not a pity that they are just dumb animals,' he added.

'Why is that, Herr Kessler?' Evans asked.

'They would have seen everything this morning,' he said. 'They would see which way your men go.'

'Of course,' Evans agreed. 'So they would.'

She had slapped his face. It had been a real, hard, stinging forehand swipe that left an angry red palm print flaring between his temple and his chin. The smacking sound at the point of contact seemed to make the very air between them tremble. Half a dozen pigeons took fright and fluttered clumsily away. Other people milling around outside the great studded doors of Notre Dame Cathedral looked round in surprise and curiosity. Somebody giggled. A few seconds later two young women of her own age who were sitting with their backs to the wall eating sandwiches and drinking from milk cartons started to applaud. She had turned round and made a low, exaggerated bow and by the time she looked up again Dale was walking away, disappearing into the tourist hordes, striding purposefully like a boy scout setting out on a long hike. She had wanted to shout Good Riddance after him but the words stuck in her throat. The reality of being abandoned in a foreign country hit her as hard and suddenly as the slap of her hand against his face. Dale was not, unlike her, given to extravagant gestures. She had never thought he would leave her. She would have to go after him and apologize if she wanted him to stay with her, but that was something she would not do. She did take a few steps in the direction of his swiftly-retreating back but then she stopped and sniffed disdainfully. Let him go, she thought. She would survive. She had a good few hundred Francs and a sheaf of travellers' cheques strapped to her thigh. She would survive without him. Come to think of it, she might even begin to enjoy herself without Dale's pervasive influence dogging her every move. After all, she had only cynically used him to get to Europe. She was here now. She would survive.

Hoisting her rucksack into a more comfortable position, she turned on her heel and walked off in the opposite direction to him. He would, no doubt, come looking for her again once he had cooled down. When he did, she would not give him the satisfaction of being there waiting for him. Paris was a big city. The weather was beautiful. She could sleep on the banks of the Seine. He would never find her. She would survive, come what may.

The wine was dry, fruity and strong. She drank more than half a bottle of the stuff before she realized it. She was sitting at a table of a pavement cafe in a quiet cobbled street with her leg through the shoulder strap of her rucksack lest anyone should try to make a grab for it. There were a number of other people in the cafe, mostly sitting in twos and threes and fours apart from the single bloke in the far corner who was staring straight at her. She had been watching him too, but much more discreetly. He was wide shouldered with dark curly hair and an almost handsome face. His eyes looked hard though, hard in a way that meant he was probably a bastard to every woman he got hold of. A real Gallic animal. His faded jeans were tight round his thighs and his biceps bulged from below the rolled-up sleeves of his tartan shirt. God, she sighed silently, would she never learn. Why was she so attracted to men like that? Why did she always go for the beefcake; no brains, no imagination, just muscle. Maybe it was because she was a piece of cheesecake herself; no brains, no imagination, just a well-packaged female. She breathed deeply so that her stomach was pulled in and her breasts pushed out. What do you think of that then, Frenchie? She bit the inside of her lip to stop a fit of the giggles.

It was a difficult job refilling her wine glass. She knocked the neck of the bottle clumsily against the rim, and then almost choked as she poured more into her mouth than she intended. She tried to have another quick look at her admirer, tried to make it a fleeting, disinterested glance. But he grinned as their eyes met and before she knew what she was doing she was smiling back. Jesus, she thought as the blood came in a sudden rush to her face and she jerked her head away.

Dale had been muscle-bound as well; star running back in the school football team while she had been senior cheerleader. What could have been more natural than such a boy and such a girl getting together. It had been great at first, extremely physical and extremely enjoyable. Then Dale had begun to get funny ideas as he suffered the birth pangs of a Born Again Christian. He began to tell her that sex only had a place inside marriage and it became increasingly difficult for her to argue with him. She only stayed with him because the long-talked-about tour of Europe was so close and she knew full well that her mother and Uncle Teddy would never have contemplated letting her go by herself. Things were cool between her and Dale when they flew out of New York and touched down at Amsterdam. They got progessively worse in the ten days it took them to hitch-hike to Paris. Frustration had a lot to do with it because she was still physically attracted to him and wanted him to make love to her. But he refused. He was too far gone down the road of sainthood to give in to the coarse pleasures of the mortal flesh. Not even in the close confines of their little tent at night could she raise any interest in him. He would just lie there with his lips going, praying for her he said. Nothing she could do, and she tried everything, could bring back the old, randy Dale she preferred, the Dale who would have uprooted the tent pegs such was the frenzy of his passion.

At Notre Dame she had lit a five-franc candle and deliberately avoided putting any money in the honesty box. Outside, Dale had pointed out the oversight and told her he had paid on her behalf. So she had slapped his face and he had walked off into martyrdom. So much for turning the other cheek, she thought. That was what she should have shouted after him, if only she had thought of it at the time. He might have given her a decent shot at his other cheek.

She took another drink. A dribble of wine ran onto her chin and she wiped it away with her thumb. She tilted the chair onto two legs and put her head back with her eyes closed. The sounds of the city swirled around her and it seemed as if the ground was rocking gently to and fro beneath her. She stretched out her legs. She did not notice as the rucksack slipped free and fell over.

'Excuse me Miss Macdonald, I think this belongs to you.'

She opened her eyes and saw that he was holding the rucksack and reading her name where it was stitched into the material above the rectangular Stars and Stripes flag. He spoke perfect English. He sounded like Sean Connery. The voice was almost as sexy as the way he looked. She smiled dumbly up into his lovely green eyes.

'We could be related you know.'

'How's that,' she replied, bringing the seat back onto four legs with a bump.

'My name is MacDonald too. MAC capital D. We're both members of the worldwide clan. We could be related.'

'Hey,' she said seriously. 'You're Scots, aren't you?'

'Born and bred in the mother country itself. You're American, aren't you?'

'How did you guess?' she said, licking her wine-stained lips.

'What do the initials stand for?' he asked, indicating the rucksack.

'P.C. Patricia Chesney Macdonald. My friends call me Peaches.' She was keen to talk and keep him beside her. 'You know why?' she added quickly.

He shook his head and sat down, accepting the unspoken invitation. She could feel his eyes roaming all over her body and she liked the sensation.

'There were two P.C. Macdonalds on the pupil roll at my elementary school in New York. There was me and there was Patricia Charlton Macdonald. So she was written down as P. Char. and I was P. Ches. Peaches it sounds like so Peaches I became. What do I call you?'

'My name is Joe. People sometimes call me Crazy Joe.'

'Why's that?'

''Cause I'm sometimes crazy.'

She had to think about it before she could laugh with him, the man was maybe ten years older than her, maybe not as much as that. There was a delightful masculine smell from him. Perhaps the prayer she had said over the candle in the cathedral that morning was going to be answered after all. She wondered why, out of all the cafes in Paris, she had had the good fortune to choose this particular one.

'So what's a nice girl like you doing in a place like this?' he said.

'We were on a grand tour of Europe,' she replied. 'We were

going to go to Scotland on our way back home. My great, great, great ...' She hesitated, laboriously counting the number of greats over in her head. 'Great, great grandfather emigrated from the Isle of Skye. Have you ever been there?'

'I've been everywhere.'

'What's it like?'

'It's a wild place, wild country. It's beautiful.'

Peaches Macdonald closed her eyes again and tried to imagine the mountains and lochs of Skye. She had seen a picture in a travel book of a huge stag, its antlers framed against a purple sky, looking out over a sheer slope and the tumbling white water of a river. That was Skye, the caption said. A wild place.

'You said we,' MacDonald reminded her. 'There are two of you?'

'Yes,' She opened her eyes and was surprised to see how dark it was. Light bulbs were strung along the underside of the awning above them, glowing alternately orange and white. The cobbles of the street shone silver. Somewhere in the distance an accordion played traditional French street music. It was Paris. She was young. The world was waiting for her to wake up.

'Where is your friend?' he inquired politely, leaning his forearms on the table and making the muscles flex smoothly under the thick browny-red covering of hair.

'My boyfriend?' she said, raising her eyebrows. 'Oh, he left me. Left me all on my own in a strange country. He just upped and left. Deserted me.'

'Now why would he go and do a thing like that?'

'You want to know why?' she said loudly. 'You want to know why?' she repeated, lowering her voice to a hoarse whisper, 'I'll tell you why. It was because he was turning queer on me. That's why.'

A mischievous smile spread all over MacDonald's face. Peaches felt a belch rising in her windpipe and held it down. She leaned forward until her nose was only inches from his. Her hair fell across her eyes and she brushed it away.

'He tried to make out it was because he had been Born Again,' she whispered confidentially. 'Born Again? Huh. He turned queer.'

'Maybe you were just too much for him, Peaches.'

She sat back a little too quickly and her head spun confusingly. She recovered, took another sip of wine, and smiled. Yes, she had decided, she would allow herself to be picked up by this handsome Highlander. The moment he had approached her she had been aware that if he whistled she would come running. Poor Dale. He was probably out looking for her at that very moment, consumed with guilt because he had deserted her. Well, let him suffer. It was him that was on his own now.

The climber wore only boots, a pair of shorts, a belt holding slings and karabiners, and a shirt that flapped open over his chest. Reaching the top of the Hochstein Nadel he sat down on a narrow ledge, coiling his rope neatly at his feet. He was in his late forties with heavily-lined eyes and a sparse covering of hair on the crown of his head. His body was tanned and well muscled. He leaned back on his hands and waited for his breathing to return to normal. All around him the undulating woodlands of the Rheinpfalz swept over the south German countryside. Several other fells, like the pink sandstone pillar he was sitting on, jutted up through the green canopy of trees that was just beginning to take on the first tinge of autumnal colouring. He had climbed them all, and dozens more in other valleys, during the first week of his holiday. In the next seven days he intended to travel even further afield and go back to the fells that offered alternative and more difficult climbing routes. He had hoped to come up the south face of the Hochstein Nadel but had arrived too late in the day and had chosen the much easier route on the other side. There was always another day.

It was late evening. Darkness was crowding on the horizon. The street lights in the town of Dahn just over a mile away were beginning to stand out in the gloom. There was a rectangular tin box cemented into the rock beside the climber's thigh, he levered open the rusty lid and took out a notebook which had a short pencil attached to it by a piece of string. There was just enough space at the bottom of a page for him to squeeze his name in, he wrote; Buster Grant, British Embassy, Bonn.

Then he replaced the notebook in the tin and closed the lid.

Grant stayed sitting where he was while the sky changed to a very dark purple, lightening to a rich red on the far horizon. Looking straight up he saw thousands of stars appearing as though they were specks of silver paint sprayed from an invisible toothbrush. He did not often go climbing these days but the fancy had suddenly taken him after he had read an article on the attraction of the Rheinpfalz crags in the region lying between Saarbrücken and Karlsruhe. The crags were relatively simple and straightforward. There were a few vertical slabs, a good many bulging overhangs, but nothing he could not handle with ease. The rock was soft, and weathering had produced an abundance of hand and footholds easily found by the most inexperienced climber. He did not try to stretch his climbing skills. If something looked too difficult he by-passed it without hesitation. Grant had not been near a proper mountain range in twenty years and had no desire to go back. A couple of hundred feet off the ground was enough for him. He did not want to go any higher.

His father had been about the age Grant was now when he fell. It had been on the Cuillins on the Isle of Skye in March. They were already in trouble, lost in the mist with the compass needle spinning crazily because of all the iron in the rock around them, when the avalanche hit. It struck with no warning at all, pushing them both over the edge of a sheer face. Grant had been saved by his rope and had been left dangling where he could watch his father falling into a deep gulley, bouncing twice off the sloping rock face, sliding spread-eagled round an outcrop of ice, and then smashing into a bare patch of rock and rolling untidily to a halt never to move again. Grant had heard his name ripping through the thin mountain air in a long drawn-out screech till it stopped abruptly, leaving the echo racing outwards to carry the sound into the distance. His father was the only person who ever called him Billy. Everybody else used his nickname, Buster.

An accident, they said. Nobody's fault. Nothing could have been done to save him. Just one of those things. Bad luck. Grant had reached out to his father in a hopeless gesture as he fell and then hung where he was to be buffeted by a stinging wind as the clouds and the mist hid the body far below him so that he thought he might have imagined it all, and then drew back to reveal it so he could not escape the truth. Gradually, the body was concealed by the drifting snow. The mountains burying their dead.

When the rescue team lifted him to safety he led them down to where his father lay and they dug him out. He followed the covered stretcher to a nearby bothy where a sudden storm forced them to shelter for the night with the body in one corner, and the next day down the mountainside to a village well below the snow-line where he had to phone his mother to break the news to her. The police had already informed her, of course, and they cried together over the phone.

Grant had been hugely ambitious before the accident. Afterwards he lost all interest in his career in the Foreign Office where he had risen rapidly through the ranks and had been marked out as a high flyer of ambassadorial potential. He drifted through dozens of overseas postings, got himself married and divorced in the space of two years, and generally let life wash over him. Ten years previously he found himself a pleasant niche in Bonn representing the interests of MI6 in West Germany. He had no ambition to rise any higher in the service. He was happy where he was, doing what he was doing.

He stood up. The lights of Dahn were much more pronounced as grey darkness washed over the valleys. He began to feed his double rope through the iron ring-peg that was embedded in the sandstone just short of the peak of the pillar. Then he tossed the ends over the edge and watched them land on the grass below. He buttoned his shirt, took a pair of gloves from the pocket of his shorts and pulled them on. He put the rope between his legs and diagonally across his chest and over his left shoulder, taking the strain against the anchor peg as he backed out over the edge of the crag. Slowly and carefully, he walked down the vertical face with the soles of his boots against the uneven rock and the uncomfortable friction of the rope rubbing round his body and through his hands. Ten feet from the bottom he released the tension and jumped onto the grass. The rope came down after him with a single jerk to coil at his feet. Looping it round his hand and elbow he carried it towards the car parked a few hundred yards away at the bottom of a heavily-wooded slope.

The faint bleeping of his radio pager was just audible when

he opened the rear door and threw the rope onto the back seat. The batteries were very low, he realized it must have been going soon after he had left the car to climb the crag. That was probably three hours ago because he had been in no hurry. He slid into the passenger seat and dialled the embassy's special number on the mobile phone. It was answered at once and he was transferred to the First Secretary's office. A voice he recognized as Adrian Smart's acknowledged his call and told him he was required to return as soon as possible. No more information could be given because there was no scrambling facility on the car phone link. Grant hung up immediately and climbed over into the driving seat. He drove into Dahn to cancel his room at the pension for the coming week and collect his clothes. He would take time to have a shower because he had been out all day and he needed to freshen himself up before heading north. He was always glad to be called in from leave. It was nice to feel wanted. Bonn was not far away. Perhaps a couple of hours once he got onto the autobahn at Zweibrücken. It would be after midnight when he got there and he might be able to snatch a few hours' sleep before settling down to deal with whatever was causing the great panic.

Peaches Macdonald was woken by a slight movement underneath her. She opened her eyes and saw a tall window with the curtains drawn back. Outside, through the grey, early morning light, she could see shutters tightly closed on the windows opposite. She could hear the traffic in the street below and the distant sound of marching footsteps. The body beneath her moved again. She raised her head a little so that a shop sign appeared above the window sill. It read, Boulangerie. She remembered she was in Paris. She remembered Joe MacDonald. She remembered what had happened and she flushed with embarrassment, quickly closing her eyes to make him think she was still asleep.

The side of her face was lying on a mat of thick brown hair, warm against her skin. A strong heartbeat thumped in her ear. The rest of her was draped down his left-hand side. One arm was over his chest and shoulder, one leg was hooked across his knees. She felt him ease himself out from below her and she flopped face down on the bed. He pulled the sheets up from the small of her back to her neck and she felt his fingers gently stroking her hair behind her ear. Then she sensed that he moved away from the bed and she opened one eye to see what he was doing, and saw that he was standing with his back to her stretching to relieve his stiff muscles, pushing his arms up above his head, almost touching the ceiling. He was completely naked and his whole body was covered in a generous coating of the browny-red hair. It was all over him apart from the soles of his feet and the palms of his hands, like some exotic animal. Framed in the light from the window his outline was not clearly defined at all. It was more like an artist's pencil-drawn figure. He stopped stretching and stood for a few moments looking out the window. Peaches remembered a little more of what had happened during the night and the flush this time was one of pleasure rather than embarrassment.

When he turned towards her she immediately pretended to be asleep again. He must have knelt down in front of her because she could feel his breath on her eyelids and then his fingers in her hair and then his lips on her forehead. She smiled as a finger traced a line across her mouth. She kissed it softly but did not open her eyes. She heard her name whispered in a hoarse voice but did not move although she desperately wanted to reach out to him. He repeated her name but still she did not react. He put a hand under the sheets and ran it down her side and over her hip. Clenching her teeth she gripped the underside of the pillow. A few more seconds and she knew she would not be able to keep the act up. Not that she understood why she was resisting anyway. She wanted him to climb back in beside her so that they could start all over again, so that the two of them could pretend together that the night had never ended. But, just as she was about to roll onto her back for him, he suddenly let go and she heard his feet padding over the carpet. A door clicked open and then closed. There was the muffled sound of running water.

Peaches sat up in the bed and rubbed her eyes. Her rucksack was propped up in the corner of the room, her clothes had been dropped in an untidy heap in front of it. If she wanted to leave, now was her chance. Dale would probably be waiting for her outside Notre Dame Cathedral, all apologies and contrition. She folded her arms and yawned. There was something unsettling about Joe MacDonald, something that was almost frightening. There was a rawness about him, a detachment that made him seem curiously reserved and at the same time coldly aggressive. It also made him tremendously exciting to her. She shrugged. First impressions, she thought, who knows what would be found when they got to know each other better. She certainly had no intention of running out on him. Not yet anyway.

The room was pleasantly warm. The radiator beside the bed was too hot to touch. Its dry heat aggravated the dryness in her throat. She was surprised she did not have a headache after all that she had drunk, but she was very clear headed, and was already laying plans to accompany her new boyfriend on a tour of Europe. She had no idea what he did, or where he was going before he met her last night. But if he wanted company, she was willing.

It was a cheap hotel room. The hems of the sheets were fraying. It consisted of nothing but the bed, which took up at least two thirds of the floor space, and a built-in wardrobe. There were shelved tables on either side of the bed and a long cut in the fabric of the headboard which had been neatly repaired with sewing thread that was not quite the right shade of blue. Getting up she looked out of the window, keeping to one side so that no one would see her if they looked up. She had no idea where they were, presumably still in Paris. The street below was getting busier by the minute. A sudden rush of people emerged from the underground steps leading up from a Metro station, funnelling beneath an intricate wrought-iron arch, and spilling out across the pavements. A newspaper vendor's stall faced the road, its front entirely hidden under columns of colourful newsprint. A line of young trees opposite had round, bushy heads of green leaves.

Peaches found her wristwatch lying on the floor and picked it up. It was just after eight in the morning. She worked out that it was around midnight back home. She reminded herself that she would have to write to her mother as soon as possible, before Dale got in first. She would say that she had met up with another young girl after Dale had left her, a nice Scots girl from the Isle of Skye. Joanne MacDonald, that was the name she would give her imaginary friend. Together they would go round Europe. She and Joanne together.

She pulled on her discarded tee-shirt and checked her jeans. The wad of travellers' cheques was still in the special pouch sewn into the inside leg. As she looked for her knickers in the heap of clothing the sound of running water in the bathroom abruptly ceased. Quickly, she scrambled back into bed, remaining sitting up against the soft headboard and watching the bathroom door for the entrance of her namesake. It was another five minutes before he came out, clean shaven and with a small white towel carelessly wrapped round his waist.

He smiled hugely as he saw her looking at him. Tiny droplets of water glistened all over the abundant hair of his chest and arms.

'Good morning Miss Macdonald,' he said. 'Remember me?'

'Oh yes, I think so Mr MacDonald.'

'How's the head?'

'Not too bad.'

He raised his eyebrows. 'Really? From the amount you put away last night I would have thought you would surface with one humdinger of a hangover.'

'No humdingers. I'm okay.'

'No regrets either?'

'Regrets?' she repeated.

'Me. Taking advantage of you when your boyfriend had just walked out.'

'Certainly not,' she said quickly, forcing herself to look directly at him. 'I enjoyed it. Didn't you?'

'Oh yes, I most certainly did. I just wondered how much you would remember when you woke up this morning.'

'I remember everything.'

'Everything? Absolutely everything?'

She looked down suddenly, blushing. She could only recall isolated moments, little cameos of tangled bodies and frozen movements. She wanted to say something about hoping he realized that she didn't do this sort of thing with every stranger she met but stopped herself, realizing how clichéd it would sound. The proximity of MacDonald's damp body was making her fidget, the smell of him and the sight of him was beginning to arouse her again.

'What do we do now?' she asked, stammering a little over the words. 'I mean, where do we go from here?'

'Wherever you want to go, Peaches baby.'

She swallowed and coughed to clear her throat. 'Where are you headed for?'

'South.' He spread his arms in an expansive gesture. 'East maybe. I've got a mate to the east of here and an invitation to visit him but I'm in no hurry. I just like to keep moving. I'm like a shark, you know. If I stop moving, I die.'

Peaches looked up into his lovely green eyes and a delicious warmth climbed up her spine. 'I don't know anything about you Joe MacDonald,' she said and she didn't know if the huskiness in her voice was caused by fear, anxiety or plain sexual excitement. Most probably a combination of all three, she thought.

'Come along for the ride then,' he said. 'You'll soon get to know me.'

'I reckon I might just do that.'

MacDonald sat down beside her on the edge of the bed, he reached out and laid a hand on her shoulder, letting it slide down onto a breast. 'I see you've started to get dressed,' he said. 'Now that is a pity. I was going to give you the chance of a traditional Scottish breakfast in bed.'

'Can we not have breakfast with our clothes on then?' she asked innocently.

'Not really, not this kind of breakfast anyway. Back home we call it the breakfast of champions.'

He leaned over and kissed her firmly on the lips. She pushed him back. 'And what happens after breakfast?'

'Lunch,' he replied, kissing her again. 'Dinner, and supper.'

She pulled the flimsy tee-shirt over her head and tossed it aside. 'I like the menu but when are we going to have time to eat?'

'We'll manage to fit it in sometime. It depends how hungry we get.'

'Okay champ,' Peaches said, clasping her hands together behind his neck and pulling him forward onto her. 'Let's start cooking.'

The weight of his body crushed her down into the mattress. There was so much she wanted to know, so much she had to find out about him. But there would be plenty of time for all that. She bit his shoulder. She would make sure that Crazy Joe MacDonald didn't go anywhere without her.

Gudrun Richter rolled over slowly and put one foot on the floor beside the bed while she remained lying on her back staring up at the ceiling. There was a spider's web in the corner above her and the top edge of a strip of the plain wallpaper was peeling away. She did not move again for several minutes. The last thing she wanted to do was wake her sleeping partner. The precaution was probably unnecessary because she knew what a heavy sleeper he was, difficult enough to rouse at the best of times. Now his breathing was deep and regular. He was lying on his side, facing away from her. He was pretty drunk as well. But then so was she. They had shared a couple of bottles of his favourite whisky, the one with the unpronounceable name. He got angry if she did not drink with him, so she had no choice. She spilled as much as possible but still managed to swallow enough to make her pass out. She had woken up in the bed, still wearing her jeans and her bra. She could see that Hugh Divers also had most of his clothes on even though he was under the covers.

Gudrun slipped another foot down onto the floor and stood up. The bed creaked loudly as it was relieved of her weight. She hesitated but there was no reaction to the sound. The room was cold. Hugging her arms round her bare ribs, she went to the door and put on the short white towelling dressing gown that was hanging there. It trapped her body heat and quickly warmed her. She stood looking back at the bed. The room seemed to revolve a few inches to the left, and then back again to the right. She leaned a shoulder against the door and clasped the palm of her hand over her eyes. On the bed Divers snorted and coughed, turned onto his stomach and settled again. He started to snore quite loudly.

Gudrun smiled. She lifted her hand to look at him as though she was shading her eyes from the sun. Franz had been right after all, the last nine months had not been wasted. She had not suffered Divers' continual demands on her for nothing. At times, several times, she had come close to abandoning the project but Franz always persuaded her to go back. And he had been right. Now, at last, the end was in sight, as soon as it could be arranged she would be rid of him for ever. He had served his purpose. She almost almost laughed out loud but quickly held a hand over her mouth to stop herself.

Twice before Divers had taken her in the middle of the night to the remote roadside near the border and left her there for several hours with the promise that he would return with the Minotaur. Twice before he had come back empty-handed saying that the time had not been right. The third time, just when she was almost convinced his boasting would once again fall flat, he brought the thing back and dumped it casually in the boot of the car. During a rest on the long, long journey back to Frankfurt she had seen it properly for herself. She had seen it and touched it. All his claims, all his boasts had proved true. Franz had been right. They had not allowed Divers, a foreigner, to join their group, but Franz had wanted him kept under observation and delegated the job to Gudrun. It had taken nine months but now it had all been worth while. Franz would be delighted.

Gudrun opened the bedroom door and went through to the living room. The Minotaur, stripped of its canvas harness, was standing on the low coffee table looking as natural a feature of the room as the television set. It was the size of an average television, maybe a little bit bigger. The metal sides were smooth and painted pale green with the stylized bull's-horns symbol stencilled on them in red. The top surface contained a number of grooves and jack-plug holes and a six-inch square of fine mesh besides a plastic cap two inches in diameter with the raised letters DIP on it. Gudrun reached out and ran two fingertips down a rounded edge. The thought of the Minotaur's tremendous power made her hand tremble. She could hardly wait to tell Franz.

Her blouse and jumper from the night before had been dumped beside an armchair. She took off the dressing gown and put them on. She opened the curtains and the sudden flood of harsh sunlight made her screw up her eyes in pain. She opened the window a little to let in fresh air. It was much later than she had imagined. She tilted the clock on the mantlepiece backwards to remove the glare from its face. It was after eleven o'clock.

She went to the bathroom and ran the tap until the water was hot, washed her face thoroughly and put on dark eye-shadow. She ran a brush through her tousled, dirty blonde hair and decided she was presentable enough to go out without attracting attention to herself. Her overcoat was in the hall cupboard. Her shoes were stuffed under the sofa. She went out into the street. A mongrel dog was standing beside Divers' car. It lifted its leg and peed on the back wheel.

The street was relatively quiet compared to the main road she reached after walking less than fifty yards. The petrol fumes from the traffic made her feel dizzy and sick but she kept moving. She knew where she was going. It was not far. It took her about five minutes to get to the public phone in a quiet corner of a small shopping mall. No one was using it. She searched for coins in her purse and dialled the Mannheim number from memory. It rang for a long time before it was answered.

'Franz,' she said.

'Yes,' a deep voice replied.

'We have it.'

There was a pause. Gudrun cupped her hand round the receiver and pressed as far as she could under the privacy hood of the phone.

'When?' Franz demanded, more alert now.

'Last night. We have it now.'

'We?'

'He's drunk. Dead to the world.'

'Keep him that way. I'll be there as soon as possible.'

'Hurry Franz.'

'I'm on my way.'

Gudrun put down the phone. There was a bounce in her step as she crossed the mall, threading her way through the crowds, and out onto the street once more. She hardly noticed the traffic as she returned to the flat. Humming quietly to herself she swung her handbag back and forward as she walked. At the front door she had inserted the key in the lock before she realized that something was wrong. For a few seconds she could not think what it was but then it came to her and her insides tightened into a painful knot. She looked back over her shoulder. The car was gone. Panic seized her. Fumbling to unlock the door she almost fell through it as it swung open. She went straight to the bedroom. The bed was empty. She ran to the living room. The Minotaur was gone too.

The balcony ran the whole length of the front of the villa which faced west over Lake Neuchâtel in Switzerland. The swimming pool was positioned right at the very edge of the balcony, down three steps from the covered terrace. It did not take much to make the water spill out and flow under the low rail to drip onto the bushes and trees on the steeply sloping hill-side below.

There were two teenage girls in the pool. One, wearing a plain red bikini, was sunbathing while floating on an air-bed. The other, in a black one-piece suit, was lazily kicking to and fro on her back across the width of the pool. Each time she reached the far side a little wave slopped up and over the edge. The falling silver drops sparkled in the bright sunshine.

The concrete of the balcony terrace was warm to the touch of Hugo Betzing's bare feet as he stepped out from the carpeted lounge. He was a tall man with disproportionately long legs and narrow shoulders. His face was bony and tri-angular with very deep blue eyes. He wore a tennis shirt and shorts. There was a half-empty packet of Gitânes in his breast pocket. Sitting down at a table where a selection of the day's newspapers were spread out beside a telephone he chose the *Financial Times* and began to flick through it.

The girl in the black swimsuit rested her forearms on the side of the pool and called up to him in French. 'Good morning, uncle.'

Betzing looked straight into the sun. He had to screw up his eyes and shade them with a hand before he could see her properly. The other girl shouted to him as well, rolling off the air-bed and swimming to the side to join her twin sister.

'Good morning my lovelies,' he replied. 'You do an old man's heart good on a fine morning like this.'

He watched them as they climbed out of the water together. They were indeed lovely girls, both slim and dark-skinned, and old enough to know it. The wetness of their flesh gave it a deep satin sheen. They grabbed towels and came up to him. Each kissed him on a separate, newly-shaven cheek.

He threw down the paper. 'Tell me,' he said. 'Have you enjoyed your little holiday here?'

'Oh yes, uncle,' they said together.

'Good. Tell your father that when you get home. Tell him how Uncle Hugo treated you and maybe he will let you come back soon.'

'It is a pity we have to go home today,' said the one in the red bikini as she rubbed her hair dry. 'I could stay in a place like this for ever.'

Betzing smiled indulgently. 'All good things must come to an end and I do have work to get on with. This villa has to be paid for, you know, and there is not much chance of getting anything done with you two around. Now you had better get your stuff gathered up. It won't be long till we have to leave to get your flight. I'll drive you to the airport myself.'

They went obediently. Betzing watched them go, self-consciously aware that he was staring at the fluid motion of their buttocks inside the tightly-stretched material of their costumes. He had thought it better to send his mistress, Anna, home to her parents in Geneva for the week his nieces were with him. Anna was not all that much older than the twins themselves and he would have been embarrassed by that. Who knows what women talked about when they got together on their own.

Hugo had spoiled the twins terribly during their stay, but in spoiling them he knew he was really spoiling himself more. He greatly envied his brother Manfred and the legitimate career he had made for himself in Paris. The week with the girls had, as it always did, made him regret never marrying, never having any children of his own. But maybe it was not too late. Maybe he would marry Anna, then there would be no need to hesitate over introducing her to his family. As his wife it did not matter how young she was, or how big the age difference between them was. Maybe he and Anna would have children. Maybe it wasn't too late, after all.

He had neglected the business badly over the past week, putting off decisions, delaying making calls, letting things pile up. There would be a lot of catching up to do, but the truth was that his heart was no longer in it. He had grown old and weary and the pressures that had once been tremendously exciting were now just another way of getting a headache. He wanted to retire and had salted away just about enough to live on. What he really needed was one big deal to bring in a large capital sum that would set him up once and for all. A lot of cash had slipped through his fingers in his time. He had wasted more than many men earn in a lifetime. If he had been more circumspect earlier he would have been able to give it all up before now. All he looked forward to was the day he could disconnect the phone and never have to fly in an aeroplane again.

Perhaps this business with the mysterious Mr MacDonald in Munich would provide him with the opportunity to finally retire. What he was promising certainly had the potential to reap substantial rewards. Mr MacDonald could well prove to be a crackpot and a time-waster but Betzing's instincts had been to give the man a run for his money. Helmut Rocher in Munich seemed to be convinced by his claims and Rocher was not an easy person to fool.

Betzing looked down on the armada of tiny yachts littering the turquoise waters of the lake. For a few moments he followed the trail of one set slightly apart from the others. Then his attention was snatched away by a speedboat and water-skier scoring across the calm surface like a crack across a sheet of coloured glass. The sound of the boat's engine was like the drone of a fat bumble bee at that distance.

He turned to the newspapers on the table and began to study them carefully. He had a hunch about this Mr MacDonald but there was nothing in the news reports to support his claims. If it was true, Betzing might be negotiating a six-figure sale. There would be a queue of eager buyers. No one had ever had anything like it to offer for sale before. It would be a fine way to bow out of the business.

A jet-black military limousine was waiting for Buster Grant when he arrived at the embassy in Bonn after the long drive up the autobahns from Zweibrücken. The impatient chauffeur allowed him barely half an hour to change into a decent suit and grab a quick cup of coffee and slice of toast. There was no hint of what the sudden crisis was about. Grant had heard nothing significant on the radio news bulletins in his own car and his mind was too tired to speculate. Twice he had to stop to go for a walk in the fresh air to keep himself awake and to ease the stiffness in his joints. He had been looking forward to a good night's sleep after his exertions on the Rheinpfalz crags. He did manage to sleep fitfully in the back of the smooth-running limousine as it whisked him further north to the main headquarters of the British Army of the Rhine at Rheindahlen near Moenchengladbach.

An infrequent visitor to the base, he recognized the building he was ushered into on arrival. It contained the offices of the Army Intelligence Corps. Grant was politely shown into a room with an old-fashioned sofa and half a dozen armchairs grouped around a projector screen in one corner. He paced up and down after being left alone and finally lay out on the sofa and went immediately to sleep. When he was woken by persistent shaking of his arm he was stiffer than ever.

'Buster,' a familiar voice said. 'Sorry to keep you waiting.'

Grant sat up and rubbed his eyes. Bright light was pouring in the window. Outside uniforms were marching to and fro. In front of him Colonel David Sellars sat on the arm of the sofa.

'Christ, David,' Grant said. 'What's all this about?'

'I'll tell you soon enough, but let's get some breakfast inside us first. Come into my office. It's on its way across from the mess.'

Grant picked up his jacket from the back of the chair where he had hung it. He noticed that there were dark circles under Sellars' eyes and little colour in his face. The uniform was immaculate but there was dark stubble on his chin.

'Tell me this, David. Do I look as bad as you?'

Sellars raised his bushy eyebrows. 'Worse, I would say. It looks like neither of us has had much sleep.'

Grant followed Sellars along the corridor into his office. It was a long, narrow room lined on one side with filing cabinets and with a large metal desk diagonally across the corner where the only window looked out onto a bed of carefully tended roses. On the back wall was a map of Europe and beside it a blown-up and elongated version of the border between East and West Germany. Both maps were covered in annotations in small print and symbols of tanks and planes and soldiers. On the desk a large, square object was covered with a Union Jack. Sellars tapped the top of it as he went round to take his seat.

'The flag is incidental,' he said. 'It was all I could find to cover the thing with. I didn't want it just sitting there for everyone to see.'

'What is it?'

Sellars was about to lift the edge of the flag when there was a knock at the door and a white-jacketed steward came in carrying a tray with two platefuls of bacon and eggs and a pot of tea on it. He stood waiting while Sellars slid the flag-draped box to one side then placed the tray in the middle of the desk. He poured two cups of tea and removed a clingfilm wrapping from the milk jug. Then he clicked his heels, bowed rather than saluted, and left, closing the door behind him. Sellars took off his uniform cap and placed it on the window sill at his elbow. He lifted one of the plates and handed it to Grant with a knife and fork folded inside a napkin. He helped himself to the other plate. Grant poured milk in the tea cups, offered sugar but neither of them wanted it.

'Have you heard of the Minotaur?' Sellars asked as he cut into the yolks of his eggs.

'Mythological beast in the labyrinth, half man and half

bull,' Grant replied. 'A piece of military hardware is it?'

'Spot on, Buster.'

'And somebody has pinched one?'

'Right first time.'

'Is this one of them?' Grant asked, pointing at the box with his knife.

'It's the casing of one. They wouldn't let me have a real one. The Minotaur is a nuclear land-mine. Somebody shot dead two of our boys yesterday morning and made off with one. We need your help to find out who.'

Grant stopped his hand with a forkful of bacon halfway to his mouth. His appetite had suddenly disappeared. 'A nuclear bomb,' he said, feeling his jaw sag. 'Somebody has stolen a nuclear bomb.'

Sellars spread his arms wide and shrugged his shoulders. 'It had to happen sometime, the amount of nuclear stuff we carry around in the kit these days. But it is not as bad as it sounds, believe me. If it was I would be choking on this breakfast. No. The thing wasn't armed. They can't set it off. They can't go and nuke the nearest city just when they feel like it.'

'You're certain about that?'

'I am assured by those who should know.'

Grant's appetite did not return. He placed his cutlery quietly back on the plate and began to drink his tea. Sellars pulled the Union Jack from the box, displaying the smooth, pale green metal and the bull's horns stencilled in red. He bundled the flag up and dropped it on the floor. Grant stood up to examine the box more carefully, particularly the top surface with its connecting holes. He screwed off the plastic cap and peered into the dark well beneath.

'Do they know it won't work?'

'That depends on who has got it,' Sellars replied. 'Doesn't look like much, does it? But it is going to be one Hell of an embarrassment to the Alliance when this gets out to the public.'

'Can it be kept quiet?'

'Two men dead. It will difficult but we can appeal to the families' sense of patriotism. You know, lost on a secret mission, bung them a couple of posthumous medals, that kind of thing. But the problem is that the new owners might start shouting from the rooftops. The Press will lap it up.'

Grant sat down again, still holding the plastic cap. He ran a finger over the raised letters on it. 'Any idea who they might be?' he said.

'We're starting from scratch. No obvious candidates. That's why we need your help, Buster. You keep close tabs on the budding terrorists in our midst. Have there been any recent rumblings? Red Army Faction getting restless?'

Grant shook his head. 'None. It's been as quiet as the grave, so quiet I decided to take my first real holiday in three years. Then you call me back here.'

'Isn't that always the way of it,' Sellars said apologetically. 'But you are the man in the know. You have some useful East German contacts as well, don't you?'

'You think it might have been a cross-border operation?'

Sellars pursed his lips. 'It has to be a possibility. Our lads were taken out by a professional hit and obviously the other side would love to get their hands on our technology. They might well have taken the risk.'

'Surely not?'

'Not themselves perhaps. But they might have hired some people on this side of the border to get their hands dirty; people that could be disowned easily if anything went wrong. Not much risk in that.'

'So the bomb could be over the border by now?'

'It could be,' Sellars said, pouring himself another cup of tea. 'It might already be stripped down and little circuit diagrams in Russian drawn up. Actually, if it is our problem is solved. The Minotaur's been around for a number of years. There is nothing particularly new or secret about it. They won't learn all that much from it and, of course, they won't want anyone to know that they have got it, we will bury our dead and that will be the end of the story.'

'And if it is not the other side?'

'Since they can't blow the thing up its only use to them will be as a weapon of embarrassment. Look, they can say, we nicked a Minotaur nuclear mine, what else could we nick if we put our minds to it? Do you really think these soldier chappies should be trusted with such dangerous items when they can't look after them properly? In fact, what are these British soldiers doing in our country? Isn't it about time they packed up their bombs and went home and took the Yanks and everybody else's armies with them. I simplify, but you see what I mean.'

'Indeed.' Grant sat back and folded his arms. He had worked with Sellars before on several intelligence projects and appreciated that his analysis was sharp and accurate. 'Why is it called Minotaur?' he asked.

'Who knows? The mythical creature, half man and half beast, that fed on people given to it as sacrifices in the labyrinth. Maybe it was invented by a boffin with an inclination for the classics? It's quite a classy name, don't you think? The other side call theirs CR 17s or something equally unimaginative.'

'The soldiers hump them about on their backs, don't they?' Grant said, then went on without waiting for a reply. 'With that on your back you might look a bit like a Minotaur in silhouette. You know, thick bull up top, human legs down below.'

Sellars narrowed his eyes and thought about it. 'No horns,' he said.

'That's true,' Grant conceded. 'You have to use a little imagination.'

'Look, Buster, I can't give you much more information myself,' Sellars said, suddenly standing up and collecting the breakfast dishes onto the tray. 'Brigadier Danny Evans of the Royal Engineers is being choppered in this afternoon to give you a full briefing, he visited the location yesterday. You can pick his brains. He is over at Wiesbaden just now calming the nerves of the top brass.

'Fine,' Grant said, reaching up to replace the plastic cap on the Minotaur casing. 'I'd like to make a couple of phone calls, just to get things moving.'

Sellars lifted the tray and put it across on top of the nearest filing cabinet. 'Of course,' he said. 'Use my phone. The line is secure.'

Grant went round behind the desk. Sellars leaned over and pulled open a drawer to show a pad of clean paper and some freshly sharpened pencils. 'Thanks,' Grant said. 'This won't take too long. If this Evans bloke won't be here till the afternoon, maybe I could catch a quick forty winks in a decent bed.'

'I'll have one made up for you,' Sellars said, moving to the door. 'Sweet dreams and all that.'

They had christened it Nowhere because it seemed to be in the middle of nowhere. In actual fact it was in the depths of a forest in the hills to the north of the town of Bamberg in northern Bavaria. They had stumbled across the place one hazy day while cruising around aimlessly on the run from the army. It was perfect for their purposes. It just needed a little modification. A week later they turned themselves in to get the formalities out of the way. Three months in the glasshouse, dishonourable discharges, and they were free agents once again, going nowhere.

Hugh Divers cursed as his foot slipped on the rocky bottom of the shallow stream he was walking along, he had to put a hand onto the muddy bank to regain his balance, helped by the stabilizing weight of the Minotaur on his back. He straightened up. Overhanging branches scraped against the harness. Bird song buzzed like radio interference in the trees around him. The cold water flowed sluggishly round his ankles, penetrating through to the skin. As he stood still the muddiness of the water quickly cleared. He took another step and it immediately clouded again. His sweat-sodden clothes chafed against his skin.

Nowhere was the ancient ruin of what had once been a forester's cottage. There were four knee-high, moss-covered walls with a gap for the door and a low, curved swelling for the chimney breast. That was all. The gnarled trunk of a mature tree rose from one corner inside, pushing the side wall out of line. There must have been an access road or a track to it at one time but the forest had long since reclaimed it. Divers wiped the damp hair from his forehead and stepped up out of the stream. He walked the ten yards through the long grass to the ruin, turned and crouched down so that the Minotaur was left sitting on the wall and he could take his arms out of the shoulder straps. He stayed where he was, resting on his haunches, for a few minutes, rubbing his tired muscles to relieve the cramp in them.

It was a long hike to get to Nowhere. He had left the car six miles away in a corner of a disused quarry, screened by a row of thick bushes. He could have parked it a couple of miles closer but the quarry was the agreed site. If it was discovered no clue would point in the direction of Nowhere. It was a hard hike but a worthwhile one to maintain the secrecy and isolation of the place. Divers had never covered the distance without carrying supplies in some shape or form, so the fifty-pound weight of the Minotaur, less than an ordinary army field pack, had posed no problem. He knew the way to Nowhere by the lie of the country and the position of landmarks that remained largely unchanged through the seasons. He knew the distinctive kink in the trunk of a particular tree, the shelving slope of an almost bare hillside, the octagonal shape of a clearing, a six-foot-high rock face like a carefully built garden wall and, for the final mile, the shallow stream that meandered its way between impenetrable undergrowth right to the doorstep.

Divers climbed over the wall into the ruined cottage. The ground inside was mostly tufted grass, nettles and bracken. A big dead branch lay diagonally across one corner. He took hold of one end and swung it round like opening a gate. Beyond it the ground appeared to be no different. Divers bent over and felt with his hand in the grass until he grasped something unseen. Grunting with the effort he stood up, pulling with him a four-foot-square trap-door that tore a hole in the springy turf. A stick fell forward on a hinge from the underside of the door. Divers grabbed it and fixed it into a slot to the side of the rough-cut wooden steps, leaving the door propped open at a seventy-five-degree angle. It had not been open for almost three months. A dry, musty smell came from the black interior.

They had found the cellar when Divers had tripped over the rusty iron ring. They had opened the trap-door and he had been lowered into the hole. It was eight feet deep, maybe five feet wide and ten long, the walls were lined with a smooth stone like slate. He had lit a fire at the bottom and inspected the cellar thoroughly by the light of the flames. It was empty apart from a thin sprinkling of earth on the floor, that had trickled in over the years. There was no hint of what it might once have been used for. They speculated that it might have been a log store, or a food store, but it seemed too large for the size of the cottage. Perhaps it had been a place of last refuge for the forester's family, a sanctuary in lawless times when the woods around teemed with robbers and cut-throats. Whatever it had been used for it was exactly what they needed now. After getting the army off their backs they had returned to Nowhere together and spent three weeks doubling the size of the cellar, lining the walls of the new section with tree bark and twigs, installing an air vent that came above ground inside a rotten log which made it totally invisible. There was also a chimney that went horizontally until it came up inside a nearby clump of bushes. One of the strict rules was that no fire was lit during the daylight hours. Inside they had fashioned bunks and shelves to take the stocks of canned food. They had tried to construct some kind of pipe system to bring water in from the stream but that had proved too difficult and the project had to be abandoned. Divers made a crude electric generator from a bicycle wheel and some other odds and ends. When the place was finished they had a very comfortable bolthole to which they could retreat whenever the occasion demanded it. It was private and bomb-proof. They reckoned they could hold out underground for at least three months if need be.

All that had happened two years before. Divers had laid his plans well in advance. His plans to steal the Minotaur dated back two years before then to a time when he was deployed to assist with ordnance supplies at Munsterlager. It had been relatively simple to steal what he wanted and cover his tracks to avoid any suspicion. Four years he had waited for the right moment and finally the time had come.

No one had believed him capable of doing it, but he had done it all by himself. No one had believed in him. Not even his best mate who had helped him build Nowhere and had eventually got tired of waiting and gone back home. Gudrun and her neo-Nazi pals had not believed him although they had sent

Gudrun to stay with him to keep an eye on him, just in case. At least, that was what they had probably told her. Divers thought it was more likely that her mad boyfriend got some kind of perverted kick out of ordering her to sleep with a man she loathed. No, Divers had done it all on his own and without anyone's help. The Minotaur would make him a very rich man.

He went back and picked up the Minotaur, holding it by the straps in front of him, and carried it over and placed it at the edge of the trap-door and dragged the dead branch into its former position behind him. Then he lowered the Minotaur down into the cellar, sliding it down the steps. It was a neat fit in the space. He descended awkwardly after it into the grey darkness until he felt it bump down on the floor. He stepped round it and fumbled blindly on a narrow table for the pair of crocodile clips he knew should be there. He found them and fixed them onto the terminals of a car battery. At once the cellar was bisected by the beam of a strong spotlight thrown from a point half-way up the far wall. Divers went back to the steps and removed the prop from the trap-door, taking the weight of it on his shoulder and easing it slowly into place. The noise of the forest and the birds ceased. Dust particles floated silently in the shaft of glaring white light as he descended again.

One whole side of the cellar consisted of floor-to-ceiling racks of food tins, plastic water bottles, and various items of clothing and camping equipment. Beneath the spotlight were two single bunks, and beside them a brick platform with a metal smoke hood set into the corner. An unlit fire stood on the bricks. Where the walls were not hidden behind racks they were covered in sacking to cut down on the chill from the bare stone. Damp patches stained the sacking where wall met ceiling. A chemical toilet was tucked in below the steps, the table with the car battery on it was the only piece of loose furniture. It was made from round branches with thin strips bound together to form the top surface. Divers lifted the battery onto the floor and put the Minotaur on the table. Its legs bowed out as it took the weight.

The Minotaur was covered by a dark green groundsheet. Divers untied the corners and removed it. Underneath the two Bullpup rifles were jammed inside the original harness and taped against the metal casing. He peeled off the tape and took the guns out, pushing them into a space on one of the shelves at his elbow alongside a double-barrelled shotgun. Then he quickly tore off the remaining harness fittings to leave the Minotaur standing naked on the table.

He reached in behind several rows of baked-bean tins and brought out a fat cylinder wrapped in a large sheet of yellowing newspaper, unrolling it to expose a two-foot-long tube painted bright red with small Minotaur symbols stencilled four times along its length in pale green. Divers held it in two hands and was unable to close his fingers round it. The cylinder was in four distinct sections, like the segmented body of some giant insect grub. Divers rolled it in his palms. The top section had an inset glass panel showing seven zeroes in a line a few inches down from the head. The middle sections had irregularly spaced ridges round their circumferences. The bottom section tapered sharply to a point. The harsh beam of light caused dark shadows to flit over its surface as he moved it round. It looked as if it was squirming in his hands, as if it had a life of its own.

Divers levered off the plastic DIP cap from the top of the Minotaur. Slowly and carefully, with his tongue pushing against the back of his front teeth to maintain his concentration, he inserted the tapered end of the cylinder into the hole. The first section slid in easily up to the first joint. Then he twisted the next section back and forward, moving it independently of the others, until the ridges slotted smoothly into place. He was quicker in finding the accommodating grooves for the third section, leaving the top part poking up like a periscope. He patted it with his fingertips as though it was a tame animal and looked at the date panel of the watch on his wrist. Counting in his head, his lips moving soundlessly as he made the mental calculation, he pressed a concealed switch above the glass panel which made a rectangular flap underneath spring open to reveal a row of seven small buttons corresponding to the displayed zeroes. His fingers were large and clumsy compared to the buttons and he had to use the point of the fingernail of his little finger to press them individually. He started on the left and the separate numbers rotated one digit with each press. 'Cutting it fine. Cutting it fine,' he muttered to himself as he methodically worked his way along the row.

When he was satisfied with the combination of numbers he took hold of the ring with the serrated edge at the very top of the cylinder and turned it to the right. It clicked twice and a red light glowed behind the glass panel. Divers closed the flap and, using the heel of his hand, pushed the fourth and final section down into the Minotaur casing. It went reluctantly, as though he was pushing down on a strong spring. When only the edge of the ring was visible he screwed it to the left to lock the whole thing in place. He let go and stood back, walking backwards all the way to sit down on his bunk, and stared at the Minotaur with his head resting against the hard wall. It shone in the spotlight, surrounded by darkness, seeming to hang in the air. He reached up and turned off the light, plunging the cellar into complete blackness. His eyes took some time to adjust then he could see the shape of the luminous Minotaur symbol floating in the air in front of him.

The agreed signal was for the window box with its overflowing load of lobelia to be taken down from the sill and placed at the edge of the doorstep. It was there on the ground when Franz Luneburg and three companions arrived in the street and drove slowly past. The car was parked round the next corner, out of sight, and Luneburg walked back alone.

Inside the flat Gudrun Richter watched him approach. Nervously, she ran her fingers through her hair. He was a sinister-looking figure, dressed all in black; black shoes, black trousers, black leather jacket. He was obssessed with the colour black. That was why he called the group Das Schwarze Leichentuch, The Black Shroud. And that was why Gudrun had put on her best black dress, and black stockings, and tied a black nylon scarf round her neck. She had painted her fingernails black as well. He liked that. He liked to see the nails moving like fat beetles all over his body when they slept together. He never tired of it, and neither did she for it gave her a great feeling of power over him as he lay completely exposed and helpless, like a junkie dependent on the addictive touch of her fingertips. It was the only situation when she did have power over him. At all other times she readily bowed to his will and to his orders. Sometimes she would press her sharp nails deep into his skin so that he writhed and grunted in pain. But he did not want her to stop. He begged her to press harder, dig deeper, until she drew blood. And that for him must have been like an orgasm because only after that was he fully satiated. Then, he would take her hands tenderly in his and lick the blood from her fingers.

Gudrun moved to open the front door as he turned to come up the pathway. Her legs felt very weak and her breathing was shallow and laboured. She was worried about what his reaction would be to the news that Divers had disappeared with the Minotaur. It was not her fault. She could not have stopped him. He must have been waiting for her to leave so that he could slip out. But even if he had gone while she was there, she could not have stopped him. Yet she knew Franz would blame her and she was ashamed that she had let him down. Divers would come back, but he would come back without the Minotaur. He was hiding it somewhere at that very moment, maybe in another flat in another town in Germany. It could be anywhere. She should have tried harder to win his confidence, should have faked more enthusiasm when they made love to make him trust her, should have made herself indispensable to him in every way, so that he would not have thought of going anywhere or doing anything without her. But she had not because she did not believe he could do what he said he was going to do. She had gone about her task half-heartedly and had suspected that he knew all along just exactly what her little game was. Only Franz had believed in Divers. Franz had insisted that she stay with him. And Franz had been proved right.

She opened the door and he was there on the doorstep in front of her, his hands pushed into the pockets of the short bomber jacket, his eyebrows a single black line across the bottom of his forehead. A curious sensation of mingled fear and delight made her whole body tremble. The scarf was suddenly too tight round her neck.

'He's not here?' Luneburg asked, looking up from the mass of purple flowers.

Gudrun swallowed hard. 'No.'

'And the Minotaur?' He went past her eagerly into the flat, straight into the living room. She closed the front door and followed him. He stood in the centre of the room, looking round. He went to the bedroom. When he came back Gudrun was sitting on one of the armchairs, perched on the edge, knees together, hands clasped tightly. 'Where is it?' he demanded.

'He took it with him,' she said quietly, not daring to look at him.

'You let him take it away?' Luneburg's voice had a distinct nasal whine which became even more obvious as he started to shout. 'You had the thing here and you let him take it away?'

'I thought he was asleep,' Gudrun said. 'I thought he was drunk. I only went out for ten minutes to get to a phone so that I could call you. When I got back they were gone. The car was gone.'

Luneburg seized her wrists and pulled her to her feet. 'You let him take it away?' he repeated.

'It wasn't my fault,' she pleaded. 'I couldn't stop him.'

He stood silently holding her wrists and staring at her. She thought she saw sympathy and understanding in his eyes and she tried to smile. She did not see the blow coming. The flat of his hand hit her cheek square on, wrenching her head to one side. Crying out in surprise and pain she tried to back away from him but he kept her where she was by holding her wrists. She saw the second blow coming as he brought his arm back, but there was not much she could do to avoid it. She managed to jerk her head back a little so that the back of his hand missed her cheek and made contact instead with the side of her nose. Blood spurted out, running into her mouth and over her chin. He pushed her back into the chair and she curled into a ball with her arms over her head to protect it.

Luneburg squatted down in front of her and put his hands on her shoulders. He shook her gently. 'I'm sorry Gudrun,' he said and she instantly believed him because she knew he had great difficulty in controlling his temper. It was not the first time he had hit her. It was not the first time he had been sorry.

'I know you couldn't stop him Gudrun,' he said. 'I know it is not your fault. It's just so frustrating to have the Minotaur so close and then to lose it. Do you have any idea where he may have gone?'

She shook her head, sobbing pathetically. 'He is always disappearing for days on end. He never tells me where he goes or what he does. He just comes and goes as he pleases.'

Luneburg tipped her chin upwards with his fist to make her look at him. 'The Minotaur was here? You saw it? It was the real thing?'

'It was here all right,' she said, wiping the blood from her top lip. Her nose was sore and tender to the touch. 'It was on that table. We sat looking at it all of yesterday and last night. He kept stroking it and kissing it like it was alive. He made me do it as well.' She shivered, remembering how Divers' attention had fluctuated between her warm flesh and the Minotaur's cold metal.

Luneburg stood up and turned to look down on the table. He was smaller than her by a few inches and his shoulders were narrower. Yet he looked bigger. His size was magnified by the air of authority and leadership that flowed from him. He was a born leader. When he spoke, bigger and stronger men did his bidding without question. Gudrun loved him totally and unreservedly. She would do anything for him. She would die for him. She hoped that one day, eventually, he would come to love her.

'Will he come back?' Luneburg asked without taking his eyes from the empty table.

'He always has. I think he will again.'

'He doesn't suspect, then?'

'No. He thinks I'm soft on him.' She untied the scarf from round her neck and held it to her nose to stem the bleeding. 'He trusted me enough to drive the car when we got the Minotaur. He didn't want the car sitting empty at the side of the road for too long. It was quite a busy road so he got me to drive around and pick him up. It worked perfectly.'

'So he will come back.'

'Yes.'

'But he won't bring the Minotaur?'

Gudrun wiped the tears from her eyes, smearing a little blood on her skin. 'I doubt it,' she said. 'He has a secret hiding place somewhere. He goes there every so often. I don't know where it is but that is where he will be now.'

'What do you think he intends to do with it?'

'I don't know. He's a strange one. Who knows what goes on inside that skull of his?'

Luneburg turned back to her, suddenly smiling. 'Well we shall just have to ask him when he gets back, won't we?'

She tried to smile back and a sob was transformed into a tiny laugh. Everything would work out all right in the end. Franz would see to it.

'We'll wait here until he decides to come back. I'll get the others. You just carry on as normal. Are you due to go to work tonight?'

She nodded.

'Then just go as normal. And you will have to get some extra food in. You think it could be a couple of days before he comes back?'

'Two days,' she replied. 'The longest he has ever been away is four days. It is usually two though.'

'We can wait. You'd better get yourself cleaned up before I bring the others in. When he comes back we will have a little welcoming party for him.'

Gudrun rose out of the chair, still holding the scarf to her nose. She could feel the warm blood through the thin material. 'What if he won't tell you what he has done with it?'

Luneburg's smile vanished and then reappeared. 'Then we will just have to ask him again,' he said.

Gudrun went to the bathroom to wash the blood away.

Brigadier Daniel Evans removed his cap and placed it beside the swagger-stick on the desk-top. From his brief-case he took a telescopic pointer and pulled it open to its full length. He went to the wall and studied the map of the East-West border region for a few minutes. Then he lifted the Union flag from the Minotaur casing and folded it carefully before laying it on the desk. He looked up and raised the pointer like a conductor calling an orchestra to attention.

'If you will forgive me gentlemen I will have to rush through this rather hurriedly because I have to fly to Mons to brief the NATO generals within the hour.' He grinned but it seemed an artificial gesture. 'There can be no rest for the wicked.'

Buster Grant and David Sellars sat in front of him on uncomfortable straight-back chairs. Sellars had tipped his onto two legs to lean against the front of a filing cabinet. Grant sat with his legs crossed and his hands hooked over his knees. He had managed to snatch only about an hour's sleep and the heat of the sun coming through the top half of the window directly onto the side of his face was already making him feel very tired again. He stifled a yawn and blinked several times to try and shake the heaviness off his eyelids.

'This', Evans tapped the empty casing at his feet, 'is the Minotaur nuclear land-mine. It has been in service for several years now. Its existence has been reported several times in the Press, but always without official confirmation because of its security classification. The reports have conflicted over details of capacity and deployment and no attempt has been made to clear up the confusion. However, the basic concept is public knowledge. The Minotaur has been the subject of inconclusive negotiations at several arms-talks sessions. The Soviets, of course, have their own.

He reached into his briefcase and took out two thick booklets with spiral ring-bindings. Grant and Sellars accepted one each and began to leaf through them immediately.

'If you will just bear with me for a while,' Evans said, 'I will summarize the contents of the manuals as best I can without getting too bogged down in technical details. The manuals are, of course, strictly classified and I must ask for their return within twenty-four hours. If you can collect Mr Grant's, Colonel, I would be obliged.'

'Of course,' Sellars replied. He closed the booklet in his lap and ran his fingers over the embossed Minotaur symbol on the top right-hand corner of the cover.

'Thank you, sir. Now, the Minotaur is a nuclear land-mine which can be transported by a single soldier to any place accessible by vehicle or by foot. It weighs a fraction over fifty pounds but has a yield equivalent to three hundred tons of high explosive which, naturally, could rip a fair-sized hole in the ground. It would also distribute radioactive fall-out over a large, but in nuclear terms relatively confined area, depending on prevailing weather conditions. There is no radiation danger to the individual soldier because the levels emitted are negligible until the detonation programme is initiated and the components achieve critical mass resulting in the nuclear explosion.'

Evans closed and opened the pointer as he turned to the map. 'In time of war the Minotaur would not just be laid down haphazardly. Although we call it a mine it is not detonated by being run over by an enemy tank for example. No, along the border from Lubeck in the north down to Bad Hersfeld at the north end of the Fulda Gap we have thirty-eight specially-constructed chambers in which Minotaurs can be placed within eight hours of any rise in tension and consequent call to arms. The Fulda Gap is reckoned to be one of the most vulnerable point on our line of defence. It is where East Germany bulges into the west and it is where the Warsaw Pact mass their elite troops. If the Kremlin ever decide to Blitzkrieg us that is the way they will come, following the river valley. A large number of our chambers are concentrated at this point. They are more thinly spread to the north.

'I should perhaps mention that the Minotaur is rather old-fashioned and is actually due to be replaced by the next generation of land-mine which we are developing jointly with the French. The new mine is code-named the Chimera and it is a little lighter with a quarter to a third more explosive capacity than the Minotaur.'

Sellars leaned close to Grant. 'The Chimera,' he whispered. 'Our boffin with the classical bent must still be on the job.'

'The Minotaur is due to be phased out in the next year or so. It would have been replaced by now but there was some technological hiccup somewhere along the line and changeover plans had to be reviewed.'

'What about the rest of the border?' Grant asked.

'We actually overlap a bit between Kassel and Bad Hersfeld and after that primary border defence responsibility passes to the Americans but the strategy remains the same,' Evans explained. 'They have their own nuclear mines called ADAMS, standing for Advanced Atomic Mine. These are in two categories, the most common of which is the MADAM which weighs in at four hundred pounds and can therefore only be transported by vehicle, but which has a yield equivalent to twelve thousand tons of high explosive. The MADAM is the one on which they principally rely. They also have a few SADAMs which are true back-pack bombs weighing just under sixty pounds with a yield equivalent to two hundred and fifty tons. You will see that this is inferior to the British version. However, the Americans like to do things their own way.

'To return to the northern sector. Although we have thirty-eight chambers it is proposed that only twenty-four would be utilized at any given time, depending on circumstances. A computer model exists to help with the selection of sites. There are eight sites which underpin the defensive line strategy and would always be used. All the others are variable.'

'What do you mean variable?' Grant interrupted.

'Well, they would only come into play with a certain angle of attack by enemy forces coinciding with a certain wind direction to dictate dispersal of fall-out.' Evans pressed the pointer into the palm of his hand as though he was stabbing himself. 'You see, the defensive strategy is known as the Nuclear Wall. The Minotaurs and the MADAMS would be used to break the communications link between East and West and also to form a radiation barrier. This would not prevent a determined invasion from the East, and the Soviets have overwhelming superiority both in tanks and troops on the ground, but it would certainly slow one down to a significant degree. The enemy has to, in effect, climb over the wall, giving NATO forces an important breathing space to prepare to meet the onslaught. It is estimated an invasion could be held up for at least two, and possibly four, days.'

'What about the civilian population?' Grant asked.

'There are contingency plans for the rapid evacuation of civilians if an invasion is imminent. However, there would be inevitable collateral damage.'

'I see. Good.' Grant folded his arms and sat back in his chair. Collateral damage was military jargon for civilian casualities. Military logic had a momentum all its own.

'Anyway,' Evans continued, 'the Minotaur can be deployed in battlefield situations by two-man Commando teams operating by helicopter which hops from site to site along the border setting them down and retrieving them after installation. British troops carry out the deployment on all territory covered by Germany, Holland and Belgium as partners in NORTHAG.

'Subsequent detonation is by electronic impulse from a pilotless plane which is launched from the RAF base at Gütersloh to overfly the sites. The code-name of the plane is Theseus. You know, of course, that the Minotaur lived in the labyrinth on Crete and Theseus was the Prince of Athens who went in to kill the monster, unravelling a ball of string as he went so he would be able to find his way out again. So the plane is called Theseus, but that is by the way. The new generation mine, the Chimera, is named after a monster with a lion's head, goat's body and serpent's tail. The detonating plane in its case is to be called Bellerophon, another mythological character but I don't know what his story is.'

Evans paused and looked at his watch. 'The Minotaur connected to the equipment inside the special chambers will respond to a signal from Theseus and detonate on command, or after a programmed delay.

'Just under forty-eight hours ago there was a full-scale deployment exercise involving twenty-four Minotaur teams, split evenly between bases at Munsterlager, Braunschweig, and Paderborn.' He touched the map to indicate the position of each base. 'At Minotaur chamber thirteen, here beside Hesleshausen at the extreme southern end of our defensive line, someone was waiting for the team as they arrived to cage the beast, which is squaddie slang for installing a Minotaur. Both soldiers were killed, or more exactly executed, by single shots to the head with their own rifles and the Minotaur was taken. The bodies were then put into the chamber. When the helicopter returned to pick up the team the alarm was raised but several hours passed before their bodies were found inside the chamber.

'You've been at the site, Brigadier,' Grant said. 'What is your impression?'

'Yes,' Evans replied. 'I have been there and it looks to me like a highly professional ambush. Whoever did this had the advantage of total surprise. Our men were shot with their own rifles, remember, and at point-blank range according to the post-mortems.' He telescoped the pointer to its smallest size. 'No one saw anything. No one heard anything. It was well planned and efficiently carried out. The Minotaur could be anywhere by now.'

'Any thoughts on who it might have been?'

'I think it is interesting that site thirteen is one of the eight Minotaur sites used in all deployment exercises, both because it is at the southern end of our part of the Nuclear Wall and because it would cut the autobahn which is one of the main transit roads from Berlin. If the ambush had been at site twenty-seven, for example, which is the next one to the north, then it would not have taken place because that site was not scheduled for the exercise that particular night. It would have been impossible to know that in advance because the computer model is only run and flight plans for the choppers drawn up two hours in advance of dispersal. It could have been pure luck, of course, that they picked a live site. But it might also suggest an element of inside information about deployment that they knew just where to wait.'

Grant nodded. Sellars shook his head.

'I should explain that Minotaur sites are not numbered in sequence, but at random from one to thirty-eight. This is just a very simple ruse to throw any Soviet Bloc agent off the scent.

All the sites are in publicly-accessible, if out-of-the-way, places and it would be fairly easy to establish their layout. Not that this would matter greatly because of the variable use made of the sites.'

'I am informed that the stolen Minotaur cannot be detonated,' Grant said. 'Is that correct? Is there no danger of a nuclear explosion? Is this Theseus plane trailing its nuclear string behind it the only means of setting one of these things off?'

'Theseus is the principal means of detonation,' Evans confirmed. 'However, there is another method which was developed to give more flexibility to deployment potential.'

He delved into his briefcase and brought out a fat, two-foot-long cylinder wrapped in brown paper. He unrolled it on the desk-top. It was red and divided into four sections, each of which had a blurred image of the Minotaur symbol on it. Evans picked it up and held it in two hands.

'This is a scale model of a Digital Initiation Programmer. The men call it a Dipstick. Here, have a closer look.'

He handed it to Grant who remarked that it was a bit like an upside-down washing-up-liquid bottle. Sellars took it from him and examined it carefully before giving it back to Evans.

'It is envisaged that in time of war the Minotaur could be deployed in strategic locations which lack the special chambers. For example, behind enemy lines where Theseus might be unable to penetrate anyway. In such circumstances the Dipstick could be inserted to initiate detonation. It is quite a simple procedure.'

Evans prised off the plastic cap on top of the empty Minotaur casing and slotted in the tapered end of the Dipstick. He fiddled with the two middle sections until they slid into place, leaving the top section jutting up. 'There is a timing mechanism which can be adjusted to give detonation in hours, days, weeks, or even months.'

'Was a Dipstick taken with the Minotaur yesterday?' Grant asked.

'No.'

'Is there any possibility of one falling into the hands of these people?'

'I would very much doubt it,' Evans said confidently. 'There are fifty Minotaur land-mines in store in Germany, and fifty Dipsticks. None are missing, apart from the one Minotaur, of course. One Dipstick was lost about four years ago but it is assumed destroyed.'

'What do you mean, destroyed.'

'Well,' Evans, said, removing the model Dipstick from the casing and wrapping it in the brown paper again. 'A lorry carrying a crate of ten Dipsticks, among other items, crashed into a tree and somersaulted into a lake. The crate broke open and its contents were scattered in six-foot-deep mud under thirty feet of water. Nine were eventually recovered but the search for the tenth was eventually abandoned.'

'You are telling me that as well as the missing Minotaur, there is one of these Dipstick things out there somewhere?'

'Yes, but it is at the bottom of a lake.'

'Provided no one has found it, or provided it was on the lorry in the first place.'

'It all happened four years ago,' Evans insisted, stabbing the pointer into his thigh. 'There was a full inquiry at the time. It was an accident. That was all. If we could not find it, what are the chances of somebody else doing so? And he would need to know how to operate it, how to run the programme.'

'Nonetheless, in the worst possible scenario, it is out there with the Minotaur.'

'Yes.'

Evans put the paper-wrapped cylinder in his briefcase, followed by the telescopic pointer. He squeezed the case shut and fastened the lock. 'If you will excuse me now gentlemen I must go and catch my flight.'

Sellars stood up and dragged his chair to one side. He returned the salute that Evans gave him as he left the room.

'Well, Buster,' he said. 'What do you think? Will we get it back?'

'I've got a bad feeling about this one Dave. I don't like it at all. The Minotaur goes, then we discover there is already a Dipstick on the lost property list. I don't like it.'

'The Dipstick was lost four year ago, remember, Buster. That's a long time in anyone's language. Surely you don't think there is a connection? I'm an optimist. It could be worse.'

'I'm a civil servant,' Grant said, rubbing his tired eyes. 'It could be better.'

Sellars took the flag from the desk-top and opened it out to cover the Minotaur casing on the floor.

In the few days that Peaches Macdonald had known him she had learned next to nothing about the personal history of Crazy Joe MacDonald, and yet she could feel herself being drawn closer and closer to him. They did not seem to have all that much time to talk anyway, having hardly set foot outside the little hotel room. They made love every day, every hour it seemed, and then would lie exhausted together on the bed, unwilling rather than unable to break the intimacy of the silence. The physical bond between them was quickly consolidated. Peaches was silently falling in love and the feeling was marvellous.

MacDonald did not volunteer much information about himself and what she did manage to find out came from his circuitous ramblings about other people and other things. Direct questions were evaded or simply ignored. She pieced together an incomplete life-story from tiny fragments and imagined the boy growing into the man. She was equally reticent about her own life-story and he did not press her. Peaches wanted to wait for the right moment when they would share their stories in the same way they already shared their bodies and their kisses.

They had left the hotel that morning, MacDonald was getting restless. He wanted to move on. They had agreed to head south, towards Lyon. Will we take a train, hitch-hike, or steal a car, he had asked her. Stealing a car would be best, she had replied, thinking he was joking. So they had taken the Metro to the south side of the city and wandered the streets there in the cloying late-summer heat, both of them dressed only in thin shorts and tee-shirts. He carried her rucksack because it was much heavier than his bag which she had over her shoulder. She didn't know where he was taking her but she did not really care as long as she was beside him. When she asked where they were going he just said that he was looking for an opportunity. Maybe he wasn't joking, she thought, as she saw him try the handles of a row of parked cars. Maybe he is going to steal a car. Or maybe he is just trying to fool me into thinking that. She had never stolen anything in her life, well, that was not quite true. There had been that candle in Notre Dame Cathedral but Dale had paid for it after her. Even so, maybe that had started her out on a life of crime.

They walked the streets for hours and finally rested at a pavement cafe and drank chilled beer and ate bread and paté. Peaches kicked off her shoes and massaged her aching feet. MacDonald adjusted the table umbrella so that they were sitting in the coolness of the shade.

'Are we really going to steal a car?' she asked over the rim of her beer glass.

'Of course,' he said. 'It was your idea, after all, and it's much more convenient than other forms of transport. You have so much more freedom and it's so much cheaper.'

Peaches still wasn't convinced he was entirely serious. 'Where will we go then, when we get this car?' she asked.

'Anywhere you like. South we agreed, so let's head south.'

'And after that?'

MacDonald drank his beer from the bottle and seemed to be concentrating on something at the far end of the street. 'East maybe. I've got a friend in Germany we could visit.'

'Have you? What's his name?'

'I told you about him. He wrote to me earlier this year. He wanted to see me. Big Shuggie is his name.'

'Big Shuggie,' Peaches repeated, wrinkling up her nose in distaste. 'It sounds like something horrible and slimy that crawls about the pumpkin patch.'

MacDonald held up a hand and waggled it from side to side. 'You're a wee bit wide of the mark there. Not much though. His real name is Hugh. He lives somewhere in Frankfurt. We were in the army together.'

'You were in the army? You never told me.' Another fragment was added to her expanding picture of his life-story.

'I was. We used to be a great team, the two of us. Then they chucked us out.'

He was still staring down the street. Peaches turned to look as well but could see nothing out of the ordinary. Cars parked on the pavement forced pedestrians to walk on the edge of the road. She spread paté on a hunk of bread and bit into it.

'Tell me about him,' she said with her mouth full, feeling an irrational twinge of jealousy.

'Big Shuggie? You wouldn't like him. He doesn't have my sensitive soul. He would cut your throat as soon as look at you. He's a good friend of mine.'

'Why did they throw you out of the army?'

'We were too independently minded for the military. Even the Foreign Legion wouldn't have us when we went to Marseilles and tried to enlist. Hey, maybe we should go to Marseilles. Maybe they would take me this time if I brought you along for company.'

'No thanks,' Peaches said, covering his hand with hers. 'I'll just keep you for myself. What happened then?'

'When?' he said without looking round.

'After the Foreign Legion said they didn't want you.'

'Oh, we went back to Germany and dug our own personal bunker for use in the event of the Third World War breaking out. We were going to keep our heads down while everybody else kills each other then re-emerge to repopulate the world.' He turned to her and smiled. 'You would be handy for that Peaches. Will I reserve you a place in this bunker of ours?'

'Where is this bunker?'

MacDonald drained his beer bottle and smiled again. 'Nowhere,' he said.

'Ach, you're just kidding me,' Peaches said in annoyance. 'The same way you kidded me about stealing a car. We should have stayed in the hotel. At least we were having a good time there.'

'I can't argue with that, Peaches baby. But I'm not kidding you. It's all true. Believe me.'

'Oh yes,' she said sceptically. 'Come on then. Prove it to me.'

'All right.' He nodded in the direction of the far end of the street. 'Look down there and tell me what you see.'

Peaches turned to look. The scene had not changed from the last time. 'I don't see a lot,' she said. 'A row of shops, a Post Office, a gas station, a small car park. Nothing very exciting.'

'The car park is a compound attached to that garage. Cars are left there waiting for repairs, the owners go into the reception area to report their arrival and then the mechanics come out in due course to collect the cars to work on them inside. When they are finished the car is parked outside again.'

Peaches looked again. 'So,' she said finally.

'Because of the small size of the compound the cars have to have their keys left in them so they can be moved about to let other ones out. All I have to do is wander in and pick a car and they will think I am an owner come to reclaim it after repair.'

'That's brilliant,' she said. 'Will it work?'

'No bother. I told you it was just a matter of waiting for the right opportunity. Now give me a pair of trousers and a jacket out of my bag.'

She bent down to pull back the zip. 'What do you need these for?'

'I can't go in looking like a tourist,' he said. 'I want to look like a local. You stay here and pay the bill so that we can make a quick getaway. Give me ten minutes.'

'You're really going to do it?'

'I really am. What colour would you like?'

'Blue is my favourite.'

'Blue it is then.'

She moved over to his seat so that she could watch him walk away down the street. He went into a doorway and came out a few moments later wearing the trousers and the jacket with the sleeves pulled back to the elbows. She called the waiter and paid the bill. The excitement was building inside her. Hardly able to sit still, she watched MacDonald enter the compound but then she lost sight of him behind the barrier of parked cars. A group of four young men came onto the cafe terrace and sat down at a table beside her, making no effort to hide the fact that they were looking her body up and down. She turned away from them and sat with her legs pressed tightly together, wishing she had put on some less-revealing clothes. They began to make comments about her. Her French was good enough to understand them, but she pretended she didn't even hear.

Two cars drove out of the compound and turned in the opposite direction before a big blue Renault turned her way. The strong sunlight blanked out the windscreen so she could not make out who the driver was. The car rolled to a halt at the edge of the pavement beside her. The passenger door opened and she saw MacDonald inside.

'Well, are you coming or not?' he shouted.

She stared at him open-mouthed. The four men at the next table were also looking at the car. She spurred herself into action, picking up the rucksack and the holdall and throwing them onto the back seat. She climbed in beside MacDonald and slammed the door shut.

'You did it,' she said, feeling her heart race alarmingly. 'You actually went and did it.'

'I said I would, didn't I?' He accelerated away sharply.

'I'll never doubt you again Joe,' she said, hugging his arm.

'Good. Did you notice it's even the colour you ordered?'

MacDonald flicked a switch and the windows opened on both sides. Peaches tilted her head back as the cool breeze filtered through her hair. They had actually stolen a car. They were criminals. Outlaws. On the run together. Grabbing MacDonald's hand she pulled it away from the steering wheel, bringing it up to her lips to kiss. She was enjoying her new life.

Helmut Rocher walked down Leopoldstrasse in the Schwabing district of Munich and stopped outside the entrance to the corridor and stairs which led to his second-floor office. Someone had put an anti-nuclear sticker on his stainless-steel nameplate, Atom Kraft Nei Danke. The irony was not lost on him as he paused to pick it off and rub the plate clean with the sleeve of his jacket.

He was a small, stout man with a shiny bald head and tiny eyes that seemed lost in the fleshy expanse of his face. He wore suede slip-on shoes, an off-the-peg suit which fitted him badly, a red silk waistcoat he had inherited from his father, and a red and white spotted bow tie. It was a hot, sunny day but it was not the weather that was causing him to perspire freely. He was just returning after a long lunch at his private club where he had spent the last two hours sampling the latest offerings of his video film production company. They had found him a new starlet, a twenty-year-old from Vienna called Eva who could certainly not be accused of lacking enthusiasm for her job. Like all aspiring actresses he took under his wing she was due to come to his private flat that evening for a personal interview so that he, as company boss, could plan her future. He was already aware that Eva was something special. She was six-foot tall and built like an Amazon, yet she had the cutest little baby face. He adored tall women, Eva would have a good future with him.

Rocher ran up the stairs to his office, misjudging his capability so that he had to rest at the top to regain his breath. There were three women sitting behind a frosted-glass screen in the front section of the office. Two were occupied on the phone taking orders for video films. The third stood up as he came in the door and wobbled over on her high heels to relieve him of his briefcase.

'That's all right, Mitzi,' he said, keeping a grip on it as she tried to take it from him. 'I have some papers to look at just now.'

Mitzi looked disappointed as she went back to her seat. She was over forty with blonde permed hair and a heavily made-up face that just about managed to retain its attractiveness. Her clothes were too tight for her, and too young. But Rocher could remember a time when Mitzi, and the other two women answering the phones, had been a lot like Eva. He kept them on working on the mail-order business because he was so soft-hearted. He could easily have surrounded himself with younger girls. Occasionally he used them for supporting roles in some of the films. They always performed well. They were experienced performers and knew what was expected of them. It was just a shame that women had to grow old the way they did. It was different for men, thank God. They could grow old gracefully. Very few women could.

Rocher opened the partition door and went through to the rear section of the office. He took off his jacket and hung it up. His armpits were damp with sweat. The shirt was stained in large circles round them. Sitting behind his desk, he could see the distorted images of the three women reflected through the glass panels. He checked his watch. Mr MacDonald was usually very punctual. If it hadn't been for him Rocher would still have been at the club.

The prospect of having Eva to himself that night was making it difficult for Rocher to keep his mind on the job in hand. He couldn't concentrate despite the fact that he hoped it might prove to be the biggest and most lucrative business deal he had ever set up. He grimaced at his lack of application. Arms dealing might bring in more money but making blue movies was much more fun. He could only think about Eva as the biggest and potentially most lucrative woman he had ever set up.

His private phone line bleeped softly. He let it do so three times before he wiped his palm dry on the blotting pad and picked up the receiver.

'Herr Rocher,' the familiar voice said.

'Speaking. Is that you, Herr MacDonald?' Rocher looked at his watch. It was the exact time he had said he would call. The conversation was to be in English.

'Is the meeting arranged?'

'It is,' Rocher said. 'Friday at eleven in the morning. Under the glockenspiel in Der Marienplatz, beside the column of Patrona Bavariae. Herr Betzing will speak to you there.'

'Is it not rather public?'

'Those are his instructions. If there is any difficulty the meeting may have to be postponed.'

'No. If that is what he wants. I will be there.'

'Good. And, of course, Herr Betzing will require proof that you are in full possession of the goods. He would prefer to see them for himself.'

'That will be impossible. I told you that. But rest assured I will supply the proof he wants.'

'I see no mention in the newspapers of your little project, Herr MacDonald,' Rocher said. 'I would have thought it would have made a big story for them.'

'They will get their big story soon enough.'

'As you say. I hope we can do business together. I will be with Herr Betzing on Friday. I remember you well from our meeting all that time ago when everything was but an idea in your head.'

'Till Friday, then.'

'Friday at eleven.'

Rocher held up the receiver as though it was a glass of schnapps before replacing it in its cradle. He remembered MacDonald very well, and his long-legged friend. The story had seemed wild and fanciful at first, but he had seen the thing called the Dipstick with his own eyes and his contacts confirmed what MacDonald told him about the Minotaur bombs. Now MacDonald was claiming that he had a Minotaur as well. Rocher believed him.

He lifted the briefcase onto the desk, took a key from his waistcoat pocket and opened the lock. Inside was a video tape. There was a television set and a video recorder in one corner below the shuttered window. He set up the equipment to play the tape and returned to his seat.

It was just a trial tape. There was no sound track. Its subject was Eva. It began with a shot of her standing looking at herself in the mirror, the camera at shoulder level at first and then panning back to reveal more and more. Rocher reached into his briefcase again and brought out a cardboard folder containing coloured pictures of Eva in various poses. He spread them over the desk-top and divided his attention between the pictures and the television screen. He used the empty folder to fan himself so that it was easier for him to breathe.

The casino was lavishly decorated with thick wine-red carpets and contoured wallpaper of the same colour. The design was supposed to be soothing. It was supposed to create a reassuring atmosphere in which the customers would not notice that they were losing all their money, or if they did notice they wouldn't care. The croupiers, if they were male, had to wear wine-red blazers. If they were female they had to wear long wine-red dresses with low-cut necks that showed plenty of cleavage whenever they leaned over a roulette table to sweep in all the gambling chips. That took the customers' minds off losing money as well.

Gudrun Richter was a floor waitress in the main gaming room of the casino. She had to wear a short red dress, low-cut, and large-mesh fish-net stockings with a single thigh garter. The light bruising around her eye was hidden under face powder. Her job was to stroll up and down and fetch drinks or cigarettes for anyone who asked. She had started work at ten that evening and her legs were aching after four hours without a seat. The casino was exceptionally busy. People were pressed shoulder to shoulder round the tables. There were queues for the stools at the blackjack games.

Gudrun had started out the evening in a good mood, delighted to have had Franz at the flat for the last few days, even if he was jumpy and irritable. They had shared the bedroom while the others had slept in the living room for the first day before going back to Manheim. Then it was just Franz and Gudrun on their own. What would happen when Divers returned, she did not know. But she had seen Franz with the pistol. He had tried to hide it from her and she made out she had not seen it, but it was there all right. Divers would get what was coming to him. Franz would see to that.

She leaned momentarily against the wall and lifted her heel to adjust the strap of the sandal that was chafing against her ankle. As she did so she felt a body press against her from behind. A hand ran up the outside of her thigh, pulled the garter out and snapped it back.

'A nice little smack for a nice little lady,' a voice said, slurring the words badly.

Gudrun took a step forward and turned, a smile fixed in position on her face. She saw a fat man in a shiny grey suit with his shirt hanging over the front of his trousers. He had thick glasses and dishevelled hair. He was smoking a large cigar, the smell of which did not quite mask his bad breath.

'Can I get you something sir?' Gudrun asked politely.

'You bet your sweet fanny you can, leibling.' He groped towards her, trying to pin her to the wall. The cigar smoke stung her eyes. 'Come on. How about you and me having a little fun?' he said.

She knocked his hands away with the tray she carried and quickly side-stepped so that he would miss her. He collided with the wall, slightly winding himself. She ignored him and casually walked away to the other side of the room, putting a screen of bodies between them.

She had already suffered too many propositions that night, too many lewd comments, too many hungry stares, too many hands up her skirt. It was all getting too much for her. The next one would get a swift kick in the groin, she silently decided. It would probably get her sacked but it would be worth it.

Somebody came up behind her. Hands gripped her waist. A chin rested on her shoulder. Warm breath touched her cheek. She stamped down hard with the sharp heel of her sandal, aiming at the man's foot. But he was too quick for her and moved it out of the way. She wriggled out of his grasp and turned ready to scream at him, ready to lash out with the tray as a weapon. She wasn't going to smile pleasantly at this one. She had had enough.

Gudrun froze as she recognized the man in front of her. Her

outstretched arm dropped to her side. The tray bumped against her knee with a metallic clunk.

'That's no way to treat a long-lost lover,' Divers said, speaking in English.

She struggled to regain her composure. 'You startled me,' she said. 'I didn't know it was you, Hugh.'

'Why? Not expecting me?'

'Of course, but you never said when you were coming back.' She stepped to one side as a group of people passed them. 'You never even told me you were going away. You just disappeared one morning.'

'Yes, I did, didn't I? You must have missed me.' She tried to force a smile, realizing at once how false it must look. 'You can't have missed me all that much though. I see your old boyfriend has moved into my place. That was quick work.'

Gudrun felt a tiny spasm of anxiety. 'You've been back? You have already spoken to Franz?'

'No. Not quite. I did have a glance through the window but I didn't go in. Your boyfriend has a very nasty temper, you know,' Divers said. 'He might have been annoyed with me for not giving him the Minotaur.'

She shook her head, not knowing what to say.

'No? You think not?' Divers raised his eyebrows in mock surprise. 'He is only staying there to renew old acquaintances, is he? Is he as good in bed as you remember him, Gudrun? It must have been a long time since you and he got together, a long time since he sent you to look after me.'

Gudrun swallowed hard. Divers had known all along. He had been toying with her all that time. She had not been fooling him. He had been fooling her. The blood rushed to her face. She felt her cheeks burning. Divers came forward and put an arm round her shoulders, steering her into a quiet corner.

'Now, your boyfriend obviously wants the Minotaur pretty badly,' he said. 'Well, I'm prepared to do business with him. I think it is only reasonable that Das Scwarze Leichentuch should have the chance to buy it.'

'We do not have much money,' Gudrun stammered. 'How ... how much are you intending to sell it for?'

'Money isn't everything, my darling. I may consider handing it over if the group agrees to co-operate in a plan I am formulating. I need their help. They need my Minotaur, perhaps we can do business. Does that sound fair?'

'Yes.'

'Excellent. I want you to tell Franz that I will meet him tomorrow night to discuss these things.'

She nodded. Franz would jump at the chance to get the Minotaur. Divers was on dangerous ground if he thought he could outsmart Franz. 'Where?' she asked.

Divers smiled and the hate inside Gudrun made her whole body go cold. 'I have thought of a very appropriate location. Tell Franz to meet me in Nuremberg. Tell him to be at Zeppelinwiese at midnight tomorrow. He will know the place. It is where his hero used to have wild nights out with the lads.'

'I'll tell him,' Gudrun said.

'And tell him to come alone. There will just be the two of us. That way there can be no distractions. All right?'

'I'll tell him,' she repeated steadily.

'Oh and you had better tell him to shake off the two men who are watching the flat at this very moment. It seems somebody is interested in what your boyfriend gets up to. See you around.'

Gudrun watched him leave, threading his way across the room through the milling crowds of people. They were watching Franz then. They were watching him because he posed such a danger. But they were fools and Franz would easily lose them. He would meet Hugh Divers at midnight as he wanted, but it would be Franz who would dictate the terms.

Somebody tapped her on the arm. It was a smartly-dressed man with blonde hair and blue eyes. He asked her for cigarettes. She switched on her professional smile and went to fetch them.

The Japanese embassy had hired a room in a Bonn hotel to hold a function to celebrate the arrival of a new ambassador. It was a very formal affair in full evening dress, medals to be worn, with white-faced, kimono-wrapped waitresses drifting like wraiths among the crowds of guests offering drinks and savouries. There had been much bowing and handshaking. The speeches had dragged on because they had to be translated, sentence by sentence, into a dozen different languages. When they were finally completed it was a relief for the guests to mingle and make pleasant small talk.

Buster Grant was a reluctant member of the British contingent at the embassy party. He had tried to get out of it, pleading pressure of work, but etiquette and diplomacy required his presence. Usually, he enjoyed such occasions but he was too preoccupied with the Minotaur business to be bothered with this one. Everybody seemed to think that because nothing had been heard since the theft, the crisis was passing of its own accord. The news of the soldiers' deaths had been reported as a shooting accident during a military exercise. The official account had not been challenged. No journalist had yet thought to ask the appropriate questions which would begin to unravel the thin veil of half-truths and bare-faced lies that obscured the real truth. No one had been told that the deaths happened beside a Minotaur chamber because no one had asked. In fact the reported location had been shifted a few kilometres to the west in case anybody went to look. No ransom demand had been received, anonymous or otherwise. There was no hint that the various groups of active and would-be urban terrorists were in any way involved. Grant had done an exhaustive round of contacts and fellow-travellers and turned up nothing except a cryptic phone call, monitored by the German authorities, to the leader of a very minor Nazi group. We have it, a women's voice had said. What? The Minotaur? But then she had gone on to say that somebody else was drunk and invited the man round. It might refer to anything; the day's shopping, the chance for a bit of sly nookie while a husband lay dead drunk. Grant was not greatly impressed. West Germany's Security Service, Budesamt für Verfassungsschutz, had assigned a couple of men to follow the recipient of the phone call anyway, but it was a long shot. The man's name was Luneburg, like the Lüneburg Heath in the north, near Hamburg, only without the umlaut. He ran an organization more rooted in romanticism than the real world. It was called Das Schwarze Leichentuch; The Black Shroud. Probably just another Teutonic dreamer.

The Minotaur had just vanished. But if it had disappeared in a puff of blue smoke it would have been difficult to hide the fact. Somebody out there had to have it. Somebody had to be planning to use it for something, even if they couldn't get the thing to go off. The East Germans denied any knowledge and he was inclined to believe them. There would be little point in them pinching a Minotaur when it was about to be replaced by an upgraded Chimera. What could it tell them? No, the crisis was not in the past. It was yet to arrive.

Grant was not in the mood to join the small talk. The reception room was packed. Guests were standing shoulder to shoulder. It was a simple matter for him to circulate on the fringe of the company, never staying in one place long enough to be drawn into serious conversation. He talked only when he was obliged to and then moved on at once. It was a well-known diplomatic technique for keeping out of everybody's way. The Minotaur was becoming an obssession with him. He believed that something terrible was going to happen, especially with the Dipstick missing as well. Despite the time lapse it was too much of a coincidence for him to dismiss lightly. But he seemed to be the only one thinking along these lines. Dave Sellars at Rheindahlen and Dirk Kasper in Cologne were adamant that the Dipstick remained buried at the bottom of the lake. Grant had gone as far as to get the army files on the personnel connected with the lorry and its accident. There had been seven men who gave evidence at the inquiry. No disciplinary action had been taken. Three men were still in the army, one had been killed in a car crash, another was in prison in Thailand for drug-smuggling. Of the remaining two one had received a dishonourable discharge for subsequent incidents detailed in his file, nothing really serious, just an accumulation of things. His army file stopped as soon as it was stamped DD. Grant had MI5 on the task of finding out where he was now, not that he expected anything to come of it, but at least it was a positive move. The last man had been traced by MI5. He ran a baker's shop in Cardiff.

The lorry accident had been four years ago. It took a sizeable leap of the imagination to connect it to the recent theft of the Minotaur. If there had been any other leads to follow that one would have been pushed well down the list. The accident inquiry did not apportion blame. The lorry had gone out of control on a twisting, downhill road and struck a tree before careering down a near-vertical slope into a lake. The driver had been killed instantly. His mate had been thrown clear. If anybody was to blame it was probably the dead driver, but the inquiry concluded that it was nobody's fault. An accident, they said, Just one of those things. Bad luck. Where had he heard that before?

Grant sighed and had to make a conscious effort to straighten his shoulders as they sagged wearily. He felt as if he was at the bottom of a sheer rock face rising up in front of him, the summit invisible from this angle. He was feeling for a handhold so that he could begin to climb but there was nothing to get a grip on, absolutely nothing. There were a few shallow bumps and hollows, otherwise everything was perfectly smooth. He needed somebody to give him a leg-up if he was ever going to get started at all.

'Ah Booster, my old friend.'

The greeting interrupted his train of thought. A hand fell on his shoulder and he could not pretend he had not heard. He knew before he turned round that it was Charles Deschaumes, cultural attaché at the French embassy, because of the Maurice Chevalier accent and the carefully manicured fingernails.

Deschaumes was a real pain in the neck. Grant took a drink from his glass of wine, almost emptying it as he prepared his excuse to move away.

'Charles,' he said politely, stepping back from the strong smell of after-shave. 'How good to see you.'

'You know Gerhard Lutzke from ze other side,' he presented a square-faced man with a severe crew-cut. 'Ve were just speaking about you.'

Grant knew Lutzke well. It was through him that he maintained his best contact with what went on in East Germany. It was Lutzke who had told him they were not involved in the theft of the Minotaur. Both men signalled their recognition by eye contact and with almost imperceptible nods of the head.

'Nothing too bad, I hope,' Grant said. A chest-high waitress floated by. He watched her disappear into the forest of bodies.

'Not bad, Booster. Not bad at all. Ve were just wondering if you have got eet back yet?'

Grant frowned and pretended not to understand. The loss of the Minotaur was an open secret in Bonn and it could only be a matter of time before the newspapers picked up the story. But the subject should have been taboo at such a formal occasion. Lutzke looked quite embarrassed as well.

Deschaumes put his hands at either side of his forehead with the index fingers pointing upwards. 'You know what I mean,' he said. 'Don't be so coy, Booster mon ami. In ziz matter you must take ze bull by ze horns.'

Deschaumes chuckled happily. Lutzke could not help smiling a bit. Grant decided to display the traditional British stiff upper lip. He muttered something about getting a refill and wandered away, following the path made by the little waitress.

Peaches Macdonald used nearly all her money to pay in advance for two nights in a fancy country hotel they found somewhere in central France. She didn't have to. MacDonald didn't force her to. She made the offer when they were passing the hotel gates and he mentioned that it looked like a grand place to stay for a while. It was then she told him about the wad of travellers' cheques sewn into the hidden pouch in her jeans and suggested that they blow the lot on some luxury living. He agreed at once. They went to a bank in a nearby town and cashed all the cheques. Then they abandoned the car they had stolen in Paris in a large car park and hired another Renault, a smaller one, to drive back to the hotel which was several miles out in the countryside. It was an expensive hotel. The receptionist was haughtily attractive in a stiffly-starched red uniform dress that rustled when she moved. MacDonald asked her if the rustling sound was caused by her silk underwear and not a flicker of a smile came across her heavily-made-up face. She counted the money slowly and methodically, dividing it into small bundles, before handing them their room key. A round-shouldered porter with arthritic fingers carried their luggage, the rucksack and the shoulder bag, after them up the sweeping staircase and along the picture-lined corridors. MacDonald gave him a five-franc tip. Inside the room, when they pooled all the money they had left, it amounted to forty-seven francs. Peaches felt a small thrill of pleasure at her recklessness. That money could have lasted for months, properly handled. Instead she had squandered it all in a moment of impulse. She was shocked at her own irresponsibility. It was great.

The hotel was a big old mansion house adorned with turrets and battlements and tall windows and lines of pale green moss on the roof tiles. A healthy growth of climbing plants layered the exterior walls. The interior was furnished with antiques and thick, dark carpets. The main hall was almost circular with a ring of antlered stags' heads surrounding the wide staircase with its mahogony banisters which led to the first and second floors. The other residents were mostly rich and mostly old. To them, Peaches and MacDonald were a curiosity.

The bedroom itself was big enough to play football in, as MacDonald described it. The bed was a reproduction four-poster. The first thing they did was to try it out. The ceiling was high with an intricate cornice which came down as far as the picture rail. A small chandelier hung in the centre. One side of a wooden sideboard concealed a miniature fridge containing soft drinks. The view from the small-paned bow window was of a gently sloping wooded valley with a château perched on a rocky ledge on the hillside opposite. The bathroom was huge. The bath was an ancient cast-iron affair supported on carved lions' paws. They could not resist having a bath together in it. There was an endless supply of hot water.

They went down for dinner in the restaurant because food, and two bottles of house wine, were included in the bill. But they escaped as soon as possible back to the intimacy of their room, taking the second bottle with them.

They sipped their wine and sat in cane chairs on either side of the window and looked out as darkness rolled like a fog along the valley. An irregular pattern of lights dotted the château wall facing them across the valley. Peaches brought her feet up onto the edge of the seat and sat cross-legged.

MacDonald stretched in his chair so that it creaked loudly. 'Enjoying yourself darling?' he asked.

She raised her glass to him. 'Thanks to you, yes. This is certainly much more comfortable than sleeping in that car.'

'It's legal too.'

She hesitated and then said: 'What happens when we've got no money left, Joe?'

'We'll worry about that at the time. We've got two clear days here. Two days is an eternity. We might all be dead in two days.'

Peaches was not worried. She had implicit faith in the man beside her although she had known him for such a short time. His attitude to life was the right one. It was an attitude she wanted to adopt. She was pleased that the rosy glow she had experienced while recklessly throwing away all her fallback cash had not faded as she had feared it would. Common sense had not intruded. Depression had not set in. She was well on the way to conversion.

'Tell me about yourself,' she said.

He poured himself another glass of wine and leaned over to fill hers. 'What do you want to know?'

'Everything. Tell me about your parents.'

'They are dead. We are not a long-lived family. Tell me about yours.'

'When did they die?'

'When I was a boy. My father was killed in an accident at his work. He was a docker. My mother stuck her head in the gas oven a few days later. I've been on my own ever since. What about you?'

'I never knew my father. He died before I was born. They didn't tell me till I was fourteen years old.'

MacDonald did not say anything. He just sat looking at her, waiting for her to continue, waiting for her to explain. She knew intuitively that the time had come for her to do so. She wanted him to know. She wanted him to understand. But she had never told anyone before, not personally. Her friends back home had heard through different versions from different people. Dale had known, but she had not told him.

The darkness was filtering into the room, gathering around them. It was still warm though, a velvet warmth that was soft against bare skin. MacDonald sat motionless in his chair. She collected her thoughts and then began.

'My mother did not realize she was pregnant with me until after my father had left to go to Vietnam. She says now that it was probably their last night together that did it. They were not married. They were hippies, you know, Flower People of the sixties. You should have seen my Pop's hair. It was way down past his shoulders before he was drafted. They had been trying for a while with no luck. It was probably the last night.'

Peaches looked away from MacDonald, out of the window.

The moon was behind the hotel casting a long shadow down across the tree-tops. Slowly it was merging to become indistinguishable from the greeny-blackness. 'He was a Marine, 26th Battalion. He was a short-timer. He just had to last twelve months and then he could come home. They sent him to a place called Khe Sanh just at the beginning of 1968. It was near the border of north and south, an airstrip with three hills, that was all it was. Nothing very special. He was dug in on Hill 881 when the siege of Khe Sanh was about two months old and they were surrounded by thousands and thousands of North Vietnamese. The air force was bombing the country round about, dropping five thousand a day to try and wipe out the enemy. Operation Niagra they called it because it conveyed the image of a cascade of bombs. Anyway it didn't work. The hill was a prime target for artillery fire and one day a shell landed right on the bunker my father was in. There was nothing left of him to send home.'

She stopped to take a drink of wine. Something that could have been a bat hovered in front of the window for a few seconds and then flew away. 'I didn't know any of this until I was fourteen and an uncle made some strange remarks at a family funeral and I got to asking questions. My mother had got married before I was born and I had always assumed the man was my father. But he wasn't. She said it had all been done for the best. They had always meant to tell me but had never got round to it.'

'I used to call Teddy father, but I couldn't after that. I cracked up, they had to take me away from school. I spent a year on a funny farm with doctors trying to see inside my head. I think they were frightened I was going to kill myself but that never really occurred to me at the time. I was in a state of shock. A whole year disappeared out of my life before I could think straight again.'

Peaches glanced over at MacDonald. He had not moved. He was still listening. 'I was shown my Pop's last letter,' she said. 'It was one he wrote from Hill 881, that was what he had in the top corner like a regular address. It didn't say much. It just described the bunker with its roof of aluminium runway matting held down with decks of sandbags. And he said the rats were as big as dogs. And outside on the low ground there was elephant grass constantly waving in the wind and there was the runway with a shell of a burned-out plane by its side. The planes didn't stop at Khe Sanh. They just touched down, poured the supplies out the back, and took off again immediately. And he complained about the noise of the bombs, the American bombs that is, at all times of the day and night. They shook the ground, shook the earth out of the walls of the bunker. And he said it wasn't that bad because they let reporters in to visit them. If things had been really desperate no chickenshit scribbler was going to risk his ass, he said. He said he would give the letter to a reporter to take out. That way his platoon commander wouldn't have the chance to read it and snigger over the lovey-dovey bit at the end. It was dated the day before they said he died. He had written not to worry about him because his time in Nam was getting shorter by the day. He didn't know then how right he was.'

She swallowed the remainder of the wine and put the glass on the floor. She hugged her arms round her body as if it had suddenly gone very cold and curled up more tightly in the chair. 'There was another letter,' she said more quietly. 'It was a letter to him from my mother telling him she was pregnant and there would be a new-born baby waiting for him when he got back. The letter never reached him. It was returned unopened. When he died he didn't know that I existed, that I was going to exist. He didn't know. He died not knowing. He was just about the age I am now. In fact, in a few weeks I will have lived longer than he did.'

Peaches stared out the window. Massive clouds were sealing off the sky and the stars like shutters closing. The darkness grew more intense all around them. Somewhere an owl hooted and a sudden breeze stirred nearby trees. A dozen raindrops appeared silently on the glass of the window. A car engine started up and the lights could be seen flickering on and off as it ran down the long tree-lined avenue to where the junction with the main road was hidden by a dip in the ground.

'Can you imagine how I felt?' Peaches asked and the question seemed to be directed in at herself. 'My whole world was turned upside down and at such an impressionable age. My roots were ripped up. My sense of safe belonging destroyed. I had never been all that close to my mother. Now I found out that the man I called father was an imposter. My adolescent psyche just couldn't handle it. That was why they had to send me to the funny farm for a time.

'Eventually I got to thinking that my life had started just as his had ended so maybe a part of him, you know his spirit or something like that, had been passed onto me. I thought that I should take over for him. That I should live for him, that I should do things with my life that would have made him proud of me. Does that sound crazy?'

She looked across at MacDonald but did not wait for an answer. 'Anyway, I convinced them to let me out of the funny farm. I went back to school and caught up on my studies and here I am the living, breathing example of the all-American girl having a summer holiday in Europe. What do you think of that?'

The switch from sincerity to levity came abruptly. She uncoiled her legs from under her and sat up straight in the chair.

'So we're not related after all. Your real name isn't MacDonald,' he said.

'Actually it is. You see, my mother married my daddy's brother so he had the same name. They wanted to keep me in the family. Teddy couldn't go to Vietnam because he has such bad eyesight. My mother as well. She can't see past the end of her nose. I'm the only one who can see. I guess I get that from my Pop.'

Peaches got up and went over to kneel beside MacDonald. She began to twist the hairs on his leg gently between her fingers. 'It's okay,' she said. 'I've got used to it now. I'm not crazy any more.'

'Good,' MacDonald said. 'We couldn't have two crazy people in this room.'

She laughed and kissed his kneecap. 'What about your parents?'

'I'm an orphan. I was much too young when it happened. I don't remember them at all. I was brought up in a local council home. As soon as I was old enough I joined the army to get away. But then they decided they didn't want me either after a while and I've been drifting ever since.'

'Don't you wonder about what they were like? Your parents?

'Sometimes. Not often.'

'I wonder about my father all the time. I've seen pictures of course. You know, he looked a bit like you, Joe. He really did.'

'Perhaps we were related. We had the same name.'

'Small D as opposed to your big D,' she said.

'A simple error in transcription down the generations.'

'Yeah. We all came from Adam and Eve originally, didn't we.'

'Was their name Macdonald as well then?'

She climbed up to sit on his lap and put her arms round his neck. He pulled her in close so that her cheek rubbed against the day-old stubble on his chin. 'If you were my father, Joe, would you be proud of me?' she asked.

'I most certainly would,' he replied.

She cuddled into him gratefully. 'Did you ever see the Jimmy Cagney film called *White Heat*?' she said. 'It was about this gangster who was a real hard case and his only saving grace was that he loved his mother. Everybody was against him and he had to fight them all just so that his mother would be proud of him. Anyway, she dies and at the end he is being chased through a gasworks by the police and he climbs up on top of a big gas tank. He is trapped. There is no way out. So he fires his gun into the tank and it explodes as he shouts, 'I made it, Ma. Top of the world.'

'And you think you are Jimmy Cagney?' MacDonald said. 'I can't see the resemblance myself.'

'But you do understand what I mean,' Peaches said seriously. 'I would like to be able to shout out, I made it, Pop. Top of the world.'

'Yes, I understand, darling.'

'Do you really?'

'Yes. Now let's go to bed.'

He stood up, still holding her against his chest, and lowered her feet down onto the floor. He went over to the bed while she went to the bathroom. She took the foil pack of contraceptive pills from her toilet bag and pressed out the next one in the sequence. It rolled off the edge of the palm of her hand, bounced on the enamel of the wash-hand basin, and shot straight down the plughole. She made an unsuccessful attempt to stop it.

She thought it was more of a nuisance than a serious problem, and could just take the next one in the sequence. She knew she was safe even if she missed the occasional pill. Pressing out the next one, taking great care that it did not miss her carefully cupped palm this time, she looked at the tiny pill nestling in the folds of flesh and then she looked up at her own reflection in the mirror. Peaches thought of her mother and father making love that last night before he had to leave to go to war and she thought of how she had been just a seed beginning to grow as his life was snuffed out. Smiling at herself in the mirror, the product of her father's seed, she slowly turned her hand upside down so that the pill fell out. It rattled round the basin and rolled down the plughole. She put the rest of the pack back into the toilet bag.

She returned to the bedroom. MacDonald was lying naked on the bed, on his back on top of the sheets. The hair all over his body made it look as if he was covered by a kind of veil. This was the kind of man her father would have been, she thought. However, she was content that this man was her lover.

He turned his head to watch her approach the bed. She undressed and he reached out to touch her as she came to join him. She climbed on top, sitting astride him, her hands resting on his chest.

'Look at me,' she whispered hoarsely. 'Top of the world.'

Zeppelinwiese was deserted. There was only one car sitting on the tarmac in front of the main white stone terrace. It was an ancient Volkswagen beetle, tilted badly to one side by the two flat tyres at front and rear. The rear window was white with smashed glass. Franz Luneburg drove round slowly, following the line of the track that was sometimes temporarily laid out for saloon car racing. His father had taken him there as a child to see the racing, and as they watched he had heard all the old stories. His father had married late, and was old when his son was born. So the stories he told were from first-hand experience. He had been a young storm-trooper at the Nuremberg rallies, and had seen Hitler on the platform. He had actually heard the famous speeches that his son could only listen to on tapes, and had raised his voice in the mesmeric chant of *Sieg Heil*, before going on to fight for the Fatherland.

A figure moved on the central elevated platform, indistinct in the semi-darkness of the late summer night. That was the platform where Hitler had stood with Hess, and Goering, and Bormann, and Goebbels, and the rest around him. What it must have felt like to be alive in those days, when the whole of Europe lay at Germany's mercy and the Third Reich was planning its thousand year reign. Luneburg felt the emotive power of history and heritage make his heart beat faster. And it could happen again. But this time the military lessons would have been learned. This time the Reich would not be defeated. The world would watch a nation rise up again. It was not impossible. All it needed was the right people and the right circumstances. Luneburg's eyes glittered in the dark interior of the car. A small circumstance towards that end stood waiting for him on the platform. It was ironic that it was an Englishman who would lift the corner of The Black Shroud to give the world its first glimpse of the new Germany.

Luneburg parked beside the abandoned Volkswagen. The gun in the waistband of his trousers pressed against his groin as he got out of the car. He looked up at the platform and saw a black silhouette on the rail with the low-pitched roof of the graffiti-scarred building behind. The silhouette put up a hand to wave in greeting. Luneburg smiled. The gesture was like a Nazi salute. He leaned back into the car and switched off the headlights, and then slipped his hands into the pockets of his black leather jacket. The lining of the right pocket had been slit open. His hand went straight through to grasp the butt of the gun. He smiled again and began to walk forward, trying to imagine the great Swastika banners and the rising swell of the chanting voices.

The Nuremberg arena was rectangular, lined by shallow terracing built from white stone. Weeds flourished in the cracks and joints. In the central part an American football pitch had been marked out on the grass. Four spotlights pointed up at a massive Stars and Stripes hanging limply from the tall flag-pole. The metalled section of ground took up about one quarter of the centre at the head of the arena. Black thunder clouds hung in the sky, their irregular edges outlined by bright moonlight as though they were giant jigsaw pieces fitted together. Through gaps in the clouds came shafts of light like flying buttresses holding up a canopy above the arena. Thunder rumbled in the distance. The air was warm but stale. Rain threatened.

Luneburg had to go twenty yards to his left to get to a gateway in the chain-link fence that bounded the terracing. He climbed up to the platform with big strides to take the steps two at a time until he reached the level where Divers was waiting for him, standing with his arms crossed and his back against the rail. He gripped the handle of the gun more tightly.

'You got my message then,' Divers said in German. 'I knew Gudrun would pass it on. She's a reliable girl.'

Luneburg stopped a few feet in front of Divers. 'I have come alone as you asked. We can do a deal, Hugh. What are your terms?'

Divers laughed at the mention of his Christian name. Franz was trying to humour him. That was probably Gudrun's idea. 'You got rid of them then?' he said.

'They followed for a while but they were not local people. It was simple to lose them in the back streets.'

'They will be waiting when you get back.'

Luneburg shrugged and cocked his head to one side like a bird. 'I have many hiding places in my country.'

'And over the border in the East as well I am told.'

'The East is also my country,' Luneburg said firmly. 'It is also Germany.'

'Of course. Of course.' Divers turned and leaned his fore-arms on the top of the rail. 'This must really have been an impressive place in its heyday, eh Franz? Imagine what it must have been like standing up here, having all those thousands of men out there eager to carry out your demands. Take over the world, he would shout, and off they went to take over the world. They didn't quite manage it but then that's another story, isn't it?'

He looked back over his shoulder. A flash of lightning seared down from the clouds, flooding the arena with vivid white light. Momentarily, it purged every last shadow from Lune-burg's face making it stark and smooth as though it was moulded from plastic. Then the dark returned, blacker than before. The thunder rolled a few seconds later.

'All we need is Wagner to blast out one of his tunes and this place would really have some atmosphere,' Divers said. He turned back and looked up at the American flag. It flapped lazily once and then fell back against the pole.

'What is it you want, Hugh?' Luneburg asked in a strained voice.

'Remember when I first came to you, Franz?' Divers said quietly. 'I came to your little group of would-be world-changers because I thought we could work together. I thought our minds operated on the same wavelength. I thought we were thinking the same things. I thought I could help lift The Black Shroud from the body of fascism so that it could be reborn. That is what it is all about, after all.'

Luneburg's shoes scraped the ground as he shifted position.

He remained silent.

'I wanted to join your group. I wanted to steal the Minotaur for you Franz. I wanted to give it to you. And what happened? What happened?'

Luneburg hesitated and then began to speak. 'It was not . . .'

'You said I could not join,' Divers interrupted. 'You said I was a foreigner. You said I did not have the required pedigree to be a member of the new master race. My eyes were not blue. My hair was not blonde. You told me to go fuck myself, Franz.'

'We did not know you then, Hugh,' Luneburg said quickly. 'You could have been trying to infiltrate the group. You could have been anybody.'

Divers turned again so that the two men were face to face. Another lightning streak scored the sky and the air between them flared and faded. 'You told me to go and fuck myself, Franz,' he repeated evenly.

The thunder, much louder than before, crashed above them. The stone under their feet vibrated with the pressure waves. Luneburg shook his head.

'Don't worry Franz. I'm not the type to bear a grudge.' He laughed. 'Besides, you put sweet little Gudrun onto my case and I got to fuck her instead. You see, Franz, you actually did me a lot of good by refusing to let me join your group. I didn't think I could steal the Minotaur by myself. I thought I needed help. But you forced me to do it on my own and in the end that is just what I did. All on my own. I was being too modest. I didn't realize just what the extent of my talents were. But now I know. I did it all alone, didn't I?'

'Why have you brought me here?' Luneburg said, flexing his hand on the gun butt where the palm was sticky with sweat.

'I was hurt Franz,' Divers continued as if he hadn't heard the question. 'I was really hurt when your little group voted to throw me out on the street. I thought maybe they didn't believe what I was telling them, didn't believe that I had the capability to deliver the Minotaur. They thought I was mad, raving mad. But you didn't believe that, did you Franz? You could see my potential.'

'I believed you Hugh. You're not mad.'

'That's right. You were the leader but you couldn't persuade your followers to follow you on that one. I know that Franz. I know you wanted me to join but were outvoted. And I know that in the end you voted against me yourself, but that was only for form's sake, so that it wouldn't seem like a defeat for you. That's the way politics works Franz. I don't bear a grudge.'

Luneburg smiled, sensing that the one-sided conversation was going in his favour. Divers was trying to tell him something but wanted to get the explanation in first. He was wrong, of course. The voting had been completely unanimous at all times. There was no room for foreigners in Das Schwarze Leichentuch.

'But even though I wasn't allowed to join you were still interested in what I had to say about the Minotaur, weren't you Franz? That was why Gudrun had to make the big pretence of falling head over heels in love with me, so that she could keep an eye on me. Don't look so surprised Franz. I knew all about it right from the very beginning. I played along because, to tell the truth, I'm a widower and I can get lonely and little Gudrun is nice to have around. And she certainly puts her heart into a job. You know what I mean Franz? She certainly kept me happy.'

'The Minotaur? You have it?' Luneburg said eagerly.

'You know I've got it Franz. Gudrun told you. She's seen it. She knows.'

'What do you intend to do with it?'

'I want to give it to you.'

The lightning flashed right on cue, adding to the sense of theatrical unreality that was creeping over Luneburg. Divers was ridiculing him, he was not being serious. He was taunting him. The thunder crashed like a huge gong at the back of his head. Fat raindrops spat onto his leather jacket. He loosened the pistol on his waistband and curled a finger round the trigger.

'What's the matter Franz? Don't you want it?' Divers said.

'Why should you just give the thing to me? Why?' Luneburg demanded aggressively.

'I told you Franz, I don't bear a grudge. I came to Das Schwarze Leichentuch because I believed it was the way forward. I still believe that. The cause is greater than the man. Don't you agree Franz?'

'I agree,' he replied thoughtfully, thinking that maybe the man was mad after all. There had to be a catch. There had to be a price. Divers was not as naive as he was trying to make out.

'How much?'

'No money,' Divers said with a shake of his head. 'Of course, you must let me become a member now.'

Luneburg relaxed a little. He had studied psychology. The Englishman was displaying the classic symptoms of a rejected member of a peer group trying to buy his way in by ingratiation. Membership and acceptance was his price for the Minotaur. The pledge was easily given. The price could be paid from the barrel of a gun once the Minotaur was theirs.

'I think that can be arranged,' Luneburg said, trying to mask the emotion in his voice.

'I thought it might,' Divers said. He held out a hand. 'Well, aren't you going to welcome me to the master race?'

Luneburg released his grip on the gun and they shook hands. The rain was slapping down around them, smacking loudly onto the stone slabs. It quickly soaked their hair and began to run into their eyes and over their cheeks. Falling drops gleamed as they passed through the spotlight beams in the centre of the arena. The flag unrolled to its full length in the steadily rising wind.

'Come on then Franz. You drive and I'll take you to the Minotaur.'

They ran down the terracing, shoulders hunched under the pouring rain. A lightning flash lit the way. An avalanche of thunder broke directly over their heads. Luneburg followed Divers, the excitement he felt making him seem to bounce over the ground. He was going to be handed the Minotaur on a plate. It was scarcely what he had expected when he had arrived. At the very least he had assumed that Divers would have wanted to sell the Minotaur and he had been prepared to negotiate a time and place for the handover. Of course, there would have been no question of them actually having to pay for it. Once they had it in their possession, Divers would have been eliminated. But now it seemed that he was not interested in money. He was going to give it to them free of charge, for the furtherance of the cause. Luneburg grinned confidently at the back of Divers' head. There was no need to change the substance of his original plan. Once the Minotaur was his, Divers would be executed.

They reached the car. Luneburg got behind the steering wheel and leaned over to unlock the passenger door. Divers tilted the seat forward and climbed into the back, explaining that he would be able to check more easily if they were being followed from that position. He told Luneburg to drive towards Fürth, an industrial suburb to the north-west of Nuremberg. The engine started first time. Luneburg rubbed the condensation from the inside of the windscreen. The wipers carved a path through the teeming rain as they left the arena.

Divers kept giving instructions from the rear seat, making the car turn left and right and describe a tortuous route towards Fürth. The journey lasted more than an hour. Divers was eventually satisfied that no one was following them. He directed the car into a side road lined by a row of tall trees and told Luneburg to stop behind a white Audi parked there. The rain had subsided to a light drizzle. The thunderstorm had moved on. Drips from the tree branches bumped heavily down onto the roof of the car.

'Is the Minotaur in your car?' Luneburg asked anxiously.

'Not exactly.'

'What do you mean?'

'Well Franz, I've actually brought you here to meet a friend of mine. Ah, there he is now.'

Luneburg stared out the windscreen. He could not see anybody. Nothing was moving except the swaying branches of the trees. The hairs on the nape of his neck suddenly began to prickle with a sense of unease. He saw a flash of movement in the rear-view mirror and felt a thin wire looped round his throat and pulled tight. His head was jerked back and his cheek jammed against the side of the headrest. He tore desperately at the wire as he choked and struggled to breathe. But there was nothing to get hold of. It had already cut deep into the flesh and his fingers were soaked with his own warm blood. He tried to push up with his feet to slacken the wire but his legs were trapped underneath the steering wheel. He could not move at all. Frantically, he searched blindly for the pocket of his leather jacket. His hand slipped in and he thrust it right down to reach the solid handle of the pistol. He yanked it free of his trousers but it got tangled in the lining of the pocket and he could not get it clear. His throat felt as if it was full of burning coal. He was growing weaker by the second. With his head half turned he could just see Divers looming behind him, his face contorted into a vicious snarl with the effort of holding the wire tight. It grew rapidly darker though Luneburg knew his eyes were still open. The pattering of the raindrops on the car roof grew unbearably loud. He made one last supreme effort to rip the gun free of his pocket, but it was hopelessly caught there. He managed only to force it up to the level of his chest. The barrel was pointing inwards. He pulled the trigger by mistake and in the split second he realized what he had done the bullet passed cleanly between his ribs, pierced his heart, and exited through his back. He died instantly in a crimson explosion of pain.

Divers snatched his hands away from the ends of the wire and clutched his left thigh where the red-hot pain had lanced into it. He rocked backwards, hitting his head on the back window before falling sideways along the length of the rear seat. He watched the blood ooze up between his thumbs and the dark stain spread up round his groin. He saw the tear in the back of the driver's seat where the bullet had come through.

'Shit,' he growled, lying motionless, listening in case anyone had heard the sound of the shot and was coming to investigate. But he had chosen the spot well. The lights of some houses were just visible through the trees but they were at least a quarter of a mile away. No one came.

He grabbed Luneburg's hair and jerked his head back to check that he was dead. Then he threw it forward again angrily. He was annoyed at himself for getting wounded when he should have had the situation under complete control. He knew now that he should have insisted on searching Luneburg before they left Zeppelinwiese. It would not have been an unreasonable request in the circumstances. He could not have objected but what would he have done if Divers had found the gun? A wave of pain made Divers feel sick, he had made a mistake. Too late to change it now.

The bleeding was not too bad. The bullet must have missed the main artery. His leg was stiffening up, muscles knotting as though with cramp. It was difficult for him to shift the front seat and climb out the passenger door. He stood by the side of the car for a while, letting his strength return as he held back his head to drink the bitter-tasting rain that fell in drops from the branches.

He limped to his own Audi and unlocked the door. In the glove compartment he found the template in the shape of the Minotaur symbol he had cut from a piece of thick cardboard. Beside it was the spray can of red paint. He went back to Luneburg's car and wiped the bonnet clear of rainwater with his arm. He pressed the template down on the surface and held it there with arched fingers while he sprayed round the edges. The paint immediately began to run. He moved it and sprayed two more outlines on the bonnet, then several more along the sides and on the boot. He leaned inside and sprayed one on the windscreen above the dashboard.

Luneburg's head lolled awkwardly to one side on his shoulder, his eyes were half open. A trickle of blood came from the corner of his mouth. Divers unzipped the dead man's jacket and eased the gun out of his hand. He slipped it into his own pocket.

'So much for the master race and the Fourth Reich Franz,' he said quietly.

Another spasm of pain cut short his mocking sneer. He closed his eyes until it had passed.

'You should have let me join you know,' he gasped as though the words would attract the pain back. 'I always was a bad loser. I always bore a grudge.'

He stood upright and slammed the door shut, and limped to his car, cursing himself for his carelessness in getting shot. Numbness was spreading outwards from the wound and the bleeding seemed to have stopped. Even if it was just a flesh wound the bullet was inside it and he would have to be careful about infection. It was bound to make things more difficult for him.

He knocked his leg against the side of his car and clenched his teeth in a grotesque smile. If it was more difficult that was fine by him, he thought. The harder the way, the sweeter the final victory.

The bed was soft and comfortable. It had been a long day for Hugo Betzing beginning with a helicopter flight to the Birmingham armaments factory for a presentation and demonstration, and ending with an excessive drinking session in the bar of his London hotel. But it had been worth it. The deal had been successfully concluded and his commission was ensured. The Arab go-between, with his decidedly un-Islamic liking for strong alcohol and female flesh, had duly contacted his masters and the hotel telex had printed out the coded confirmation. Ten crates of lace tablecoths would be on their way within the week. The documentation was all in order. The end-user certificate was a formality. It had been a good day's work. Now Ali, the curly-haired Arab, had retired to the room next door to be serviced by the visiting masseuse he had selected from the adverts at the back of Penthouse magazine. All Betzing wanted to do was sleep. He kicked off his shoes and lay out flat on the bed. Ali certainly had tremendous stamina, he thought wearily. Or maybe it was just that he was getting old.

Betzing reached behind his head without looking and fumbled for the switch to turn on the radio which was set into the side of the headboard. He would catch the late news and then he would sleep. His plane flew out just before noon the next day. That would give him the chance to have a long lie.

There was classical music on the radio when he turned it on. It almost lulled him to sleep, but then it finished and the crackling applause of the concert audience was loud enough to keep him awake. A smooth-voiced announcer gave a list of future programme details before handing over to the news studio. The time was exactly midnight.

'NATO commanders today admitted that a nuclear land-mine was stolen in a carefully-planned raid in West Germany at the end of last week,' the newsreader said. Betzing immediately sat upright and swung his feet round onto the floor as he turned to look at the silver radio speaker grille.

'Two British soldiers were killed in a terrorist ambush and the Minotaur land-mine was taken during a military exercise in the Hessen State north of Frankfurt near the East German border. Military sources were anxious to stress tonight that the mine was not armed and was incapable of detonation without special equipment which was not being carried by the soldiers and which is not missing.

'The admission came after several anonymous messages were sent to different German newspapers, and also in the wake of the discovery of the body of a suspected terrorist who may have been involved in the ambush. Here is our correspondent in Bonn, Timothy Randall.'

A different voice took over. Betzing leaned closer to the grille as if straining to hear, a thin smile stretching out on his lips.

'The sensational news was released here after several newspapers had received cryptic messages consisting of only the spray-painted outline of the Minotaur symbol, a stylized pair of bull's horns, and the simple question: Ask them if they have lost one?

'A further twist was added with the discovery of the body of Franz Luneburg in a car on a quiet road on the outskirts of Nuremberg. It is believed the same type of stencilled outlines had been sprayed all over the car. Luneburg, who had been shot through the heart at close range, was allegedly the leader of a shadowy neo-Nazi group known as Das Schwarze Leichentuch, The Black Shroud. This afternoon police raided houses in Mannheim and Cologne and arrested several people. They also took possession of arms and explosives.

'The Minotaur nuclear land-mine has been in service with NATO troops for several years and experts say it cannot be detonated without additional equipment which is never carried by soldiers involved in an exercise. There is therefore no danger to the public, they say. The Minotaur is in effect a small nuclear bomb with an explosive capacity equivalent to more than three hundred and fifty tons of TNT, but compact enough to be carried on a man's back like a rucksack.

'The two soldiers who died were earlier said to have been killed in an accident. It is now known that they were shot, perhaps with their own rifles, in what is being described as a highly professional attack that could not have been carried out without considerable advance planning.

'Tonight in Bonn German politicians were demanding an immediate inquiry into the events surrounding the stealing of the Minotaur and a formal statement on the extent of the use of nuclear weapons by NATO troops based in the Federal Republic. The East German government was quick to condemn the deployment of nuclear weapons during exercises, although it is known that Warsaw Pact forces have similar land-mines.

'Sources in Bonn said no ransom demand had yet been received for the return of the Minotaur which is in any case, according to them, completely harmless. Nor has there been any threat against specific targets although security has been stepped up at military installations throughout the country.

'It is being suggested that the shooting of Franz Luneburg at Nuremburg may reveal an internal dispute among the members of The Black Shroud over how the Minotaur should be handled to their advantage. Little is known about the group although police did have several members under surveillance prior to last week's ambush. This is Timothy Randall in Bonn returning you to the studio in London.'

Betzing switched off the radio as the report ended and rubbed the palm of his hand across his mouth. So Mr MacDonald, he thought, this is the proof you promised to provide. Perhaps the rest of what you say is true also. He stood up and began to unbutton his shirt. He was no longer tired and he knew it would now be difficult to sleep with his mind so active. He undressed and put on a pair of pyjamas he took from under a pillow. Then he walked over to the table by the window on which was placed his briefcase. He thumbed round the combination numbers to open it and lid sprang up. He lifted out a sheaf of photocopied pages. On the first one, in the top right-hand corner, was the Minotaur symbol. He went back to the bed, got between the sheets, and began to read through the pages.

The chair was hard and uncomfortable but Gudrun Richter refused to move to give some relief to her aching muscles. The police had picked her up earlier in the day at the flat in Frankfurt where she was becoming increasingly worried by the failure of Franz to come back. Twice she had gone out to phone the alternative address in case he had gone there, not wanting to go back under surveillance. But there had been no answer.

She had seen them follow her along the street, ridiculously conspicuous in their trench coats and dark glasses. She had even waved to them as she stood making the calls from the public phone. But there had been no answer.

Then the uniformed police arrived on the doorstep. She had not believed them at first when they told her that Franz was dead. She had thought it was some kind of strange, perverted trick. They took her in for questioning and she still refused to believe it. She laughed in their faces and ignored their endless questions. So they showed her some photographs and it was impossible for her to avoid the truth. She saw Franz slumped in the driving seat of his car with the Minotaur symbol painted on his chest. She stared at the picture and she imagined she could feel the blood slowing down in her veins. She thought her heart was beating slower and slower, like the sound of a tape played at the wrong speed. Her body was hardening all over until she felt as if she was carved from stone. She did not move, or speak. The picture of Franz lay in front of her. He was dead and she was alone. The man she had loved was dead. He had been shot through the heart, they said. Killed instantly. No chance of survival. And she had sent him to his death. It was she who had arranged the meeting with Divers. It was she who had encouraged him to go to Nuremberg. She had thought Franz was more than a match for the arrogant Englishman. But somehow he had been tricked. Somehow he had been killed. Divers had probably had a gang of thugs waiting to ambush Franz. It had probably taken half a dozen of them to kill him. He would not have died without a fight.

Gudrun did not want the policemen to see her cry. They kept asking her questions but she just looked over their heads and said nothing. They knew about Divers because they mentioned his name. But she was going to say nothing. She knew that Divers had at least two false passports and driving licences. He had boasted about it once when he was drunk, when they were in bed together. The thought of him touching her body made her squeeze her hands into tight fists. She had endured so much because Franz had asked her to. It had been distasteful and difficult but she had carried out his orders and it had been a real shock for her to find out that Divers had known all along about what was going on. He had used her, abused her, played with her. And now he had killed the man she loved.

They showed her a picture of Divers, asking if she recognized him. She recognized him all right. He was much younger and his hair was much shorter but there could be no doubt it was him. She said nothing as she stared into his eyes. The saliva collected in her mouth and she almost spat in his face, but she controlled herself at the last moment.

She noticed that they were watching her curiously as she looked away from the picture. Divers would outrun them easily. But she knew a lot about him. She knew things that might help to find him. She would find him and then she would kill him. Inside her head she swore a silent oath. Lifting her eyes to the small, square-shaped mirror set into the rear wall of the room she saw the slight, fragile smile that had appeared on her lips. They could not guess what she was thinking. No wonder they were looking at her strangely.

Dirk Kaspar stood a little way behind Buster Grant as both men watched Gudrun Richter through the one-way mirror. They were in a narrow room with no furniture and a door at either end. An extractor fan hummed in the ceiling. The floor smelled of polish.

'She's smiling at you Buster,' Kaspar said. 'She must be glad to see you.'

Grant did not react. He was in no mood for joking. The crisis was developing. As he had feared, things were beginning to happen; the letters to the newspapers, the killing of Luneburg, the ritual plastering of the car and the body with the Minotaur symbols. It did not look at all healthy.

Earlier in the day he had been quietly sipping coffee in Kaspar's fifth-floor office in the featureless glass and concrete building which housed Bundesamt Für Verfassungsschutz on the Barthelstrasse in Cologne. They had been putting their heads together to try and make sense of events after the discovery of Luneburg and the spray-painted warning, or boast, or threat. Fragmented items of information trickled in over the telex as the rounded-up terrorist suspects were interrogated at various places around Germany. There was a fifteen-minute gap between reception and decoding. Grant had almost choked on his coffee when the name of Hugh Divers was first mentioned. He recognized it immediately. Divers had been the name of the driver of the truck which had crashed into the lake when the Dipstick was lost four years previously. Now he was being told that someone with the same name had offered to steal a Minotaur nuclear land-mine for the Black Shroud if they would help him to do it. It was not a German name. It was not even a common British name. There was no chance it could be a coincidence. It looked as if Divers had taken the Dipstick. Now he had the Minotaur as well.

Grant's face had gone so pale Kaspar had asked him if he was ill. He managed to mumble some excuse about not being accustomed to the heat. Kaspar did not know about the missing Dipstick. British Intelligence had decided at a high level that that particular piece of information should not be passed on to NATO partners. The official reason was to avoid confusing the issue by what could only be wild speculation. So only Grant and a handful of other intelligence staff were aware of what was now the real possibility of a Minotaur land-mine and Digital Initiation Programmer being together in unauthorized, unfriendly hands. In fact, Grant realized, he was the first person to know because he was getting the information hot off the press. Everyone else seemed to think that it was just a great game, that it was something harmless that was missing out there. That was how Kaspar was able to keep making bad jokes.

Kaspar was roughly the same age as Grant but looked much older with his full head of aristocratic silver hair. When he spoke he always held his head well back and all but closed his eyes.

'We could hold onto this young lady but we think it might be a good idea to release her and then keep a close eye on her,' he said. 'It might be interesting where she could lead us.'

'You think she and Divers might be planning to meet up somewhere?' Grant asked.

'It is possible. She's a strange one. Just look at her.'

Grant looked, frowning back into Gudrun Richter's smiling face. It had been her voice on the tape taken from the phone tap on Luneburg's Mannheim flat. We have it, she had said. It; the Minotaur. We; her and Divers. But if it was Divers why was she calling Luneburg to her? Hurry Franz, she had said. Why? To kill Divers and take the Minotaur for themselves? Then why hadn't that happened? Maybe she had been calling Luneburg in so that Divers could kill him. But then why the delay? What had happened in the days between the first phone call and the eventual killing of Luneberg? Grant sighed in frustration. The footholds were there for him to begin the climb towards the truth of the situation but he just could not get a grip on them. They had known about Divers and about Luneberg before the murder and the weird announcement of possession of the Minotaur through the painted symbols. But it had done them no good. Perhaps if the leads had been followed up more assiduously there might have been a better conclusion, but hindsight always made things seem ridiculously obvious. Perhaps they already knew other things, things that would direct them straight to Divers' hiding place. Grant shook his head, then turned to Kaspar and nodded.

'It is a good idea. She's a hard nut by all accounts and it doesn't look as if she is going to crack,' he said.

'She hasn't told us a thing,' Kaspar said and there was a trace of admiration in the words. 'Not a thing.'

'It's a good idea as long as you don't lose her.'

Kaspar shrugged and ran his fingers through his hair. 'It will be a gamble. We lost Luneburg but new men will be briefed. They should stay awake this time.'

Grant turned back to face the woman through the mirror. She moved her eyes slightly to the side as though acknowledging his look. 'I doubt if she and Divers are in this together,' he said.

'She has not mentioned him. Not once,' Kaspar said. 'All our information has come from the others. She pretends not to recognize his photograph, but she can't hide it then, not completely. She either loves him or hates him.'

'The two things are pretty close. If she was Luneburg's woman she will hate him.'

'She might have switched loyalties. They were living together you know. We're told it was on Luneburg's instructions but maybe she did a little thinking for herself after Divers whispered a few sweet nothings in her ear.'

'Give me even money and I would bet she hates him,' Grant insisted.

There was a gentle tap on the door to their right. Kaspar went to answer it and disappeared outside. Grant remained where he was staring into the eyes of Gudrun Richter, trying to read her mind. Her face seemed to keep changing between blank indifference and, with a twitch of her lips, wry amusement. A shirt-sleeved policeman with greasy black hair sat in front of her, the light shining wetly on hs hair as he continued to ask questions she simply ignored. Grant almost smiled back. He had flown the short distance from Cologne, intending to question her himself. The German police had no objection. They were willing to try anything. He wanted to learn more about Divers and she had refused legal representation, so there was no problem. But now, having seen her, he had decided not to go in personally. She intimidated him. She frightened him. He decided to stay on the outside and just observe her, like watching a wild animal through the bars of a cage.

Kaspar returned to the room and to his position behind Grant's shoulder. 'I've just been shown the full post-mortem and ballistics reports,' he said. 'They paint a different picture from the one we thought we had.'

'What?' Grant said disinterestedly, unable to look away from the woman.

'Well, the shot through the heart killed him all right. It was a 9 mm bullet from a Walther P38. A German make. He was patriotic to the last.'

'We already know that.'

'Yes, but they can't find the bullet. It passed through the soft tissue of his internal organs, out through his back and then right through the driver's seat of the car as well. There is a blood stain on the rear seat but no tear in the fabric, indicating that it may have wounded somebody there.'

Grant turned slowly to face Kaspar. 'So there were two people involved in Luneburg's murder?'

'At least two,' Kaspar replied. 'Luneburg was being strangled with a thin piece of wire by somebody in the rear seat. The wire had sliced into his throat and was found embedded there. If they hadn't shot him, they would certainly have throttled him to death.'

'So why shoot him at all?'

Kaspar scratched the corner of his mouth. 'Amateurs?' he suggested. 'Sudden panic? One thing is sure, Luneburg didn't shoot himself.' He laughed stiffly.

'Divers has a friend out there with him then?'

'It looks that way. And one of them has a bullet in his leg. We think it is the leg because that was the angle of the shot, downwards. We have begun checking hospitals and doctors.' He nodded at the mirror. Miss Richter is ruled out. She was under constant surveillance at the time.'

'Divers and a friend eh?' Grant said quietly, thinking back to the army files and wondering if any of the names he had seen there would soon confront him again. 'How bad is the wound?'

'There was no great loss of blood. A flesh wound. It will be painful but not serious as long as it is treated properly. Of course, that is presuming it didn't hit a vital spot.'

'You mean he might have had his balls shot off?'

'We didn't find them on the rear seat either. It was a real piece of bad luck apparently. The ballistics people say it was a thousand to one chance that the bullet should pass through Luneburg's body without hitting bone and then right through the back of the seat without hitting any of the metal frame.

'Let's hope they have some more bad luck soon,' Grant said, feeling his attention drawn back to Gudrun Richter's smiling face.

'We have more information on Divers himself,' Kaspar said, handing a small photograph over Grant's shoulder. 'This is a more up-to-date likeness taken from his identity card. He seems to have changed quite a lot. He got married to a German citizen shortly after he was thrown out of your army, that is how he has been able to remain in this country all these years. She was a rich widow, a Frau Maria Hetz, much older than him. She died in a car crash six months after the wedding. He inherited her money.'

'That was handy for him.'

'Nothing suspicious about the crash apparently. Divers was driving and was injured, not too badly though. Their car had a blow-out at speed on the autobahn between Nuremberg and Munich. It somersaulted into a field. She suffered a broken neck.'

A persistent tingling sensation spread from the base of Grant's spine through his body to the fingers that were holding the photograph. He realized now that Divers had been patiently laying his plans for years; the diguised theft of the Dipstick, then the marriage to a wealthy widow and her subsequent death leaving him financially secure, now the blatant theft of the Minotaur land-mine itself. The stencilling of the symbols on Luneburg and the car was as if Divers was shouting out, It's me, it's me. Come and get me if you can.

Grant looked up from the photograph. Gudrun Richter was still smiling at him. Perhaps, he thought obliquely, she was reading his mind.

The long summer's heat had confined the shallow river to the centre of its stony bed. The crystal-clear water was flowing over less than one quarter of the width it could have occupied, with small offshoot streams which had detached themselves from the main body of water, trickling along at the side. The round, dry stones between the edge of the river and the grassy banks lay baking in the sun. MacDonald greeted the chance discovery of the river with a loud whoop and set off running towards it, throwing his clothes behind him as he went. Peaches followed, stripping down to nothing but a pair of bikini briefs. The water was only knee-deep but ice-cold and they had to lie flat to get a decent cooling effect all over.

At one point, where the land began to slope down quite sharply for about fifty yards, a natural barrier of huge six-foot and eight-foot-tall boulders ran horizontally across the path of the river. The water was deeper behind the boulders where it divided into two separate channels which, accelerated by the funnelling action, raced down the incline like two strands of plaited hair. The water foamed white, twisting in and out of the jumble of rocks, sending spray flying into the air where it crashed against or glanced off an unyielding wall, before finding the easiest route round it. At the bottom of the slope the river formed again into what was more or less a single unit and calmly continued its journey.

They could not find the river on their map so they did not know its name. All they knew was that they were somewhere near Lyon, heading by mutual agreement for Nice and Cannes on the Côte D'Azur. They had taken to hitch-hiking again after their stay in the expensive hotel and returning the hired car. Peaches had wanted to keep it but MacDonald had refused. It would be too easy to trace them, he explained. He had had to use his passport as identification when he originally hired it and they had the number which would quickly go on a list at every police station, at every border crossing. You should never steal anything that can be linked to you, he said. That is the way to keep one step ahead. Peaches appreciated the logic. She was learning all the time.

MacDonald shouted to her as she lay half floating, half resting on the river bed. 'Watch this, baby.'

She paddled herself round so that she could see him over the top of her toes. He was standing at the side of one of the biggest rocks where the water was almost up to his chest as it swelled to enter one of the narrow channels. As she watched he took what looked like a running jump and disappeared from sight. She heard him cry out once, a sustained shout that rose above the constant rush of the tumbling water. Then it abruptly stopped as if a switch had been thrown. She hesitated a moment, listening to make sure she was not mistaken, then she was clambering to her feet, an impulse of fear making her move urgently. She slipped and slid on the smooth stones as she ran clumsily downstream, kicking sheets of water high in the air. She reached the spot where she had last seen MacDonald and scrambled up the side of the rock. A tremendous feeling of relief washed over her when she saw him coming back up towards her, leaping from boulder to boulder. She was close to tears and she wiped her eyes quickly so that he would not notice.

'Come on,' he said when he got to her. 'It's great fun. Have a go.'

'What is?'

'This. Watch me.'

He dropped down into the water at the entrance to the channel and let the current sweep him away. It carried him along at a steady speed with the water up to his neck and then dumped him into a square-shaped pool. He went completely under for a few seconds before his head bobbed up and he was gasping for air and turning round to wave at her. The current pushed him the last few yards through the rocks into the tranquil flow of the river beyond.

He stood up and shouted to her. 'Come on baby. Dive in.'

Peaches lowered herself from the rock uncertainly. She felt the tug of the water where it swirled round her in the mouth of the channel. There could be anything under the surface; jagged edges, jutting stones. But she did not want to turn back. MacDonald had already been down safely, twice. Once she let go and was in the grip of the current she would not be able to stop. MacDonald was at the bottom, shouting to her, encouraging her. So she took a deep breath, closed her eyes, and launched herself.

The endless passage of water had worn the rock underneath into a satin-smooth chute. Her backside and her legs shot down the greasy underwater surface. She tried to control her speed but the current just kept her going at its own rate, getting faster and faster towards the bottom. She yelled out in exhilaration and the sound trailed behind her like a flying scarf. Then the avalanche of water plunged her into the deep pool and her mouth was suddenly full of the cold water and there was nothing beneath her and she thrashed around furiously not knowing which way was up, desperate for something solid to give her a sense of orientation. She broke the surface and was gulping air instead of water and her hair was matted over her face and the sunlight blinded her. She was still in the grip of the current and she did not see MacDonald as she was bowled into him and his arms closed round her as he fell backwards with her on top of him. They got to their feet in the shallow part of the river and splashed each other like children at the seaside. Then they laughed and hugged and splashed some more.

'It's great, isn't it?' MacDonald said.

'Marvellous,' she agreed.

'Let's do it again.'

They raced back up the rocks to the head of the channel and launched themselves one after the other down the chute. They did it again and again throughout the afternoon until they were bone tired and barely had the energy to raise a shout as they jumped into the torrent of white water.

The oven heat of the day had passed by the time they dragged themselves up onto a flat section of the rock and lay dozing and sunbathing. It was still pleasantly warm with a gentle breeze to keep the insects away. MacDonald lay face down and the wet hair on his shoulder blades and legs glistened in the sun as it dried. Peaches lay on her back, her breasts flattened out, luxuriating in the dry warmth of the rock against her skin. She smiled at MacDonald although he was not looking at her and reached out languidly to caress his arm. She knew she had fallen a little more in love with him that afternoon.

The forty-seven francs had lasted remarkably well once their stay at the fancy hotel had come to an end. They only needed food. Twice, when they had to fill up the car with petrol they waited until the service station was really busy with queues forming at the pumps. Then they drove up, filled up, MacDonald would go inside and look round the shelves before coming out without paying, and they would drive away. It worked perfectly both times. No one chased them. No one seemed to notice. And then when they did return the car to the hire company they were handed back a deposit of one hundred francs they had completely forgotten about. It meant they could afford more than bread and cheese for a while. It got them quite a few bottles of wine. But it was almost gone as well now.

They left the river when it got too cold and pitched their tent in the corner of a meadow not far away. MacDonald carved out a square of turf with a small penknife and collected a pile of dry twigs to make a fire. There was no real need for the fire, there was nothing to cook. All they had with them was some cold meat and a litre of coarse red wine. And they did not need it for heat because the meadow was well sheltered and the evening air was still and balmy. But the crackling flames made a pleasing focus for their campsite. MacDonald sat cross-legged feeding the fire with fresh sticks as it burned down. Peaches sat beside him with her arm hooked possessively through his. The rushing sound of the river rapids and the clicking of the crickets in the long grass was constantly in the background. Smoke from the fire kept away the flies.

'Where will we go tomorrow?' Peaches asked.

'Anywhere you want darling,' MacDonald replied.

Peaches watched the glowing embers at the heart of the fire.

When she was a young girl her Uncle Teddy had taught her to look for prowling animals there. She made out the rippling shape of a striped tiger, and the pointed face of a wolf. MacDonald poked the fire and the black framework of burning twigs collapsed inwards sending a shower of sparks up into the air.

'What will we do for money?' she asked.

'We'll maybe have to rob a bank,' he answered and then turned to look at her when she laughed. 'I'm serious, you know. Maybe not a bank, they are too well protected these days, but we can always do a supermarket or a little shop, or a cafe even. We don't need much money, just enough to get by.'

'Who do you think we are? Bonnie and Clyde?'

'No. We'll do better than them. We won't get caught for a start.'

MacDonald stared back into the fire and she wondered what he was seeing there. The tiger was still visible to her, pacing to and fro across the mound of embers. The wolf had gone. There was no more wood to feed the flames. The fire was beginning to die. Peaches slapped a mosquito that had settled on her neck and felt its body like a speck of grit between her fingers.

'You are serious, aren't you?'

'Of course. They have got the money. We need the money. They won't miss a little bit. Where's the problem?'

'I was a respectable East Coast girl before I met you. I had never stolen so much as a library book. Now look at me. We have already stolen one car and here we are planning to rob a bank. If my friends could see me now.'

'Kismet, Peaches, Kismet. We were destined for each other. Do you want to know how I figure things?'

'What things?'

'All things. Life in general.'

'Tell me then.'

His attention was fixed on the embers. There were more mosquitoes in the air around them now that the smoke had dwindled to a thin column. Peaches watched the tiger march away and waited for MacDonald to speak.

'We have a saying where I come from; De'il tak the Hindmost, Devil take the Hindmost. What it means is that we're all in this world together, running together, scrambling over each other, bursting a gut to stay in front of everybody else. Because every so often Auld Nick himself, the Devil to you, raises his horned head and reaches up out of his pit with blood-encrusted claws and sweeps away the host of bodies stuck at the rear, the hindmost, so that they tumble down into his gaping mouth where they splash about in an acid saliva that burns off their skin, before they are ground to powder by his teeth and swallowed in a single gulp.'

He paused. A gust of wind somehow got past the sheltering trees and made the embers of the fire glow more brightly for a few seconds. Grey ash was creeping in from the edges to smother the yellowy-orange centre.

'What a lurid imagination you've got,' Peaches said. 'You'll give me nightmares.'

'We all end up as the hindmost sooner or later Peaches baby. There is no escaping it. Sooner or later we're going to feel those claws digging into our tender flesh and it will be our turn to die. It doesn't matter who you are or what you are or where you are. Young and old, rich and poor, if you are the hindmost you have got to go.'

He picked up a half-charred stick and broke it in two. 'Well, that's what it is like out here in the big wide world. We call ourselves the human race, don't we? We're all in this race together whether we like it or not and every day, every minute, somebody has to be the hindmost and be taken out of the race for good because the Devil has a healthy appetite. And the rest keep on running till the next time.'

'What is the point of running if we're going to lose out in the end?' she aked quietly, feeling the chill of the evening air.

'You just keep running, one foot in front of the other. There's no end to this race. The prize is staying alive.' He turned his head to Peaches and grinned broadly, showing his teeth. 'I've managed to stay with the pack all this time but you don't always know when you start to slip behind. I get the feeling that I'm somewhere near the back now. You never know when the actual cut-off point is going to be. You never know when you are going to be the hindmost. You've just got to keep running while you can.'

They sat together in silence for a while. Peaches was thinking of her father in the Vietnam bunker writing his last letter, not knowing that he was to be one of the hindmost in the next few hours. She held onto MacDonald's arm more tightly, pressing her cheek against it. 'Let's go to bed,' she said finally.

Peaches crawled into the tent, took off her clothes and got into the sleeping bag. MacDonald kicked earth over what remained of the fire, extinguishing it completely, then followed her to the tent. The curve of his back pushed out the sloping tent wall as he zipped down the doorway and squirmed awkwardly to remove his clothes in the confined space. When he was naked he climbed into the sleeping bag beside Peaches, already aroused and passionate as he rolled on top of her. She was ready for him with none of the usual preliminaries but she could hardly open her legs wide enough to accommodate him in the tight circle of the bag. There was a ripping sound as his movements became more insistent and a seam gave way. That allowed her to force a leg out the side so that he could sink into her. She moaned softly and rubbed her forehead against the hair on his chest. His hands were spread out on her hips. His weight rose and fell over her and although she grasped her wrist in her hand behind his back and squeezed as tightly as she could it was impossible for her to stop the slow, powerful rhythm driving down on her. She didn't want it to stop anyway. She wanted to be smothered by him, crushed into the ground. She was thinking that they were running together, side by side, hand in hand, and as long as they stayed together they would be able to stay ahead in the race.

The bullet was lodged deep in his thigh. Divers could feel it like a piece of grit caught under the smooth surface of his skin, grating against the hip bone. It hurt a lot but the unbearable pain of the previous night now seemed to have passed. He had cleaned up the wound with alcohol and then cauterized the ragged edges with the blade of a knife heated against the cylinder head of his car engine. The shock of the hot metal touching the raw nerve ends had knocked him unconscious but it had been worth it. He had had to do it himself. He could not go for medical help, not without giving himself away to the authorities. And he would not do that. So he had to subject himself to drastic treatment to prevent infection setting in. It seemed to have worked. He could stand the constant burning pain now. He had been able to make the long drive south to Munich.

The bullet had just missed the femoral artery and buried itself in the flesh and muscle at the rear of the thigh. If it had burst the artery he would certainly have died. He would have bled to death before Luneburg's body had had time to grow cold. But he had been lucky. He had heard stories of old soldiers dying in their beds with pieces of shrapnel still inside them from long-forgotten wars. He would survive.

It had been a headstrong and foolish thing to do. It had been sheer arrogance to go to meet Luneburg unarmed and then to allow him to keep a weapon in his possession during all that time. The only precaution he had taken was to hide in the shadows till he was sure that Luneburg had come alone. Yet Divers knew, despite all the cursing at himself, that he had done it deliberately. He had gone to Zeppelinwiese in Nuremberg and deliberately exposed himself to the danger to prove that he was a better man than Luneburg. He had given him a clear advantage and then snuffed him out like pinching a candle flame between finger and thumb. Divers had proved he was the better man, the better candidate for the master race. Luneburg had almost managed to save himself, but he had ended up shooting himself in order to threaten Divers. It was the only way he could hurt him.

Divers walked with a pronounced limp as he left his hotel on the Hotterstrasse and headed towards Marienplatz. He had lain in his bed in his room for twelve unbroken hours, willing his leg to heal. He had sat in the bath for hours on end with the warm water subduing the fierce throbbing of the open wound. He walked slowly because the movement caused fresh soreness. He clenched his teeth tightly together. Each step resulted in a little flashing stab of pain.

It was not far to the pedestrianized area of the Kaufingerstrasse with the twin-domed towers of the cathedral rising behind the tall line of buildings. Marienplatz itself was only a few minutes away and he had given himself plenty of time to get there. It was another warm day and the streets were cluttered with early shoppers and tourists. He stopped on the fringe of a group gathered round a guitar-playing busker and listened to the music. A woman by his side glanced at him and then immediately looked away.

The face that had appeared on the front pages of all the newspapers and on all the television channels was a very bad likeness. He had known that other members of Das Schwarze Leichentuch would be rounded up after Luneburg's death, Gudrun for one, and that his name would be touted as the killer. He had planned for that on being issued with an identity card soon after getting married and applying for German citizenship. Before having his picture taken he had grown his hair long and cultivated a Mexican-style moustache with drooping corners. He had worn large-framed spectacles and stuffed some cotton wool inside his mouth to alter the shape of his cheeks. He had even stuck some chewing gum behind his ears to make them more prominent. The result had been the creation of a total stranger who had disappeared several months ago when he got his hair cut short and shaved off the moustache. He had expected them to use the identity card picture when they started hunting for him, so he had acted in advance to short-circuit that threat. Only a couple of the papers he had seen had used an old army picture of him. That one was much more recognizable although again the hair was a different style and the face was much chubbier and younger looking than his present-day gaunt and lined appearance. He was confident no one would recognize him. No one would expect him to be deliberately mingling with shoppers in the centre of Munich. No one would believe he would be so foolish and so arrogant. He tilted his face upwards to catch the full warmth of the sun.

The press had given blanket coverage to Luneburg's murder and the startling revelation of the theft of the Minotaur land-mine. All the stories he had read constructed their own theories of what had happened and why, and all the stories centred the conspiracy on Das Schwarze Leichentuch with Luneburg as the victim of an internal power struggle and Divers as the leader of a team of assassins recruited by a dissident faction within the group. Divers liked that. Everybody thought it was a team that was necessary to kill Luneburg, and a team that had stolen the Minotaur. And it was only him. All by himself.

Luneburg would have lapped up the publicity. He had always been the kind who dreamed of dying with his boots on, a battlefield death in a blaze of glory. Speculation in the stories also agreed on the supposed fact that the Minotaur was harmless without a DIP to initiate the chain reaction for the nuclear explosion. Long, detailed articles on the actual mechanics of the land-mine explained how it worked, and how it could not work without certain parts. The authorities appeared to have done their job well and the writers seemed to have readily swallowed the propaganda. Nowhere was there any mention of a Dipstick being unaccounted for.

Divers left the busker's audience and limped towards Marienplatz. An old man with only one leg was seated against the wall between two shops. His head nodded in sleep. There was a piece of cardboard balanced on his lap with the words Habe Hunger written on it. The upturned hat beside his foot had very few coins in it. Divers poured in a handful of marks.

He entered the square and joined the crowds milling around at the side of the mock-Gothic town hall. There was a smell of flowers in the air. He passed the newspaper stall and went to lean against the marble wall surrounding the golden statue on its column with four guardian cherubs at each corner. He could see there were a few empty seats at the open-air cafe tables behind but he stayed where he was, glad to be able to take the weight off his leg.

The bells in the tower of the town hall struck eleven and everybody looked up at the glockenspiel expectantly. The carillon rang out and after a pause the top rank of figures began to rotate stiffly. A medieval jousting tournament was acted out by the colourfully painted figures high above the heads of the crown. Two knights on horseback passed each other and a procession of jesters, heralds and trumpeters. On the second pass as the two knights confronted each other one suddenly fell backwards on his horse as though struck by his opponent's lance. There was a little gasp of surprise from the crowd and then a ripple of quiet applause which ran across the square like an eddy of wind. In the same instant Divers felt a touch on his arm. He looked round to see a small, fat, bald man wearing a spotted bow-tie and a red waistcoat smiling up at him.

'Herr MacDonald,' the man said, 'it is good for us to meet once more. I hope you are enjoying the glockenspiel.'

'It reminds me of the army, Herr Rocher,' Divers replied.

'Hah,' Rocher looked from side to side in an exaggerated manner. 'You do not have your lady friend with you this time?'

'No. I'm afraid she couldn't make it.'

'A pity. I very much liked your friend. Gudrun was her name, was it not?' He nodded his own answer.

'You are alone?' Divers demanded.

'A slight change of plan, Herr MacDonald. My client is a very careful man. He is waiting to meet you at his hotel. He has asked that I bring you to him. We can take a taxi.'

The glockenspiel was still playing. The figures in the lower window began to move round in their mechanical dance. Rocher looked up at it. Divers followed his example.

'We call it the dance of the barrel makers, Der Schäffler-tanz,' Rocher explained. 'It remembers a time in the sixteenth century after a terrible plague when the guild danced through the streets of Munich to show the citizens it was safe once more to come out of their houses.' He lowered his voice and added: 'You will be searched at the hotel, Herr MacDonald. You understand.'

'A wise precaution,' Divers said. 'Unncessary in this case, but wise. Let's go.'

They walked to the taxi rank on Rindermarkt, threading their way through the static crowd and round the obstruction of the cafe tables. Divers tried hard not to limp too badly. Rocher matched his slow pace. A taxi was sitting at the head of the rank with the driver drumming his fingers on the roof. He saw Rocher's signal and came round to open the rear door. Divers had difficulty bending his injured leg to get in through the doorway.

'You have hurt your leg, Herr MacDonald?' Rocher said. 'Are you all right?'

Divers ignored the sharp, slicing pain that made his eyes water as he twisted his leg to sit down in the back of the taxi. 'It is nothing,' he said firmly. 'Nothing at all.'

They woke at dawn, still lashed together by the torn sleeping bag, and made love again before getting up. It was fairly cold so they put on warm clothes. The sky was already a light blue, promising warm weather later on. Peaches went to the river and washed her hair before they packed up their tent and walked across the fields to the nearest road. The grass was wet with dew, soaking the legs of their jeans right up to the knee. They sat on a sandy bank and Peaches let the newly-emerged sun dry her hair. The first vehicle to come into sight seemed to be slowing down even before Peaches stood up and stuck her thumb out.

'The wind must be in our back today,' MacDonald said as he pushed her up into the cab of the furniture van.

The driver was wearing oil-stained trousers and a tight-fitting vest that dug deep into the flesh of his rounded shoulders. Hair sprouted from his armpits as though some plump, furry animals had crawled in to make their home there. He lifted his black beret in greeting as Peaches slid over the torn leather seat towards him, leering unashamedly with a gap-toothed smile at her legs.

'He says he is going to Grenoble,' Peaches told MacDonald as he climbed in after her. 'Where's that?'

'It's to the west, I think, near the Swiss border.'

'Do we want to go there?'

'Why not? That's the way the wind is blowing us.'

'Grenoble it is then,' Peaches said firmly, turning back to nod and smile at the driver.

The cab contained a fog of Gauloise smoke that caught in

their throats and stung their eyes. Even when the van got going again, after much crunching of gears, and with both side windows open, the air did not clear very much. The heater blasted hot air onto their lower legs, drying the wet material quickly.The driver lit cigarette after cigarette and dangled them from the side of his mouth. The loud roar of the engine made it very hard to have a conversation. He spoke no English anyway, but Peaches was able to communicate with him in her schoolgirl French. She would lean over to him while he shouted in her ear and then she would lean over to MacDonald to relay what had been said.

'He says he has to get back to Marseilles tonight if he can.'

'Good for him,' MacDonald replied. 'Why don't we help him by knocking him on the head and throwing him in the nearest river so that he will float back. Meanwhile we will hijack this van and take off into the wide blue yonder.'

Peaches wriggled between them and removed her sweater. The driver looked over and grinned at MacDonald, ash falling from his cigarette onto his chin. He glanced at Peaches' chest and the shape of her breasts outlined by the tee-shirt, then he rolled his eyes towards the roof with a sharp intake of breath. MacDonald smiled back over Peaches' head and placed his hand on her thigh to show that she belonged to him.

'On second thoughts, I don't believe that would be a good idea,' MacDonald said, his lips so close to her ear that they brushed her skin. 'My secret for being a successful criminal involves avoidance of all human contact if at all possible. My targets have to be things, not people. You see, my theory is that your average policeman or gendarme won't get too excited about a little petty theft here or there, but spill a few drops of blood and they will really begin to take an interest in you. No, our friend is safe with us.'

'We can still rob a bank though, can't we?'

'Maybe some day, Peaches baby. Who do you think we are, Bonnie and Clyde?'

The driver grunted to attract her attention above the racing engine as the van negotiated a sharp downhill bend. She moved over to him like the swinging pointer of a metronome. After an expressive exchange lasting several minutes she swung back again.

'He wants to know if you are interested in earning some money,' she said.

'How much is he offering for you?'

'Not like that.' She punched his arm gently. 'His buddy did not turn up for work this morning so he needs help with his deliveries. He only has three to make, he says.'

'Great. That means we will be able to afford some lunch. Tell him I'm his man.' MacDonald saluted across the cab. 'Didn't I tell you Peaches baby, the wind is in our back.'

'I've already told him you'll do it,' Peaches said, laying her head sleepily against his arm.

'A hard night?' MacDonald said, putting the sole of his shoe against the dirty windscreen to keep himself steady in the seat.

'Very hard,' she mumbled.

The van was carrying antiques. The first stop was at a big country house somewhere between Lyon and Grenoble to deliver a large wardrobe that broke down into three still sizeable parts. Peaches stayed in the cab while MacDonald and the driver sweated and struggled to get the heavy pieces up a tightly-twisting staircase and reassemble them at the top. A stout middle-aged woman in a floral pinafore and a head-scarf fussed around them as the worked. She yelled a stream of instructions and warnings that MacDonald could not understand and that the driver chose to ignore. Eventually the wardrobe was in place, the receipt was signed and the woman ushered them quickly out of the house.

'How the hell was he going to deliver that by himself?' MacDonald asked when they were back in the cab.

Peaches translated. The driver wrinkled his top lip, took off his beret to scratch his head, and lit another cigarette. 'The same way you were going to buy our lunch today,' Peaches said.

The second delivery was much easier and this time they were treated to coffee and hot croissants by the home-owner. It took no more than ten minutes to set an oak dining table and eight chairs up in the ground-floor room waiting to receive them. The third delivery was in Grenoble itself. It was only a small bookcase and two small tables but the address proved hard to find. The driver cursed and swore as he got lost in narrow back streets. He had to ask three different people before they finally arived at the correct place.

It was the middle of the afternoon when he dropped Peaches and MacDonald in the town centre with a one-hundred-franc note that bought them a good meal in the rear room of a busy cafe. When they had eaten they took their coffee out onto the pavement terrace and sat in the sunshine.

'Well, that's us all but broke again,' Peaches said. 'What now?'

'We find our way out of this town,' MacDonald replied.

'Which way?'

He shrugged and pointed up in the air. 'That way?'

'The wind doesn't blow that way.'

'But before we go I think we should take the chance to replenish our depleted resources.'

'So now we rob the bank?'

'Not quite.'

MacDonald gestured to a table in the corner of the cafe area. A young woman in a white cotton dress was sitting at it alone with her arms crossed and her head sagging forward. Her sunglasses had slipped to the end of her nose. Her eyes were closed. The neck of her dress hung loosely, showing a lot of cleavage. She was not wearing a bra. The shadow cast by the table umbrella ran down the centre of her head and body.

'Very nice,' Peaches said sarcastically. 'We sell her to white slavers, do we?'

'Look on the table,' MacDonald said quietly.

Peaches looked. She saw a wine glass and an empty half carafe. Beside them was a large, soft, white leather handbag lying on top of a couple of tourist brochures. She nodded to herself, realizing MacDonald's intention.

'She is sleeping like a baby, Peaches baby,' he said. 'All you have to do is walk right up to that table, take the bag and walk away. Do it as if you own it and nobody will give you a second glance.'

'Me?' Her voice trembled. 'You want me to do it?'

'We're a team. I've done my bit for today. Now it is your turn to bring in some money. Let's go.'

MacDonald pushed back his chair and stood up. He took her rucksack and swung it up onto the same shoulder as his holdall. She stood as well, suddenly breathing hard, suddenly conscious that everybody in the café must be staring at her. You can do it, she told herself uncertainly. You can do it. It will be simple. You can do it. MacDonald smiled his encouragement and she tried to smile back.

'I'll be strolling down the street ahead of you,' he said. 'Don't hesitate. That can be fatal. And don't trip over her feet.'

He moved away from her and went slowly down the tree-lined street, leaving her no choice. She looked round. The cafe was not as busy as she had imagined. Only a few of the tables were occupied and the people at them seemed engrossed in themselves. No one was looking at her. She felt a surge of unexpected confidence. She walked towards the table and the young woman whose head was nodding gently. The sunglasses were balanced right at the tip of her nose, ready to fall at any moment. Peaches did not break step as she passed the table and picked up the bag in a single, fluid motion. She tucked it under her arm and followed MacDonald. Her legs felt rubbery as she walked quickly away, resisting the temptation to break into a run. The back of her neck burned. She expected to hear a shout at any instant. Stop thief. She expected to feel a hand on her shoulder and an angry accusation. But no one shouted except some children in an enclosed playground. And no one grabbed her except MacDonald who put his arm casually round her as she drew level with him. She leaned into him and rubbed herself against the side of his body like a friendly cat, knowing she was safe.

'You are now a paid-up member of the criminal classes, Peaches baby,' he said. 'How does it feel?'

'Pretty fine.'

'Just keep walking,' he ordered. 'Don't look back. Let's not spoil it now.'

They walked the length of the street and turned right at the junction at its end. They kept going, turning left and right at random through a maze of side streets, taking care always to be travelling away from the cafe. After fifteen minutes they arrived outside a small park with sunbathers sprawled lethargically over the undulating grass. Finding a bench partially hidden in a fold of bushes they sat down. MacDonald took the bag and delved inside it.

'It maybe wasn't a bank but you did a good job,' he said.

'What have we got?' Peaches asked eagerly.

'Three bells. The jackpot.' MacDonald held up a fat roll of banknotes tied with a thick rubber band. 'She must have been going to have a good holiday on this.'

'How much is there?'

'Enough to last us a week or so if we don't get too extravagant.' He unrolled a single note and held it up to examine it.' 'There is one slight problem. I don't think this will buy us a bed for the night here. It's all in German money, Deutschmarks.'

'Then we'd better head for Germany,' Peaches said quickly. 'We can go and visit your friend in Frankfurt, Big Shuggie.'

'We better had. That seems to be the day the wind is blowing us.'

'Anything else of interest?'

'A few French francs to get us an evening meal, a passport and a few other bits and pieces,' MacDonald said. 'She has been good to us, has Fraulein Genscher, so I don't think we should be nasty and take them. We'll leave them here on this bench in her bag.'

'That's very thoughtful of you, darling,' Peaches said, kissing him on the cheek.

'Isn't it? We'll just have to hope it is an honest person who finds them.'

Hugo Betzing sat in the foyer of the Munich Sheraton and watched Helmut Rocher walk past him with the man called MacDonald at his side. Rocher glanced sideways and his eyebrows arched slightly but he made no obvious sign of recognition. Betzing stared straight through both men, pretending not to see them while actually studying MacDonald's appearance and manner very carefully. He immediately liked the look of the man and that pleased him. He did a lot, if not all, of his business purely on the strength of first impressions and his own instincts and gut reactions to the people he was dealing with. They had stood him in good stead over the years. MacDonald looked a good bet. He looked an honourable man, a man you could reason with, a man you could trust. And all this from the briefest of looks. It was likely they would be able to do business together.

The surface of the grey leather sofa was smooth and warm to the touch as Betzing stretched his arm along it and slowly turned his head to watch Rocher lead MacDonald to the lifts beyond the concierge's desk. MacDonald had an awkward stiff-legged walk with a pronounced limp as if one leg was shorter than the other. Or perhaps he was carrying an injury. One of the gang who had killed Luneburg had been wounded according to the police. This man MacDonald could well be the Divers who had been named in the papers, even though he looked nothing like the pictures. Or perhaps Divers was sitting somewhere with the Minotaur pulling MacDonald's strings.

In total contrast to MacDonald, Rocher fairly bounced along, walking on the balls of his feet as if he was crossing a trampoline. Rocher was an unpleasant man, unattractive in both a physical and a social sense. Betzing detested him, but was prepared to ignore his own sensibilities and used the man as a go-between and a fixer because he had proved himself to be unfailingly efficient in the past. He did not have to like him to respect his organizational and business ability. He had not brought Anna to Munich with him because he knew Rocher would be hanging around a lot this time. Betzing did not like Rocher being close to her, or the way his little piggy eyes stared at her and at any other woman who happened to be around, probably imagining them as star performers in one of his bad-taste blue movies. The top of Rocher's bald head sweated like a melting lump of lard whenever a female came within ten yards of him. It could be quite amusing, as long as the female was not connected with you.

They disappeared into a lift. Betzing gave them five minutes' start, then slowly got up and went over to where they had been waiting. One of the four lifts opened its doors with a tiny ping as he arrived and disgorged a group of five Dutchmen who stepped the same way as Betzing as they tried to get out of each other's way. There was much apologizing and smiling as they sorted themselves out and finally Betzing managed to enter the empty lift. He touched the button for the seventeenth floor and the doors closed in front of him. There was only the vaguest sensation of movement as it whisked him upwards, covering the distance in seconds. He stepped out onto the landing. There was an ice store on the right. He raised the flap and selected a small ice cube from it to pop into his mouth. Then he walked along the thickly-carpeted corridor and stopped outside one of the plain wood doors at the far end. He tapped three times on it and the door opened to reveal two large men in open-necked shirts and sports jackets. They had been recruited by Rocher but, now that he had seen MacDonald, Betzing knew that they would not be needed. Still, it was better to be safe than sorry.

'I am going in now,' he said and their heads nodded in unison. 'Just ensure that we are not interrupted. I do not think you will be called on to do any more but be ready anyway.'

Betzing turned abruptly and went over to the door diagonally opposite. It was unlocked. He went straight in. The man called MacDonald was seated at the table by the window rubbing his thigh. Behind him the white gauze curtains fluttered in the air stream of the ventilation system. The table was loaded with plates of cold meat and salads. Rocher rose from the foot of the bed where he had been sitting, his thumbs hooked into the pockets of his red waistcoat. The bottom half of his face spilt in a huge grin and a complementary band of wrinkles appeared on his forehead.

'Herr Betzing,' Rocher said, half bowing and indicating the table with a sweep of his arm. 'Herr MacDonald.'

'Thank you. We will speak alone,' Betzing said dismissively. He crossed the room and took the seat on the opposite side of the table from his guest. Rocher left without another word. The door bumped shut but the lock did not click into place.

'It is good to meet you at last, Herr MacDonald,' Betzing said, looking directly into his eyes, confirming his first assessment. 'I have been reading about your exploits. You seem to have a flair for the dramatic.

'You wanted proof,' Divers said simply. 'I had an old score to settle and I needed to draw the attention of the Press to provide you with proof, so it seemed the only way to go about things. I didn't want the authorities to be able to hush anything up.'

'You certainly managed that. And this other person, this Divers that the whole country is seeking. He is an associate of yours?'

'A friend of mine. We were in the army together.'

An honest man, Betzing thought. He had passed the first test. 'Yes, indeed. I have taken the precaution of finding out all about you and Mr Divers. You are, as you say, old friends. The Royal Engineers, was it not?'

'My parents always wanted me to learn a proper trade.'

'And then you were part of the special Commando detachment seconded to the task of deploying Minotaur land-mines in the NATO strategy of the Nuclear Wall defence. Yourself and your friend formed a single two-man team for a time.'

'That was before our little difference of opinion with the army.'

'Of course. But I am forgetting my manners.' Betzing waved the fingers of one hand over the table as though he was sprinkling salt. 'Please help yourself to some of this delicious food. I did not know if you would want lunch. Would you like some wine?'

Betzing stood up and lifted the already-opened wine bottle from its basket. He poured two glasses of the rich red liquid. Divers took the jug of water and filled his glass to the brim.

'Now,' Betzing resumed, after swilling some of the wine round in his mouth and holding his head well back to drink it down. 'Through the good offices of our mutual friend outside you are offering to sell me one Minotaur land-mine which was recently stolen during a military exercise in the Hessen region near the East German border. The newspapers report that two soldiers were shot dead in a carefully planned raid.'

Divers sipped his wine and licked his top lip. He remained silent.

'The newspapers also report that the stolen Minotaur is harmless without the external electronic pulse which would be transmitted to trigger detonation at a given time. This pulse would come from a robot aircraft. It is also mentioned that the only other way of priming the Minotaur is by means of a Digital Initiation Programmer, known to those in the trade as a Dipstick. There is no danger, the newspapers say, because all Dipsticks are accounted for.'

'You shouldn't believe everything you read in the papers,' Divers said.

Betzing paused for thought and helped himself to a slice of ham, putting his head back and lowering it into his mouth. 'However,' he began again as he chewed, 'when you first approached Herr Rocher some four months ago you were able to show him a DIP unit or a Dipstick and he tells me he is satisfied it was authentic.' He reached for another slice of meat.

'And you trust Herr Rocher's judgement?' Divers asked.

'Rocher, you may agree, is not the most likeable of men. Yet despite his personal failings I have always found his professional judgement in these matters to be sound. He is not an easy man to fool and I believe him when he says you have possession of the Minotaur and the DIP. If you were a member of the opposite sex I would very seriously doubt his judgement. He is a different man in the presence of female flesh.'

'So I've noticed.'
'Naturally, I would like very much to see the Minotaur for myself and the DIP with it.'
'Not possible.' Divers shook his head. 'I told Rocher that. You know I have it. That should be enough.'
'I believe you do have it, Mr MacDonald,' Betzing said reasonably 'Then perhaps I could see the Dipstick. It is more easily transported.'
'Absolutely not possible.'
'And why not?'
'Well, I'm afraid it is already inserted in the Minotaur and is ticking away as we speak.' Betzing frowned and drew his head back sharply. 'Not to worry,' Divers said quickly. 'I know what I am doing.'
'I hope so, Herr MacDonald. I certainly hope so.' Betzing paused for thought again. He took a few grapes and popped them into his mouth, biting down on the pips. He stared through the transparent curtains at the Englischer Garten for several minutes before turning back to face Divers across the table. He poured another two glasses of wine. 'And so,' he said, 'I will trust Rocher and that puts us in the position of you having something to sell, Herr MacDonald, and I wishing to make a purchase. What is your price?'
'You are very direct, Herr Betzing.'
'I find it the best way to do business.'
'I could not agree more,' Divers said. 'I want five million pounds sterling.'
Betzing drew back even more sharply. His frown grew darker and then disappeared completely as he laughed. It was a harsh braying laugh and he saw that it made the colour spring to the other's face. 'Come now,' he said pleasantly. 'Let us try to establish some common ground here. I am afraid that five million pounds is not a figure I regard as a realistic opening gambit.'
Divers shrugged. 'How about three million then?'
Betzing laughed again. 'You have a novel negotiating style, Herr MacDonald, and at least we are moving in the right direction. Your motivation in this matter is financial, I take it. There is no hidden political dimension?'
'You're right. I just want to be rich and live happily ever after.'

'I only ask because of your unhappy relationship with Das Schwarze Leichentuch. They do not appear to have taken you to their heart. It was, I assume, a purely practical relationship from your point of view in that they helped you to steal the Minotaur. Am I correct?'

'Perhaps. Perhaps not. But I am on my own now. Believe me, I am all on my own.'

'I see,' Betzing said, letting the point pass. 'I hope I can help you in your quest to become a rich man but we must maintain a sense of proportion. I am prepared to offer you four hundred and fifty thousand pounds for the Minotaur.'

It was Divers' turn to laugh. 'The Minotaur is a nuclear land-mine. It is a one-off. It is a very valuable property. You can hardly buy a hand grenade these days for the kind of money you are talking about.'

'My friend,' Betzing said patiently with a theatrical sigh. 'Our transaction is taking place in a very difficult and restricted market. Many people would like to buy the Minotaur but could not possibly raise the necessary funds. Its very nature excludes them from the market place. Potential customers are few and far between. I could buy the Minotaur from you and then find no one willing to take it off my hands. I am no politician, Herr MacDonald. I want to be a rich man too.'

He clasped a hand over his mouth and rubbed his jaw. 'You are a Scotsman, Herr MacDonald. I once tried to buy a country estate in your Highlands of Scotland. I like to shoot and stalk deer. I travel to a place called Knoydart each year to indulge in these pleasures. I thought it might be a good idea to buy my own personal estate. Unfortunately there were other bidders and I lost out. It was too expensive for me.'

'There are plenty of other estates. No one is ever going to offer you the chance to get your hands on another Minotaur. If this one is too expensive for you maybe I should sell it to someone else.'

'There are many dishonourable men in my line of business. You chose well in coming to me. I am a fair man, but I have to be coldly realistic in what might be obtained for the Minotaur.' He grimaced as though someone had stamped on his toes. 'I am prepared to raise my offer to five hundred thousand.'

'I don't think I can go below two million.'

Betzing nodded seriously. He rose and began to pace up and down at the foot of the bed. 'Two million pounds is very rich. Very, very, very rich. I too must make a small profit for my involvement and my risk. Two million pounds?' He shook his head.

'What about my risk?' Divers asked.

Betzing sighed. 'Five hundred and fifty thousand.'

'At least you are moving in the right direction.'

Betzing laughed again, shaking his head. 'I am stretching my resources to the limit. I really cannot go any higher.'

'Talk to your bank manager,' Divers said, diluting what was left in his wine glass so that the deep red colour changed to a light pink.

'What would you do with all this money? Buy a Highland estate perhaps?'

'I think I'd prefer something in a warmer climate.' He straightened his injured leg under the table and swallowed hard to control the pain.

'You drive a hard bargain,' Betzing said, noticing his discomfort.

'I bet you say that to all your clients,' Divers replied.

Betzing ran his tongue round the inside of his teeth. 'Six hundred thousand.'

Divers leaned forward over the table. 'When I was young I always wanted to be a millionaire. This is the only chance I am going to get. I'm not going to throw it away easily.'

Betzing returned to his chair and put his hand over his eyes for a few seconds. Then he took the hand away and grinned like a child playing peek-a-boo. 'Seven hundred thousand will take you within spitting distance of your ambition, Herr MacDonald.'

'One million would be better.'

'No. Seven hundred thousand is my limit. I can go no higher.'

Divers picked up his glass and drained it. He refilled it and Betzing's with fresh wine and took a drink. 'All right then,' he said. 'We have a deal.'

Both men rose simultaneously and shook hands over the table. The sudden pressure on his leg made Divers grunt with pain and quickly sit down again.

'Your leg?' Betzing inquired politely, remembering again the newspaper story about one of the killers of the Leichentuch terrorist possibly being shot. 'You are injured.'

'It is nothing,' Divers insisted. He reached into his trouser pocket and brought out a small piece of paper, determinedly ignoring the pain. 'Here is the name of my Swiss bank and the number of my special account. I want you to pay my money in there.'

Betzing accepted the piece of paper and read it. 'An excellent choice of bank, if I may say so. I, too, have an account there. But when shall I receive the Minotaur?'

'I will bring it to you.'

'May I ask where the Minotaur is at this moment?'

'No.'

'Very well then. You will excuse my suspicious mind but what guarantee do I have that you will deliver the goods once the money is paid?'

'I have had a long time to think about this. If I hand over the goods before you hand over the money what is to stop you tucking the Minotaur under your arm and never handing over my cash?'

'Aha,' Betzing said, clinking his wine glass against his bottom teeth. 'The eternal problem of human nature. You have a solution? How should we do it then, Herr MacDonald?'

'I suggest this: that I bring the Minotaur here to Munich and meet you again in an appropriate place. Not here. It is too private. I want somewhere much more public, with plenty of people around. The Minotaur is large but easily disguised as a suitcase or a rucksack. It will not attract attention so it will not matter if we are surrounded by crowds. I will bring the Minotaur to the Oktoberfest and meet you on the steps below the statue of Bavaria at the Theresienwiese.'

'It is most certainly not a private place.'

'I want the meeting to be at nine in the evening on the twenty-second of this month. That should give you ample time to raise the money. I want it in sterling notes; no drafts, no cheques.' Divers paused and Betzing nodded curtly to signal agreement. 'I will telephone Rocher in one week's time to confirm this.'

'You will bring a radiophone to the Wies'n so that you can phone the bank in Switzerland where you will arrange for an associate of yours to be ready to deposit the money in my account when you give the word. I have already instructed a Mr Sabaroff at the bank to be ready to accept the money. I can then phone Sabaroff to check that it has been lodged in my account. The Minotaur will then belong to you.'

Betzing smiled and folded the small piece of paper into a neat square. He was about to speak when Divers continued. 'I forgot to mention that the Minotaur will have the Dipstick in place and will be armed. Only I know the digital combination necessary to cancel the detonation programme. I will provide you with that once the money is paid into my account. if anything goes wrong I will simply walk away and leave you with a nice surprise.'

Betzing's smile grew wider. 'As I said earlier Herr MacDonald, you do indeed seem to have a flair for the dramatic. I think these arrangements may well prevent human nature from indulging itself.'

'I also forgot to mention that the Minotaur is armed at this very moment. If you were planning to have me followed when I leave here, I would forget that now. It would just result in our deal being cancelled with a very loud bang.'

'You seem, as they say, to have thought of everything. You will not be followed, Herr MacDonald, I guarantee that.' Betzing rose and held out his hand again. 'Phone Rocher in one week's time for the final go-ahead and I look forward to meeting you again on the twenty-second.'

Divers stood up and took the offered hand, swaying a little.

'Are you all right?' Betzing asked.

'It is lack of sleep, that is all. I am tired. I must go.'

'Are you sure? Can I order a car for you?'

'No. I will manage, thank you.'

Betzing escorted him to the door and watched him limp along the corridor towards the lifts. Goodbye for now Hugh Divers, he thought. We shall meet again.

Rocher emerged from the door opposite. 'Everything all right, Herr Betzing?' he asked. 'No problems?'

'Call off your man downstairs. I don't want him followed.'

'At once.' Rocher shouted an instruction into the room.

'Come with me,' Betzing said. 'I need your help. Then I will take Mr MacDonald's advice and have a word with my bank manager.'

Hugh Divers could feel the eyes of the tall arms dealer boring into his back as he walked away from the hotel room, trying hard not to limp too badly. The pain had been suddenly excruciating but was now gradually fading. When he had stood up quickly in the room to shake hands and seal the deal it had seemed to stay behind on the chair and then snap back into its proper place as if it was on a piece of elastic. For a moment he had thought he was going to faint but that had passed and it had just been a question of keeping a straight face and getting out as quickly as possible.

He had to lean against the wall as he waited for the lift, rubbing his leg above the wound to try and soothe it. He could feel it hot and damp, with the bandages bulging beneath his trousers. It was probably bleeding again but no blood had yet soaked through the material. He took a handful of ice cubes from the store and rubbed them across his forehead and eyes.

He was satisfied with the deal he had struck. He had gone in prepared to hold out for the full million pounds, prepared to walk out if Betzing had consistently refused his demands. But the pain in his leg had weakened his resolve. He could see that Betzing was ready for a long session, and half-way through the meeting all he wanted to do was take what money he could get and run. Seven hundred thousand pounds was not too bad anyway. Besides he was not really interested in the money, he had always told himself, only in stealing the thing and then getting rid of it. It was all just to show that he could do it.

Take the money and run. So he had got the promise of his money and now he could run. He laughed at his predicament as the lift doors slid open and he stepped inside, dragging his bad leg. A wave of pain fanned out from the wound. His legs gave way and he had to clutch at the walls to stop himself falling. He did not know how much further he would be able to run though, not in his condition. He gritted his teeth and stood up straight, shaking his head to clear it. All the pain fell away. He was strong and healthy once more. Then it began to gnaw quietly at his leg again.

He took a taxi waiting outside the Sheraton and ordered the driver to go to Schloss Nymphenburg. He settled down in the back with his leg stretched out along the seat. He planned to take three taxis in different directions before he finally got back to his hotel, just to make certain he was not being followed. Despite all that Betzing had said he knew there was no such thing as an honourable man.

Der Schäfflertanz it was called and, according to the guidebook, the knights' tournament of 1568 to honour the marriage of Duke Wilhelm of Bavaria and Renata of Lorraine had gone before. The glockenspiel in Der Marienplatz came to a halt after its second ten-minute performance of the day, ending with the golden cockerel above it crowing and flapping its mechanical wings. The crowds below began to drift away. At his table outside the cafe Gerhard Lutzke took off his sunglasses and hung them on the breast pocket of his short-sleeved shirt. The breeze was freshening and beginning to lift the edge of the tablecloth but it was still very warm. He took a sip of his Weissbier and put the tall glass back down, watching the strings of tiny bubbles stream to the foaming top.

He had never been to Munich before. He rarely got out of Bonn and the main Rheinland conurbations, so he had taken the opportunity to play the tourist. His feet were sore with tramping round the city sites but he preferred to kill time by doing something rather than sitting in his hotel all day. Now it was nearly time for the rendezvous. He looked at his watch and then up at the clock face on the town-hall tower. There were still a few minutes though. He did not want to be early.

It was a tremendous stroke of luck for Agent Bavaria to turn up such an important piece of information so early in her assignment. Helmut Rocher was considered to be a long-term project, the kind of small businessman with fingers in all sorts of juicy pies who might throw up something useful in the long run. Lutzke had been doubtful about the value of the assignment when it was requested by Berlin. It was after all based on what might easily be a wild rumour, but he was now extremely glad that he had kept those doubts to himself. He hated asking female agents to operate among the low life, having to abuse their bodies in the name of the State, but then he was only the regional controller, not the overall strategist. On reflection, he had to admit the assignment was fully justified anyway, even without the early bonus it seemed to have produced. Rocher frequently acted as a middle-man for arms dealers and as such regularly came into contact with influential officials of many Western governments, whom he would supply with prostitutes and other personal services. It was believed that he had secretly filmed some very important people in some very compromising positions and stored the pictures away in a safe place for future reference. Agent Bavaria's assignment was to find out if this was true and to acquire the films if possible. It was the methods she was required to use that offended Lutzke's innate sense of prudishness.

The routine coded message she had sent in to the embassy had greatly excited Lutzke when he read it. If it was true, then he saw it as an excellent way of forcing his name to the notice of the hierarchy. He was still young and intensely ambitious. He wanted to move on from Bonn, to Paris or London, or Washington perhaps. He liked the West, and rather fancied that if he had been born on the other side of the border he would have become the kind of free-booting entrepreneur that got rich quick and then enjoyed it. In the East, the only real means of self-advancement was through the party machine and that was the way he had chosen to go. His career had stalled somewhat in Bonn after a couple of successful tours of duty in Africa and he needed something major to get him moving again. For one of his agents to discover the whereabouts of the stolen Minotaur land-mine when the whole of Western Europe was searching frantically for it would result in a great deal of credit being reflected on him; he would make sure of that. The decision to travel to Munich personally had not been a difficult one to take. He wanted to be certain that it was true.

He finished his beer and left the cafe, throwing his red sweater over his shoulders and tying the arms round his neck. That was to be the signal by which Agent Bavaria would identify him, that and the passwords. He had never met her before, although he had seen many photographs in the file. She was to wear white ankle socks and open-toed sandals so that he could be sure it was her. It was his attempt at a little joke.

Lutzke descended to the underground station from Marienplatz. It was five-thirty. The main rush hour was past but the place was still very busy. He had bought his ticket earlier in the day and he cancelled it in the machine before going down to the north-bound platform of the number six line. He saw her almost at once, leaning against a pillar reading a copy of Bild. She was taller than he had imagined although he knew her height from the files. He looked down and, through a forest of bodies, saw the white ankle socks neatly turned over at the top, and the brown leather sandals. He smiled and walked over to her.

'Excuse me,' he said. 'I am a stranger in this city. Do I take this train to Kieferngarten?'

'Yes,' she replied, looking at him shyly over the top of the paper. 'Kieferngarten is the terminus.'

'May I follow you onto the train?'

'Yes. I am travelling in that direction.'

He moved away to stand ten yards along from her and she resumed reading her newspaper. She was prettier than her official photographs, but then they were always terribly unflattering. She was not conventionally attractive but had a pleasant face surrounded by a bob of straw-blonde hair. Other men close by kept casting admiring glances at her. She was wearing a yellow blouse and a loose summer skirt slit up one side. Her body was well proportioned with relatively small breasts. She had exceedingly long fingernails, painted silver. He tried to remember her real name but it eluded him.

The train drew up at the platform and the carriage doors opened with an explosive hiss. Lutzke followed her in and stood beside her in the crush, his leg touching hers. The train was very full and stayed that way through the next three stations. At the fourth there was a great exodus and several seats became vacant. He nudged her with his knee and they went to sit together. The doors slid shut and the train started up again. It was very warm and stuffy. Lutzke ran his thumb over the closed pages of the guidebook he was carrying and fanned cool air onto his face.

'Repeat to me what you know about the Minotaur landmine,' he demanded.

'Rocher, my target, has mentioned that he is working for an arms dealer who is negotiating to buy the stolen Minotaur. The exchange is to be made here in Munich.'

'When?'

'I do not know.'

'Where exactly?'

'I do not know.'

'Can you find out?'

'I can try.'

The next stop was Dietlindenstrasse. More people got off. The train started up again with a jerk.

'Do you believe Rocher when he tells you this?' Lutzke asked, watching her face for her reaction.

'It could be idle boasting but I think he his speaking the truth. I think he is involved with this Minotaur.'

'Do you know the name of the arms dealer in question?'

'No sir.'

'Or the names of the sellers? Is it this group Das Schwarze Leichentuch?'

'It is not the terrorists. Rocher was laughing at the newspaper stories. He said it was a good smokescreen.'

'Then could it be this ex-British soldier, the man Divers?'

'I do not know.'

Lutzke put his arm along the back of the seat and let his hand rest on her shoulder. He could see why she made a good actress. The train stopped and started again. There were only three other people in the carriage, all with their backs to them.

'Listen, my dear, I want you to give this matter the utmost priority and find out all you can as quickly as possible. It is essential that you do this. Do you understand?'

'Yes sir.' She sat straighter in her seat. A soldier receiving orders.

'I want the truth or falsity of Rocher's claims established beyond doubt. I also want you to bypass the normal channels of communication and contact me directly once you know more details. Use this emergency number.' He took a small card from his shirt pocket and handed it to her. 'I will leave the necessary instructions. Speak to no one but me and do not mention the Minotaur on the phone. I will understand what you are talking about. If this is true I just want the name of the buyer, the name of the seller, and the time and place of the handover. What is your name, my dear? Your real name?'

'Gretchen.'

'Ah yes. Now I remember. Use that name to identify yourself to me. Now I think you should leave me here.'

The train pulled into Alte Heide. No one got on or off. 'There was one thing I would like to ask you sir,' Gretchen said hesitantly.

'What is that? Quickly girl,' he snapped immediately regretting his impatience.

She stammered a little and coughed to clear her throat. The train doors closed and it moved out of the station. She was sitting on the edge of the seat. Her skirt had fallen away from her leg showing a tanned thigh, but she did not seem to notice.

'The money that I receive each month at my home in Dresden.' She looked down at her feet, summoning up courage before continuing. 'I wonder if it would be possible to have a little more each month.'

Lutzke was surprised by the request. His first thought was that he did not know how to go about changing an agent's remuneration. He only had limited powers to make single payments in exceptional circumstances and that generated a mountain of paperwork, so he did it very rarely.

'Wage bargaining, are we?' he said, disapproval implicit in his tone. 'You must have been influenced too much by the capitalist West.'

'I hope to get married when I leave the service,' she explained. 'We want to set up a little business for ourselves.'

'We?'

'My boyfriend and I. He is a carpenter in Dresden. He hopes to begin restoring old furniture. There is a growing market within the republic.'

Lutzke nodded. He wondered if her boyfriend knew exactly what her work entailed while she was away from him. 'I can make no promises. Gretchen,' he said. 'All I can say is that I will do my best for you if you do yours for me.'

'Thank you sir.'

'Now get off here and remember what it is that I need to know.'

He watched her get off, along with the three other occupants of the carriage, leaving him on his own. The doors closed and the train rolled away from the platform. Lutzke bit the back of his hand. If he could retrieve the Minotaur his reputation would soar. He would be able to choose virtually any posting he desired. He laughed out loud. He would certainly get a wage rise.

The bunk was in the rear section of the giant tanker's cab, above and separated from the driving seats by some heavy curtains and a narrow ledge that served as a step up. Peaches Macdonald lay on her side on the lumpy mattress writing a letter. The sheet of paper was balanced on the back of a folded map of Europe. Her top shoulder was within an inch of brushing the ceiling. Her breathing had caused a fine film of condensation to gather on the metal surface. Larger drops formed in the corners and ran down the vertical wall she was facing. A battery-operated lamp was clipped to a flange by her head, shedding a faint, poor-quality light onto the paper. It swayed constantly to the rythmic motion of the speeding lorry. The vibration of the engine gently shook the whole of Peaches' body, massaging right through to her bones.

They had been travelling in the lorry for almost four hours after finally managing to hitch a lift outside a big transport cafe on the outskirts of Grenoble. The driver was a New Zealander who had returned to work and live in his mother's native country, and who was pleased to have the chance to speak English again for a while. The lorry was taking a load of chemicals up through Switzerland and Germany on its way to Copenhagen. He had agreed to drop them off in Frankfurt. Peaches had been happy to let MacDonald do all the talking on their behalf. She had kept dozing off as she leaned against his arm. After crossing the border near Geneva the driver had suggested she would be more comfortable in the bed behind the seats. However, once she was in the bed, with a coarse blanket that smelled of alsatian pulled round her, she found she could not sleep. Instead she got some writing paper out of her rucksack and began to compose a letter.

It was the first letter she had written in eighteen months and she knew it would never be sent. It was a letter to her father. It was a letter that rambled on over several sides of the paper, telling in intimate detail about her meeting with Joe MacDonald and their subsequent relationship and her hopes for the future. Letter-writing to her father was a habit she had formed while in hospital during her nervous breakdown. She had done it every night when they locked her away in her room, under the bedclothes, by torchlight, so that none of them knew what she was up to. She would write simple things, everything that had happened during the day and what she had been thinking about. Often it took her two or three hours to copy it all down because she wrote very slowly, but she always felt it was worth it. The letters linked her to her father in a spiritual way. It made her feel better to write to him, to share her problems and to share her joys. It was a contact with her father that she had been denied as a child. She believed that it helped her regain her sanity.

Her writing was cramped and childlike with little joining up of the individual letters. Everything was always laid out formally with the address and date in the top right-hand corner and her full signature to finish it off, Patricia Chesney Macdonald. Then, when a letter was completed, she would gather all the individual pages, line up the edges and tear them up again and again until the paper was reduced to tiny pieces. She would sleep all night with the pieces clutched tightly in her hand and then in the morning, at the first opportunity, flush them away down the toilet.

From the front of the cab she could hear the muffled sound of the radio. MacDonald was listening to the BBC World Service. He wanted to find out what was going on in the world, he had said. She did not care what was happening outside in the world. She had not listened to a radio or read a newspaper since landing in Europe. She did not care what was going on in the world of other people because it could not be more important than what was happening in her own personal world.

The address on her letter was Switzerland, September. She

did not know the exact date. *Dear Pop,* she wrote. *It was love at first sight. I'm pretty sure you would understand. Maybe it was like when you first met Mummy. There is an electricity between me and Joe. I can feel it. It crackles in the air when he is near me. When he touches me it is just like turning up the gas ring beneath a pan of milk. My blood bubbles and boils like mad. I'm certain that Joe is just the kind of person you would have been at his age Pop. And I love him terribly. I want to marry him. I want to have his children. You understand, don't you Pop?*

Peaches went on to describe in detail how they had met each other in the Paris cafe and then how they had stolen a car to get away from Paris and how they had recklessly blown all their money on a room in a fancy hotel for only a couple of nights. She carefully described the furniture van that had taken them into Grenoble and how MacDonald had helped with the deliveries so they would have money to buy lunch and how she had stolen the woman's purse and all the Deutschmarks from under her very nose.

I'm lying on my side in the back of a lorry cab heading north into Germany, she wrote. *Joe is just a few feet away from me. I can't see him but I can sense his presence. He radiates a kind of warmth to me. I feel safe with Joe, Pop. Life seems to make some sort of sense when I am with him. I never want to be more than a few feet away from him ever again. I'm really living now, Pop. It really is wonderful. I don't know what it would be like if I lost him. I wouldn't want to go back to what it was like before. Not now.*

She signed her name with a flourish and rolled over onto her back, holding the pages above her face so that she could read them over. The arm she had been leaning on was stiff and sore. She flexed her fingers as she read to pump blood back into the muscles. Her closely-spaced writing covered both sides of five pages in all. After reading the whole letter she turned the sheets onto their side and tore them in half, placed them on top of each other and tore them in half again. She repeated the process until the pieces were too small to be shredded further. Then she swept them all into a neat pile on her flat stomach and squashed them into the palm of her right hand until she could close it into a fist. After that she lay for a while where she was with the fist resting lightly against her cheek.

Her father would have understood, Peaches thought. He would have known that she and Joe were kindred spirits. But it would be a different story with her mother. She must have changed a lot from the woman who loved the man who was her natural father. Peaches could not imagine her mother acting the way her daughter was behaving after finding Joe MacDonald. Her crazy daughter, she had once heard herself described as, to a relative on the phone. Peaches liked that description.

Her mother was bound to know she had taken off by now, of course. Dale would have phoned home to confess that he had lost her and to hang his head in guilty shame as he was shouted at for his failure to keep her in check. Dale would enjoy being a martyr. He would insist that it was his fault and that no blame whatsoever should be attached to Peaches. Dale would not lie. Untruths were compliments to the Devil, he always said. Teddy and her mother had only allowed her to come to Europe because Dale had solemnly promised to look after her. She was still supposed to be in a fairly delicate state of health, with regular check-ups from the psychiatrist who always had soup stains on his tie. But they had finally agreed to let her go abroad, persuaded that it might do her some good. Peaches smiled and rubbed her knuckles over her lips. It certainly had done her some good, a great deal of good. If only they realized. She was a different woman now.

Peaches was seized by a sudden overwhelming desire to see MacDonald at once. She scrambled off the bed and parted the curtains with her feet before sliding down onto the seat beside him. The radio had been turned off.

'You didn't sleep for very long,' the driver said.

'It's too claustrophobic back there,' she replied, twining her arm round MacDonald's and pressing it against her breast. 'I couldn't get comfortable.'

There was a grey darkness outside. The countryside all around was visible but there were no sharply-defined edges or contours anywhere. It was like a furnished room under a thick layer of dust. The window beside her was half open. She stretched out her arm and felt the cold wind tug at her hand. She opened her fingers and the pieces of paper were whipped away into the lorry's slipstream like a flurry of snowflakes. One solitary piece lingered on the palm, stuck there by the perspiration until it was snatched away.

'What was that?' MacDonald asked.

'Oh nothing,' she said. 'Just some bits and pieces I cleared out of my rucksack. When will we reach Frankfurt?'

'Well, Peaches Baby, there has been a change of plan. I don't think we should bother going to Frankfurt any more.'

'No? Where then?'

'I've arranged with our driver to take a little detour to let us take in the sights somewhere else. I think Shuggie is more likely to be there.'

'Where?' Peaches asked, ready to sleep now that she was beside MacDonald again.

'Nowhere,' MacDonald said, grinning hugely. 'Nowhere anybody has every heard of. Somewhere well off the usual tourist routes.'

'You lead Joe, and I will follow,' she said sleepily.

'That's my girl,' he said, reaching across his chest to stroke her hair.

Her eyes closed and her head nodded forward. I'm your girl, she thought, and you're my man.

She knew they were watching her. They had let her go despite all the reasons they must have had for holding onto her. All smiles, they had been. All friends. Look after yourself, Gudrun, they had said. Mind the company you keep out there. Behave yourself. Auf Wiedersehen.

The contents of her handbag were poured from a large brown envelope onto the table in front of her, a pattering shower of coins and lipsticks and keys and pens. And right in the centre of the jumble of items was the heart-shaped locket that Franz had given her soon after they first met. The chain was broken now. His picture was inside. She imagined that his eyes were looking up into hers from beneath the smooth gold of the locket's face. She remembered the picture they had shown her of Franz's lifeless body in the driving seat of his car and for the first time since she had arrived at the police station the tears pricked at her eyes. A huge sob began to rise in her throat like an air bubble rushing to the surface. She gulped it back down and scooped all the stuff off the table into her bag. She would not let them see her cry. She kept her head down as she signed the form and surreptitiously managed to wipe away the tears that had leaked out with the back of her hand. When she finally lifted her head her face had become a mask of stony indifference.

They were more subtle this time, much more professional, but she knew they were there. They did not wear trench coats and dark glasses. They did not blatantly park on the other side of the street at all times of the day and night. When she went out during the day she was barely aware of them, but she knew they were there. Only a hurriedly-averted glance sometimes gave one away, or the conspicuous window-shopper who was reluctant to move on when she simply stopped on the pavement and stood there for five minutes for no obvious reason.

They were watching her now as she sat at the window looking out, as she did every night. She could see no one but they were watching her, probably from one of the windows in the wall of the tall block of modern flats opposite. There she is sitting at the window again, they would say. Sitting there knitting like one of the women round the base of the guillotine. She must be mad, they would say.

Gudrun looked down at the closed locket in the palm of her hand. The chain snaked off and dropped down through the gap between thumb and first finger. It had been Divers who had broken the chain, ripping it off her neck and throwing it at her during one of his temper tantrums. I'm going to fuck your boyfriend, he had shouted. I'm going to make him pay.

And she had sent Franz to him so that he could be shot through the heart. She could cry now because they were too far away to see the tears. As long as she sat upright and held her head high they would not know about her secret weakness. She closed her hand tightly round the locket and wept silently, the tears on her face running like the raindrops on the window pane in front of her.

She had accepted his death. She was not inconsolable or helplessly distracted by the intensity of her grief. She was thinking clearly all the time. She was pragmatic enough to realize that the shedding of tears was a necessary outlet for her emotions. It would be too painful, too dangerous to keep them bottled up inside. This way she could let the grief flow away naturally so that she would have the strength to go on alone.

Franz had always warned her that the life-style he had chosen to follow was an extremely high-risk one. He had tried to prepare her for his death and she had, to a certain extent without fully realizing it, been prepared. But it had come so soon, before they had a real chance of enjoying each other, before she had told him all the things she wanted him to know, before she had managed to break down the barriers he placed round his real feelings. He had never been able to tell her that he loved her but she knew it would have been only a matter of time before he did. But then she had sent him to his death. Somehow, she had to atone for that.

She was not mad. She had a good reason for sitting in the window. She wanted them to see her there, to get a really good look at her. Soon, she intended to leave but they would still think she was sitting there. She would remain in front of them like an after-image which refuses to fade from eyes which have stared at the same spot for too long. She was not mad. Soon, she would dye her hair black and go out into the big city to lose those who sought to follow her. Franz had taught her how to go about such things. He had had the foresight to prepare her for such a course of action even though, at the time, she had thought it silly and unnecessary. But, as in so many other things, Franz had been proved right and she was ready to employ all the cunning at her command to break free. He had taught her well.

She would also need to get to one of the secret caches that Franz's foresight had created all over the country. There were dozens of them but she could not be sure how many had already been revealed by other members of the group arrested after Franz's death. However, there was at least one which she knew would still be intact. This is one just for the two of us, he had told her. No one else is to know of its existence. It is just for the two of us.

A tear splashed onto her closed fist. It was almost as if Franz had known he was going to die and had arranged for everything to be ready for her when he was gone. It was almost funny that they were watching her because they thought she and Divers had worked together in killing Franz so that they could have the Minotaur for themselves. She laughed through her tears as she carefully laid the locket on the window sill, spreading out the chain in a graceful curve. Franz would have appreciated the joke.

She picked up her knitting from her lap. She was making a sweater for herself; a nice, close-fitting black sweater, very fashionable. It would soon be finished. The needles clicked quietly as she stared up at the flats opposite. The lights of the windows were diffused by her water-filled eyes. Rainbow colours radiated out from them.

They were watching her because they wanted her to lead

them to Divers. She laughed again, a small grunting noise. They would never manage to find him for themselves. The picture they had put in all the papers was nothing like him. She had barely recognized him.

Well, she thought, she would not lead them to Divers. She intended to find him herself. She knew the place to start looking. They could have him once she was finished with him.

Divers booked into his hotel in Munich for an extra night after his meeting with Betzing. His original plan had been to drive north immediately afterwards but it was impossible for him to do that. He was sick. The wound was poisoning his blood, numbing his brain, affecting his co-ordination. He had to sleep it off before he tackled the long journey. He just could not drive in that condition.

He managed to get to his room without attracting too much attention to the state he was in. The receptionist thought he was drunk and frowned disapprovingly when he asked her to get him a bottle of vodka to take up with him. Safe behind his locked door, he started to shiver uncontrollably. He took off his clothes and soaked away the sodden bandage that was stuck to the wound. It had become badly swollen, a deep scarlet and black slash in the centre of a massive purple bruise. He cleaned it up as best he could and poured neat vodka over it in the hope of killing any infection before it got a proper hold on him. The pain came at him in waves, so intense was it that he had to bite down hard on a towel to stop himself crying out, reducing the sound to a pathetic whimper. Tears poured from his eyes. His senses would clear momentarily, but then the pain would come rushing back with redoubled force.

He lay the whole night in a warm bath, continually topping up the level with fresh hot water. The warm cocoon helped a lot. It soothed the pain and allowed him to doze fitfully. By the morning he still felt unwell but he managed to eat some breakfast. He had stopped shivering. The pain was bearable. He hoped he might be over the worst of it.

His leg with the bullet embedded in it was stiff and sore. He found he could walk as long as he kept the sole of his foot curled inwards. In any other position it was like standing on needle-sharp spikes every time a little pressure was applied. He thought about abandoning his car and taking a train or a plane north but quickly decided against it. He could bend his knee well enough and the clutch in his car was very light. He would manage. He needed to be alone. If he was going to pass out he could always park the car in some secluded lay-by and take his chances there. On public transport he would not be able to escape notice.

It did not take him long to get onto the autobahn. He let the car cruise at a steady speed to avoid changing gears as much as possible, staying in the inside lane except to overhaul slow-moving lorries. He kept his window open to have a stream of cold air into his face. A song began repeating itself inside his head.

We're busy going Nowhere, having a lovely time. We'd like to be unhappy but ... We never do have the time. Da da, daddidy da, daddidy daddidy daddidy da.

He grinned stupidly as the words and the tune kept replaying themselves.

Two thirds of the way to Nuremberg he had to stop. His leg began to throb. He broke out in a cold sweat. He held his hand to his forehead and it was burning hot. A dizzy spell blurred his vision and the car began to creep over to the right before he realized what was happening. He pulled over into a rastplatz and just managed to get his door open before he was sick. Another driver standing beside his car which was parked further along on the near side peered at him curiously, unable to see what was actually going on. Divers hurriedly got back on the road again, wincing each time he had to press down on the clutch. The dizziness had passed but he had started shivering again. His body was drenched in sweat.

Having a lovely time. We'd like to be unhappy but ... We never do have the time. Da da ...

Divers knew that it was a race against time for him to get back to Nowhere before he collapsed. The bullet was gnawing away at him inside his leg. It felt as if it was entering and re-entering the channel it had carved into his flesh in endless repetition of the moment he had been shot. It was only his will-power that kept him going. He was draining his reserves. It was touch and go if he would make it, and even when he left the car there was still the strength-sapping cross-country hike to follow. He groaned and leaned right forward over the steering wheel so that his forehead touched the windscreen and the vibration rattled his teeth. When he did get back he would just lie still and let his body repair itself. His nervous system would purge itself of the debilitating poison in his blood. It might take a couple of days, perhaps a week. That gave him plenty of time to recover fully and get back to Munich to complete the bargain. A line from a new song started up spontaneously in his mind.

Who wants to be a millionaire? I do.

He hummed the tune.

The traffic was very quiet on the interchanges just south of Nuremberg. He managed to switch onto the autobahn to Bamberg, only once having to drop below fourth gear. He began to feel better. The journey seemed to pass more quickly. He built up his speed. The old car shook and the engine whined its complaint at what it was being asked to do. When the autobahn ran out and he emerged onto the ordinary road, skirting round Bamberg and still heading north, he kept travelling fast, confident now that he could make it. He swung to the north-west, into more hilly country, recognizing the increasingly familiar landmarks. The roller-coaster road was empty. He accelerated even more, taking corners at dangerous speeds, ramming on the brakes at the last moment as the car threatened to side-slip. Then the engine would labour as it pulled away still in top gear. At last he saw what he was looking for a few miles beyond Staffelstein, the distant steeple of a church sticking out above a line of tall trees. He turned into the concealed entrance to the disused road which led to the old quarry and went too fast over the pot-holes, jarring his injured leg so that what new-found strength he had fell away like a piece of discarded clothing. He ran the car into its hiding place and lay slumped over the wheel for a long time before he could rouse himself. There were still six miles to go. This was the part of the journey he had really been dreading. With his leg, he could not expect to keep up any sort of reasonable pace. He would just have to take it as it came. At all costs he had to keep moving. There was, after all, nowhere else for him to go. He had nowhere else he could hide. Opening the car door he almost fell out. *We're busy going nowhere*, he sang , snarling the words.

From the boot he took a pair of strong walking boots and replaced his shoes. He covered the car with the pile of dead branches and dried ferns and set off without a backward glance or a moment's hesitation. Following the steep path out of the quarry, he crawled through a ditch to avoid jumping over it, and marched away. The pain chased him like a pack of hounds.

Divers tried to concentrate totally on walking, looking down at his boots falling one in front of the other. Each step is another yard closer, he kept telling himself. Every hundred yards he stopped for a brief rest, never for more than a minute lest his leg muscles should seize up. He never looked far ahead, just enough to keep him on the right track, and he sang to himself to keep his spirits up. It was like the forced marches they had made them do in army training, only this was easier because he was not in full combat gear with a fifty-pound pack weighing him down. Just keep moving, he repeated. One foot in front of the other. Another step. And again, And again. You'll get there soon enough. Don't give up. Only the weaklings give up.

The stiffness was spreading out from the wound. He could not bend the knee now and the limp was much more pronounced. It was spreading up through his hip and along the side of his body, under his arm and over his chest. The pain was making him weep. One foot in front of the other. You can do it. Come on boy. Keep going. Soon be there. Yo can do it.

Having a lovely time. We'd like to be unhappy but ... We never do have the time. Da da, daddidy da ...

He reached the strangely-shaped tree trunk and draped himself over it. Getting closer, he told himself. Not far now. Keep going. Another step. And another. One foot in front of the other. He staggered on. The bag he had looped over his shoulder suddenly became intolerably heavy. He threw it away.

He reached the top of the bare hillside with shelving platforms at various levels. Searching around for a suitable stick he leaned on it like a crutch as he began to feel his way tentatively down the first steep slope. His teeth chattered loudly and his whole body shook in increasingly violent spasms. Keep going boy. Keep going. Keep going. We're almost there. At the foot of the hill he took off his jacket and threw it away.

The next thing he knew he was lying on his back, staring up at the sky. Swaying tree-tops formed an octagonal shape above him. Got to keep moving, he muttered. Can't give up now. Only weaklings give up. One foot in front of the other. You can do it. You can make it. He got to his knees and then to his feet with his hands still supporting him on the ground. When he took his hands away he fell and a surge of pain thumped him like a hard punch in the stomach. He tried to stand again and fell over again. The wound on his leg was pulsing as though it was alive, as though it was a parasite attached there to suck away his strength and his life. It throbbed in a regular beat like the ticking of a bomb. Divers laughed. Like a time bomb, he thought. He tried to stand up again and this time he made it.

The rock face was coarse against his cheek. He leaned against it, arms outstretched to embrace it. He stood there for minutes, or it could have been hours. He had lost all sense of time. All he knew was that it was growing darker, but that might have been because the forest was blotting out the sun. He placed the palms of his hands flat on the ground at the top of the six-foot-high rock face and, with a supreme effort, began to raise himself inch by inch. The toe of his right boot scrambled for a hold. His left leg dangled uselessly, scraping the rock, holding him down like an anchor. He channelled all the strength he could summon into his arms and pushed. He stretched his neck back so that he was looking up at the sky and he howled like a wounded animal.

He made it to the top, dragging his injured leg over the edge so that the bandage was almost ripped off it, and rolled over to lie totally exhausted in the dusty soil. Not far now, he thought, forcing himself to move when all he wanted to do was lie down and sleep. He couldn't afford to stop now. Not now. There was dust in his eyes and in his mouth. Clambering awkwardly to his feet, his shoulder bounced off a tree, spinning him round. A branch whipped across his face. No time to rest, he thought. Can't stop. Only the weaklings give up.

The wound had started to bleed. He was aware of the

warmth flowing down his leg. Then it hardened and solidified, forming a crust. It seemed to take the pain away as it flowed out. It made it easier for him to walk, much easier. But it was as if he was walking in a mist. All he could see were grey shadows shifting around him. The trees seemed to be moving, dancing in a circle round him. It was like the games he had played as a child in the school playground. The trees danced round him calling his name and he reached out to try and grab them, but they avoided him, swerving away from his clutching fingers, teasing him, tauntng him. He staggered on.

He splashed face down into the shallow water of the stream. Its coldness revived him briefly. He drank the water and it ran through him encouraging him, coaxing him a little further on. He could no longer use his left leg at all so he half crawled, half dragged himself along the bed of the stream. The trees lined the bank on both sides of him, calling his name, tugging at his hair with their overhanging branches, tearing his clothes. The dried blood round the wound squeezed his leg like a vice. He was so close, he thought. So close. He had almost made it. He had given it his best shot, but now the last of his strength was going. It was being washed out of him and borne away on the running water. His face was wet too, but the water there was different. It was hot and salty and burned liked acid.

He could no longer move either leg so he pulled himself along on his hands, lumbering like a seal stranded on dry land. The water around him seemed to thicken and coagulate. He imagined he must be lying in the mud at the entrance to Minotaur Chamber Number Thirteen. His arms could not bear his weight. He slumped down and twisted onto his side. There was not much pain any more, just an all-pervasive ache that seemed to be centred inside his skull. The trees had stopped moving on the banks. He could make them out quite clearly now, standing in orderly rows like a guard of honour, forming an avenue leading up to the Minotaur chamber. The eye of the beast looked out at him, a solitary glow of light in the darkness. He lay on his side passively and watched it. One of his eyes was blinded by the water. He opened his mouth and thick, glutinous mud oozed in to gather in the hollow of his cheek. The mud seeped into one nostril.

The eye of the Minotaur blinked shut, vanishing instantly.

The avenue of trees narrowed. Divers could see that something was emerging from the chamber. He stared in dumb wonderment as a strangely-shaped figure with human legs and a large hunchback came out and began to approach him. He heard his name spoken like a faraway shout. The trees chanted it, taunting him again. The beast moved silently againt the background of the forest.

'My God, it's,' Divers said and then he was choked by the mud flowing to the back of his throat. His face sank deeper. The blackness filled his second eye, mud trickled into his ear and he could see and hear no more.

Joe MacDonald threw off the rucksack and rushed into the stream. He stumbled to his knees as the spray flew around him in sheets and grabbed Divers just as his face was rolling under the water. He looped his arms round his chest and hoisted him clear, trying to stand up at the same time. The dead weight of the body pulled him off balance and both men collapsed into the water, falling over each other. MacDonald went right under and came up coughing and spluttering. Peaches had waded in and was at his side, helping him. Divers had landed on his back and was half floating in the shallow water, his legs slowly swinging round in the current. They took an arm each and dragged him to the side until only his boots were trailing in the water. MacDonald knelt beside him and put the flat of his hand on his chest.

'He's alive,' he announced. 'Christ, look at his leg.'

Peaches had already seen the trouser leg stained black at the thigh. In the stream at the bottom of the leg the water was a dirty pink colour and gradually becoming redder and redder as the disturbed mud settled. She watched as MacDonald produced his small penknife and slit the trousers over the bulge on the thigh to reveal a filthy bandage that had slipped off the wound it was supposed to be protecting. MacDonald whistled loudly through his teeth. The skin around the wound was black and purple and yellow. Fresh scarlet blood was seeping from the raised centre like lava down the slopes of a volcano. Peaches clapped a hand over her mouth and looked away to stop herself being sick.

'God knows how much blood he has lost,' MacDonald said.

'And God knows how he managed to walk nearly six miles on a leg like this.'

'It looks like a bullet wound,' Peaches said tentatively, not really knowing what a bullet wound looked like. 'Has he been shot?'

MacDonald nodded. 'I was worried that he might have been shot. The reports all said somebody was shot and injured when the German was killed.'

'What are you talking about? How could you have known he'd been shot?'

MacDonald looked up and wiped some mud from his mouth. 'While you were kipping in the back of that lorry last night I was hearing the whole story on the radio. Big Shuggie has been busy recently and I never thought he would actually do it.' He looked down at his friend lying unconscious in front of him. 'Well, I believe him now.'

'What do you mean?' Peaches demanded. 'You're not joking then. All that you've told me is true? You're not making it up?'

'Would I lie to you, Peaches baby?' he replied. 'I was deadly serious. Do you believe me now?'

She shook her head, looking between MacDonald and Divers. Her lips moved but no sound came out.

'No time for arguments just now. We've got to do something about this leg and get him under cover as soon as possible. Have you got anything that would serve as a bandage? We'd better try to stop this bleeding.'

He cut away the remains of the old bandage and tossed it into the stream. Peaches searched in her rucksack and found an old jersey. She also took a face-cloth and some sanitary towels from her toilet bag and handed them to MacDonald.

'You had better wash off the worst of the dirt,' she said. 'Then these should soak up the blood.'

He dipped the cloth in the water and tenderly dabbed at the exposed wound. Divers groaned only once and the whites of his eyes showed beneath almost closed eyelids. When it was as clean as he could get it, MacDonald placed two pads over it and wrapped the jersey round the leg.

Peaches tore a tee-shirt down its side seam and gave it to MacDonald. 'For a tourniquet higher up. It will slow down the blood flow.' she said.

He applied the strip of material right up in the groin, hard against the pelvic bone. Peaches broke off a thin branch and used it to twist the ends together as tightly as possible. They watched anxiously as some blood soaked through but the worst of the bleeding seemed to have been stopped.

'Hold that,' she said, directing his hand onto the tourniquet. 'Don't let up on the pressure.'

She took a foil blanket from one of the pockets on the rucksack and unfolded it on the ground alongside Divers. It was a huge sheet of silver paper. They lifted him onto it and wrapped it round him. Then they raised him into a sitting position and hauled him right up onto his feet. Peaches balanced him there while MacDonald went down on one knee and took the body across his shoulders with one hand between his legs holding the tension on the tourniquet and the other clutching an arm and a handful of silver blanket. He straightened his legs and stood up.

'Right. Let's go,' he said,' he said. 'The bunker is about a mile from here if I remember rightly. We have to use this stream as a path. The forest gets too thick to move through soon. It will be like walking through a tunnel. The undergrowth will catch us as we go along. You follow behind, Peaches, and try to make sure that nothing rubs on the leg if you can. I think he is suffering enough without that.'

'Should we not take him to a doctor?'

'Not a good idea, Peaches baby. Not a good idea at all.'

She blushed, realizing her foolishness. 'Do you think he will live?'

MacDonald shook his head and the blanket flashed in the fading light. 'He's not dead yet. Come on. Let's go.'

Peaches picked up the rucksack and the holdall and followed MacDonald as he splashed clumsily along the uneven bed of the stream. She was in a state of mild shock, still uncertain about what exactly was going on but slowly beginning to make sense of it all. She had laughed at MacDonald, lost her temper when he stuck to his story, convinced it was all a bad joke on his part. Now she could see only too well that he must have been telling the truth. Divers' injured leg stuck out from under the blanket. She reached forward to prevent a springy branch lashing back across it.

The tanker that had brought them from Grenoble had obligingly taken a detour round by Stuttgart instead of going directly up the Rhine valley. The driver said it made no difference to him but MacDonald had insisted on paying him one hundred and fifty Deutschmarks for his trouble anyway. Instead of Frankfurt as originally planned they had got off a Würzburg seventy miles to the east. MacDonald was being mysterious and refused to tell her where they were going. She had not bothered to push him. They quickly got another lift, taking them further east, and another one which dropped them off at a remote crossroads somewhere well to the north of Nuremberg. She had asked why they were standing in the middle of nowhere, and he had replied that they hadn't yet got to Nowhere, but it wasn't far away. He reminded her of the underground bunker he had mentioned once. She could not decide if he was joking. They set up camp in a forest clearing and made love under the stars before sleeping in separate sleeping bags inside the tent. They had a long walk in front of them the next day, MacDonald said.

At first, she was content to trot obediently behind when they set off on a cross-country hike. MacDonald set a fast pace and it was all she could do to keep up with him. They travelled for miles and they didn't seem to be getting anywhere. He just kept repeating that they would be there soon. Be patient, he told her, it can't be far.

As Peaches got more and more tired as the day wore on, she got more and more irritable. He carried both the rucksack and his holdall when she began complaining about the weight. Finally he admitted he was lost and didn't know where he was going although he was sure they were in the general area of the bunker. She decided she had had enough. She sat down on a fallen tree trunk beside a stone wall and refused to budge. It was then he told her about Hugh Divers and the theft of a nuclear land-mine called a Minotaur and his plans to ransom it for a small fortune. She had laughed sarcastically and told him to go and tell it to the Marines. He had repeated the story, straight-faced, adding how Divers had written asking him to help with the scheme before going ahead and doing it all on his own. She had laughed again in a more subdued tone, searching his face for some sign that it was still a joke.

It was then the sound reached them, carrying across the forest from a great distance, echoing eerily through the walls of trees. It was like the howl of a wounded animal, momentarily silencing all other life in the forest.

'That's him,' MacDonald said and began running in the direction of the sound. Peaches had no option but to follow. She did not want to be left alone with night approaching. MacDonald seemed to have got his bearings. He knew where he was going. They came upon Divers face down in the hidden stream, going under just as they arrived. He would have drowned if they had not found him.

Ahead of her, MacDonald ducked to get under a particularly low branch, but he could not get down far enough to stop its underside scraping the silver blanket. Divers jerked a couple of times and then lay still. MacDonald adjusted his burden as he stood up on the other side and continued at once. Peaches bowed under the branch.

It was all true then, she thought. This Big Shuggie person had stolen a nuclear bomb and had somehow got himself shot in the process, it was a different league from stolen cars and stolen purses. And now she was an accessory. Every last hair on her body bristled with excitement. She liked the feeling. For some reason it made her feel very sexy. Her legs were weak with desire and if MacDonald had not been busy she would have had him there and then. It really was the big time. Scooping a handful of water from the stream at her feet she splashed it in her face, licked her lips and smiled. She liked being in the big league. She liked it a lot.

They stopped together, glancing sideways as something large lumbered noisily through the trees on the bank. 'A deer,' MacDonald said, although nothing was visible. 'This is the place. It is just another fifty yards or so.'

He climbed out of the stream where the trees thinned to let more light onto the forest floor and where the ruined walls of an ancient house were shrouded in moss and undergrowth. He laid out Divers' body beside one of the broken-down walls. Peaches knelt beside him and checked the tourniquet. She put a hand on his forehead. It was burning hot beneath a layer of cold sweat. She looked across at MacDonald.

'We have to get him out of these wet clothes,' she said.

'Okay. You start undressing him. I'll light a fire.'

'Out here? Where's your secret bunker then?'

'It's so secret you can't even see it when you are standing right on top of it.' He stood up and grinned down on her. 'In fact, that's where I am going to light the fire.'

Peaches looked around but could see nothing. She began unbuttoning Divers' soaking-wet shirt. MacDonald went through the gap in the wall. He moved a big dead branch from one corner of the ruin and turned to face her.

'Welcome to Nowhere,' he said, bending down to pull up the trap-door. He balanced it for a moment and then let it fall open. Then he stepped down into the hole and disappeared.

Peaches smiled. It was all true. How much more evidence did she need? She got the shirt off fairly easily. She ripped the trousers along the cut in the left leg and then managed to pull them off the right one. The makeshift bandage was thick with blood. She tightened the tourniquet a little more and tucked the silver blanket around the bare body. Then she left him and went inside the ruined wall, looking into the black square that led underground. A rectangular beam of light cut across just below the surface. She could make out what seemed to be rows of shelves. There was a damp smell. The light vanished and MacDonald's head popped up.

'It's here all right,' he said.

'What?'

'The Minotaur, that's what. A beautiful beast. Let's take Shuggie down to join it.'

They lifted the body between them by arms and ankles and carried it to the entrance. MacDonald went down the steps holding the legs while Peaches lowered from above. MacDonald moved out of sight and took Divers with him. She turned round and descended backwards into the bunker.

At the bottom of the steps she was dazzled by the white beam but gradually her eyes became accustomed to the dimness around it. She noticed the rows and rows of food tins, and the car battery with wires trailing from it, and the walls lined with sacking, and the spotlight glaring at her, and MacDonald bent over beside a fire in the far corner that was just beginning to grow into life. She saw that she was standing beside a home-made table with a large box on it. She reached out and touched it with a fingertip. The metal was very cold. There was something painted on the side, some kind of symbol. She traced its outline and her excitement swelled outwards in an audible gasp. It looked like the horns of a bull. The Minotaur.

'He's in a bad way but he's alive,' MacDonald said. Peaches went over to him. 'He could be on his last lap.'

Divers' face was grey. Flecks of spittle foamed at the corners of his mouth. His breathing was loud and laboured. They rubbed his skin dry and put on a new dressing that MacDonald produced from one of the shelves.

'What else can we do?' she asked.

'We might try getting some antibiotics for him but I'm no doctor.' He took some of the woollen blankets down and spread them over Divers, tucking in the edges except over the injured leg. 'I think we should give him till the morning to see if that fever is going to break. If it doesn't I might have to head into town to see what I can find.'

'And leave me here?'

'It's okay. I trust you.'

The flames had got a proper hold. The foil blanket lay in a heap in front of the fire, its surface sparkling. Peaches stood closer to MacDonald, rubbing herself against him, desperate for him to hold her. He kissed her on the cheek and she turned hungrily to return the kiss on his lips, keeping her eyes open so that she could watch his face.

'Meanwhile,' she said, 'I think we should dispense with our own wet clothes before we catch our deaths of cold.'

'What? Now?' he said and his eyes gleamed.

'There is nothing we can do for your friend at the moment. Maybe there is something I can do for you, or maybe that you can do for me.'

She stripped naked and then helped MacDonald out of his clothes when he was too slow for her. Her hands trembled with anticipation. The fire flared and was hot against their sides. She lifted a leg and curled it around his back, resting it on his hip bone. He grabbed the back of her knee and raised her off the ground. He walked with her in that position until, with an intense thrill of pleasure, she felt her buttocks touch the cold metal surface of the Minotaur. The table wobbled and tilted onto two legs. The Minotaur touched the wall and jammed there. She was sitting on the narrow ledge of the table, pressed back against the Minotaur. She sighed as she spread her legs wide and pulled MacDonald forward, sliding her hands down to his backside.

'Come on, you beautiful beast you,' she said. 'Let's see what you can do.'

She threw her head back as she felt his teeth nip the flesh of her neck and, through the open trap-door, she saw the first faint stars swirling above in the evening sky. He was warm between her legs. The Minotaur was steely cold behind her back. She could not imagine anywhere else in the world she would rather be.

Dirk Kaspar came round from behind his desk and shook Buster Grant's hand without saying a word. He returned to his chair and swivelled sideways to look out the window, nodding curtly to dismiss the secretary from where she stood hovering just inside the door. Grant put his briefcase down at his feet, opened his jacket, and settled comfortably into the high-winged chair. He was surrounded by the pervasive smell of leather and polish. The sun shone on an antique silver inkwell on the desk where two stags battled, heads down, antlers locked. Kaspar's hair also shone silver.

'This conversation is off the record for the time being,' Kaspar said evenly without looking round. 'We can begin again more formally when we are ready.'

'Agreed,' Grant said, knowing exactly what was coming.

Kaspar cleared his throat as if he was about to begin a speech. 'You did not tell us about the loss of your DIP unit, Buster. My people are most annoyed. There are likely to be repercussions. We should have been told.'

Grant nodded contritely, casting his eyes down like a child caught out in a lie. It was the Americans who had unearthed the truth about the missing Dipstick and the internal inquiry into its loss. And the Americans had big mouths. Now all the allies knew. Britain was in the doghouse for concealing the information. Grant was obliged to eat humble pie and accept the blame on behalf of his country. He was the whipping-boy.

'We should have been told,' Kaspar repeated. 'There are arses that will have to be kicked.'

'What can I say?' Grant spread his arms wide, indicating

helplessness. 'The judgement of my superiors was not to confuse the situation with information that was considered unlikely to be directly relevant. It was decided that it was too much of a remote possibility that the Dipstick and the Minotaur could be united. Officially, the Dipstick is still regarded as being on the bottom of that lake. It remains lost to everyone, not just us.'

Kaspar swung round to face him, his cheeks highly coloured. 'And that line did not change when it became known that a certain Hugh Divers was suspected of being involved in the loss of the DIP unit, this Dipstick as you call it. The same man who is now responsible for the theft of the Minotaur from under your noses?'

Grant put out his arms again, but this time they felt a lot heavier. Diplomacy was all about justifying decisions you did not believe in and knew to be foolish. The truth to a diplomat was a strange animal like Dr Dolittle's Push-me-Pull-you. It faced two ways and wanted to go in opposite directions at the same time.

'Divers was cleared by the inquiry. The loss was accidental.'

'You believe that now?' Kaspar's eyebrows disappeared under the sweep of his fringe.

'I believed the information should have been passed on initially,' Grant said defensively. 'I was over-ruled. I have been suffering from chronic indigestion ever since Divers' name came into the picture.'

'We should have been told, especially after the implication of this former soldier,' Kaspar insisted. 'We believed the Minotaur was harmless. Now, at this late stage, we discover it is far from harmless. We should have been told. This is not good for the digestion. It is not good to think that this madman is out there with an operational nuclear bomb in his pocket. This creates a whole new perspective. We will have to redouble our efforts to find this man Divers.'

'Yes,' Grant said simply, crossing his legs and folding his arms.

Kaspar shook his head and brushed away the hair that fell down into his eyes. 'It is bad, Buster, very bad,' he said softly. 'There is much panic at high levels in my government.'

'A lot of indigestion.'

'Indeed. This small bomb is capable of a very big bang. It is you, the British, to blame and yet already our politicians are looking for scapegoats amongst themselves.'

'But surely it is nobody's fault? Nobody on your side anyway.'

'It always has to be somebody's fault. You know that, Buster. Always.' He sat back, looking down his nose. 'If my government did not find somebody here to take the blame the people might begin to think that their government was not fully in control of what went on in their own country.'

'Blame us, the British.'

'Oh, we do. It is your fault after all. But we have to blame at least one of our own as well. It is a way of keeping our self-respect.'

'Grant smiled sympathetically. 'Any news of the police investigation?'

Kaspar sat forward again, brisk and businesslike, leaning on papers scattered over the top of his desk. 'We are withdrawing the photograph of Divers taken from his identity-card records. Feedback from his former neighbours in Frankfurt suggest that it is not a good likeness at all. A detailed scientific examination of it revealed that some of the facial muscles and tissues were held in apparently unnatural positions. It appears he was not actually making funny faces at the camera but he may have had his cheeks and his upper lip padded out with something like cotton wool. Then there is the moustache, of course. He has been clean-shaven for at least six months. And he does not normally wear glasses like these.'

Grant took the blown-up copy of the picture which Kaspar removed from a plastic envelope and handed to him. There had also been comments from former army colleagues that the picture was a bad resemblance. They had been passed on to the police.

'He must have been planning this several years in advance to have arranged something like this,' Grant said.

'Yes,' Kaspar acknowledged wearily. 'First of all the clever theft of the DIP unit, so clever that no one realizes it has been stolen. Then the doctoring of his identity-card photograph, easily done because people just send them in and there is no real check. The police always take the pictures of wanted criminals from that source. And finally, the coup de grâce, the theft of the Minotaur itself. A well-laid plan.'

'And it has all run pretty smoothly for him so far.'

'We are officially withdrawing this photograph and issuing this much earlier one from his army file. It is said to be a much better likeness.'

Kaspar held another picture between finger and thumb as he leaned forward to give it to Grant. Grant had seen them both before. There was a degree of similarity, but it took a close examination to find it.

'Psychologists point out that the distinctive features of the moustache and the thick spectacles grab the attention of a viewer and become an integral part of the image that is carried around in the mind.' Kaspar flicked at the edge of the first photograph with a fingernail. 'The much plainer face in the earlier one is unlikely to be related to it.'

'He's not stupid, is he?' Grant said grudgingly.

'On the contrary, he is obviously highly intelligent. He has managed to fool us with this dummy picture for a week now. God alone knows where he has been or what he has been doing in that time.'

'The army picture was sent out to the Press as well, wasn't it?'

'Yes, but it was not given as much prominence as the first one. Coverage was dominated by the moustache and glasses, just as he had planned. We should have realized at the beginning. It is easy to be wise now.'

Kaspar took back the photograph and placed it with the other one in the plastic envelope.

'I assume there has been no ransom demand or anything of that sort?' Grant said.

'Several, but none that we regard as authentic,' Kaspar replied. 'Our assumption at the moment is that Divers and his friends are looking for a customer. They may have had one lined up before the event, of course. Either that or they intend to use the Minotaur personally.'

'Well, I have some reasonably good news for you Dirk, and I have been authorized to pass it on.'

'Something else the British army has lost recently?'

'No.' Grant laughed dutifully. 'But I can tell you the reason why the Dipsticks were being moved when the lorry crashed and one was lost. The information was and is highly classified and was not released at the inquiry.'

'You intrigue me.'

'The units were being transported to Hamburg for shipment back to Britain because of doubts over the reliability of the thermal batteries built into them. Obviously, we could not let this become common knowledge or it would have detracted from the deterrent value of the Nuclear Wall strategy.'

'Just what are thermal batteries?' Kaspar asked.

'A thermal battery is the integral power source of military hardware like Minotaurs and missiles and rockets and stuff like that which provides instant power when triggered. It is just like any ordinary battery only it is much more powerful, of course, and has a very long storage capability. Fifteen years is the current specification. The batteries providing the initial power are distinct from the radioactive elements contained in nuclear devices which cause the chain reaction resulting in a nuclear explosion. The latter usually have a life of about two years. The one in the stolen Minotaur was replaced six months ago.'

'I see.' Kaspar slowly rubbed the tips of his fingers together and stared unblinking across the desk.

'The battery is not in the Minotaur casing itself. It is contained either in the detonation chamber or the DIP unit. It is a collection of electro-chemical cells in a hermetically sealed case. There is a solid salt electrolyte which is non-conductive in that state and the battery is therefore inactive. When chemical heat sources are ignited the electrolyte melts and immediately becomes highly conductive making power available. So, bang goes your Minotaur or whoosh goes your missile.'

'Come to the point please, Buster,' Kaspar said impatiently.

'Four years ago a batch of Dipsticks were recalled after faults were discovered in the thermal battery manufacturing process. It was subsequently discovered that the suspect batteries were only fifty per cent reliable compared with the ninety-nine point nine per cent reliability figure required. In other words, any Minotaur fitted with the Dipstick containing one of these batteries only had a fifty-fifty chance of detonation.'

'And the missing or stolen DIP unit is one of these?'

'Yes, but I must add that even if the battery in it is faulty it will still precipitate an explosion, but only a small conventional one. It would not be too healthy to be close to it, but not enough power would be transmitted to initiate the nuclear explosion.'

'But there is an even chance that a nuclear explosion would result?'

'I'm afraid so. That's why it is only reasonably good news.'

'Why were we not told this before as well?'

'I've only just found out myself, Dirk. It has the highest classification because of its embarrassment potential. It wasn't just Minotaurs that were affected four years ago. It was our whole range of missiles and rockets and other equipment. We had our pants at our ankles for at least three months till replacement parts were installed and all the faulty batteries were weeded out. We're still pretty touchy about it.'

'What do we do with this information then?'

'It can only be a matter of time before the media find out about the lost Dipstick so I have persuaded our people that when the story breaks it would be useful to make the fact known that the Dipstick was a faulty one being taken for repair when it went missing. This can be done without revealing the full extent of the equipment problems we suffered at the time.'

'I suppose something must be better than nothing,' Kaspar said philosophically.

'I know it is not a complete cure for indigestion but it has to help a little. If we put out this story about a faulty Dipstick, potential customers might be frightened off. We won't even say that there is a fifty-fifty chance of the thing operating properly. We can just say it is faulty. Full stop. That should be enough to convince a sceptical buyer not to get his fingers burned.'

Kaspar swung round in his chair to look out of the window again. He pressed his hands together and tapped the tips of his index fingers against his chin. 'And what if Herr Divers is not interested in selling?' he asked quietly.

'That is a possibility,' Grant conceded. 'As far as we know he is not aware that the Dipstick he may have is faulty. He could either treat the news as crude disinformation, or he might try to set the Minotaur off just to see if it will work. But if he is not interested in selling then that is presumably what he is going to do anyway.'

Kaspar nodded slowly and continued staring out the window.

'We want your government's agreement before we do anything, of course,' Grant said.

'Of course.' Kaspar moved smoothly round to face Grant, smiling at him over the pyramid of his fingers. 'I will pass on the request.'

There was a silence between the two men lasting more than a minute. The moving reflection of the sunlight on the silver stags made the surface shift as if the wind was blowing over them, rippling their hairs.

Grant said: 'No leads have been thrown up by the terrorist connection, this group of would-be Nazis that Divers seems to have taken a dislike to?'

'None so far. Blind alleys every one.'

'The woman?'

'Under surveillance. Apparently she sits at the window of her flat knitting most of the time.' Kaspar laughed weakly and suddenly stood up and began to pace round the room. 'Tell me, Buster. What do you think is going to happen?'

'Dirk, your guess is as good as mine. We must hope we get a breakthrough somewhere, and quickly.'

'It is interesting that our friend has given the country a new hobby since he killed Luneburg and painted the Minotaur symbol on him. Now everyone with a can of spray paint is doing it.'

'I've seen the grafitti,' Grant said.

'It is like the country has come out in a rash. You see it everywhere you go. You just can't get away from it.'

Monsieur Yves Sabaroff had known Manfred Steinmetz for the best part of twenty years and had done very well out of the relationship. He himself had a numbered account at his own bank's Berne branch into which payments were regularly channelled and it was a very useful source of capital that had served him well in the past. The arrangement in no way compromised his position at the bank. Officially, he was providing a financial consultancy service in his spare time but there was no danger of it ever becoming public knowledge anyway. The beauty of the Swiss system was its unassailable tradition of secrecy. There were no names, only numbers, but he used a false name anyway to be doubly secure. Steinmetz's money came from some very dubious sources. More than once he had arrived on the doorstep with a bag of used notes for deposit. Sabaroff asked no questions, but neither did he do anything illegal. He simply accepted the deposit and a few days later a sum would be credited to his Berne account, usually one per cent of the amount in the bag, sometimes more. Steinmetz was not the only customer who did it, but he was by far the most frequent. He came to the bank at least twice a year and at least once Sabaroff took him out to lunch. So he had thought nothing of it when Steinmetz had phoned and invited him out as the guest for a change. It had been a suprise, and a pleasant one, that was all.

Sabaroff was a big man. He had to press his soft belly against the edge of the table to reach the meal in front of him. He placed his knife and fork together on the plate beside the untouched fillet steak and sat back in his chair. Now that he knew the real reason for the lunch invitation he had lost his appetite.

'It was a fantastic piece of luck that this man MacDonald should come to you, my friend,' Steinmetz said. 'I found it very hard not to react when he handed me this piece of paper with your name on it.'

'What you are asking is completely unethical, Herr Steinmetz. I could not possibly contemplate such an action.'

'Come now Yves, ethics are for the saints. This man I am doing business with is a thief and a murderer. Should he be allowed to profit from his crime?'

Sabaroff opened his mouth but could not speak. He thought of getting up and walking out but he did not want to create a scene. Besides, the last thing he wanted to do was leave. The shock of being asked to participate in a criminal act rooted him to the spot. But it was more than shock. He was flattered that a man like Steinmetz should take him into his confidence, and he was excited at the prospect of joining him. He could not just blurt something like that straight out. He had to make a show of indignation and permit his integrity to slip away only gradually. The truth was he was desperately keen to do what Steinmetz asked. His emotional self had always admired the people who turned up with suitcases of dirty money. His professional self had duly processed the cash without showing the slightest curiosity about where it came from. His romantic self had imagined him doing the same thing some day. He knew it was perverse, but he had a recurring dream about being a bank robber.

Steinmetz was probing inside the claw of a pink lobster. 'I have known you for quite some time Yves,' he said. 'I would not ask you if I did not think you would do it. Am I to be proved wrong?'

Sabaroff closed his mouth and swallowed the saliva that had collected behind his tongue. Of course Steinmetz was right. It was a question of presentation; how he was to retain his dignity in abandoning his principles. Also, there had been the mention of seventy thousand pounds sterling, not a fortune but a significant sum. Sabaroff was a rich man. He was a fat man too. Over the years he had found that just as a fat man needs more food to keep him going so a rich man needs more money.

Seventy thousand pounds would be very welcome. He had lost quite heavily on a land speculation deal in Portugal recently. Such a sum would go some way towards recouping his losses.

'So you see Yves,' Steinmetz continued, snapping the lobster claw in half, 'I thought I would give you this chance as a favour. This is to be my last big transaction, my last sting if you like. I am going to retire and I need as much money as possible for my old age. I will make money whatever happens. With your help I can make more, a few seconds on the phone and you can make a little for yourself.' He piled the remains of the lobster on his plate and reached over to the finger bowl. 'Not so little,' he added as an afterthought.

Sabaroff slowly leaned forward and picked up his long-stemmed wine glass. He took a tiny sip and replaced it on the table. He spoke German with a curious French accent. 'You must be very sure that I will go along with your plan before you ask me,' he said.

Steinmetz finished wiping his lips with the napkin. 'If you do not agree I have a team outside who will gun you down before you get back to your office.' He patted the back of Sabaroff's hand as the fat man's eyes flashed with panic and he half rose from his chair. 'A joke Yves,' Steinmetz assured him. 'Just my little joke.'

Sabaroff slowly sank back to a seated position. 'Not so little,' he said, and a smile broke out on his face. 'What is it that you intend buying from this thief and murderer?'

Steinmetz noted the expression on Sabaroff's face and knew he had been right to approach him. He would acquiesce and he would play his part. He would be handsomely rewarded but then so would Steinmetz. There could be no gain without risk. He had virtually doubled the selling price of the Minotaur by cutting out the middle man.

'His ill-gotten gains naturally. I honestly believe that his sort of crime should not be allowed to pay.'

'What exactly is it you want me to do?' Sabaroff asked eagerly.

The waiter moved in to clear the plates, Sabaroff's steak still untouched. They both declined dessert and ordered coffee. Betzing waited until it had been poured before answering.

'On the twenty-second at around three o'clock you are due

to receive a call from our Mr MacDonald to ascertain that my representative has handed over to you seven hundred thousand pounds which has then been deposited in his numbered account.'

'I have these instructions but I did not know you were to be involved Herr Steinmetz.'

'You will simply state that everything has passed off without any problems. There will, of course, be no representative and no seven hundred thousand.'

Sabaroff ignored his coffee and drank the wine. It would be ridiculously easy. He grinned over the rim of the glass, enjoying himself immensely.

'That is all. I will take care of everything else. A few days later I will transfer seventy thousand pounds to the usual account and you will be richer man for a few seconds' work. I think a ten per cent cut is a reasonable return for the effort required.' Steinmetz raised his glass over the centre of the table and Sabaroff brought his up to meet it. 'Don't worry about it Yves. Trust me. I am an honourable man.'

Gertrud Richter was sitting at the window of the cafe sucking orange juice through a green and white straw as she watched people pass by in the street. She was wearing red running shoes and faded demins, a Southern Comfort sweat-shirt and a thin red jacket. Her scalp was itchy where her hair was chafing under the heavy dark wig she had been told to wear but she resisted the urge to scratch in case she attracted undesirable attention. Two middle-aged women in winter boots and belted raincoats sat at the same table oposite her, their feet hemmed in by bulging shopping bags. Every time Gertrud caught their eye they smiled benignly at her as though she was a small child. They were drinking coffee and seemed absorbed in their whispered conversation which, as far as she could make out, was about their various health problems.

Physically, Gertrud was tired after the journey down from Hamburg that morning, but mentally she was acutely alert. She had not been able to sleep for days after receiving the phone call asking for her assistance. It was a request she never thought for a moment about turning down. In fact, it was a request she had been hoping might come her way for a very long time. The police had briefly taken her in for questioning after the killing. They had not kept her long, of course, because she was only a small cog who turned no wheels in the machine. They had nothing against her so they had to let her go. She was really surprised to hear from her sister so soon afterwards because she had thought they would have kept Gudrun in custody. She was a cog who turned many other wheels. But Gudrun explained the situation and asked for her help. How could she refuse?

She saw her elder sister pass the window, looking directly at her but giving no sign of recognition. Gudrun's hair was tied up and hidden in a wide, white scarf round her head. She had on a black jumper, loose calf-length trousers with a colourful flowery pattern and white plastic sandals. She was carrying a nylon shopping bag, full to overflowing, on one side and a leather shoulder bag on the other. Gertrud got up as soon as she entered the cafe, said goodbye to the two women and went to the ladies toilet.

Gudrun Richter saw her little sister disappear through the toilet door. She sat down at the window table where Gertrud had been and ordered coffee. The cafe was not quite half full. There were plenty of free places. She balanced her two bags on the empty chair at her side and looked round.

Two people had followed her into the cafe, a man and a woman. They sat down at a table near the door and seemed lost in an animated conversation. Gudrun knew that she had been followed all day. She had to admit they had been quite clever about it, using dozens of different people, switching them again and again so that no one person needed to be near her for more than about twenty minutes at a time. Even so, the couple were familiar despite having changed their clothes and appearance regularly during the day. There would also be somebody out on the street, observing her through the window. She could not see anybody but they were there all right.

Gudrun took her time drinking her coffee, like any other housewife resting after a hard day out shopping. When the cup was half finished she asked the women to watch her bags and went to the toilet. It was a long, narrow room with four cubicles and three sinks fronted by a strip of mirror above a shelf. A woman was bending over one of the sinks, standing over her young daughter as she washed her hands. Gudrun went to another sink and began to fill it with water. The woman ushered the little girl towards the hot air blower and held her hands under it. Gudrun watched impatiently until at last the mother was satisfied they were dry and they left. She turned and went to the only cubicle with a closed door.

'Gertrud,' she whispered.

The door opened. The two Richter sisters were very alike.

As children they were constantly being mistaken for each other. There was only an eighteen-month age difference and the similarity remained as they grew into adulthood. The most obvious difference was that Gertrud usually chose to grow her hair long while Gudrun kept hers short. Otherwise, they were the image of each other.

Gudrun squeezed into the cubicle beside her sister and locked the door. Gertrud was already stripped down to her bra and pants. She lifted off the wig by its crown to display ner newly-cut short blonde hair.

'I wouldn't have done it for anyone else,' she said.

'It's perfect,' Gudrun answered, struggling to get her jumper over her head in the confined space. 'You look more like me than I do.'

They exchanged clothes quickly. Gertrud dressed first while Gudrun stood back out of the way to give her as much room as possible. She put on the black jumper and the flowery trousers and the plastic sandals. Gudrun unwound the scarf from her head and handed it over. It was lightly stained in places where it had been pressing against the black hair dye she had applied the previous night. She took the wig and dropped it into the small disposal bucket.

'Black hair quite suits you,' Gertrud said. She left some of her own hair sticking out from under the edge.

'That's fine,' Gudrun said approvingly. 'It looks as as if you've been adjusting it in the mirror. Have you done all I asked?'

'The suitcase is in a left-luggage locker at the station. The key is in my jacket pocket.'

'Good. 'Quick now. Any longer and they will start getting suspicious out there. My bags are at the table you were at. Those women are watching them. The house keys are in my purse. Sit down and finish my cup of coffee. Take five minutes. You know what to do after that.'

'Just sit and knit. That's what you want, isn't it?'

'That's it. Sit in the window. Don't try to hide. That will keep them happy. Go now.'

Gertrud opened the door and hesitated. 'Good luck sister,' she said, leaning back to kiss Gudrun on the cheek. 'Good luck with whatever it is you are going to do.'

'Thanks. Go now.'

Gudrun sat down in the cubicle with Gertrud's clothes bundled in her lap. She waited ten minutes, listening to women come and go and imagining her sister walking back through the streets of Frankfurt with the squad of plain-clothes policemen in hot pursuit. She got dressed slowly, finding it difficult to get into the jeans because they were so tight. Then she sat down again and waited another ten minutes.

There were two women standing at the sinks when she flushed the toilet and left the cubicle. She saw them both glance at her in the mirror as she joined them to wash her hands. She paced the hand-washing and drying so that she was able to follow the second of the two women out into the cafe. The tables seemed much busier, but there was nobody she recognized. The table by the window was occupied by a couple with two young children. No one took any notice of her. The waiter excused himself as he brushed against her carrying a tray of drinks.

She went straight to the door and out into the street. She walked with a spring in her step, elated by the successful switch of identity. Looking over her shoulder she saw people moving on the crowded pavement. Nobody was watching her now. She was free to go wherever she wanted to go and to do exactly what she wanted to do. Nobody was following her now. She took a deep breath and headed for the station.

Peaches Macdonald sat cross-legged on the floor with her back against the wall close beside the flickering flames of the fire in the corner. At her eye level Divers slept restlessly in his bunk. The sound of his breathing was very loud. It seemed strangely magnified, filling all the space in the bunker before pouring upwards through the faint grey square of the open trap-door.

They were alone. MacDonald had gone to try and find some antibiotics to kill the infection that had set in on the wounded leg. He had been gone more than twelve hours. Divers was getting worse. He couldn't last much longer. The last lap, MacDonald had said. The hindmost. Not much longer now.

The fire was hot against the side of Peaches' face but she could not move any further away without being unable to see what she was writing. She could have turned on the spotlight but she preferred the firelight. It was warmer and more intimate and gave her a sense of well-being and safety. The luminous Minotaur symbol glowed dimly in the moving shadows at the other end of the bunker. With the edge of her hand, she smoothed the sheets of paper resting on the board balanced against her leg. She chewed the top of the pencil and wished MacDonald would come back so that they could make love again. She wanted him badly. The prospect had her pulse racing. She bit hard on the pencil and it splintered. She took a tiny sliver of wood from her tongue and flicked it into the flames.

I guess this place is maybe a lot like your old bunker on Hill 881 in Vietnam, Pop. No rats here though and it is pretty peaceful, just the forest and the animals. We've only got one bomb and it has been silent so far, but Joe says if it was to go off it would make Operation Niagra look like a spit in a bucket.

Peaches smiled as she put the full stop to the end of the sentence. This could be our big chance baby, MacDonald had told her. This could make us enough money to keep us in luxury for the rest of our lives. How do you fancy buying a yacht and sailing round the Mediterranean, maybe take a trip over to the Caribbean sometime? She fancied it a great deal, especially with him. She wanted to suggest that they should just let Divers die naturally so they could share the proceeds between the two of them. But MacDonald seemed fiercely loyal to his old friend. He had committed himself to saving him if he could. He would not just stand aside. She could appreciate that it was different for him. But in her view, there was no room in their lives for a threesome. She wanted all of MacDonald's affection and attention for herself. She wanted Divers dead.

This Minotaur bomb is going to make us rich, Pop. Joe's friend here had it all worked out before he got himself shot in the leg. He has already made the contacts and arranged the sale. One million pounds. That is what we are going to sell it for. Pounds, not dollars, Pop. We'll be rich and we'll be able to travel as far and for as long as we like. I will never have to go home again if I don't want to. We'll just keep running. We'll never have to stop. Never.

A shadow passed over the trap-door entrance. Peaches looked up, hoping it might be MacDonald returning. She quickly realized it was not, just the wind buffeting the trees, or a cloud passing in front of the moon. She sighed resignedly and turned to the fire where she could make out the head of a magnificent deer with tall, many-pointed antlers. She raked at the ashes to encourage the flames and the deer fled. The heat against the side of her face intensified for a few seconds as the embers became bright red and then slowly faded to a dull pink. She tossed some more thin sticks on the fire and they crackled and hissed softly. On the bunk Divers groaned and twisted under the blankets.

Joe's friend has told him all about it. Since we found him floundering in the river here in the forest and brought him back to the bunker he has been lapsing in and out of consciousness. He is delirious. Sometimes he wakes up, sitting bolt upright with his eyes staring wide, and starts to ramble on. At other times he just lies with his eyes tight shut and shouts out things. I can't make much sense of what he says, but Joe can. He takes notes of names and times and places and he tells me that everything is arranged, all we have to do is go and hand the Minotaur over. It will be no problem, Joe says. It has all been laid on a plate for us.

He is going to die, Joe's friend. The wound in his leg is really ugly now. The poison from it must be diluting his blood. It is a miracle he has lasted this long. He must be incredibly strong. Joe says he came all the way north from Munich on the day we found him. Munich is hundreds of miles away. Maybe it's not true. Maybe it is the fever talking when he claims that. But if he is strong enough to make a journey like that he might be strong enough to pull through despite everything.

There is not all that much we can do for him, except feed him the little he will take, keep him warm, and bathe the wound every so often. Basically we are just keeping him as comfortable as possible. He is going to die. Joe has gone off to try and steal some drugs that might help him. He has also been talking about us operating on the leg, cutting open the wound to try and remove the bullet that must be in there. If we try that the shock will probably be enough to kill his friend. He is going to die. It is inevitable. I think Joe knows it too.

It seems his bad luck is our good fortune, Pop. His name must have been on the bullet in his leg, the same way your name was on that shell that dropped on your bunker at Khe Sanh. You can't hide from it. You can't escape it. If your name is on it, it is going to find you wherever you are, whatever you do. Joe says we are all taking part in the one big race, the human race, and at the end of every lap some people have to be eliminated. The Devil takes the hindmost he says. All you can do is keep running till your turn comes. You have got to keep running with the pack, running as fast as you can until you can't go any further.

People die all the time, Pop. It's no big deal really, is it? Everything that is born is destined to die, so why do we have to make such a fuss about it? The race can't last for ever. I'm going to die too, Pop. Someday, I'm going to die. Someday. Somewhere. Maybe then I'll be able to join you and get to know you after all. Maye the Devil is reaching out with his claws to take me at this very moment. Maybe I'm one of the hindmost today. Maybe it will be my turn tomorrow, or the next day, or next week. I don't know how far I have left to run. But I'm running to you, Pop. I'm running to you.

Peaches realized that she was saying the words out loud as she wrote them. She could not keep up with the speed of her own thoughts so she stopped writing and laid her head back against the sacking on the wall. She felt exhausted, as if she had been physically running, and took long slow breaths to fill her lungs and calm herself down. She had been crying as well she was surprised to find. Her cheeks were wet with tears. She wiped them dry and rubbed her eyes.

Only gradually did she become aware that something had changed in the bunker. She could hear the fire crackling and she could feel its heat, but there was something different about the atmosphere around her. Listening carefully, she tried to discern what was wrong. Outside, she could just hear a faint rustling of wind and, even fainter, the night sounds of the birds and insects. Nothing unusual. Nothing out of place. Looking from side to side she saw nothing but the familiar darkness. She looked straight into the fire and it hurt her eyes, and across at the shadows thrown by the dancing flames writhing on the blankets covering Divers. He was lying completely still. That was what had changed, she realized. His breathing had stopped. The sound, like a voice whispering too close to a microphone, had stopped.

Peaches did not move for a few moments then rose slowly from her seated position, using only her legs to push herself up. Divers' body was tensed under the covers as if it was being stretched on a rack. She stepped forward and looked down on him, leaning close so that her own shadow fell over his face and she had to move back a little. His face was ghostly white, and his eyes were squeezed shut. His teeth were bared and clenched together. The adam's apple bulged in his throat, threatening to tear through the skin. The bandage on the wound was clean, not yet stained by blood. She frowned and took the cloth from the bowl of water beside his head and laid it gently over his forehead. The eyelids trembled. The lips closed over his teeth. She was certain he was not breathing. She leaned close again. His face disappeared under the dark swathe of her shadow. She could just hear something, a very small noise, a very distant noise. She tilted her head more to one side so that her ear was over his mouth. A sound emerged like a sharp blade slicing across glass. Gradually, although it happened in only a few seconds, the pitch fell and she could feel his breath on her skin. Suddenly, he coughed violently and his whole body jerked making him jack-knife up from the bunk. His dry lips hit her ear. She snatched her face away and staggered backwards until she hit the wall, clutching at the loose sacking to steady herself which tore and fell over her head. The whole bunker seemed to spin round her. Her heart pumped furiously. Divers coughed and jerked twice more and then settled with a long, drawn-out sigh. The sound of his breathing re-established its regular monotony.

Peaches remained where she was for several minutes, backed up against the wall with the torn, sour-smelling sacking hanging over her shoulder. When she was calm enough to laugh at her panic reaction she wiped the ear where his lips had touched her, rubbing hard to remove the sensation. A kiss before dying, she thought abstractedly, not sure if she was remembering the title of a book or a film. She allowed herself to slide down the wall until she was once more sitting cross-legged on the floor. She picked up the pencil and paper and began writing again.

It is strange, Pop. I sometimes like to think that Joe MacDonald is you and that I am Mom. I'm sure you know what I mean, not a reincarnation or anything like that, more a sort of reflection. It's not the sex either. That is incredible but it goes much deeper than that. I like to think that what Joe and I have found is what you and Mom had before I was born. It's something real special, Pop. I hope it is the same for Joe as it is for me. He doesn't say very much and sometimes he can be awful offhand with me but I guess that is the Calvinist in him, being raised in Scotland as he was. Grandaddy Macdonald told me all about that before he died, I remember. He said that Scotsmen might not say much but they were always thinking. And although they might often try to pretend one thing, it was often the exact opposite they were feeling. It's part of their upbringing. They can't get away from it. I guess that must mean that Joe is just longing to tell me how much he loves me. I reckon he will get round to it in his own good time. I can wait.

I bet you told Mom you loved her a few times. But then you're an American Scot, aint you Pop? I guess that makes a big difference. The passing generations must have smoothed your rough edges down a bit. Joe is an original model. It's up to me to smooth down his edges.

Peaches glanced up at Divers. He was lying still, breathing steadily. She stoked the fire with new fuel so that the flames were smothered. The darkness pressed in round her and then retreated as the flames regained their hold and began to leap up through the framework of sticks. She felt much better, much happier with herself. Letter writing always helped. She moved onto a new sheet of paper.

There is not much wrong with my Joe. His heart is in the right place. He is terribly concerned about his old friend and is taking all this trouble even though he must know it is hopeless. He doesn't show it, of course, the sadness he must be feeling. He keeps making bad jokes as if he is trying to keep my spirits up. I can see that it is affecting him a lot and the quicker it is all over, the better. Then Joe and I can get on with selling this Minotaur bomb and booking our cruise in the Med. That should keep us going for a few years and who knows what we will do after that. I have this wild idea that one day I might go back to the Isle of Skye. We could get married, settle down, raise kids. That would be a full turn of the circle, wouldn't it Pop? Everything would be beginning all over again.

I don't know what I would do if I lost Joe now. I've known him for such a short time and yet I can't imagine a future without him. I think I am just beginning to understand how Mom must have felt when she heard that you had died Pop. I don't think I would be able to carry on the way she did. I'm sure I couldn't live in this world without Joe. I don't think I would want to live without him. We're running together, me and him; running together hand in hand. If the Devil wants to take one of us, he has got to take both. Then maybe we can all meet up Pop. You will like Joe, and I just know he will like you.

The page was filled up with the closely-spaced lines of writing. Peaches signed her name at the bottom. Then she shuffled the pages into order and read through them, having to hold them at an angle to catch the light from the fire. When she had finished she rearranged the pages again and evened up the edges before tearing them in half, then in half again. And again. And again, until she did not have the strength to make the pieces any smaller. She cupped the heap of torn pieces in her hands and rose to her feet. Divers was sleeping peacefully. She went over to the steps, suddenly cold as she left the cosy circle of heat beside the fire.

The natural shape of the fat chestnut-tree branch fitted the slight curve of MacDonald's spine almost exactly. It was very comfortable and, propped upright at an angle of sixty degrees, he was able to doze in spite of the ever-present cloud of flies round his face. His feet rested on the fork of the main trunk and his head rested at a point where the branch split into smaller divisions above him. He was perched twenty feet above the forest floor, sheltering among the confusion of branches and hanging canopy of broad leaves. He had tied back the twigs and leaves directly in front of him, hooking them out of the way to create a window through which he could watch the old ruin on the other side of the stream. He could easily make out where the hatch to the bunker lay open. Flickering shadows, like smoke against a grey background, marked its position. He had warned Peaches to keep the hatch closed but it had been open for the six hours he had been hiding in the tree. The Bullpup rifle on the strap over his shoulder lay along his thigh with his hand resting lightly on top of it.

MacDonald had never had any intention of going to find drugs to help Divers. It had been a stupid idea to begin with, but he had gone through the motions because he thought Peaches might expect it of him. The kind of drugs Divers needed were not available over the counter and if he had managed to break into a German pharmacy or hospital he would not have known what to look for. Divers was a dead man, probably sooner rather than later. The Minotaur was ticking silently away, set to go off on the twenty-fourth if he read it correctly. If Divers had died and they hadn't come to

Nowhere it would have gone ahead and ripped a big hole in Germany. MacDonald could disarm it whenever he wanted to but there was plenty of time for that.

MacDonald had gone all the way to the old quarry to refamiliarize himself with the landmarks so that he would know the route out of Nowhere. He found Divers' car there as well before turning back. Divers, slipping in and out of delirium, had given him enough information for him to be able to take over the sale of the Minotaur. He was confident about that. At the Oktoberfest, under the statue of Bavaria on the twenty-second at nine in the evening. The arrangements seemed to be straightforward but with Divers rambling so much it was hard to be sure. It was more than the product of a fevered imagination though. The Minotaur was real enough. He had seen it and touched it. Presumably the buyer would hand over the million pounds in a direct exchange. He would just have to play that part by ear. MacDonald wondered how heavy one million pounds would be.

The deal was the opportunity of a lifetime. Everything was neatly wrapped up. The money was there for the taking. Enough money to propel him right to the front of the pack and, once there, not much effort was required to keep going. He would be able to look over his shoulder and laugh at the poor bastards trailing behind.

It was impossible for him to ignore it yet he was frightened of the opportunity even though Divers had done all the spade-work. It was too big, too easy. If he had been by himself he would probably have thought about leaving the Minotaur buried with Divers in the bunker and stuck to his wandering life. He wanted to remain in the small time because that was what he knew and he was happy there. He enjoyed floating around, taking each day as it came, and had no real ambition to be a millionaire. He had scoffed at his friend's wild dreams, and the chance to join in, because the scale of them terrified him. Yet, somehow, he had been sucked in and could not ignore it now. He would never forgive himself if he did, and would for ever be dwelling on what might have been. He just had to make sure that there were no mistakes, no loose ends. If he was going to do it, it had to be done properly.

Divers was not a problem. He had exhausted his entitlement

to miracles by dragging himself all the way back from Munich with that bullet festering in the wound in his leg. He would not last more than a few days. Hopefully, he was already dead. Peaches was the problem.

He had seriously thought of abandoning her as soon as he had heard the news about Divers and the Minotaur on the radio in the cab of the tanker bringing them into Germany. His first idea was to get to Nowhere and team up with Divers just like his letter had suggested. If she had stayed sleeping in the back he might have done it. The driver was the type who would have sided with him in a lovers' tiff. But she hadn't stayed in the back. She had slid back down beside him and hung onto his arm like a limpet. And he had got to thinking that she was young and pretty and good in bed and extremely eager to please and he hadn't known her long enough to tire of her. Besides Divers might not be at Nowhere. It might take him long enough to return there. MacDonald would need somebody to help him pass the time if that was the case. His mind was made up in a flash. He would take her with him.

Now Peaches knew all about the Minotaur. He had not told her about it to begin with but the temptation to impress her, to see her mouth fall open with disbelief, to see his own stature rise in her eyes, proved too much and he revealed the whole story. She would have heard about it anyway on the news bulletins punctuating the country and western music played by the American army channel received on the radio in the bunker. Now she expected to share everything with him. That didn't bother him too much. What worried him was that when he eventually dumped her she might take offence and talk out of turn. Women were funny like that. No amount of money made up for hurt feelings. He didn't plan on sharing the rest of his life with Peaches. Another month maybe. No woman lasted longer than that. The talk of yachts in the Mediterranean was just a good line in patter. He was a loner and he wanted to stay like that. He had never been to prison because he had never been caught. He was always supremely careful, taking no risks, absolutely none. Long-term involvement with other people was a preventable risk. Logic dictated what he had to do. So he had taken the rifle when she was not watching, trekked to the edge of the forest and worked it all out. He should never have brought her here in the first place. He should have known better.

A head and shoulders appeared above the ruined wall of the cottage. Moonlight was flooding into the small clearing but the criss-cross web of shadows wiped out most details. Everything was smudged and indistinct. MacDonald watched as the figure rose fully out of the ground, moving gracefully like a genie out of a bottle. It was the second time he had seen her emerge since taking up his position in the tree. The first time she had gone to squat in the bushes at the side. This time she came straight towards him, wading through the waist-high grass till she reached the gently sloping bank of the stream.

MacDonald braced himself firmly against the tree and lifted the rifle to his shoulder. The forest seemed to grow darker. Peaches was nothing more than a silhouette, black on grey, like a cloud of smoke drifting on the breeze.

She seemed to be looking straight up at him. He frowned when she raised both arms in the air as if in surrender. He screwed up his eyes to try and see more clearly and had a brief impression of small things fluttering like butterflies down to the water and then they were gone. She dropped her arms but stood for several moments staring at the tree. MacDonald sighted along the short barrel and aimed for her head. Such a pretty head, such soft hair. A single shot and his problem ceased to exist.

She turned and began to retrace her steps. He aimed between her shoulder blades. His finger tightened marginally round the trigger. A tree obscured her outline, then a bush, then another tree. His finger was hard up against the trigger. The muscles in it were stiffening as he prevented himself from applying the extra ounce of pressure that would fire the bullet that would kill Peaches. A single shot and his problem would cease to exist. He had a clear view as she reached the ruin and turned again to look back. Moving firelight from below shone on her face. A single shot was all it would take.

He slackened the muscles of his hand and lowered the rifle. He had changed his mind again. There was no need to dispense with Peaches just yet. She might still be useful to him in many ways. He could get rid of her at his leisure once she had helped him to sell the Minotaur. He would have to kill her eventually, of course, if he was to be totally safe in the future. She was a loose end. It was a pity but he could see no other way.

The leaves around MacDonald stirred. The clouds blotted out the moon. Darkness swept in with the wind. He could still just see Peaches, descending into the ground.

The trap-door closed with a heavy thump above her and some loose earth trickled down into her hair. Peaches brushed it away and went down the steps, using the Minotaur to lean on as she reached the floor. It was primed to blow, MacDonald had said. She still hadn't learned to tell when he was joking.

The fire crackled and glowed in the corner of the bunker. She went towards it, holding out her hands to heat them. The air outside had been very cold. Now the flames rapidly warmed her as she stepped into their circle. It was like a blanket being wrapped round her. She hugged herself with her arms and swayed from side to side.

The stag had been a good omen, she had decided. She had noticed it among the trees as she stood by the stream. It had raised its head, crowned with a massive set of antlers, and sniffed the air. It was the same as the stag's head she had seen in the embers not long ago. The dream become life. A good omen. She had stood motionless not wanting to frighten the animal away. But it seemed to sense danger and had faded into the forest, just as it had faded from the embers.

MacDonald would be back soon. She smiled. She was looking forward to his return. It was the longest time, in fact the only time, they had been apart since their first encounter in a Paris cafe. She wanted him badly. She was desperate to make love to him to demonstrate how much she cared. She would make his homecoming a memorable occasion. She closed her eyes and imagined what would happen. The heat of the flames was like his fingers stroking her all over. Her smile grew wider.

A sudden thought troubled her; supposing MacDonald came back with the drugs he was after. Supposing they stopped the infection spreading from the wound? Supposing Divers recovered? Supposing he and MacDonald decided to team up again? Supposing there was no place for her in their plans? Supposing they ditched her?

She looked down on Divers' face, almost hidden beneath her own shadow. His breathing was shallow and laboured. The sound of it seemed to swell around her as she stood there. MacDonald had said he would not be surprised if his friend was dead by the time he got back, but there he was, still stubbornly alive. If Divers did manage to survive everything would be changed. Nothing could be the same. His survival implied that she would lose MacDonald, that the order of things would be restored to a time before she and MacDonald were even aware of each other's existence. That frightened her. That was the very last thing she wanted to happen.

The solution was obvious to her but she did not know if she was capable of carrying it out. But then, until recently, she had not known she was capable of stealing cars, or of blowing all her money with no thought of the future, or of robbing people in the street. She was a different woman now thanks to Joe MacDonald. And it wouldn't really be murder anyway, she told herself, not with the way things were. Not with Divers in this condition.

She smiled again and the expression froze onto her face. Boiling sap in the sticks on the fire hissed like a snake behind her. It would be an act of mercy. It would be a relief for him to escape the constant pain. He was going to die anyway. Of course she was capable of doing it, and it had to be done quickly before she weakened and changed her mind. Before MacDonald returned.

A sense of urgency gripped her. She fumbled in the darkness to find the pile of thick blankets on the rack at the foot of the bunk. She counted three, each folded double, and pulled them out. Divers was sleeping peacefully. The fire flared briefly, throwing out an orange light that flooded over his pale face. His eyes seemed to open and close as the shadows moved and fell back in the same second. Peaches bent down and touched her lips against his forehead. A kiss before dying, she said softly and the muscles round her mouth ached with the effort of maintaining the smile.

She laid the blankets over his face, muffling the sound of his breathing, spreading her fingers wide and leaning on her hands. It made no difference. She leaned more heavily, the sound of breathing stuttered and then restarted. She leaned still more heavily. Divers did not struggle. She flopped down so that her chest was pressing hard against the surface of the blankets. The breathing stopped abruptly. She lay where she was, forcing her fingers between the edge of the bunk and the wall so that she could exert downward pressure by pulling with her arms. Beneath her breasts she felt faint stirrings, like weak punches into the underside of the blanket. It reminded her of the movements of kittens about to be drowned inside a sack. Her Uncle Teddy had made her hold the sack when she was nine years old, and then he had made her throw it into the water with the iron bar tied to it so the sack was dragged under. And the kittens had drowned.

Divers stopped moving. Peaches turned her head so that her left ear was up against the coarse wool of the blanket. There was nothing to hear but the noise of the fire behind her. All she could feel was the heat of the flames on the back of her legs. She was comfortable in the position she was in. Tired and sleepy, she could hardly keep her eyes open. In the distance, in the darkness, she could see the faint gleam of the Minotaur, like a single far-off star in an empty sky. She thought she could hear it ticking like a heart beat. An immense sense of space overwhelmed her, making her dizzy. She had to close her eyes.

A new sound disturbed her. The hatch was being opened. Light and fresh air were spilling in. She straightened up. Her legs were sore, and her back stiff. It took her a few seconds to realize where she was, to realize what she had done. She had no idea how long she had slept. The fire was out. The ashes were coldly grey. It must have been a long time.

MacDonald was coming down the steps. Peaches snatched the blankets away from Divers' face and threw them back onto the rack. His mouth was partly open, the tongue swollen and slightly protruding. A thin channel of dried blood ran from his nose, curling round the corner of his mouth. MacDonald was fixing the crocodile clips to the battery. The spotlight came on, dazzling her. She turned her head away, hiding her face in her hands.

'What's the matter?' MacDonald asked.

She felt him approach, reach out and touch her shoulder, and then move away. She narrowed her eyes and opened her hands so that she could see what he was doing. He was stooped over Divers, searching for a pulse. She hid her face again as he began to turn to her.

'He's dead,' MacDonald said, taking her in his arms. She put her arms round his neck and laid her head on his shoulder. 'It's just you and me from now on, Peaches baby.'

She could see Divers lying dead on the bunk, blank eyes staring up at her. She squeezed herself as tightly against MacDonald as she could. Just you and me, she thought.

Hugo Betzing slowly disentangled himself from Anna's naked body without waking her. She sighed and turned away from him, dragging the cream-coloured covers with her. He stood up at the side of the bed, placed his hands in the small of his back and stretched to ease the stiffness. He yawned and rolled his neck, smiling wryly down on the sleeping figure and the splash of auburn hair on the pillow. Too much bed and not enough sleep, he thought. I really am getting old.

He pulled on the pyjama trousers he found lying at his feet and slipped into a red towelling dressing gown that had his monogram woven on the breast pocket. Taking his wrist-watch, lighter and packet of Gitânes from the bedside table he padded across the warm pile of the carpet to the adjoining bathroom. He filled the sink and dabbed cold water round his swollen eyes, then stuck out his tongue and examined it in the mirror. With two fingertips he pulled down the flaps of skin under his eyes and saw the dull orange of the veins there. Reaching into the wall cupboard he took out a brown plastic bottle of iron tablets, pouring out two and swallowing them with a mouthful of water sucked from the palm of his hand. Then he lit a cigarette and coughed as the smoke flowed down his throat and into his lungs.

It was his first night back at the villa since his meeting with Divers in Munich. He had hardly paused for breath in between, having been to Zurich to enlist Sabaroff and then on a whirl-wind tour of potential Minotaur buyers. It was not his usual style to handle things in such a personal way but the special circumstances warranted it this time. There could be no gain without risk. The time-scale was limited and he had to take the risk of putting the word out and he had to go himself so that he could explain that there was a detonating device for the Minotaur available despite the claims of the British Government. MacDonald or Divers, or whatever his real name was, had convinced him and he was sure he could convince the buyers, using his reputation as a guarantee; money refunded if not absolutely delighted.

He had been very selective in the people he had approached and was pleased that all three had shown interest. Three bids would be coming in, a one-hundred-per-cent return on his time. He already had a good idea of which would be the highest, but he was ready to be proved wrong.

It had been non-stop travelling over six days, shuttling back and forth between the different countries, snatching sleep when he could in the hastily chartered Jetstream, being passed from official to official, biting his lip when frustration and impatience almost became too much for him. On the last day there were stories in the papers about a long-lost Dipstick, confirming his sales pitch and probably pushing up the value. After that he knew he would not have to argue about the veracity of his case any longer.

Betzing rubbed the stubble on his chin but did not have the energy to begin shaving. He drew the strong tobacco smoke deep inside him and his head spun. He had known Anna would be a very demanding bed partner last night when what he really needed was total rest, but that had not stopped him. He had briefly considerd taking a room at a hotel beside the airport and leaving his return until this morning, but only briefly. He had only himself to blame for the condition he was in.

He stubbed out the cigarette in the sink and went back into the bedroom. Anna had moved into the centre of the bed and was lying face down with her arms above her head and the sheets wrapped round her middle so that her ankles were exposed at the bottom. Betzing felt a little tug of emotion as he pulled the sheets down over them and went to the door. He walked along the corridor to his office. It was a relatively small room, furnished with tubular-steel chairs, two large desks topped with green leather and scattered with phones, two computer terminals and display screens. A free-standing teleprinter sent a long tongue of paper curling do',n to the floor, and a row of filing cabinets were built into one wall, opposite the tall windows that overlooked the swimming pool. Landscape paintings in brass frames hung on the walls. He had given his personal secretary two weeks' holiday so that he could handle the Minotaur business himself.

It was still very early in the morning. The sky was eggshell white. The lake below was a cold slate grey. Betzing went over to his desk, lifted one of the phones and ordered coffee when the housekeeper answered in the basement kitchen. He lit another cigarette and went over to the teleprinter. He tore off the tongue of paper and began to scroll through it until he reached the first item he was looking for. The numerical code at the top told him the bid had come from Damascus. The message below was printed in English. It read: Bull sale — bid for prize exhibit 2.3 units. Terms as discussed.

Betzing smiled. He put down the cigarette and folded the paper above and below the message and carefully tore along the creases, discarding the remainder into a basket beside the desk after checking everything else that was on it. As he was doing so another telex message emerged from the almost silent printer. He read it before it had finished running. Bull sale — estimated price for prize exhibit 1.9 units. Terms cash as agreed. The bid was from Tripoli. He pursed his lips and nodded wisely to himself. It was as he had expected. He doubted if the bid from Barcelona would be close when it arrived. Still, he had to give them their chance. They had been good customers in the past.

A bell rang and a small hatch slid open on the wall behind the desk to reveal a tray with a coffee set and some hot croissants on it. Betzing went over and moved it down onto the desk. He filled a cup, leaving it black, and buttered one of the croissants. He heard a movement outside and looked out the window. Anna was standing at the side of the pool, shivering in the cold wind that was shaking the trees on the mountainside. She had put on a bikini and tied her hair back. Seeing Betzing she waved to him and dived into the water in the same movement. He wached her body arch through the air and disappear under the surface. This was definitely to be his last big deal. It was all getting too dangerous now. It was a young man's game.

He would take his profit from the Minotaur and retire. He would marry Anna and live happily ever after.

Her head came up and she rolled onto her back, swimming lazily. Yes, he had made his decision. It was time to retire. He had had a long run of good luck. The odds were beginning to stack up against him. The Minotaur would make a pretty spectacular end to a career.

Every morning when he was in Bonn and working at the embassy, Buster Grant liked to put on his blue and white track suit and jog the half mile down to the Rheinaue Park. He always followed the same route, although the security consultants to the embassy had twice warned him that he should vary it as much as possible. He always ran along Friedrich Ebert Allee and then down through the houses to the pedestrian bridge that took him over the traffic and into the park to the north of the Adenauer Bridge. Then he would go straight down to the edge of the Rhine itself and follow it up towards where the pleasure boats moored close beside the Bundestag and the other Government buildings. There he would circle round the other side of the park and follow the paths back to the pedestrian bridge. Then up through the quiet streets and along to the embassy.

He did not always run the full distance. More often than not he would slow to a walk or, depending on the weather, stop altogether on the river bank for long periods. It helped him think, and it helped him face the day. It had become a necessary ritual for him. If he did not manage to find the time for his morning run before settling down to his office work he believed he was always irritable and short tempered.

Grant stopped by the riverside and stood watching a huge, slow-moving barge as it fought the Rhine current on its way south. It was very low in the water. The gunwales were almost submerged. A pale green car was parked on its stern. He breathed deeply in and out through his nose to refill his lungs. The wash from the barge lapped over the stony shore. Some leaves drifted down to the ground to join the growing piles. It was the first time he had managed to get out for a run since being recalled from his climbing holiday. He had gone much too fast too soon and was feeling the lack of exercise. He was frustrated by his lack of progress in the Minotaur case. The political turmoil it was causing was creating shock waves all the way down the line. The German police were reluctant to share what information they had, which seemed to be precious little, if any. Even his usual contacts on the diplomatic circuit were being cool towards him. Britain was not the world's favourite nation at the moment. The switch of photographs in the media had produced mixed results, a host of sightings throughout Europe which all had to be checked, taking up valuable time. None of the alleged sightings had so far proved authentic.

Grant turned away from the river and began to walk across the grass with his hands on his hips, still breathing heavily. It was a relatively cold morning and dirty-grey clouds lined the sky. The grass was wet with dew. Gradually, he broke into a shambling trot. A wooden bridge shook below him as he crossed one of the small lakes. Where are you, Hugh Divers? he thought. What are you doing? What are you thinking?

He again slowed to a walk as he reached the footbridge over the speeding cars on Ludwig Erhard Strasse and strolled all the way back to the embassy grounds. On the main road just before he got to the corner of the security fence he started jogging again. The sun was already bright on the white-painted walls and the cars in the car park. The security guard in his little booth grinned at him through the glass as he ran round the vehicle barrier and the retractable bollards. He went round the rear of the low, flat-roofed building and in through the back door which led to the small gymnasium. In the changing room he took off his track suit and running gear. He turned on a cold shower at full blast and stepped under the powerful jet. He had to gasp for breath with the shock of it hitting him. After a few seconds he turned the heat up and washed himself thoroughly. After that he got dried, took a hair dryer from his locker and spent five minutes in front of the mirror arranging his hair. He put on a clean white shirt, a plain blue tie and his normal dark suit, and polished his shoes with the track-suit top before bundling it and the rest of the gear into a holdall. It was exactly eight-thirty.

Dirk Kaspar was waiting for him in the main entrance hall behind the glass screen beside the reception desk. As Grant came out of a side door into the main hall Kaspar rose to his feet and waved him over. Kaspar's silver hair was at a jaunty angle across his eyes and he seemed nervous and agitated. Grant signed an entry authorization chit and the guard opened the electronic lock. Kaspar pushed open the door at the side of the screen and the two men shook hands.

'You're an early bird, Dirk,' Grant said. 'I'm only just getting my breath back after my morning constitutional.'

'Good news, Buster. The breakthrough we have been waiting for perhaps.'

'Aha. Things are beginning to happen at last.'

Grant put his arm round Kaspar's shoulder and steered him up the stairs and along the corridor to his office. It was a large, square room. There was a Victorian-style oak desk in one corner and one wall was lined with books. The window looked out over the main gate to the embassy. Two underground trains passed each other on the surface line running in the middle of the road outside.

'Have you had breakfast?' Grant asked as they sat down opposite each other.

'Yes. I have no time, Buster. I can only spare five minutes to put you in the picture.' He fidgeted impatiently, sitting right on the edge of his chair.

'Fire away then,' Grant said.

'We have a report from Israeli intelligence that the Syrians may have been approached as possible buyers of the Minotaur nuclear land-mine.'

'We're getting hot,' Grant said. 'When did this happen? How reliable is the report?'

'A few days ago. Four days it may have been. The offer was being seriously considered according to the Israelis who say the information comes from a well-established source. The Syrians are annoyed that the Soviets won't give them any nuclear hardware and this Minotaur could be just the thing they need to solve the Middle East problem once and for all. In other words, nuke Israel. Take that last bit with a pinch of salt, if you like. It could be inspired by Israeli paranoia, but the main thing is that someone is trying to sell the Minotaur.'

'Do we know who made the approach?'

'Yes.' Kaspar brushed his hair out of his eyes. 'It was an arms dealer known to them as Manfred Steinmetz. Our security services know the same man as Hugo Betzing, a Swiss citizen. He is a legitimate dealer but also likes to operate outside the law every now and then. He has one conviction some years ago for his part in the supply of arms to South Africa.'

'Do we know where he is now?'

Kaspar sat back 'We do. He lives at a villa overlooking Lake Neuchâtel. The moment we heard about him we put men onto him. We are trying to get a tap on his phone but you know what the Swiss are like when it comes to breaching a person's civil liberties. It might take a while. He was there last night though. He can't move now without us knowing about it.'

'Do we know where he has been? Who else he has approached?'

'We are trying to find out right now. It appears he chartered a jet to travel around in the last week. We will check its flight details today.' Kaspar clenched both fists and shook them in front of his face. 'It is a big breakthrough, Buster. It looks like Lady Luck may have changed sides.'

'It is good news. But what was it that he offered for sale?'

'A fully operational Minotaur nuclear land-mine with DIP unit attached. Asking price is two million pounds.'

Grant whistled through his teeth. 'So now we know that Divers did have the missing Dipstick all along.'

'Yes. Now we know for certain.'

'Are the Syrians in the market?'

'They are thinking about it.'

'Anybody else?'

'It may be that Steinmetz is running an auction.'

'Presumably Divers must have met this man Steinmetz or Betzing at some stage to sell him the Minotaur.'

'Steinmetz was in Munich last week. We know that much.'

'Munich eh. Divers must have sold him the Minotaur outright or he may be using him as a selling agent to get the best price.'

'Yes. That is the assumption. We cannot be sure if Steinmetz actually has possession of the Minotaur yet. It could be that Divers still has it, wherever he is.'

'But at least we are off the mark. Thanks for coming to tell me, Dirk.'

Kaspar stood up abruptly. 'I must go Buster,' he said. 'I have a lot to do this morning. My official reason for coming this morning is to pass on my government's approval for the disinformation package on the missing DIP unit being faulty. We want it out as soon as possible.'

'Everything is prepared. We can make tomorrow's papers. And it's not strictly disinformation. The thing is faulty. Remember it is a fifty-fifty chance that it will only go off like a damp squib. Then all our problems would be solved.'

'I will keep you up to date as soon as we know of any new developments,' Kaspar said. 'You have nothing to add from the British end?'

'There is some stuff through in last night's bag from London but I haven't had a chance to look at it yet. I doubt if it will take us much further anyway. You seem to have all the good news.'

Grant escorted Kaspar as far as the main door and then returned to his office alone. He sat behind his desk and pushed the pile of morning newspapers to one side. The in-tray contained a sheaf of papers and a single envelope. He took the envelope and slit it open, turning it upside down to shake out two thin sheets of MI5 report paper and a small black and white photograph. He read the information and studied the picture.

Joseph MacDonald, aged thirty-two. Formerly of same Royal Engineers company as Hugh Divers. Formed specialist Minotaur team with Divers for nine-month period. No known contact since dishonourable discharge from service. Both men admitted joint charges of insubordination and indiscipline. MacDonald returned to his native Scotland soon afterwards. Worked as a labourer in oil-rig repair yard in Inverness-shire until early part of this year when he was made redundant. Unmarried. No children. Present whereabouts unknown. Only known relative, an elderly aunt, says he has gone to London to find work.

Grant distilled the essence of the sketchy information that was spread thinly over the paper and tried to assess its significance. MacDonald, nicknamed Crazy Joe, was the only old army mate of Divers they had so far been unable to trace. So what? He had got fed up working on oil rigs and gone AWOL. There was nothing sinister in that. It didn't mean he had rushed over to Germany to help Divers pinch the Minotaur. He may not have even seen Divers since being thrown out of the army. There was the fact that MacDonald and Divers had made up a Minotaur team at one stage and now he could not be traced. Neither could Divers. It was an uncomfortable fact that made Grant uneasy. But it was not as if MacDonald had left his job voluntarily, he reasoned. He had been paid off and then travelled down to London where he had probably got a new job on some building site. It was easily done. Men working like that were virtually impossible to find if they didn't want to be. Maybe he had got a big redundancy payment and was hiding from the taxman. Grant made a note at the bottom of the report to get MI5 to ask the Inland Revenue if they had any interest in Joe MacDonald.

No. Grant had decided. Events were gaining momentum by themselves. He did not want to obscure the issue at the moment by running too many hares. It would serve no good purpose to have MacDonald's name and picture circulated to the Press. At least, not at the moment when there were other leads to be followed. Maybe next week if he still hadn't been traced. Any additional revelation might detract from the impact of the story about the stolen Dipstick being faulty. It wouldn't be too clever to let that happen.

Grant unclipped the photograph and balanced it against the front of his telephone. He interlocked his fingers and placed both hands at the back of his head. 'Way to go Joe,' he said. 'We're onto your friend.'

It was Peaches who came up with the idea of using the dead body as a diversion. It would confuse the authorities, she said. It would have them running round in circles scratching their heads and imagining all kinds of new plots and conspiracies. It would also serve the purpose of demonstrating to the buyers that the new Mr MacDonald was a man to be taken seriously. The diversion would not be employed until satisfactory contact was established with the man Rocher, a name Divers had mentioned several times and one which had a phone number next to it in the small notebook he carried. Peaches had it all worked out and MacDonald could not damp down her enthusiasm. He was reluctant at first, though he could see the sense in the plan. It would, perhaps, not be too smart just to turn up in Munich and say he was taking over and demand payment. It had to be established in advance that he was now in possession of the Minotaur so that they could get used to the idea. After that, there was no reason why they could not do business with him rather than with Divers. The price was the same. The outcome would be the same. Peaches' advice was sound. It was a good idea. Perhaps it was just as well he hadn't got rid of her too soon. She was proving useful.

Divers' body was wrapped in a groundsheet and hidden six feet off the ground in the branches of a nearby tree to keep it out of the way of inquisitive animals. Down in the bunker Peaches and MacDonald lay in the separate bunks making their plans and waiting for nightfall. The radio station was playing country and western music. They built the fire up to huge proportions so that the flames were licking round the edge of the smoke-hood. The dry heat filled the bunker and they were able to lie without clothes or blankets, sweating freely.

'Why do you think Big Shuggie used your name when he was setting up this deal?' Peaches asked.

'We always used to swop names when we were out on the town trying to pick up women,' MacDonald explained. 'It was a game we used to play, a kind of security system to keep us out of trouble. I've been him and he's been me a hundred times.'

'That's not a very nice way to treat the ladies. How do I know you really are who you say?'

'You'll just have to take my word for it.'

Peaches rolled onto her front and changed the subject. 'I think we should dump him at this Zeppelinwiese arena place he was mumbling about. That's where he said he killed that Nazi guy.'

'I'm not too sure about that. According to all the reports I've heard it was on the other side of the city that Luneburg was bumped off. Hughie always was a bit of a romantic though. I'm sure he would have liked it to be the scene of the Nuremberg rallies. An element of poetic justice in that, there would have been. He must have planned it that way and maybe changed his mind at the last minute.'

'It would make sense for the Nazis to leave his body there if they had killed him in revenge for their leader's death, don't you think Joe?'

'It might do, I suppose.'

'Well, we'll dump the body there then. What do you think?'

'It's as good a place as any.'

During the long, lazy afternoon they adjusted Peaches' rucksack to take the Minotaur casing. They had to remove the internal aluminium frame and split a seam to insert it but it was a relatively simple job, and from the outside the rucksack looked no different from what it had been before.

Then Peaches watched in fascination as MacDonald turned the raised disc anti-clockwise on the top of the Minotaur. It clicked once and he rotated it the other way. It clicked again and sprang up six inches. She saw the red glow of the panel of numbers. The final digit in the row was moving quite quickly upwards as the figure seven replaced the eight.

'I told you she was ticking away,' MacDonald said. 'It is set to blow not long after Shuggie was due to collect his money. I don't know if he intended telling them or not.'

'Are you going to switch it off?'

'Can do.' He pressed the concealed switch above the panel and the rectangular flap below it came open. Immediately the red glow vanished and the seven digits all rolled round to record zero. 'But I think we should leave her running.' He pressed all the buttons at once and the numbers and the red glow re-appeared.

'Why did you do that?'

'A live Minotaur is more intimidating than a dead one. It should prevent any funny business at the handover. I think we should keep it armed.'

'All right. You're the expert. How does it work?'

'It is a pretty simple system,' MacDonald explained. 'It has to be so that the army thickheads can work it. You just feed in the number of seconds to the time you want it to go off and retire to a safe distance. I can still remember the numbers from my training; three thousand six hundred for one hour, eighty-six thousand four hundred for a whole day, six hundred and five thousand or thereabouts for a week and so on.'

'It's amazing to think that this thing would have exploded if we hadn't come here and switched it off?' Peaches said. 'If you hadn't been listening to the radio in that lorry. If your friend had not managed to get back here by himself. If we had never met in Paris. If we had stolen French francs instead of Deutschmarks.'

'That's about the size of it.' He pushed the Dipstick into the casing and screwed the disc into place.

'Gee, wouldn't that have been something.'

'It would indeed. It might have attracted a lot of attention to this neck of the woods.'

They were standing round the makeshift table with the beam of the spotlight passing between their shoulders onto the canvas material of the rucksack. He put his hand round the back of her neck and pulled her in against him and kissed her on the top of the head. The fire had died back a bit. The sweat had dried on her skin and she felt cold.

'There are built-in booby-traps of course,' MacDonald explained. 'It all has to do with the way the ring at the top is turned to release the Dipstick. You have to lift and turn in the proper sequence but don't you bother your pretty head about that, Peaches baby. I'll do the disarming if we get to the stage of having to stop the thing.'

'And how do you stop this?' Her hand slipped down over his stomach and grabbed his genitals. He turned to face her.

'I'm afraid there is no way of stopping it,' he said, moving her backwards towards the bunk and the warmth of the fire. 'There is going to be an explosion in the next few minutes. There is no escape. There will be no survivors.'

It was midnight when they left Nowhere, carefully lowering the trap-door and removing all signs of human presence from the area. Peaches carried the Minotaur on her back as well as MacDonald's bag now stuffed with both sets of their clothes and all their money. MacDonald lowered Divers' body out of the tree onto his shoulder. It was very stiff and he had to bounce it up and down vigorously before it sagged and bent in the middle. Each of them carried one of the Bullpup rifles. They walked in silence, MacDonald leading, Peaches keeping close to him in the pitch darkness of the forest, unable to see him even a few yards in front. She kept reaching out to touch him just to check that he was there. They did not hurry, stopping for frequent rests. Four hours later they reached the old quarry and MacDonald uncovered the rusty white Audi. The keys were in the off-side rear hub cap.

'The car is registered in a false name,' MacDonald said. 'Hugh wouldn't have chanced driving it all the way back from Munich if it hadn't been. It's clean. That's handy for us.'

The dead body fitted snugly into the boot. The rifles went beside it. The Minotaur in its new rucksack went on the back seat. The car started first time. With dawn breaking they drove slowly towards Nuremberg.

The traffic was beginning to build up when they reached the outskirts of the city. They stopped for breakfast and let the worst of the morning rush hour pass before continuing. MacDonald bought a map and worked out a route to Zeppelinwiese. They got onto the ring road and followed it round the north side. American army jeeps and lorries seemed to be everywhere, the shirt-sleeved soldiers staring at Peaches. Little pizza huts seemed to be set up every few hundred yards along the rows of barracks. When they were stopped at one set of traffic lights a black soldier leaned out of the passenger seat of his open jeep to tap on the window and flutter his fingers at Peaches. She replied by kissing MacDonald on the cheek and hugging his arm. The soldier conceded defeat by shoving his cap to the back of his head and shaking his head. The jeep driver roared with laughter as he accelerated sharply on the green light, screeching the tyres. MacDonald moved off more sedately.

They found Zeppelinwiese with no difficulty, not far from the main ring road, opposite a railway station. A tractor-drawn mower was cutting the grass in the centre of the arena. The sun was bright on the white stone. The Stars and Stripes flag drifted limply in the soft breeze.

'Up there,' Peaches said, pointing to the platform which jutted out from the weed-cluttered terracing. 'That's where we'll leave him.'

'If you say so, Peaches baby,' MacDonald murmured.

They drove towards the city centre and found a small, reasonably-priced hotel with parking spaces in the Galgenhof area. MacDonald paid for one night and went straight to bed. Peaches took some money and said she was going shopping for new clothes. She came back a few hours later and woke him up. He supported himself on his elbows as he watched while she changed into a knee-length blue dress with a low neckline and pinched waist.

'What do you think?' she asked, pirouetting in front of him.

'Very nice,' he answered. 'Why don't you take it off?'

They had agreed that they would not phone Rocher until after six o'clock.

Helmut Rocher was wearing only a pair of tight yellow boxer shorts. The elastic of the waist cut deep into his fleshy belly. The room was in darkness. All the shutters were down. He sat on the red satin sheets, propped up by half a dozen pillows at the top of the bed, drinking beer from his personal pewter tankard. Eva, in a short see-through night-dress of frothy lace, was curled round in a loose circle at his feet, one arm thrown over his ankles. The changing light from the wide, flat video screen at the bottom of the bed made patterns of shadows ebb and flow over her pale skin. It was a close-up of Rocher's face on the screen, his eyes closed, his lips pouting. In the foreground the blurred outline of Eva's naked back gradually came into focus as the camera moved back to take a wider angle. She was crouched over him, her head shaking like a dog worrying a bone. The film was silent. There was only the gentle hiss of the tape in the machine.

It was a weakness of his to star in his own films now and then, especially when he had a special relationship going with an actress. This one was called Working for the Boss. He only watched the final product once, maybe twice, and then he made certain that the tape was destroyed. On the bed, Rocher stroked Eva's hair with his pudgy toes and drank the sweet-tasting beer. Sex always made him thirsty.

When the phone rang with a soft burring sound he knew by the tone that it was a call to his office patched through to the flat. He did not answer it straight away, but finished his beer before reaching over to place the tankard on the table and move the receiver aside, activating the loudspeaker control. Eva did not stir. She was sound asleep.

'Rocher?' said a voice in a familiar accent.

'Ah, Herr MacDonald. You are one day late in phoning. It is most unlike you. I hope there are no problems.'

'Nothing that cannot be overcome. To begin with I am not the MacDonald you met in Munich. I am a different MacDonald and I am taking over the Minotaur sale.'

Rocher frowned. His eyes never left the video screen. 'And what has happened to the first Herr MacDonald?' he asked.

'You know his real name. You must have read it in the papers. It was Hugh Divers. He was an old friend of mine. We were in this together. We were partners.'

'Were?'

'I'm afraid so. He is dead. I am now in sole possession of the Minotaur and you must deal with me.'

'I see,' Rocher said slowly, drawing out the words to give himself time to think. 'How do I know that you are telling me the truth?'

'Does it matter? I have the Minotaur. If you want it you have to pay me. The price is the same. One million pounds sterling.'

'The agreed price was seven hundred thousand pounds. How can I be sure you have the Minotaur?'

'We were in it together. I was his partner behind the scenes. You didn't think he did all that by himself, did you? He was the front man who was to do all the negotiating. We didn't allow for him getting killed so now I'm having to come out of the back room and take over. So now you're going to have to deal with me.'

'I see. How did he die? Can you tell me that?'

'The Nazis got him. They were after him ever since he took out Luneburg. He didn't look over his shoulder often enough.'

'It wasn't the leg wound then?'

'No. That slowed him down but that wasn't what killed him.'

It seemed plausible. The assassination of Luneburg might well have provoked a reaction in kind. Divers must have had some back-up to kill Luneburg in the first place. The Nazi had been shot while someone was strangling him from behind, the newspaper reports had said. There had to be at least two people involved. If Divers had been the one in the back of the car, the one who had been shot, then this new MacDonald had to be the number two. On the screen another female appeared and knelt down beside Eva. She was young and thin and her blonde hair had dark roots.

'My condolences on the death of your friend. I hope you are not next on their list.' Rocher said.

'That particular argument is over. I can concentrate on the business in hand.'

'Are there any more partners?'

There was a slight hesitation. 'Just one who prefers to remain behind the scenes.'

'And how much did your late partner tell you?'

'Just about everything.'

'Excuse my suspicious nature, Herr MacDonald but could you expand on that a little?'

'He told me about the handover at the Oktoberfest on the twenty-second, at nine, on the steps under the statue of Bavaria, and the fact that he had programmed the Minotaur for detonation so that you could not double-cross him. He told me you were going to pay him one million pounds. By the way, the programme is still running.'

'I see,' Rocher said. He pressed a switch and the video screen suddenly went blank. He looked down on Eva, still sleeping soundly. 'The agreed price was only seven hundred thousand pounds.'

'The price has gone up then. The loss of my partner has meant I have incurred certain expenses, funeral expenses. I want the million pounds in used Bank of England notes, in a suitcase ready to be handed over to me at the Oktoberfest.'

'You are going too fast for me, I'm afraid,' Rocher interrupted. 'That was not the agreement. The price was seven hundred thousand and it was to be paid into Herr MacDonald's Swiss bank.'

'It's a new set up now.'

'I do not know if that is a valid proposition, Herr MacDonald. It is most regrettable that you choose to alter the terms of our gentlemen's agreement. I am not empowered to make a decision. I myself am not the buyer. I will have to speak to my client.'

'You talk to him, Rocher. You tell him that there is nothing to worry about. We can do business together, I am sure of that.'

'Perhaps.'

'No perhaps about it. You be there on the twenty-second with the money and I will be there with the Minotaur. What could be simpler?'

'It may prove impossible to find the extra cash in the time remaining, Herr MacDonald.'

'Nothing is impossible, and to make it easier for you, I tell you what I'll do. I'll accept the seven-hundred-thousand-pound figure that my partner negotiated and forget about my expenses. How about that?'

'It may make a difference,' Rocher said soothingly. 'May I repeat that I am sad to hear of the death of your friend.'

'It comes to us all sooner or later.'

'You sound remarkably like him. If you had not told me I doubt if I would have been able to tell the difference. You are not brothers by any chance?'

'Blood brothers maybe. Do we have a deal?'

'I must consult my client. He will not be pleased with the changed situation. He may wish to renegotiate.'

'The negotiations are over. I have made one big concession. I will be at the Oktoberfest at the appointed time, at the appointed place. Tell your client to be there and to have the money if he wants the Minotaur. Otherwise I will find another buyer.'

'All I can do is pass on the message. If he should prove agreeable how are we to recognize you?'

'You sit on the steps under the statue at nine. Sit on one copy of Die Welt and be reading another. I'll find you.'

'Okay,' Rocher said. 'If my client is agreeable.'

'Very well then. By the way if you don't believe that Hugh Divers is dead those Nazis will provide some proof for you soon.'

'I do not understand. What do you mean?'

'You'll see.'

Rocher was sitting bolt upright in the bed by the time the connection was broken. He switched on the room lights and rubbed his chin. If Divers was dead then it was conceivable that the new MacDonald should emerge from the background to take over. Betzing would not like the change in arrangements and might conceivably decide to withdraw on principle. He was extremely wary of interruptions to the smooth running of an operation. But then again it would be foolish to throw away the opportunity to buy such a piece of merchandise. If the suppliers were fighting amongst themselves or with rival groups it made no real difference. That was their problem. If the new MacDonald had got rid of Divers then that was his business. Divers had tried to give the impression that he was in it alone but that obviously had not been the case. The new MacDonald was aware of too many facts to be an imposter. Perhaps Divers had boasted to him that he was to get the full million. That was why he had got that bit wrong. It was a strange mistake to make, but an understandable one, and that suggested to Rocher that the new MacDonald was genuine. Anyway, the Minotaur was the important thing. It was still for sale, at the same price, to be had at the same place. His advice to Betzing would be to go ahead with the deal.

Rocher carefully extracted his feet from under Eva's arm and rolled off the big bed. Eva stirred a little but did not wake up. She seemed to curl into a tighter ball. The video recorder had rewound the tape. He switched the machine off and lifted the yellow dressing gown from the floor where it had been thrown. The bedroom walls were decorated with an erotic mural of larger-than-life naked girls supposedly dancing and frolicking around maypoles. The door was almost invisible until he turned the concealed handle and walked out between a pair of widely spread legs.

Eva did not open her eyes until she heard the door close behind him. She remained where she was on the bed, going over all that she had heard said on the phone. Her English was not that good but it was sufficient to make sense of the conversation. She would relay the information to her control at the next opportunity and the date of her final return home to Dresden would come even closer.

Peaches was lying along MacDonald's side in the hotel bed, listening to his phone conversation with Rocher. She held her hand over her mouth to stifle the sound of her breathing. When he hung up he stretched out from the bed and slammed the receiver into the cradle, letting his face fall into the pillow at the same time. Peaches lay on his back with her head resting between his shoulder blades. She had liked it when he had turned to look at her when Rocher had asked if there was another partner, and then answered that there was. Partners. She liked that.

MacDonald raised his head. 'Well partner,' he said. 'How did you think I handled that?'

'You should have held out for the million,' she replied.

'Let's not be too greedy. Let's just take what the Good Lord has seen fit to drop in our laps.'

'You should have asked for dollars as well.'

'The dollar is pretty weak these days. Sterling is good value.'

'Why do you think Shuggie said it was a million pounds when it was only seven hundred thousand?' Peaches said, smoothing out the hair on his shoulders with the palm of her hand.

'Maybe he was raving.' MacDonald turned over so that Peaches was lying on his chest and they were face to face. 'Maybe this bloke Rocher thinks fast on his feet and just cut the price he is willing to pay by a quarter. Who knows?'

'Do you think he'll be there in Munich?' Peaches asked seriously.

'If he wants the Minotaur, he'll be there.'

'What about this client he was talking about? Do you think

he is just the middle-man for a bigger fish?'

'I wouldn't be surprised. It doesn't matter to me where the money comes from, as long as it comes.'

'What are we going to do with all this money? How are we going to get it out of Germany?'

'One thing at a time,' MacDonald said. 'Let's get it first.'

Peaches dropped her head and kissed him in the hollow where the neck joins the chest. She looked up again. 'We're going to bring this off, ain't we partner?'

'Keep saying so Peaches baby. Keep saying so.'

They fell silent. Peaches rolled onto her back with MacDonald's arm under her neck curled round so that his fingers played with some strands of her hair. They both stared at the ceiling and listened to the sound of the city outside the shuttered window.

'What are you thinking partner?' she said eventually.

'I was thinking that poor Shuggie will be cold out there in the boot of his car.'

'Don't be so morbid. What else are you thinking?'

'Me? I'm thinking where I might go when we get the Minotaur off our hands once and for all.'

'Where we might go Joe. Remember, we're partners.'

'That's right. We're a team, you and me.'

'Any ideas where we might go?'

'It depends which way the wind is blowing.'

The house was quite near the centre of Augsburg not far from the Thommstrasse in a narrow, winding, cobbled lane. Gudrun Richter took a long time to find it when she arrived by train at the station. She would not ask anyone and she only had a vague memory of the layout of the streets. But she persisted and in the end she recognized a butcher's shop window with a large red plastic model of a cow's carcase labelled with all the different cuts of meat. That told her she was close and pointed her in the right direction. Then she saw the tiny run-down cafe on the corner and she had found what she was looking for.

It was an old house, set well back from the pavement with clumps of curious, stunted trees in untidy rows on either side of the overgrown path leading up to the front door. There were not many like it in the street, most of which was taken up by small, modern blocks of flats. Cars were littered the length of the street, parked half on and half off the pavement.

When Franz had taken her there it had been late at night and in the darkness she remembered thinking how it seemed a perfect setting for the witch's house in the Hansel and Gretel story. The squat trees were like an avenue of bloated sentry toads lining the approach. The door was made of ancient wooden boards, like cardboard to the touch, held together by rusty iron crossbands. It creaked loudly as it was opened and they had to duck to get inside without bumping their heads. Frau Schaller had only added to the impression; a small, hunched figure with her grey hair scraped back into a tight bun and a black shawl like a giant spider's web round her shoulders.

In the clear light of day what had been sinister became merely quaint. Gudrun was rather disappointed to find that the roof was not thatched but had modern tiles and plastic guttering. Franz had tidied up the garden a bit and oiled the door hinges. Frau Schaller showed Gudrun the lovely woollen shawl she had crocheted herself and promised to make her one.

Gudrun had only been to the house once before. Frau Schaller was Franz's grandmother's half-sister, a widow since the second world war. He had taken her there because he wanted to show her, and her alone, his final hiding place. It was the last bolthole he would retreat to if circumstances ever obliged him to do so. No one knew about the Augsburg house, he had told her. Not the authorities, not his fellow travellers in Das Schwarze Leichentuch. No one, absolutely no one. He was admitting her to the secret because he trusted her. She had been proud that he had trusted her before everybody else and she had loved him for it. They had gone to elaborate lengths to ensure that they were not followed. The secret remained secure and completely safe with her.

She walked up and down past the gate a few times before she was satisfied that the place was not under surveillance. Not that there was any reason it should be, but she was being ultra cautious. It was dark as she went up the path through the unkempt garden, carrying the suitcase Gertrud had left for her in the locker at Frankfurt station. A bat flapped close to her head, startling her. She raised a protective arm and backed away. Then, smiling at her foolishness, she continued to the door. The windows were shuttered and there was no sign of light or life. She tapped at the door gently with her knuckles and then more firmly with her fist when that did not seem to make sufficient noise. She waited several minutes, knocking at regular intervals, and was about to leave the door and go round the house to check for other means of access when she heard a faint sound from inside. It was like a tiny bird cheeping. She pressed her ear against the coarse wood and listened.

'Who is it?' the voice asked, trilling like the sound of a tuning fork.

'It is Gudrun, Frau Schaller,' she replied, surprised by the strength and loudness of her own voice. 'I need your help.'

There was a pause and then the sound of heavy bolts being

drawn back. The door swung inwards silently and pale yellow light flowed out. Frau Schaller stood in the entrance wearing a white quilted dressing gown and fur-edged slippers. Her hair was down and straggling over her face. Pink skin was visible where it sprouted from her scalp. The black shawl was round her shoulders and held at her chest by one hand. She looked much older, much more bowed than Gudrun remembered. The lines on her face seemed deeper. Her eyes seemed cloudier. She held out her free hand in greeting and when Gudrun took it between hers it was frail and delicate like a piece of bone china.

'I wondered if you would come,' the old woman said.

'You know what happened to Franz?'

'Yes, I heard about it. I wondered if you would come. I have your room ready for you.'

'I need your help, Frau Schaller,' Gudrun said. 'I need a place to stay for a little while.'

'Of course, of course. Come in, girl. Come in. You must tell me about Franz. I had not seen him for such a long time and now he is dead.' Her mouth creased in a humourless, toothless smile. 'You are a widow now as I have been for so many years. Come in. Come in.'

Gudrun bowed her head and entered the house. Frau Schaller closed the door and bolted it before showing her into the living room. Then she insisted on going through to the kitchen to make coffee leaving Gudrun sitting in an armchair. It was a low-ceilinged room with a large dark wood sideboard taking up the length of one wall, a corner cupboard full of porcelain ornaments, and a marble fireplace. The sofa and chairs were arranged round an electric fire sitting in front of the empty grate. There were two photographs in ornate silver frames on the mantlepiece. One was of a young man in the full dress uniform of the Waffen SS; Frau Schaller's only son. His name had also been Franz. He had been captured at the end of the war but had taken poison rather than face trial. The other photograph was of his father, also Franz, a bomber pilot in the Luftwaffe shot down and killed during a bombing raid on London a few years before his son.

Frau Schaller came into the room carrying a tray. 'I am sorry I took so long to answer the door,' she said. 'I go to bed very early these days and my old bones do not respond very quickly when I have to get up again quickly.'

'Think nothing of it,' Gudrun replied, accepting a thick slice of chocolate cake and a cup of coffee with cream.

The old woman lowered herself into an armchair. It was an old-fashioned suite, stuffed with horse hair, and her slight weight barely made a dent in the seat. She sipped the hot coffee once and put the cup back on the tray at her side. Her face hardened.

'Tell me about Franz,' she demanded.

Gudrun told the whole story, leaving out the fact of her enforced occupation of Divers' bed. She kept it simple, making it out to be a straight feud between Franz and Divers with Franz on the losing side only because of deceit and trickery.

'Now,' she said, watching the old woman's mouth stretch in a smile of encouragement. 'I intend to avenge Franz.'

Frau Schaller nodded. 'It is good that this Englishman should not escape without paying the penalty. It is sad that Franz had to die. He might have been one of the new generation of leaders that this country so clearly lacks. You must make the Englishman pay.'

'I will. I know how I can find him.'

The old woman rocked on the seat of the chair. 'This Minotaur bomb will lead you to him, my girl. Believe me, you just have to follow the trail that he has left behind and it will lead you straight to him.'

'I hope so.'

'It will happen. There is a pattern in the order of things that you may perhaps begin to see as you grow older. I can see it now. I can feel it. The killer of our Franz; psssht.' She spat a fine spray of spittle. 'He is already dead.'

Gudrun made exaggerated efforts to stop a yawn. 'If you do not mind Frau Schaller, I am very tired. I would like to retire to bed now.'

'Of course, my girl. We will talk more in the morning.'

She was shown to the bedroom that she had shared with Franz on her last visit to the house. The bed was always kept in readiness, Frau Schaller explained, as she pulled down the corner of the freshly laundered sheets. The bedroom was small, low-ceilinged again. The bed took up most of the room except for the old wardrobe in one corner and a small fireplace opposite it. It was stopped up with a plain wooden panel standing on the colourful tiles of the hearth. As soon as she was left alone, Gudrun began to lever the panel out of its fixed position. It came away easily once she had freed the top. She removed the iron grate and prised out the loose stones underneath. It took her only a few minutes to expose the parcel wrapped in black plastic in the space below the stones. She lifted it out and picked impatiently at the knotted cord and sticky tape which kept it sealed. It took her five minutes to undo all the wrapping and reveal the contents. There were two separate items, each contained in its own clear plastic bag. One was a Walther P38 pistol with ammunition, the second was a nine-inch-long, stiff leather sheath with three buckles.

She tore open the first bag and examined the gun, filling and then emptying the magazine of bullets. She strapped the leather sheath to the outside of her right arm with the top buckle looped round her thumb. She held her arm out straight and when she flexed her thumb a six-inch-long, double-sided blade shot out. She tried the edges. They were razor sharp. The point was only slightly blunter. She placed it against one of the tiles and compressed the spring so that the blade re-entered the sheath and clicked back into place.

She quickly re-wrapped the gun and the leather sheath in their individual bags and in the black plastic and replaced them in the hole below the hearth stones. Carefully replacing the panel she checked to see that it did not look as if it had been disturbed. She did not know if the old woman knew about the secret cache. Perhaps she did. Perhaps she did not. Franz had never mentioned it. All he had said was that only the two of them knew about it. It was their personal secret.

She cleaned her hands as best she could and began to unpack the suitcase. She was undressing when she heard the knock at the door and went to answer it wearing only her sweatshirt and knickers. Frau Schaller grinned her toothless smile.

'I promised you this the last time you were here, my girl,' she said, handing over a shapeless bundle of black wool before shuffling back across the corridor to her own bedroom.

It was a crocheted shawl, exactly like the one Frau Schaller wore herself. Gudrun closed the door and took it inside, throwing it on the bed where it fanned out to display its intricate pattern. She finished undressing and picked up the shawl to drape over her shoulders, pulling it in tightly so that her white skin pressed through the holes. Franz would have liked it, she told herself. The colour black suited her so well.

MacDonald would not have gone through with it if Peaches had not accompanied him to Zeppelinwiese. Privately, throughout the day as he reconsidered the idea in the hotel room, he had grown increasingly sceptical about its value. It seemed to him to be deliberately tempting fate to be carting Divers' body round the city in the back of the car. It was an incredible, and totally unnecessary, risk to then try and dump the body in such a public place. He had decided that if he was doing it alone he would just leave it in some deserted back street, or go out into the country and abandon it on the verge of a lonely road, and say that there had been too many people about. But he couldn't do that with Peaches sitting beside him. There seemed to have been a subtle change in their relationship. She seemed to be leading now and he was following. She did not seem to have any doubts about Zeppelinwiese, or if she did she was keeping them very quiet. MacDonald was too proud to make the suggestion that it was too risky. He did not want her to think he was somehow lacking in courage. So he had to go through with it.

The arena was completely empty when they drove into it with the car's headlights turned off just after midnight. They had stopped a few streets away to blank out the number plates with black insulating tape. There was not a soul to be seen, only the wreck of the old Volkswagen beetle. The wind had grown quite strong during the evening and it was laced with light rain from the solid ceiling of clouds. The white stone terraces were just visible in the darkness, stretching away from where MacDonald parked the car right under the main platform. They could not see the giant American flag flying high above the central grass area as it rustled and snapped in the wind. MacDonald switched off the engine and it ticked loudly as it began to cool. He glanced sideways at Peaches and wished he had never repeated Divers' version of his encounter with Franz Luneburg. Even Divers had had the sense to take him well way from the arena before bumping him off.

The call to the man Rocher in Munich had gone well. He thought he had handled the situation very well and convinced Rocher of his sincerity with hardly any trouble at all. They were half-way there. All they had to do now was hand over the goods and take the money. It was silly to jeopardize that by taking needless risks.

'We're in luck,' Peaches said quietly. 'We have the place to ourselves.'

'Then let's do it before company arrives,' MacDonald said, desperate to get it over with.

They got out of the car, leaving their doors open. The boot sprang open on the turn of the key. It was an awkward job getting the body out of the confined space. The groundsheet was coarse and slippery and difficult to get a grip on. MacDonald managed to get the legs out first and to pivot the body on the rear ledge so that they swung down to the ground and the head came up to be level with his own. He went down on one knee and the heavy body fell stiffly over his shoulder. He stood up and looked round. Peaches had slung one of the rifles over her shoulder and was standing guard. Nothing had changed. There was no one to be seen.

'Hurry,' she whispered urgently and MacDonald ran towards the gap in the fence.

He stumbled once on his way up the terrace but quickly regained his balance and reached the central platform. Peaches and the car were hidden from him under its edge. He threw the body down unceremoniously and pulled the groundsheet open to expose Divers lying on his back. MacDonald looked down at the ash-grey face. The yellow eyes were half open and the top lip had been pushed up to show the teeth. He did not look like himself at all, MacDonald thought as he took a piece of paper the size of a magazine page from his jacket pocket and unfolded it. The words Das Schwarze Leichentuch were printed on it in black felt-tip pen. They would have preferred to leave a more detailed message but neither of them could speak German well enough to ensure that it had not obviously been written by a foreigner.

From his other pocket, MacDonald took one of the wide-bladed hunting knives they had brought with them from Nowhere. He slid the blade through the centre of the piece of paper, then he crouched down beside Divers and laid the point on his chest. From the corner of his eye he caught a glimpse of the whole arena. The weeds on the terracing were like the shadowy ghosts of thousands of spectators gathered to watch a human sacrifice being made. And MacDonald was the high priest.

'Sorry Shuggie, old pal,' he murmured, 'but it's all in a good cause.'

MacDonald held the knife in two hands and pressed down. The blade struck a rib and would not go any further. He tried to force it then lifted it off, moved the point half an inch up the way and pressed again. It entered the skin easily and sank in right up to the hilt. There was no blood. The wind caught the underside of the piece of paper and it flapped against the handle. MacDonald stood up and backed away. The rain began to fall more heavily, stinging against his face. He turned and ran down the terrace. Peaches was already in the car waiting for him. He got in the driver's side and started up the engine.

'Not too fast,' she ordered. 'Take it nice and easy.'

He drove out of the arena, turning on the lights only when he reached the road. Three cars passed them, travelling slowly in single file. Half a mile away he stopped and got out to remove the tape from the number plates.

'We did it, Peaches baby,' he said as he got back behind the steering wheel. 'We're home and dry.'

She leaned over and kissed him. 'It's just a step along the way, Joe. Come on now, let's go to bed. We've got a long journey tomorrow.'

'When do you think they will find him?'

'It will be hard to miss him when it gets light.'

They drove back to their hotel, a happy couple returning from a pleasant evening out on the town.

Hugo Betzing paced restlessly up and down in his office in the villa. Outside, the cold wind was thrashing the surrounding trees and causing little waves to rise on the swimming pool, slopping the water over the edge. He stubbed out one cigarette and immediately lit another one. On the lake most of the boats were huddled together in a sheltered bay as though they were flotsam driven there by the wind and tide. There was a bottle of brandy and a half-full glass on his desk. Every second or third time he passed the table he would lift the glass and take a drink, then begin pacing again.

He did not like it; a new and unknown Mr MacDonald taking over the deal; Divers himself, the first MacDonald, found dead that morning, apparently the victim of Nazi fanatics; changes in the way the money was to be handed over which would mean him losing the extra six hundred thousand or so he had planned to make by using Sabaroff. He did not like it at all. His instincts told him to pull out. He had been happy to do business with Divers after meeting him in Munich. He had not been convinced that Divers was working on his own and had been proved right. Divers was probably the leader of the gang which had snatched the Minotaur and now his friends were taking over. The new MacDonald and the rest of them did not seem to have the same sophisticated groundwork of organization. They did not have access to a numbered Swiss bank account. They had no system to short-circuit any attempts at a double-cross, apart from the Minotaur being armed. They had lost their leader and were trying to make the best of things, simply wanting the money handed over in a suitcase stuffed with notes. Originally they had asked for one million but had backed down quickly when Rocher had questioned the amount, according to Rocher. If they were to be offered a smaller sum they might well settle for that; say half the original seven hundred thousand pounds, or as low as two hundred thousand perhaps. It was more than Divers himself would have ended up with. The simple approach had its advantages.

Betzing smiled and rubbed the tiredness from his eyes. He stubbed out his cigarette after only a few puffs and tapped another free of the packet, drawing it out with his lips. There was another reason why he should back away from this one. His customer was having second thoughts. The stories put out by the British about the missing Dipstick being one of a defective batch incapable of detonating a Minotaur were having the desired effect. The authoritative New Scientist magazine, published in London, was claiming that the fact had not been revealed before because virtually all of Britain's contribution to NATO in Europe had been rendered potentially ineffective for a period of three months by the suspect thermal batteries and there had been fears about destabilization in West Germany if that had become known at the time.

The revelation had entailed a hastily-arranged rendezvous with his main Syrian contacts in Vienna where he had tried to convince them it was crude disinformation deliberately designed to stop them buying. He believed that himself so he argued forcefully. He pointed out that the story said the Dipstick had a fifty per cent chance of initiating the chain reaction necessary for the nuclear explosion. That was to cover themselves when it did go off, he told them. They were far from convinced. They talked about reneging on the deal altogether. Finally he was forced to agree to take a mere ten per cent on delivery, instead of the originally agreed sixty per cent, with the remainder coming once the Minotaur's capability had been established beyond doubt. He was not happy but it was the best deal he could negotiate in the circumstances. He thought about going back to the two unsuccessful bidders but they, too, would know about the faulty batteries and would not be so ready to commit themselves.

It never rains but it pours. He had flown back from Vienna

only to find Rocher adding to the complications of the deal with the news that the arrangements had been unavoidably changed. Rocher did not like it, but it could all be logically explained. There was no hint of deviousness from the new Mr MacDonald. All he wanted was his money. Even if it was no longer possible to obtain the Minotaur for the one-hundred-thousand-dollar payment to Sabaroff and Rocher's commission it was still an attractive deal if he could get it for less than half a million pounds. That would leave him with a clear profit of at least one and a half million pounds which would help to finance his comfortable retirement. All this was dependent on the Dipstick being in working order and the Syrians keeping faith with him once they had used it. He had some influence in circles which could make arms deals problematical for them, but he didn't know if it was two million dollars' worth of influence. Besides, the Soviets would always see the Syrians all right for arms. But then the Syrians were doing business with Betzing because the Soviets wouldn't give them any nuclear hardware. If the Syrians did set off the Minotaur they might be disowned by Moscow and have to rely more on the open market for arms supplies. In that event, Betzing was more likely to get his money. They would want to maintain their credibility with other suppliers.

It was a gamble now but Betzing reckoned that if he just handed over a suitcase with two hundred thousand pounds, maybe two hundred and fifty, the new MacDonald would have to take it or leave it. If he could get the Minotaur for that amount the risk was acceptable. He would recoup his outlay at once. And he was confident that, with the technical manual available, he had a man who could disarm the land-mine. It was still a gamble though, and a big one.

Betzing emptied the brandy bottle into his glass and stood at the windows looking out over the swimming pool and down onto the lake. Let's roll the dice and see what we get, he thought.

MacDonald raised his arm and hit the steering wheel with the heel of his hand as the *Stadt München* sign flashed by.

'Yee ha,' he shouted. 'The end of the road.'

Peaches woke up. It was late afternoon on another hot day. She yawned and stretched, arching her spine over the back of the seat so that she could touch the rucksack containing the Minotaur. She was wearing shorts. MacDonald reached over and ran his hand up and down her bare leg.

'There is an old saying, you know,' he told her. 'It is better to travel hopefully than to arrive. But here we are.'

'Robert Louis Stevenson,' Peaches said. 'To travel hopefully is a better thing than to arrive, and the true success is to labour. My analyst was always quoting it at me for some reason.'

They followed the road-signs in towards the city centre, taking a diversion round by Theresienwiese just to see what the Oktoberfest looked like, driving past without stopping. The site was dominated by the big beer tents, the giant ferris wheel and the undulating steel frames of the roller-coaster rides. There were crowds of people milling round the tall entrance gateway and thronging the main avenue leading into the grounds.

'My God, it's so big,' Peaches said.

'The bigger, the better,' MacDonald said. 'The more, the merrier on the night after next. There is safety in numbers.'

The Munich Tourist Office in the main station provided them with a booklet on accommodation and they chose to go to the Thalkirchen camping site on Zentralländstrasse beside the

River Isar. It was almost full when they finally found it, but they managed to squeeze into a space in a secluded corner between two large family tents. Peaches bought a five-day ticket which entitled them to take the car in as well. She used her real name on the form but put down a false registration number and nobody bothered to check it against the vehicle.

It was fairly late by the time they had their tent pitched. They ate cold Bratwurst and bread and drank bottled beer. Taking the Minotaur from the back seat they locked it in the boot, reversing the car into one end of the tent so that no-one could get at it without disturbing them. Then they settled down for an early night, squeezing together into the sleeping bag with the torn seam. A baby cried loudly in a neighbouring tent and they listened to its mother sing it a soft lullaby.

'No sex tonight,' MacDonald said. 'Let's save our energy.'

'You're getting past it, old man,' Peaches teased, cuddling against him as she breathed warm air into the side of his face.

She was asleep within minutes, but MacDonald lay for ages looking up at the ridge where the sharp angle of the tent's triangle was formed. It grew colder as it grew darker and darker. His body was warm where it touched Peaches and cold elsewhere. His breath was a dark fog in the blackness. Around them the campsite gradually quietened and slept. MacDonald's eyes remained open. He thought he must be the only person in the whole world who was still awake.

The trees in the Rheinaue Park seemed to have taken on their full autumnal colouring overnight. From being slightly dark at the edges, the leaves had suddenly turned brown and red and yellow. And the piles of fallen leaves were growing bigger. Buster Grant kicked at them as he jogged past. He turned to his left as he reached the Rhine, nodding to a fellow jogger going in the opposite direction, and following the curve of the path to run with the current. It was a warm morning. It was going to be a hot day. He was running in a vest and blue track-suit bottoms.

Grant looked ahead and saw the man in the light raincoat standing beside the path at the rear of the canoe-club building. He thought nothing of it until the man came down the small slope and stood in the middle of the path when Grant was only ten yards away. He recognized the square-shaped face of Gerhard Lutzke as he came to a halt. He looked around. There was no one else in sight apart from a cyclist on another path a few hundred yards off, travelling away from them.

'Good morning Buster,' the East German said.

'Well Gerhard. Fancy meeting you here. Small world, isn't it?'

Lutzke's hands were deep in his pockets. For a moment Grant thought he might be about to produce a gun and shoot him. He laughed uncertainly, feeling the sweat dry on his bare shoulders. There had to be some reason for this contrived encounter. Lutzke was very relaxed. Grant had never seen him in such a good mood.

'I knew I would find you here this morning Buster.'

'Our security people keep telling me to vary my route.

Maybe I should listen to them.'

'Don't worry. What I have to tell you is something to your advantage, as you Englishmen would say. I didn't want to phone the embassy. I wanted to see you face to face. There is a certain urgency.'

'Here I am. Fire away.'

'Let me ask you something first. Are you any closer to recovering your stolen Minotaur land-mine?'

The question surprised Grant. The murder of Hugh Divers by Das Schwarze Liechentuch had re-opened interest in the case but they were no further forward than on the day it had been stolen. He shook his head and tried to guess what was in Lutzke's mind. He jogged up and down on the spot to keep warm.

'For instance, do you know where it is? Or even who has it now that this Divers has been killed?'

'Not a clue, to be honest, Gerhard. Do you?'

'Yes actually. That's what I want to tell you.'

Grant stopped running and stood flat-footed. He must have let his mouth fall open in astonishment because Lutzke grinned at his reaction.

'Don't look so shocked,' he said. 'I know the entire resources of NATO and the West German police force couldn't find it but we managed to.'

'Why tell me?'

'You want it back, don't you? Go and get it.'

'Where is it?'

'It will be exchanged for cash at the Oktoberfest in Munich tomorrow night. The handover is set for nine o'clock, on the steps under the big statue of Bavaria at Theresienwiese.'

'Tomorrow? You're sure about this?'

'It comes from a very reliable source. I can't tell you where I got the information, of course, but I would stake my life on it being accurate. If you want the Minotaur back, go and get it.'

'Come on Gerhard,' Grant coaxed. 'You're just dying to tell me how you know all this.'

'Good contacts Buster. That's how. That's why I am passing it on to you. You're a good contact of mine.'

'It's the Syrians who are buying it. I know that much.'

Lutzke nodded his agreement. 'It wouldn't be in our interests for these volatile Middle Easterners to have a nuclear land-mine at their disposal. We have always refused to play that particular game. That is why they have gone onto the open market.'

'And you want to shut the door on them.'

'We are not involved. You shut the door Buster. We've not gone soft you know. As I said, it is in our interests for this Minotaur to be taken off the market.'

'Why don't you take it for yourselves?'

'We would if we thought it would be of some value to us. I am being perfectly straight with you Buster. But you and I both know it's yesterday's weapon. Technology has moved on. I believe your scientists are working on a new type to be called after another mythological monster. The Chimera, isn't it? Now we would be interested in obtaining one of those.'

Grant started running on the spot again. He hadn't realized they knew about the Chimera. He hadn't known himself until the briefing session after the Minotaur was stolen. He would have to send that nugget of information back to London.

'Thanks for the tip then Gerhard. But why me? Why didn't you go to the locals with this?'

'I thought you could do with some cheering up, you looked so miserable at that Japanese reception. Besides I know I can rely on you not to reveal me as the source of your information. We want our noses to be kept clean. I must go. It wouldn't do for me to be seen with you.'

'You can rely on me, Gerhard.' Lutzke turned to walk away and Grant caught his arm. 'Nine, at the Oktoberfest, tomorrow?'

'Correct. See you around, Buster.' He took his hands out of his pockets for the first time and put both index fingers up at either side of his head. 'The bull by the horns, Buster. The bull by the horns.'

Grant watched Lutzke walk away from him. He almost shouted after him, realizing he had forgotten to ask who would be making the exchange, but a woman walking her dog appeared close by and he stopped. It didn't matter anyway. They would find out soon enough. He turned and ran back the way he had come, moving fast to cover the distance to the embassy. He would have to get onto Kaspar immediately. They did not have long. Tomorrow night. At the Oktoberfest.

It had to be a trick. There was nobody left in Das Schwarze Leichentuch capable of killing Hugh Divers. The group had always been a one-man band under Franz's leadership, the others had simply made up the numbers. It had to be a trick. The picture in all the newspapers had certainly been him this time, but then he had fooled the papers before. It was a clever trick designed to convince the authorities he was no longer a problem. Gudrun Richter knew that it had to be a trick. Divers was not going to deny her that easily. She would find him. She would have the pleasure of killing him. He could not get away from her.

Frau Schaller agreed with her. She had given encouragement to her plan. The old woman with her rounded shoulders and her toothless smile had laughed at the stories about the discovery of the body at Zeppelinwiese in Nuremberg, supposed to be Divers. She, too, did not believe that the message pinned to the body with the knife was genuine because, without Franz, there was no one to do such a thing. The only two group members who could conceivably be involved were both still in prison on firearm-possession charges after the police raids on safe houses soon after Franz had been killed. But Frau Schaller thought it might be the police who were trying to be clever. She thought they might be trying to flush Divers out of hiding by pretending they were no longer interested in him. Gudrun preferred her own interpretation. Divers had used Zeppelinwiese because that was where he had tricked her into sending Franz to his death. Now he was trying to trick everybody into believing he was dead. Nobody knew where Franz had been the night he died except her. Nobody but her knew that Divers had come to the casino and told her to send Franz there. He could not fool her with his tricks any longer. She knew he was still out there. She knew that he was still alive. She still had to find him. She still had to kill him.

Gudrun was wearing a simple grey raincoat, a wide-brimmed hat and a pair of flat-heeled shoes. The P38 was in her clutch-bag. Underneath she had on a plain black, long-sleeved dress and the new black shawl. The leather strap was buckled to her right forearm. She had painted her eyelids black, and her fingernails and her toenails. Combined with her dyed black hair it gave her face a curious luminosity. On the busy train in from Augsburg she stared out the window all the time, hardly noticing the rapidly darkening landscape, fascinated by her own reflection shining like the moon as it hovered a few feet beyond the glass.

In Munich Hauptbahnhof she crossed the concourse and went down to the U-Bahn. She bought a ticket from the machine and took a train three stops out to Josephsplatz station in Schwabing. From there it was only a short walk to her destination on the tree-lined Elizabethstrasse. She had only been there once before, as in Augsburg, but it was easier for her to find because she knew the name of the street and the number of the flat. Divers had driven her there and she remembered it well. It was the only time she had ever accompanied him on one of his trips. He had been using the pseudonym MacDonald. She had wondered why he had wanted her with him, especially when he told her just to sit in the car outside. But after an hour he came to get her, bringing a horrible little fat man with tiny, glittering eyes that leered at her unpleasantly, and lips like thin strips of rubber. Divers made her get out of the car and the two of them took her back upstairs. It was only when she was shown into the bedroom with the pornographic mural on the wall that she realized what was going on. The little fat man began to paw at her. Divers winked as he closed the door to leave them alone. She was trapped. She could not leave. Divers would force her to return. Franz would not want her to blow her cover. The fat man's brain hung between his legs and she was the sexual seal on the bargain he and Divers had just struck. Sex was never more repulsive to her but she had to go through with it. There was nothing else she could do even though every touch by the fat man seemed to be the touch of some vile, scaly reptile. Her blood was running cold as he led her to the bed. It was not a man and a woman, it was two reptiles that copulated there.

Gudrun recognized the doorway and found Rocher's name on the list of occupants on the entry-control panel. His flat was on the third floor. She stepped back to stand beside a tree and looked up. There were a few pot plants on the balcony. The shutters were pulled half-way down. Nothing moved. No lights could be seen. 'Be in, you bastard,' she whispered. 'Be in.'

Standing under the tree on the sparse carpet of fallen leaves she opened her bag and took out a lipstick. The colour was matt black. She applied it to her lips smoothly and evenly. Then she stepped forward to the door again and pressed the call button beside Rocher's name.

Eva was in the bath and Rocher was looking forward to joining her when the bell rang. He had worked a long day making the final arrangements for the handover of the Minotaur at Wies'n the following evening. He had recruited two good men to escort Betzing and his suitcase full of money and another four to remain in the background to be called on if necessary. He had left the recruitment to the last moment to prevent gossip spreading. He was pleased the deal was going ahead despite the last-minute changes. Betzing seemed satisfied that everything was in order. There may be a whole dynasty of MacDonalds involved in this but we only need one to give us the Minotaur. There was no reason to suspect that the second Mr MacDonald, whoever he was, was interested in anything other than getting rid of the Minotaur as quickly as possible.

Rocher was just folding away his clothes and putting on his yellow dressing gown when the bell interrupted him. He cursed silently and went bare-footed to the intercom link beside the main door.

'Who is it?' he said into the speaker.

'Remember me, Herr Rocher? MacDonald sent me to talk to you. I have something for you. Are you alone?'

He remembered her immediately. The long-legged friend of Divers who had been such a passionate lover after he had first seen the DIP unit and heard all about the plans to steal the Minotaur. But what was she doing here now?

'You say MacDonald sent you to me. Don't you mean Hugh Divers.'

'That's right.' She smiled up at him. 'You know his real name now, don't you. Remember how I came here with him before. He said you liked me. My name is Gudrun. Don't you remember?'

'But he's dead.'

'Is he?' Her voice purred electronically.

'Yes,' he said uncertainly. 'It's been all over the newspapers.'

'You shouldn't believe all you read in the papers. He sent me to see you.'

Rocher was confused. Maybe Divers wasn't dead after all. Maybe he had faked his death for some reason. Maybe there was to be yet another last-minute change in arrangements. Maybe it was some kind of trap.

'What is it you want?' he asked, playing for time.

'I want to speak to you.'

'About what?'

'Mutual friends. Are you alone?'

Rocher moistened his lips with his tongue. What the Hell was going on? What was this woman doing arriving on his doorstep like this? If she really had been sent by Divers then he had to discover the truth before tomorrow. If Divers was alive then he had fooled absolutely everybody with a brilliant piece of trickery. But if he was alive who was the second MacDonald? It couldn't be a trap if she was alone. He could handle a lone woman easily enough. He had no choice in the matter. He had to find out what was going on.

'Yes, I'm alone. Come on up,' he said, releasing the electronic lock.

He went to the bathroom and told Eva to get dressed and keep out of sight. He did not explain who Gudrun was or why she should suddenly arrive at the flat. He did not know himself yet. He got his personal handgun from the bedroom and slipped it into his dressing-gown pocket. Then he went back to the door and peered through the spy-hole which gave a clear view as she emerged through the sliding doors of the lift, turning to close them behind her. A woman. An attractive woman. A sexy woman. A desirable woman. And she was on her own. No problem.

The black and white face looked straight at him as she approached the door. For a brief second, she looked threatening, somehow sinister. Rocher shrugged off the feeling. It was the distorted image caused by the lens. She was only a woman after all. She couldn't hurt him, but she could tell him a lot.

Gudrun smiled when the door opened as she approached it. She saw the look of surprise on Rocher's face as he noticed the black lipstick and the black make-up. She walked past him into the flat and waited while he replaced the bolts.

'May I take your coat?' he asked politely.

'Thank you.'

She could see that he was having difficulty keeping his eyes off her. The black dress was deliberately tight-fitting to show off her slim figure. She wanted to have him distracted. She wanted him to have only half his mind on their discussion. She needed to have the advantage if things started moving fast. She was not at all sure that she was capable of doing what she planned to do. She adjusted the shawl on her shoulders.

'Black is my favourite colour,' she offered in explanation when he continued to stare. 'Unusual, I know, but I like it.'

'So do I. So do I,' he said and his eyes almost disappeared in the wrinkled skin as he beamed a huge smile of approval.

He ushered her into the living room and switched on the light. She felt his fingers brush lightly over one buttock and a shiver of loathing went right through her. The room was sparsely furnished with just a sofa and a single chair. There was a white sheepskin rug on the polished wood floor and a standard lamp in one corner. The radiator was disguised as a cabinet. Large sliding doors filled most of one wall and a light burned behind the opaque glass panes. She placed her bag in her lap. Gudrun sat down on the sofa, letting her dress ride well up above her knees. Rocher remained standing. The cord of his dressing gown hung in a loose knot. The two sides only just met in the middle.

'Well, Gudrun. What is it that you want to tell me?'

'I want to tell you that Hugh Divers is alive and well.' She was controlling herself well. Her hands would have been shaking if she did not have them gripping the bag.

'Really? Then why does everybody else tell me he is dead?'

Rocher had both hands in his pockets. If she could reach her gun he would be at her mercy. Her fingers were clumsy. The stud which held the flap of the bag would not open. Panic simmered under the surface of her calm demeanour. It had been easy up till now. It had been all talk and no action. Her body wouldn't do what her mind told it.

'Here. Let me,' he said, and before she could move he had snatched the bag away from her. He took out the pistol and held it up. 'Now I can see why you've come dressed as an undertaker.'

Gudrun sat staring in horror at Rocher. The sudden flurry of movement had separated the sides of his dressing gown. She could see the rolls of fat at his stomach and hanging breasts almost like a woman's. His penis was erect, sticking out above small testicles like a cannon on wheels. She was suddenly very calm, very clear headed. She took a corner of the shawl and rubbed the soft wool against her cheek.

'Why did you come here Gudrun? What is it you really want?' He was holding the gun in the palm of his hand, moving it up and down as if weighing it.

'I want you to tell me the time and place of the Minotaur handover,' she said.

'Why don't you ask your boyfriend?'

'I came here to ask you.'

'And use this to persuade me?'

He had his finger on the trigger. He brushed her hair with the muzzle. She felt the hard metal ring bump against the bone of her skull. He was standing a few feet in front of her, his legs apart. His nostrils flared wide. His tongue ran slowly over his bloodless lips. With his free hand he untied the cord. Then he slipped off one shoulder of the dressing gown. He swopped over the gun and removed the other shoulder, letting it slide to the ground which it hit with an incongruous thump. Naked, he resembled a partially-deflated Michelin man. She bit the inside of her mouth to stop herself laughing.

'There are other ways of making me talk,' he said. 'Much more pleasant ways. Don't you remember?'

Gudrun remembered. She reached out with her right hand and grasped Rocher's penis. She felt his body shudder. His eyes glazed over and his head went back. The gun was lowered to the side of his leg. She smiled. She was no longer afraid, no longer even nervous. Her black fingernails curled slowly round the fleshy cylinder and then pulled back so that she was holding it by the very tip. She squeezed her thumb inwards. Rocher moaned loudly. The silver blade shot out, tearing through the sleeve of her dress and slicing along the top of the engorged penis. The point pressed deeply into his abdomen but only just broke the skin. Strawberry-red blood spurted over her hand and gushed up Rocher's stomach. He jerked himself backwards with a roar of pain. He dropped the pistol and it rattled over the floor and bounced off the radiator cabinet. He doubled over. Gudrun picked up his discarded dressing gown and wiped the blade clean.

'I'll ask you again now, Herr Rocher,' she said slowly. 'Time and place. That's all I want to know.'

His forehead was almost on the floorboards. He twisted his head round so that he could look up at her. 'Bitch,' he snarled. 'I'll kill you for that.'

She raised a foot, put it against his neck and pushed him back. He fell on his backside and slid on his own blood until he bumped into the back wall. The insides of his legs were scarlet.

'I'll ask you once more, Herr Rocher, and then I'll cut your balls off one by one and teach you to juggle with them.'

His breathing was rapid. His eyes had narrowed to pin-points. His teeth were bared. She saw his tongue move as he struggled to form coherent words. 'Eva,' he yelled. 'Save me.'

Gudrun had heard the rumble of the sliding doors behind her before Rocher managed to shout out. She whirled on her heel and brought her right hand slashing round at head height. She glimpsed a tall, well-built woman in a flimsy nightdress charging at her. She heard a high-pitched scream. Then she saw the blade sweep across the gaping mouth. It caught the corner and ripped open the cheek. Blood flowered from the wound, spattering in a horizontal line along the wall above

Rocher. The woman collapsed and curled into a tight ball on the sheepskin rug, her face hidden in her hands. She sobbed like a child.

Gudrun turned back to Rocher. His tiny eyes glared at her. Drops of sweat trickled over the dome of his bald head. All the colour seemed to be draining out of his body and seeping through the hands clutching his groin. On the wall behind him thin trails of blood were beginning to branch off from the thick line and run vertically downwards.

'Do I have to ask again?' Gudrun said quietly as she cleaned the blade for a second time.

'Tomorrow night at nine,' Rocher gasped. 'On the steps under the big statue of Bavaria at the Oktoberfest.' His head sagged weakly.

She found his pistol in the pocket of the dresing gown and used the butt to compress the spring and return the blade inside the leather sheath. 'You wouldn't lie to me, would you Herr Rocher?' she said.

'It's the truth. I swear it.'

'She squatted down in front of him and took his chin between finger and thumb, forcing his head up so that he had to look at her. 'You wouldn't lie to me?' she repeated.

'The truth. The truth.' His face screwed up in a grimace of pain. 'Call a doctor. Please.'

'You're not lying, are you?'

'No.' He tried to shout but the effort was too much for him and he began to weep. The truth. I've told you the truth.'

'I believe you,' Gudrun whispered. 'I believe you.'

She stroked his chin as he cried, still holding his head up. She extended her thumb a little and ran it over his bottom lip. Then she snapped the thumb down. The blade sprang from its sheath. The blunt point punched a hole through the front of his throat. A jet of blood leaped over Gudrun's shoulder. She moved to one side to avoid it. Rocher trembled violently. His eyes protruded and then sank back to disappear. His heels drummed on the wooden floor. A liquid gargling sound came from his mouth, awash with bubbles of foaming blood.

Behind her, Gudrun heard the woman give a little shriek of fear. She quickly turned and saw her trying to scramble on hands and knees to the sliding doors. One hand held her mutilated face in place. Gudrun raised the gun and fired once. The bullet hit its target low down on the back. The lace night-dress creased in a spiral round the wound. The woman fell spread-eagled on the floor and lay still.

Gudrun dropped the gun. An overwhelming sense of panic returned like a long-forgotten memory. She had to get away from here. Rocher was dead, sitting propped against the wall with his hands still clasped to his groin. He had told her what she wanted to know.

She cleaned the blood from her hands with the dressing gown, grabbed her bag and ran for the door, hastily ramming the blade back into its sheath and pulling on her coat over her blood-stained dress. The lift was not at that floor level so she ran down the stairs, wiping away the black make-up from her face with a tissue. She could hear people moving on the floors above. She burst out into the street, surprised that it was still reasonably light and that there were a lot of people around. Forcing herself to slow down, she licked another tissue and wiped her eyelids. Gradually, the panic subsided and she regained her self-control. She could see the sign over the steps to the underground station.

She should have at least shut the flat door, she thought. All that noise was bound to attract the attention of neighbours, and a wide-open door was an invitation to the curious. She should have rearranged the scene inside the flat to make it look like Rocher and the woman had killed each other in a bloody fight. A crime of passion. That would have been the smart thing to do.

Too late now. She had what she wanted. Hugh Divers must already be somewhere in Munich preparing for tomorrow night's rendezvous. She would return from Augsburg again tomorrow night. She smiled and rubbed off the last of the black lipstick with her thumb. They had a date.

The vast beer hall had five thousand people packed together under its canvas roof. The atmosphere was riotous but friendly. When the band on the raised central stage began to play many of the people climbed onto the tables and waved the big glass Steins of beer in the air. Everybody sang the familiar songs, swaying from side to side and stamping their feet on the wooden boards. Couples waltzed in the walkways. Bread sellers in white aprons lugged their baskets of pretzels up and down the aisles. Waitresses in traditional Bavarian costume bawled *Vorsicht* and forced their way through the unruly crowds carrying fistfuls of the litre Steins.

Peaches and MacDonald had squeezed in at a table not far from the entrance to the hall. Behind them a whole ox was being roasted on a spit. Half the meat had already been picked from the bones by a team of chefs. They could feel the heat of the cooking on the back of their necks and smell the flavour of the meat in the air. It was the third beer hall they had visited and the first where they had managed to find seats. No one else at the table seemed to be able to speak English so they just smiled and nodded when something was said to them. A few men had tried to take Peaches up to dance but she had always refused. MacDonald had drunk three Steins in quick succession. Peaches had hardly touched a drop.

They had arrived at the Oktoberfest in the late afternoon. MacDonald had wanted to come alone but she had insisted on going with him. He just wanted to get his bearings, study the geography of the place, he said. He wanted her to stay with the

Minotaur but she was adamant that she was to go with him. In the end they paid the ten-year-old Dutch boy in the next tent five Deutschmarks to guard their car while they were gone the promise of the same again if it was untouched when they got back.

At the Theresienwiese the first thing they had gone to see was the statue of Bavaria, half-way along and one hundred yards to the side of the main avenue running between the big beer halls. A steep flight of steps ran up the slope to where she stood looking out over the Oktoberfest site. She was more than sixty feet high on top of a thirty-foot stone plinth. One hand rested on a lion's mane. The other held a crown of laurel leaves. She stood in front of a Greek-style Hall of Fame containing busts of Bavarian heroes of the past. When it got dark floodlights were switched on to illuminate the statue and its background.

They walked all round her. They sat on the steps eating Bratwurst among the crowds of other festival-goers, and on the tiers at the foot of the plinth. They paid to go inside the statue and climb the circular staircase which led up to her head. From there they could look out through her eyes over Wies'n. MacDonald surveyed her from all angles. They left the Oktoberfest and walked round the streets within a half a mile's radius. They discussed how they would go about the exchange the next day. When they were finally satisfied with what they had seen they went to the fair.

Peaches persuaded him to go for a ride on the big dipper and then on a ghost train. They tried to go on the huge ferris wheel but decided the queue was too long. He won her a soft toy at a shooting gallery. They wandered among the souvenir stalls. A lot of people were wearing face masks of famous people. He bought one of the Pope while she chose one of Marilyn Monroe and they kissed passionately through the plastic holes. Then they decided to go for a drink and ended up in the beer hall watching the festivities.

MacDonald leaned against her to attract her attention. 'It's almost nine,' he said. 'Let's go and see what it looks like now.'

They slid out from the bench in the middle of a song. Nobody seemed to notice them go. One person grabbed MacDonald's hand and shook it enthusiastically for no particular reason. Peaches held onto the masks and the soft toy.

Outside, they joined the slow-moving throng which clogged the avenue.

'Safety in numbers,' he said as they allowed themselves to be carried along in the motion of the crowd towards the statue of Bavaria.

The road leading up to the statue was much quieter than the main thoroughfare. There was room to walk at your own pace. The steps were below the level of the floodlights and in deep shadow. The nearest sideshow was a small sawdust ring offering children pony rides, twenty yards away. Some of the light from that reached the steps but they had to go quite close to be able to see that a few people were sitting on them. About a dozen were gathered round the plinth.

'That's good,' Peaches said. 'You'll come here to collect the money. I will bring the Minotaur on my back and we'll find a nice quiet spot just outside the entrance for me to wait at. Once you've got the money you'll bring them to collect their end of the bargain.'

'It sounds easier than robbing a bank.'

'It is.'

'Okay, let's go home. We've got a busy day ahead of us tomorrow.'

'Can't we try again for a go on the big wheel?' Peaches asked, pointing over the fairground to where the brightly-coloured wheel was spinning. 'Please Joe. I've never been on one of those things. Please Joe.'

'All right then. Since it's you.'

They had to queue for ten minutes outside the ticket box and another ten minutes inside before they got into one of the cabins with another eight people. They sat opposite each other and Peaches rested her hands on MacDonald's knees. The wheel moved smoothly round and their cabin stopped right at the peak of its circle, swinging gently, as more were loaded down below.

The lights of the city spread out on every side. Peaches moved one hand and secretly pressed it against her flat stomach. Her period was only two days late but she was usually as regular as clockwork. She was sure in her own mind even though they had been together such a short time. She could sense the difference in her body. But she would wait a while before telling MacDonald. There was no hurry.

He was staring out of the cabin window. She followed his gaze down onto the brilliantly-lit statue of Bavaria far below.

'Top of the world Pop,' she said in a low voice that was drowned by the chatter of the other people around them. 'Top of the world.'

The news of Rocher's death reached Hugo Betzing just before midnight. Mitzi sounded as if she was in a dreadful state, talking in rapid bursts between body-racking sobs, but she still retained enough presence of mind to let Betzing know. He paid her to keep an eye on Rocher and she wanted to be sure of a last payment.

'Dead,' she wailed. 'Murdered. The police came and got me to identify the body. It was terrible what she did to him, terrible. What is going to happen to me now? What am I going to do?'

Betzing took her number and said he would call her back straight away. He splashed his face with cold water first, giving her time to calm down and himself time to think. Anna asked drowsily what was happening and he told her to go back to sleep. Just business, he said. There were plenty of people who might want Rocher dead with no reference to the Minotaur deal. He must have acquired a lot of enemies in his particular line of business. He had phoned Betzing the previous day to confirm the arrangements. Everything was in place. The flat for temporary storage of the Minotaur had been rented. The flight to Munich left Basle at noon. Sabaroff had an associate meeting him at Munich airport with the money. Rocher was no longer necessary.

He went through to his office and sat behind his desk, leaving the lights off. He lit a cigarette and looked out over Lake Neuchâtel where the moon cast a silvery path across the black waters. When he drew on the cigarette the red tip glowed fiercely and created a momentary reflection of him, orange-skinned, in the window glass. He punched the number and Mitzi answered it on the first ring.

'Tell me everything you know Mitzi,' he said. 'Take your time.'

He listened carefully as she related what she had been told about Rocher's death and that of his most recent girlfriend. She described how they had died and how the police were now looking for a mysterious woman in black who was seen running away from the flat just before the bodies were discovered by neighbours investigating the noise. Police were working on the theory that it must have been one of Rocher's extensive stable of blue-movie actresses who had a grudge against him. Mitzi had been a suspect until she produced proof of where she had been at the time. Then they had asked her to identify the bodies. It was awful, she said. There was a hole in Rocher's throat she could have put her fist into, and one side of Eva's face had been slit open.

'Thank you for phoning me, Mitzi,' Betzing said.

'What's going to happen to me now?' she said pitifully. 'Helmut always looked after me. What will I do now?'

'I'll see you all right for the time being, Mitzi. Don't worry about it. You will survive.'

He put the phone down. Mitzi knew nothing about the Minotaur deal. Rocher was known in Munich first and foremost as a pornographer. The nature of the injuries inflicted on him suggested an attack that was somehow connected with his business. It looked like a crude attempt to destroy the tools of his trade. Very probably somebody with a grudge, as the police thought. Somebody who had been exploited a little too blatantly by Rocher. A woman probably, a mysterious woman in black. The newspapers would lap it up.

It had certainly not been a professional murder. The screaming and then the gunshot that brought the neighbours running. The flat door left wide open. The woman seen running away. It had been an amateur at work, driven by hatred of the fat, bald man. Or maybe it was just set up to look like that.

Poor Rocher, Betzing thought as he lit another cigarette from the burning tip of his last one. He had it coming to him. He's done all this work for me and now I won't have to pay him any commission. The profit margin has just shot up.

Still, it was an added complication to a deal that was beginning to worry him. His instincts warned him to pull out while his obstinate streak told him that if anyone could pull it off successfully it was him. He had not met the new MacDonald, and could not be sure of him. He could not be sure if he would take the three hundred thousand Betzing intended to hand over. And the Syrians were being difficult as well, threatening not to go through with the deal. The publicized doubts over the effectiveness of the Minotaur's DIP unit had dampened their enthusiasm. Was it all worth it?

There could be no gain without risk. He was convinced the Minotaur and the Dipstick were the genuine article. It would blow. Somebody would buy it. And this would be the last big arms deal before he retired and settled down with Anna to enjoy spending all the money he had made. Still, he was not happy. He was undecided, and needed something to tip the balance one way or the other.

He began to straighten a stack of magazines hanging over the edge of his desk and discovered a pile of small change, Belgian francs, that he had emptied out of his pocket after a trip to Luxembourg and forgotten all about. He took a twenty-franc coin and balanced it on his thumbnail.

'Heads I do it, tails I stay at home,' he said.

He flicked the coin up, caught it in mid-air and slapped it down on the back of his other hand. Uncovering it slowly he sighed long and hard. Tails. A piece of broom, was it? The deal was off then. It was as simple as that. He would retire the next time round.

The pretty young woman and the bow-legged old lady sat on a bench in the railway station at Augsburg. The station was busy with crowds of people waiting for the Munich train to take them into the Oktoberfest. The young woman helped her companion to her feet as the train drew in to the platform and passengers immediately began boarding. They were among the last to reach the train. The old lady did not get on. Instead, she patted the young woman on the arm and grinned a toothless smile.

'Take care, my child. Take care,' she said and closed the door.

Gudrun Richter watched Frau Schaller standing, hunched and round-shouldered, on the platform as the train started up. She waved just once. The image of the empty, wide mouth remained in her mind long after it had receded into the distance and disappeared from sight.

Gudrun had no difficulty in finding a seat on the packed train. At least three men volunteered to stand up before she chose a window seat beside an inoffensive-looking teenage girl reading a paperback book. She sat looking out at the passing countryside with her hands resting lightly in her lap, swaying gently to the motion of the train as it quickly gathered speed.

There was no black make-up this time. Her fingernails were painted with clear varnish. She wore a white ribbon in her hair, a white jacket, and a bright red, low-waisted dress that smelled of moth balls. Frau Schaller said it had been bought for her a long time ago, just at the beginning of the war. Now it had come back into fashion. She had cackled merrily and smacked her gums as she rescued it from a wardrobe to spend hours pressing the creases flat. It was good to see it gracing a fine female body once more, she said as she admired it. Under the jacket Gudrun wore the black shawl, newly washed of the blood that had soaked into it. The leather strap was once more buckled to her forearm. The P38 was in her handbag.

Gudrun appreciated just how lucky she had been to get away from Rocher's flat without being captured. The police were hunting the woman in black seen running from the scene. How she had made it to the underground and then the train out to Augsburg without being recognized was a mystery to her. She had made no attempt to hide, apart from wiping off the make-up. She had been very lucky.

It had not gone as she had planned inside the flat although, in the end, she got what she wanted out of Rocher. She had imagined she would be more in control of the situation, more cool-headed, more efficient. She would just walk in, threaten him, get the information, kill him, and walk out. Instead, she had been forced to respond instinctively. She had been forced to fight for her life, and had come off best.

She remembered the evil smile on Rocher's face and the animal stench of his breath in her nostrils when he had raped her, and the trembling of his blubbery flesh as he slapped the hanging folds of his stomach and chest against her. Then she remembered Rocher's terrified eyes and his face, twisted in agony, as she stood over him the previous night. She remembered the thick, creamy blood oozing so slowly across the floor and she licked her lips like a cat. Franz would have been proud of her.

She was fully in control now as she sat in the train which was taking her towards Munich and her last meeting with the man she most wanted to kill. But the fear and panic were not far away. She could feel it fluttering raggedly on the fringe of her consciousness, fraying the boundaries of her field of vision. When she stared out on the parks and houses it was like looking down on a page carelessly torn from a book. Behind that page, eating away at its edges, was nothing but blinding white light.

Peaches lay alone in the tent. She was on her stomach with her feet up and resting on the bumper of the car where it jutted into the material at the rear. MacDonald had gone to Theresienwiese for another reconnaissance. She had let him go by himself this time. She wanted to write a letter.

This is just a short note, Pop, to let you know that all systems are go for tonight. Joe and I have it all worked out. We have considered every possibility. It's going to be a cinch, Pop. Like taking sweeties from a bairn, Joe says.

She scratched the side of her nose with the end of the pen and then tapped it against her teeth. It was hot and airless inside the tent. Outside there was bright sunshine. She could hear people all around talking and laughing.

I suppose I can tell you Pop. You're not going to tell anyone else. But it will be our little secret for now. Just you and me. No one else must know. Not even Joe. Not till I am ready.

I'm going to have a baby Pop. It's too early to be absolutely certain but I'm as sure as a woman can be about these things. I feel different. I can feel the baby beginning to grow inside me. I can feel my spirit beginning to flow into it to create the new life. Joe is the father, of course. Who else?

Isn't it wonderful Pop? How does it feel to know you are going to be a grandfather at last? I bet you're really pleased. I know I am. It's the best thing that has ever happened to me. And now we are going to have all this money and the baby will never want for anything. It's all working out perfectly. It's almost all too good to be true. I'm worried that maybe I'll wake up and all this is going to turn out to be just some kind of wonderful dream.

She stopped writing and signed the bottom of the page. There were many other things she wanted to write but the mood had suddenly left her. It was not hard to think why. She had worked it out a long time ago, when she was recovering in the sanitorium. She had tried to ignore the knowledge, especially since meeting MacDonald, but it was getting too close now. It demanded that she take notice of it. In two days time, on the twenty-fourth, she would be the exact age in years and days that her father had been when he was killed. Eighteen years and ninety-nine days. That was how old he had been when he died. That was how old she would be two days from now. She did not know the time of day the shell had soared up into the sky and down through the roof of the bunker. That had never been established. She did not know the exact moment when she would become older than her father.

Peaches tore up the letter she had just written and squashed the pieces in the palm of her hand. She crawled out of the tent and stood up. The sun was warm on the top of her head. She walked slowly over to the plastic litter bag hanging from its metal frame and lifting the lid she dropped the pieces in.

MacDonald had not gone to Theresienwiese. He had walked to the underground station at Implerstrasse and taken a train into Marienplatz. He went up the escalator into the square and sat at an outside table drinking Weissbier and watching the good-looking girls parade in their summer dresses. He should just keep on going, he thought idly, leave Peaches and the Minotaur and ride into the sunset. He should never go back.

It wasn't going to work tonight. It was too much for him. It would be too much luck at one time, in one place. He just wasn't that lucky. There had been no premonition of disaster but he felt no confidence in what he had to do. He did not believe he would wake up as a rich man the next day. It wasn't going to work, so he should just keep on running.

He would go back though. And he would go through with the deal as far as he was able. All his life he had grabbed opportunities as and when they cropped up and so far he had had the sense to shy away from any where the risk was too great. He had lived by his wits. He was always careful, always rational, always sensible. But this opportunity, the Minotaur, was the biggest thing to come his way. He had tried to ignore it and it had come looking for him. It would not leave him alone. The risk was enormous. If he was careful, rational, and sensible he would not touch it. However, the normal rules did not seem to apply to this one. It was not just about the money either. There was the challenge of it all too. What are you, Joe MacDonald, a man or a mouse? He could not ignore the challenge. Not now, even though he knew it wasn't going to work.

Then there was Peaches. He could not just walk away from Peaches. What would she think of him? If she was caught in possession of the Minotaur she might implicate him out of spite and they would come looking for him. There was no other course of action for him to take now that he had come this far. The wind had blown him into this corner. It was the only way out.

The bells rang out over Marienplatz and the crowds looked up at the tower on the side of the town hall, shading their eyes from the strong sun. Divers had told him about the glockenspiel, while barely conscious, the whites of his eyes showing, not recognizing his friend, in words that never rose above a whisper. MacDonald had leaned very close to listen as he described the mechanical knights in armour and the shock of the touch of Rocher's hand on his shoulder. Then, after a second's pause, as though he was seeing new images and thoughts emerging through the mist of pain, he had said, *Beware the Minotaur. It's free. It's free.* The words seemed to float out on his breath so that MacDonald could not be sure if he heard them properly. He had turned to Peaches for confirmation. She was standing back against the wall beside the fire. The flames threw shadows upwards, distorting her features, moulding her pretty face into that of a hideous devil. It was at that precise moment that MacDonald knew that his time was running out.

It would all have been so different if he had never got that letter and never left Scotland in the first place, if he had never gone into that Paris cafe, if he had never seen Peaches, if she had not been so attractive, if the name MacDonald had not been on her rucksack, if she had told him to get lost, if they had gone north instead of south, west instead of east, if they had never got a lift to Grenoble, if the bag they had stolen had contained French francs instead of Deutschmarks, if Divers had not howled in pain and drawn them to Nowhere when they were hopelessly lost, if he had not died.

The crowd in the square murmured appreciatively as the glockenspiel began to play. The colourful figures began to move. A gust of wind ruffled the hairs at the back of his neck. MacDonald finished his beer. It was time to go back.

Buster Grant was pleased with himself. He was taking all the credit for breaking the impasse. He just hoped he was right in accepting Lutzke at face value. He could see no reason for him to lie. He could see no point in it. The West German authorities had reacted with commendable speed and efficiency when he passed on Lutzke's tip-off about the Oktoberfest rendezvous. They did not question its credibility when he insisted it came from an utterly reliable source. They were desperate for some hard information to act on. Dirk Kaspar had been impressed.

'You've been busy Buster,' Kaspar said. 'Do you fancy coming south to witness the end product of your labours?'

'I've never been a field agent, Dirk. I'm strictly management. I would just get in the way.'

'Nonsense, I'm management too. We'll take ringside seats and watch the action unfold.'

It didn't take much to convince Grant that he should go to Munich. His only worry was that nothing at all might happen. If it did, he was keen to see it all for himself. The Germans did not want any outside help to set the trap for the Minotaur. They were relying on their alert forces, Bereitschaftspolizei, backed up by their crack counter-terrorist unit, Grenzschutzgruppe 9. Grant would be the official British observer.

They flew down overnight. The plan was to completely encircle the statue of Bavaria with plain-clothes agents at a radius of one hundred and fifty or two hundred yards. People would be observed and allowed to percolate in and out of the circle until nine, when all those leaving would be quietly taken aside for questioning. If a positive identification was made the circle would close in on the target.

Hidden cameras with night sights had been erected at strategic points so that the darkened steps and the illuminated area around the statue could be observed. Six monitor screens were installed inside the free-standing trailer of an articulated lorry with the Hacker-Pschorr brewery crest on the side standing fifty yards to the south of the steps. A discreet oblong slit had been cut in the canvas side as a vantage point for two pairs of powerful binoculars on tripods. Access was at the rear, concealed by a tent pitched behind the pony-rides stall. Another six monitor screens and a communications centre were contained in a large van alongside the tent. Grant and Kaspar had reserved positions inside the trailer.

Kaspar had been called away twenty minutes ago leaving his cardboard plate of Leberknödel and Sauerkraut to get cold. Grant ate his meal and sipped at the glass of Spezi. In front of him two engineers were fiddling with the controls. On one of the screens the picture zoomed in on Bavaria's imposing face. People could be seen crawling like maggots inside her head. Another screen took in the whole flight of steps. There must have been more than one hundred people scattered up and down them.

Kaspar returned, ducking under the flap at the tail, followed by a uniformed police inspector and the GSG-9 commander in jeans and Oktoberfest tee-shirt. He was in overall operational control. Grant had been introduced but had already forgotten their names.

'Steinmetz is on the move, Buster,' Kaspar said.

Grant felt a surge of confidence.

'He has just boarded a flight from Basle in Switzerland accompanied by an unidentified woman. The flight is to Paris.'

'Paris? But he's going in the wrong direction.' The confidence he had felt evaporated.

'It could be a deliberate move to try and fool us,' Kaspar said. 'There is no reason why Steinmetz should expose himself to unnecessary risk. He will have plenty of foot-soldiers to carry out his orders.'

'Of course he will.'

'There is something else you should know, Buster.' He gave

Grant a copy of that morning's *Süddeutsche Zeitung*. 'The story there at the bottom of the front page, about the murder. It has relevance for us.'

Grant read it through quickly. 'Nasty,' he said. 'What is the relevance?'

'The police found Gudrun Richter's fingerprints all over the flat where these two people were murdered.'

'Gudrun Richter? But you said . . . '

'I can't explain it. Last night at the exact time of these murders she was sitting at the window of her Frankfurt flat, knitting. The surveillance team swear to it. But then, we have her fingerprints.'

'She can't have been in two places at once.'

Kaspar's silver hair shone in the electronic glow from the monitor screens. He held his arms out in a gesture of incomprehension. 'We're going to take her in for questioning.'

'It should be interesting to hear her answers,' Grant looked down at the paper again. 'This Rocher was into pornography. She was never involved in anything like that was she?'

'Not as far as we know but Helmut Rocher was more than a blue-movie maker. He sometimes worked as a middle-man for arms dealers; small-time stuff mostly, just oiling the wheels, setting up meetings, things like that.'

'Setting up meetings,' Grant echoed.

Kaspar nodded wisely. 'Exactly. Just like tonight's exchange. And the woman who was murdered is interesting too. One of Rocher's more recently-acquired actresses, known here as Eva Fischer, allegedly from Vienna but her Austrian identity was a front. Her real name was Gretchen Pfaff, an employee of Haupt Verwaltung Aufklärung, the East German intelligence service.'

'So our friends on the other side were watching Herr Rocher.' Now Grant knew where Lutzke had got his information.

'It would appear so. Unless, of course, he was working with them willingly. But I doubt it. The HVA may have been after the archive of compromising films of influential civil servants he is said to have built up. It is a persistent rumour that refuses to go away, our people down here tell me. We checked him out ourselves at the beginning of the year. Nothing,'

'Any link between Steinmetz and this Rocher character?'

'It is believed Rocher has worked for him in the past. No court would accept the evidence though.'

Grant rubbed his forehead to ease the tension headache that was settling over his eyes. Gudrun Richter in Munich. Manfred Steinmetz linked with a man perhaps murdered by her just last night. His confidence had returned. He looked up and smiled at Kaspar.

'I don't know what it all means, Dirk, except that maybe we're in the right place after all'.

The small patch of grass beside the children's playground, not far from the Hacker Keller, was on a mound a few hundred yards from the main entrance to Theresienwiese hidden behind a row of trees and bushes. The raucous music from the fairground was clearly audible. MacDonald stepped over the low rail marking the edge of the concrete pathway. He took the Minotaur off his back and balanced the rucksack against the trunk of a young tree. Peaches threw her arms round him and kissed him on the lips. He pushed her away. It was hardly surprising that he was agitated and nervous, she thought. He had been the same all day. Now there were only thirty minutes left before the appointed time.

'Be careful darling,' she said, holding onto his hand until the very last minute.

'Don't worry, Peaches baby,' he said as he walked away. 'I'll be back soon.'

Peaches sat down beside the Minotaur, her back to the tree. The path was brightly lit and the grass round her was a deep emerald green. It was relatively quiet compared to the main routes down to the Oktoberfest. Small groups of people strolled past, and couples, and individuals. A few of them glanced at her curiously, but most took no notice at all. It was a dry, warm evening. She was dressed in jeans and tee-shirt. She was a foreign tourist waiting for a friend. Nothing out of the ordinary in that. A pair of policemen walked past. One smiled down at her. She forced herself to smile back.

She and MacDonald had walked all the way from the campsite. She had formulated the whole plan and selected this spot for herself. MacDonald would make contact at the statue and make Rocher come back alone for the exchange. She did not like the idea of doing business at the statue. Rocher had had too long to prepare a trap there. They needed to be on their own territory. MacDonald had wanted to bring the rifles but she had talked him out of that. They would have had to wear coats to conceal them and it was too warm to wear overcoats. They were unarmed. The Minotaur was the only weapon they had with them. She reached out, without looking, to touch it.

The policemen were walking back along the path. They smiled at her again, coming closer. Peaches felt a sudden cold chill spread through her bones. One stepped over the rail, holding the holster of his gun against his leg to stop it flapping. He had a fair moustache and a line of smooth scar tissue above one eye stretching up to the hairline and under the rim of his peaked cap. He stood over Peaches, bending forward slightly. His companion was thinner, his cheeks sunken, the bones of his face and neck almost skeletal. He remained on the path with his arms folded.

'Sprechen Sie Deutsch?' the policeman asked.

Peaches almost screamed out loud as his fingers touched the top of the rucksack. The sound died in her throat. Her body tingled. A pulse of blood began to beat at the side of her forehead.

'American?' he said in a pleasant voice. 'American?'

His shadow was over her, pressing down on her, cutting off the heat and the light. She shivered. He tapped the miniature Stars and Stripes sewn onto the rucksack. She understood what he was asking but she could not answer him. Her tongue refused to move.

'Name?' he said, indicating the letters below the flag and pointing at her. 'Name?'

Peaches still could not speak. Her hands began to twitch and she squeezed them together. The pulse of blood tugged at the muscles round her right eye. She felt it tremble. She had the absurd impression that she was winking cheekily. Perhaps they were just trying to chat her up, she thought desperately. European policemen were notorious for it. More than once traffic cops had whistled at her in Paris. She should be nice to them, talk to them, laugh with them. They would go away soon.

'P.C. Macdonald,' the policeman said slowly, struggling with the foreign pronunciation. 'Patricia Chesney Macdonald?'

He knew who she was. He knew her name. The realization caused her to start back. She almost wet herself. Her head struck the tree. They knew who she was. They must have been watching her all the time, waiting for the right moment to move in. They must have seen MacDonald leave her there. They must be after him as well. He might have already been arrested. The elaborate plan had been a complete waste of time. It had never had a chance. They had been watching them all the time.

'Alone?' he asked. 'Yourself?'

Surely they had seen MacDonald with her? But perhaps not. Perhaps they did not know about MacDonald after all. Perhaps it was only her. She did not want to betray him. She could not say she was waiting for a friend. They would want to know who. She could not speak but she nodded her head.

The policeman took hold of her arm. Gently but insistently, he pulled her up onto her feet. He lifted the rucksack from the ground, showing surprise at the weight of it. He said something to the other policeman who stepped over the rail and stood on the other side of Peaches.

'Much heavy,' he said to her, grimacing as he hoisted the rucksack onto one shoulder. 'Lot of things inside.'

She could not reply, she thought her legs were going to give way. They were on either side of her. Each held an elbow. She could not run. It was all over before it had even started.

'You must come with us. We have a car.'

They eased her forward. She did not resist. She tripped on the rail. Their grip tightened, holding her up. Her head was spinning. Her insides churned. The air she breathed was like swallowing ice. The music from the Oktoberfest faded further into the distance as she allowed herself to be led away along the path. They spoke across her in German. She could not understand them and her own thoughts were equally unintelligible to her. She could make no sense of what was happening.

Gudrun Richter felt extremely exposed and vulnerable as she walked through the fairground. All of her senses were acutely tuned. Noises seemed louder, smells more pronounced. It was impossible to avoid contact among the swirling mass of people and each touch was like brushing bare skin against coarse sandpaper. The shawl was pulled tightly round her shoulders. She kept a firm grip on her handbag.

She had been to the statue, had walked up the steps and round the plinth and then back down again. But she didn't want to stay too close. It was too early, and she did not want to remain in one place too long. It was too dangerous. She did not want to attract attention to herself. She had to keep moving. So, she drifted slowly with the crowds between the different stalls, feigning interest in watching the people trying their luck at shooting or dart throwing and other trials of skill. She paid to go into a Hall of Mirrors and saw her face and body distorted out of all proportion and it felt like the same thing was happening to the brain inside her skull.

Loud music waxed and waned as she walked with the never-ending flow of people. Neon lights flashed on and off. Voices bellowed from loudspeakers to compete for customers. The screams of the roller-coaster riders scythed through the night air.

The sights and sounds merged into one continuous roar in her ears. The flashing lights pushed further and further in from the periphery of her vision. But she had control of herself. She knew where she was and what she was doing. She had been walking round in circles for long enough, and could delay no longer. It was time now to head for the meeting place.

Gudrun stared straight ahead. It was like looking down a tunnel and the walls of the tunnel were made up of faces that loomed up before her and rushed past. Laughing faces, curious faces, indifferent faces, leering faces, young faces, old faces, ugly faces, pretty faces, sad faces. But there was never the face she wanted to see. The face of her lover and her tormentor, Hugh Divers. When it did come, she was ready for him.

Joe MacDonald stood at the crossroads in the middle of Theresienwiese and looked up at the illuminated statue of Bavaria. Hordes of people flowed round him in both directions.The light shone wetly on the blue-dark surface of her robes, contrasting sharply with the glaring paleness of the Hall of Fame behind. His intention had been just to look and to walk on, to return to Peaches and tell her that no one had turned up to meet him. Then they could dump the Minotaur somewhere and head south again. They would be no richer but certainly no poorer for the experience.

The statue refused to let him pass. She seemed to beckon him towards her. He was mesmerized by the upraised hand and the blank face which singled him out from all those around him and returned his stare. She was daring him to come to her, just as Peaches was daring him to complete the deal. If he didn't go he would never know if the contact with the money was there waiting for him. Perhaps he was not there. Then the whole thing was a useless academic exercise. Even if he was there it would be simple just to ignore him but it would be interesting to know what he looked like. MacDonald was aware that nobody knew what he looked like. He was perfectly safe, just another anonymous face in the crowd. Nobody would be able to recognize him. He had nothing to lose.

At exactly two minutes to nine he began walking purposefully towards the statue. The angle of the light shining on her face changed as he approached, giving the impression of a welcoming smile. He could see silhouettes gathered round the bottom of the plinth and as he got closer he was able to see that the darkened steps, too, were far from deserted. A Bavarian drinking song blared from loudspeakers among tables placed outside one of the vast beer halls. He recognized the tune as *Wild Rover* and he began to sing the version he knew.

I've been a wild rover for many a year
And I've spent all my money on whisky and beer.
But now I've come home with gold in great store
And ne'er will I play the wild rover no more
And it's no, nay, never . . .

He reached the foot of the steps as the chorus, swollen by the thousands of singers inside, roared lustily from the distant speakers. He started to go up, threading his way through the groups of people, carefully examining every person he passed. It was after nine. His contact should be waiting for him.

I went to an ale-house I used to frequent
And I told the landlady my money was spent.
I asked her for credit; she answered me nay
Saying custom like yours I can get any day
And it's no, nay, never . . .

MacDonald stopped just beyond the half-way point of the steps. He was breathing heavily. Above him, at the top level, he could see the shapes of people stuck like cheap colour transfers on the floodlit background of the statue's plinth. Now that he was so close he could make out every detail of their clothes and their faces. In front was a thin photographer wearing torn jeans and a straggly beard. He had his camera on a tripod and was taking long-exposure pictures of Wies'n. Behind him there was a gang of sleepy teenage boys who had drunk too much and were spread out over one corner of the tiers leading up to the vertical wall. Beside them a fat man in baggy shorts and open-necked shirt sat with his elbows digging into his knees and his chin cupped in his hands. There was a courting couple with the girl's face hidden in the boy's long hair, and two middle-aged women writing postcards. An older man was asleep, using the surface of the highest tier as a pillow. His wife beside him was dangling some kind of animal puppet between her legs, making it jump and dance. The only one who looked as if she was waiting for anybody was the attractive woman in a red dress and white jacket with a white ribbon in her jet-black hair. Lucky man whoever it was, MacDonald thought.

There was no one who looked suspicious, no one reading a newspaper, no one with a bag full of money. MacDonald continued to climb more slowly. He felt slightly drunk. Maybe he would be able to tell Peaches the truth after all.

He reached the top of the steps. The woman in the white jacket studied him closely and then looked away. She seemed to be nervous. Her fingers were drumming silently on her handbag. There was a faraway, haunted look in her eyes. She must have been stood up, MacDonald thought. Any other time he would have been tempted to pick her up himself but not tonight.

He turned and looked out over the bustling fairground for a few seconds and then turned again. He walked towards the woman and past her, going round behind the huge plinth. There were a few other people scattered about in the shadows. MacDonald came round the other side into the field of the floodlights again. Nothing had changed. No one had moved. He looked at his watch. It was quarter past nine. The contact had not shown. The deal was off. The world was a safer place for him. He rubbed his mouth with a hand to hide his spontaneous smile of relief and started down the steps again.

It was crowded in the command trailer. The row of tungsten bulbs strung from the ceiling gave off as much heat as they did light. The heat, added to the stale air permeated with cigarette smoke, made the whole interior intensely uncomfortable. The ventilation was very poor. The light reflected from the monitor screens made the pictures there difficult to observe easily. But it was too late to change the set-up now. There had been a flurry of excitement. Things had begun to happen.

Buster Grant screwed up his eyes and tried to decide if the face on the screen in front of him did belong to Gudrun Richer as Dirk Kaspar claimed. There was a definite similarity despite the colour of the hair. Grant cocked his head to one side and the white glare thrown by the bulbs immediately obscured half of the picture.

'It is her, isn't it?' Kaspar demanded urgently.

'It looks like her,' Grant conceded, pulling the sweat-drenched material of his shirt away from where it was stuck to the skin at the small of his back.

'Here, take a look through the binoculars, Buster. You must see it. It is her, I tell you.'

Kaspar had already bent his tall frame down to the eye-pieces of one pair of binoculars mounted on their tripod. A policeman backed away from the second pair and indicated that Grant should move in. He did so. The lenses were already sharply focused on the face at the top of the steps. It was a much clearer image; the black hair, the white ribbon, the staring eyes. He thought back to Frankfurt and the face on the other side of the one-way mirror in the police station. It was

Gudrun all right. It was unmistakably her. He straightened up. Kaspar was looking across at him, waiting for confirmation. Grant nodded.

'I see it but I don't know if I believe it,' he said.

'She seems to be defying reality by being in two places at once.' Kaspar replied. 'She was arrested in Frankfurt two hours ago and now here she is. I don't think I believe it either.'

'What the Hell is going on, Dirk?' Grant asked, experiencing the same sense of foreboding he had felt during his first encounter with her. 'And where the Hell is the Minotaur?'

'I reckon we will find out soon enough. Like you said earlier, Buster, at least we seem to be in the right place and she has walked right into the middle of our little trap.'

'We don't even know whose side she is on yet.'

The smoky atmosphere was making Grant's eyes water. He squeezed them tightly shut and blinked rapidly, then looked through the binoculars again. Gudrun had frightened him in Frankfurt and she frightened him now. He was unaccountably reassured by the knowledge that she did not know he was watching her. She had never even seen him. She did not know that he existed.

Grant was annoyed when another figure entered his field of vision. A blurred face superimposed itself on Gudrun's face. He reached up and made an adjustment so that the nearer face sprang into focus. He was totally unprepared for the shock of recognition that made him jerk forward and knock over the tripod. He hurriedly reset it and refocused the binoculars. His heart hammered painfully inside his rib cage as he remembered Joe MacDonald's photograph in the file on his desk in Bonn. My God, he thought, you and Divers did keep the team going.

'What is it Buster? What's the matter?' Kaspar asked.

'That man who has just arrived at the top of the steps, I've seen him somewhere before.'

'Where? Who is he?'

'I'm not sure,' Grant said, instantly deciding to withhold the details of what he knew until later. 'But he has some connection with Divers. I've seen that face before.'

'He could be the delivery man,' Kaspar suggested. 'Look. Look. He is going over to her. Look.'

They watched as MacDonald walked right up to Gudrun.

She appeared to ignore him but there was the smallest pause on MacDonald's part as he drew level with her. A movement of the eyes, an incline of the head, perhaps a whispered word. Some form of secret signal seemed to pass between them. Then he was past and out of sight behind the statue.

Grant and Kaspar left the binoculars and ran to the monitors. The one in the bottom right-hand corner of the bank of six showed the area to the rear of the statue. The poorer quality of the light meant that the figure was little more than a moving shadow as it went slowly across the screen.

'MacDonald is his name,' Grant said, resigned to being blamed for not acting on the information when he first received it. 'He was in the army with Divers. I've seen his face in the records.'

MacDonald emerged onto all three brightly-lit monitor screens on the top row. He hesitated briefly and then began to descend the steps. He became a ghostly image on the two monitors on the bottom row receiving pictures from the night-sight cameras. He moved down through the other scattered bodies.

'He could be going to collect the Minotaur,' Kaspar said in a shouted whisper. 'Let him through the circle. Follow him.'

Kaspar's instructions were repeated. The trailer rocked as some men rushed out. A radio crackled acknowledgment. MacDonald disappeared from the screens altogether.

'Have we got him?' Grant asked simply.

Kaspar listened to the incoming messages on the radio. 'We're with him,' he said finally. 'He can take us wherever he likes now.'

Grant returned to the binoculars and readjusted the focus until he could see Gudrun clearly again. She had not moved. She just stood there waiting and staring back at him.

MacDonald did not look back once as he walked quickly to join the crowds funnelling up and down the avenue of the Theresienwiese fairground. He whistled in time to the music of the constantly-changing tunes as he headed for the main entrance and exit gate. He was relieved and delighted that he had gone to look and there had been no one to meet him at the statue. He wouldn't have to lie to Peaches now. There had been no contact, no money, no prospect of a deal. He was in the clear.

As he walked he thought he could hear his own, individual footsteps tap, tapping on the tarmac above all the other raucous sounds. He also thought he could hear other footsteps following behind. He looked back over his shoulder and saw hundreds of anonymous faces bearing down on him. Don't get paranoid, he told himself. There was no one following him because no one knew who he was or what he looked like. He was safe. They could get rid of the Minotaur now and go back on the road as if nothing had happened. The money wasn't really important anyway. You can't miss what you've never had.

He passed under the tall archway and weaved his way around the ranks of taxis parked on the road outside. A policeman was holding up traffic at the junction to let people cross the road. MacDonald glanced back over his shoulder again and shook his head at his own stupidity. He crossed over the central tram lines and over the opposite carriageway to the far pavement and then up the slope into the cover of the bushes and trees on the small hill.

He was surprised he could not see Peaches when he reached the top of the slope. The surprise turned to apprehension and then to outright fear as he went round the pathway skirting the patch of grass. The sound of his footsteps seemed to grow louder. She was supposed to be there, standing under the tree where he had left her, ready with the Minotaur. That was the plan. That was what was supposed to happen. Yet she was not there. Where was she? What had happened? He half expected her to emerge like a cartoon character from behind the thin tree trunk, rucksack on her back. Just kidding, she would say. Did you get the money?

MacDonald halted at the spot where he had left Peaches. Looking down at the brightly-lit grass he thought he could make out the indentations where she and the Minotaur had been. His hands shook and he pressed them against his thighs to steady them. She had vanished. He looked round helplessly, not knowing what to do next.

There were suddenly several groups of two or three people loitering in the near vicinity. Before there had been only a few passers-by who had seemed totally innocent. Now the static groups took on a sinister appearance. Perhaps he had been followed from the statue. They seemed to be deliberately avoiding looking in his direction. They shuffled around, talking and lighting cigarettes. But why should they stop there to talk and to smoke? Had they already taken Peaches and now they were going to get him?

He looked from group to group. There were at least ten people in all, strung out round the path and the grass area. There was one way to find out if they were after him. MacDonald lowered himself into a crouching position and ran.

Dirk Kaspar leapt to his feet in the command trailer. Everybody else followed suit making the floor shake.

'Alive,' he screamed into the radio handset. 'We need him alive.'

'What's happened?' Grant shouted above the babble of voices, unable to understand the thick Bavarian accent coming over the radio.

'Our man is running. He must have realized he was being followed.'

'No sign of the Minotaur?'

'None.'

'Oh my God,' Grant said to himself as he pinched the bridge of his nose between finger and thumb.

'Don't worry,' Kaspar said. 'We'll get him.'

Grant turned to the monitor screens. Gudrun Richter was still standing motionless beneath the statue. One camera had zoomed in on her face. It filled one screen. On her lips, a curious half-smile appeared and faded. A breeze ruffled the white ribbon in her hair.

'What about our friend here?' Grant said.

'We've sealed the circle and are ready to move in,' Kaspar replied. 'We'll take Gudrun first.' He turned and spoke into the radio. 'Bring her to me.'

They all watched as the old couple sitting on the tiers of the statue's plinth rose to their feet, drew their guns, and went over to Gudrun. She showed no surprise except for an initial step backwards. The photographer abandoned his equipment and went over to help his colleagues. He searched Gudrun, finding a weapon in her handbag and untying something from her wrist. Other people began to crowd round curiously. More plain-clothes police officers appeared and began to herd them down the steps. Gudrun was the last to be led away. The top row of monitors in the command trailer were emptied of all activity. Grant's own face stared back at him and when he moved his head to the side the white glare of the tungsten lights gradually obscured it, as if it was being covered by drifting snow.

Gudrun Richter was pleased when the two police officers identified themselves and said she was under arrest. She did not notice the guns levelled at her at first, just the moulded ear-pieces they each wore. It was well past nine o'clock. Divers would never have been late, if he had been coming in the first place. She was beginning to think that Rocher must have lied to her about the rendezvous. Now, at least, she knew that he had spoken the truth.

Another policeman came over and searched her. He found the gun in her handbag and she briefly considered using the spring-loaded blade attached to her forearm to cut his throat but she was too late. He had found it and gripped her arm tightly to prevent any sudden movement. She allowed him to remove it without resistance. She allowed herself to be escorted down the steps, her hands deep in the pockets of her jacket. She was neither afraid nor nervous. She didn't really care what happened to her. Not now.

The neon-lit spokes of the giant ferris wheel expanded and contracted as she looked out over the sprawling fairground. The undulations of the roller-coaster were traced in a glowing line against the blackness of the sky. A million other lights flashed and sparkled. Hugh Divers was dead. She realized that now. If he had been alive he would have been there at nine. Punctuality was an obsession with him. If Rocher had lied to her there was always a chance that he was still alive somewhere. But, with the police lying in wait, she now knew that Rocher had spoken the truth.

Gudrun smiled. She was alone. Divers was dead and there

was nothing else she had to do. Just as in Frankfurt when they had shown her pictures of Franz's lifeless body, she felt the beating of her heart change rhythm and the blood beginning to flow more sluggishly in her veins. Her body was hardening all over, becoming as solid and outwardly unyielding as the surface of the huge statue behind her. She was a foreign presence inside a body that functioned mechanically only, safely lodged inside her own skull just like the tourists who climbed the stairs to the very top inside the statue of Bavaria. She had retreated into her mind, looking out from eye sockets that no longer seemed to belong to her. And what she saw was a blaze of whirling coloured lights.

They could not hurt her now. She could live inside herself for ever if need be; untouchable, inviolable. She would answer no questions, tell them nothing. She would never speak another word again.

Joe MacDonald ran. He put the sole of one foot on top of the low rail to give him impetus and pushed off, heading across the grass. He had taken two strides before he heard the first shout. A bullet whirred through the air at the side of his head. The sharp crack of the pistol shot following behind spurred him to move even faster.

MacDonald ran. They yelled at him to stop. The flesh on his back itched furiously where he expected the bullets to strike. They fired again but into the air. He kept running.

He saw someone coming at him from the side, head lowered, charging like a bull. He put out a hand and forced the head down so that the man overbalanced and pitched down onto his face. MacDonald stood on the neck as he launched himself blindly into the wall of bushes. Branches and leaves ripped and slapped at his face as he careered down the slope. He thumped against a tree trunk, winding himself. Then he was out onto the roadway, staggering with the force of the momentum of the downward plunge, losing his footing, converting it into a forward roll from which he came up running again. They were close behind him. He could hear them thrashing through the bushes. A tram was approaching fast from his left, the chain of square window lights straightening as it rounded a slight curve. He dived over the track in front of it, catching a glimpse of the driver's horrified face, hearing the grating, metallic squeal of the brakes. He felt a bang on his ankle just before he landed on the road on the other side.

The passengers watched him as he instantly got to his feet. The policeman controlling the traffic at the junction was staring at him with his hands held up as if in surrender. The people crossing the road had stopped in mid-stride. MacDonald did not hesitate. The tram had come to an abrupt halt, giving him a few extra seconds of advantage over his pursuers. He went straight for the slow-thinking policeman, swinging a punch that broke his nose and knocked him over, kneeling on his stomach, unbuttoning his holster and snatching the gun from it. People round him began to scream. They began to run in all directions. Somebody grabbed his arm. He swung it savagely backwards. The side of his hand connected with a rib-cage, hitting the bone, breaking it.

MacDonald ran. He headed for the entrance to the Oktober-fest. There was safety in numbers. He could lose himself in the mass of people. More shots were fired behind him, the sound of them almost drowned by the loud music. He realized he was limping. He could not feel his ankle. It only slowed him a little. He passed under the archway. The crowds parted in front of him as he barged his way through. He had to keep running, he told himself. As long as he kept running he would be all right. He had to keep running. He was like a shark, if he stopped moving he died.

Somebody tackled him from behind. Arms tightened round his waist and slipped down to his thighs making him fall. His cheek hit the tarmac, stunning him, loosening his teeth. He seemed to bounce to his knees. He twisted, clubbing brutally at the round bald patch on the head below, seeing blood splash outwards in a ring like water being stamped from a puddle. Then he was free and scrambling up, running again. He blundered into a souvenir stall, kicking over a stack of soft toys. They were gaining. He imagined he could hear their footsteps getting closer, their hot breath on the back of his neck. He couldn't run any faster.

He ran into a beer hall. It was the one he and Peaches had been in the day before. He recognized the huge mechanical model of a cow being rotated on a spit above the entrance. The place was seething. The band was playing, people were singing, rocking from side to side in time to the music. The passage-ways were crammed with bodies. There was nowhere to run. He could hear the rumble of the boards outside as his pursuers followed him.

He jumped over the waist-high partition and onto the first row of trestle tables, sending glass Steins crashing to the floor. He bounded across the tables, using them as stepping-stones. He slid on a surface where beer had been spilled, falling sideways into a young woman's lap, feeling his face press briefly against her soft breasts, wondering if he stayed where he was if they would ever find him in the crowd. Then he was up again, still running, the heavy revolver in his hand. He swung it above his head, firing into the roof of the tent.

The band stopped playing in a cacophony of clashing notes. More shouts. More screams. More shots behind him. People close by dived for cover. Others further away stood up and cheered him on.

MacDonald ran. Suddenly he flew. His feet no longer touched anything solid. He was flying through the air. Looking down, well beneath him, he could see the closely-packed tables and the upturned faces. Then he was plunging down into their midst, smashing right through them to lie exhausted and helpless on the hard floor. He was on his back. His legs would not respond when he tried to move them. There was a terrible pain at the bottom of his spine as if it was being squeezed ever tighter between the jaws of a pair of pliers. He coughed and the thick blood that was gathering in his throat sprayed outwards to fall back on his face like drops of warm, gentle rain. His whole body burned. He couldn't run any further. This time he was the hindmost.

He opened his eyes and there was a ring of faces above him, looking down. Mouths moved silently. Hands reached down and touched him. He felt as if he was in a river, caught and borne along by a powerful current, gaining speed by the second. The faces retreated getting smaller and smaller and fainter and fainter. They soared away until they were barely visible, specks on the horizon. Then he went under.

The formica top of the table in front of Peaches MacDonald was pitted and scarred with dozens of cigarette burns. The chair she was sitting on had one short leg which made it rock every time she made the smallest movement. The door was closed but not locked. The shutter was down on the outside of the window. The walls were painted a featureless pale green. The single light bulb hanging from the centre of the ceiling was masked by a spherical shade. Thick patches of dust clung to some areas of the curving sides like the outlines of countries on a globe.

It must have been after midnight. She had been in the room since being brought to the police station. Various people had come in to look at her but no one would tell her what was going on. They would only tell her that her name was listed on an Interpol circular but would not say why. They all seemed to be preoccupied with some emergency that was more important than her. There was the continuous sound of running feet and shouted commands.

She assumed that MacDonald had been picked up as well. They were probably interrogating him at that moment, trying to get him to incriminate himself and her. She remembered his advice if faced with police questioning; just keep your mouth shut. It is the police who have to prove you are involved, he had told her. Let them get on with it. Don't give them any help. So MacDonald would be sitting tight, probably in a room identical to this one, ignoring all the questions they fired at him. She would do the same when it was her turn.

She was surprised at her calm attitude. They had the

Minotaur, of course. There was nothing she could do about that. That was probably proof enough. They had carried it in from the boot of the police car and deposited it behind the main reception desk. They had even given her a numbered ticket and informed her in broken English that she should present it to reclaim the rucksack before she left. It seemed a strange way to act. Perhaps they were testing her in some way, trying to break her by confusing her. Whatever the reason for their little game it would not work. Meanwhile, the Minotaur was ticking away relentlessly on the ground floor, unless they had already disarmed it.

The door opened and a large man in a dark blue suit entered alone. He smiled at her and sat down on the chair opposite. He was in his mid-thirties. There was an air of good-humoured efficiency about him. His brown hair receded sharply from both sides of his forehead leaving a spear-point in the centre. He reached into his briefcase and brought out a clear plastic wallet containing some papers and the passport that had been taken from Peaches on her arrival.

'Patricia Chesney Macdonald,' the man said, reading the name from her passport. She recognized a New England accent. 'My name is Samuel Norris and folks call me Uncle Sam. I am tonight's duty assistant at the US consulate here in Munich. The police have called me in to resolve this little matter. My pleasure, I assure you.'

Peaches folded her arms and looked directly at him. His cheeks were like squirrel pouches and he had no ear lobes. When he wasn't speaking he pinched his lower lip between finger and thumb. He wasn't wearing a wedding band.

'Sorry about the time it took me to get here but the police have got roadblocks all over the city. There was some excitement at the Oktoberfest apparently. They shot down one man in one of the big beer tents and now they are out chasing the rest of the gang.'

The sense of shock was like a huge weight crushing her chest. She struggled to breathe. She rocked on her chair and sat forward. She felt completely hollow inside. When she finally managed to say something the words came out in a high pitched squeak.

'What happened?'

Norris shrugged, seeming not to notice her discomfort. 'Rumour has it the police tried to ambush the gang which stole this nuclear Minotaur. You know what I mean?'

She nodded weakly.

'Things went wrong. There was a shoot-out.' He gave his bottom lip a squeeze as a full stop to the sentence.

'You're sure he's dead?'

'At least one. They shot one right in the middle of a beer tent, in front of thousands of people. Can you imagine it. Shot him dead. It must have been like the gunfight at the OK Corral.'

'Who was it?' she asked so softly she could barely hear herself.

Norris shrugged again. 'Can't say. A foreigner they tell me. A British citizen, according to the bosses here but that is still unofficial. Thank God it wasn't an American or I doubt if I would ever get to my bed tonight.'

Norris laughed and his head nodded backwards and forwards. Peaches looked down at her hands resting in her lap and slowly intertwined her fingers. MacDonald was dead. The short time they had known each other stretched like a lifetime behind her. He had known he was going to die. She had seen it in his eyes the first night they met. She had shut it out of her mind then though and gone along with him. She had loved him deeply after all but she had always known it would not last for all her wild dreams of living happily ever after. Now he was dead and it was over and she accepted it. When it's your turn you have got to go, he would have said. He had been the hindmost in that fleeting moment. She was still running and the prize was that she stayed alive.

Norris cleared his throat to catch her attention. Peaches pressed her hands against her stomach and held back the tears welling up in her eyes. Not completely over, she thought. Not completely.

'You were found just outside the Oktoberfest, weren't you Patricia? I think you may have been the victim of an over-enthusiastic Schandi. You're not a criminal. They had no right to bring you here against your will.'

'They didn't speak much English,' she said in voice that sounded strangely impersonal. 'I couldn't really argue with them.'

'How on earth were you recognized? The Schandi must have a memory like an elephant to recall faces from Interpol lists.'

'He saw my name on my rucksack.'

'Ah, I see. Your name. Patricia, do you know a Dale Farmer?' he asked.

The question threw her. It was totally unexpected. It shocked her more than the fact that MacDonald was dead. She rocked on the chair, trying to make sense of it. The consul was reading a piece of paper from the plastic wallet.

'Dale Farmer is the source of the missing person's report filed with Interpol a few weeks ago. I take it you know him?'

Norris looked over at her, inviting an answer. She almost laughed in his face. She had just realized that if MacDonald was dead they didn't know about the Minotaur. They didn't know they had it downstairs. They didn't know about her connection with it and MacDonald. They had no reason to think there was a connection. She would not be going to prison. She would be free, running free.

It was Dale. Good old dependable Dale, refusing to go away, tracking her down and now riding to her rescue like an old-time chivalrous knight on a white horse. He must have gone to Interpol in Paris and persuaded them that she was a lunatic on the loose, a danger to herself. Every policeman in Europe had her name in his notebook but they didn't know about MacDonald and the Minotaur. And what about MacDonald? What must he have thought when he discovered that she was gone? Did he ever find out?

'You know him?' Norris repeated.

'Of course, I know him. He was a boyfriend,' she said. 'We had an argument in Paris and went our separate ways.'

'Mr Farmer claims that you disappeared in Paris and he was afraid you may have wandered off in a disturbed mental state. Interpol agreed to issue a bulletin on you because of your . . . er . . . your medical history.'

'Mr Farmer and I had a difference of opinion, that is all. My doctors approved my trip to Europe because I was fully recovered from my breakdown. We just fell out . . . '

Peaches burst into tears, suddenly and dramatically. She collapsed forward onto the table and cried in huge sobs that shook her whole body. She did not know if she was weeping with grief at MacDonald's death or relief that the police did not know about her involvement. She heard the chair scraping over the floor as Norris stood up and she felt his hand patting her on the shoulder.

'It's okay, Patricia,' he said awkwardly. 'Don't cry now. I tell you what we'll do. I've got a Paris number as a contact for Mr Farmer. It must be the hotel he is staying at. Would you like to speak to him right now? I'm sure he will want to talk to you even if it is quite late.'

Peaches lifted her head. 'That would be real nice, Mr Norris,' she said between sobs.

'Uncle Sam. Call me Uncle Sam.'

'Uncle Sam,' she said.

He left the room for a few minutes and came back with a telephone. He looked around and found a wall socket and plugged it in before sitting down at the table opposite her again. She had stopped crying and was wiping her eyes dry. He smiled indulgently and winked at her as he punched out the number. 'I know the code for Paris by heart,' he explained. 'I have a friend there.'

So do I, Peaches thought, quickly giving shape to the idea that was growing in her mind. A real friend.

Norris spoke a few words in French and then handed her the receiver. 'They are ringing the extension in his room.'

It rang several times before it was answered. Peaches immediately recognized Dale's voice, deep and slow with sleep.

'Hello Dale,' she said. 'How are tricks?'

'Peaches,' he shouted back, instantly awake. 'Where have you been?'

'Nowhere,' she replied, allowing herself a tiny smile. MacDonald would have enjoyed the joke.

'Where are you now?'

'Munich.'

'In Germany? How did you get there?'

'It's a long story. Why don't you come and get me, Dale?' She hesitated. 'I missed you,' she added.

'Of course I will. Straight away. I'll get a train or a plane. I'll get there just as soon as I can.'

Norris was beaming at her across the table. He nodded approvingly at the happy resolution of the lovers' tiff.

'One thing, Dale.'

'Anything honey.'

'You've got to make love to me when we get back together. I want you to make love to me. No excuses. No nonsense. I want you to promise.'

Norris's jaw dropped open. After a few seconds his cheeks went bright red and he looked down at the floor to hide his embarrassment.

'I promise,' Dale said.

'Cross your heart.'

'Cross my heart.'

'Good,' she sighed. 'Come and get me.'

'Where will I find you?'

'I'll be at . . . ' She looked questioningly at Norris who understood what she wanted immediately. 'Marienplatz, under the glockenspiel,' she repeated after him as he mouthed the words. 'It's easy to find. It's right in the centre of the city. I'll wait there all afternoon.'

'I'll get there just as quick as I can, honey.'

'Hurry please, Dale. I don't like being on my own.'

Norris had regained his composure. He gave her back her passport and replaced his file in his briefcase. Then he took her down the corridor to an office where a uniformed officer sat behind a desk. They had a brief conversation in German while Peaches stood in the doorway. After a few minutes Norris bent down to sign a form. He came across to her and led her away.

'I am now officially responsible for you Patricia, but I trust you. It's not as if you are a criminal after all. Where are you staying in Munich? I'll give you a lift back.'

'At the Thalkirchen camping site. I have a tent there.'

'Ah yes. It's on my way home. I'll go round by the back way to avoid the roadblocks. You are there by yourself?'

'Yes.'

'Young women who look like you look shouldn't travel round by themselves,' he said. 'I don't mean to sound patronizing but it really is asking for trouble.'

'Thanks for the advice Mr Norris. You're right, but Dale will be here tomorrow and he will look after me.'

'Fair enough. Did you have any belongings?'

'Just my rucksack. They gave me this ticket.'

Norris took the ticket and collected the rucksack from behind the reception desk. He remarked on how heavy it was as he carried it to his car and slid it along the back seat. Peaches climbed in the front. She willed him to hurry up as he stood with the driver's door half open talking to some policemen. She was desperate to get back to be alone. When he did get in beside her and started up the engine she pretended to have fallen asleep, sitting with her eyes closed and her head resting on the back of the chair.

'It was a British citizen they shot at the Oktoberfest. A former soldier apparently. They didn't get the Minotaur though. It's still out there somewhere.'

Peaches made no reply. Norris chattered away to himself but after a while they drove in total silence. Her mind would not work. She did not feel grief or pain or misery or even guilt. She could not feel anything at all exept the blood in her veins warming the underside of her skin.

Norris stopped at the Thalkirchen entrance. She said she wanted to walk in to get some fresh air. He helped her pull the rucksack onto her shoulders.

'Take care now,' he said. 'This is my card with the consulate number on it. Ring me if you've any problems. Good luck with the boyfriend.'

She walked into the almost-silent campsite towards their little tent. She expected MacDonald to be lying inside, wrapped in his sleeping bag. He would rise, bleary-eyed, and demand to know where she had been. But he wasn't there. The tent was cold and empty.

She crawled inside and removed the straps so that the Minotaur fell to one side. She pulled the sleeping bags and blankets around her but she could not get comfortable. She turned and put an arm over the Minotaur, rubbing her cheek against it. She raised a leg and put it over. She pulled down the edge of the rucksack to reveal the casing underneath and pressed her lips against the bitter coldness of the metal. The tears came again, large and round, running away from her eyes, leaving river trails down the surface of the Minotaur. She was very tired but she could not let herself fall asleep. She had to get away before it was light.

The white Audi with the rusty wings was parked diagonally across the narrow side-street running parallel to Landsbergerstrasse, blocking it completely. There was only a space of a few feet between its front and rear and the parked cars lining the edge of the kerb. The entire area had been sealed off by police. Only now was the traffic being allowed to run again on the main roads. The immediate vicinity was still cordoned off by untidy rows of uniformed police.

The rear door of the Audi was open and on the back seat was the pale green bulk of the Minotaur. The early morning sunlight was channelled into the street by the tall buildings on either side. It streamed through the grime-streaked windscreen and played around the outlines of the bull's horns symbols painted in vivid red. Lying beside it on a sheet of polythene was the two-foot-long cylindrical shape of the DIP unit with the colour scheme reversed, pale green symbols on a bright red background.

'The car was abandoned here like this early this morning,' Dirk Kaspar said over his shoulder.

Buster Grant peered past him into the back of the car. His head was spinning from lack of sleep and too much drink. He had almost finished the clutch of miniature spirits bottles in the little fridge he had found in his hotel room before Kaspar had come to tell him the good news.

'It was left here just like this,' Kaspar said. 'Obviously we were meant to find it and its contents. Your bomb experts took only a matter of minutes to disarm the thing and we all breathed a collective sigh of relief. They said we had another twelve hours before it was due to go off.'

'Nobody saw anyone leaving the car, I suppose?'

'We haven't found any witnesses yet but we're checking.'

Grant nodded and rubbed his eyes. 'It was nice of them to wrap up all the loose ends for us like this. Why do you think they did it?'

'They probably panicked when MacDonald was shot and Gudrun was arrested. Maybe they think we'll be so glad to get the Minotaur back we won't bother going after them.'

'And will we?'

'Oh yes, but they've got a head start and unless we get some fingerprints or some other evidence from this car we don't have much to work with. We won't be getting any help from Joseph MacDonald and I can't see our old friend Gudrun Richter suddenly becoming very talkative.'

'No, she's a hopeless case. I doubt if we'll even find out whose side she was on. It was a pretty smart switch with her sister up in Frankfurt,' Grant shook his head ruefully. 'It is a pity they shot MacDonald. We might have got the real story from him.'

'They had to stop him when he started shooting back. The shot was aimed at his legs but he slipped at the vital moment and was hit in the back instead. At least that is the official line.' Kaspar laughed. 'You know what they say, if it's got your number on it.'

'We'll never know all the facts now.'

Grant realized he was looking down on the Minotaur on the back seat of the car as he had looked down on MacDonald's dead body in the empty beer hall with the false clouds hanging from the roof, and as he had looked down on Gudrun's impassive face in the bare interrogation room with the glowing orange bar of the electric wall heater burning the side of his face. None of them would reveal their secrets. His head ached and his throat was dry.

'Well, at least we've got the Minotaur back. That's the main thing.' Kaspar said, tossing back a few loose strands of silver hair that had fallen over his eyes. 'If whoever left it for us is on the run now, good luck to them. They could just as easily have left it hidden till it detonated. We would have been blown to atoms and we still wouldn't have known the full facts.'

'There is that,' Grant agreed.

'So let's be grateful for small mercies and take the credit for all this with a good grace.' Kaspar grinned and put his arm round Grant's shoulder and began to lead him away from the car. 'Come on, Buster, I'll run you back to your hotel. You look as if you could do with a rest.'

'Thanks Dirk.'

'We can all sleep easy in our beds tonight.'

Grant stumbled and then regained his balance. He was so light headed that for a few seconds he could not throw off the feeling that he was falling, tumbling through space. Instinctively he braced himself for the impact but he just seemed to keep falling and falling until his feet touched the ground softly and he found himself walking along beside Kaspar.

It had all been no one's fault, he thought. No one could have stopped it happening. Nothing could have been done to prevent it. It was just one of those things. Bad luck that it had been stolen in the first place. Good luck that it had been returned unused. He laughed with Kaspar.

'A job well done,' he said.

Peaches Macdonald sat cross-legged on the ground with her back against the wall at the base of St Mary's Column in Der Marienplatz. She leaned slightly to one side, resting against her rucksack and wrote on a sheet of paper resting on a magazine balanced on her leg. She had been there for two hours and had already filled half a dozen sheets. It was a sunny day. The square was crowded with tourists casting long, dark shadows.

There is not much more to say, Pop. I've told you just about everything. I guess I'll never know what Joe must have thought when he discovered I was gone. Maybe he thought I had run out on him. I would never have done that. Never in a million years. He should know the truth by now. Maybe he is with you now. I'm sure you two will get along real fine.

She raised her head and looked round. She was beyond tears, using them all up in the few hours she had remained in the tent at the campsite before packing up and leaving before dawn broke. She had left the car and the Minotaur so that they were bound to find them and nobody saw her steal away through the silent streets. There was nothing to connect her with MacDonald, nothing to bring them chasing after her. She was starting another new life. Rubbing her stomach with the flat of one hand she raised the pencil.

Joe did warn me that he didn't come from a long-lived family. But I did have him for a short time, didn't I Pop? I guess I'm going to have to settle for that. It's a whole lot better than never having known him at all. Joe would probably make some comment like, We had a good run for our money.

I was just a seed starting to grow inside Mom when you were killed Pop. Now there is a seed growing inside me. I guess I know now how Mom must have felt when she heard you were dead Pop. I've just got to carry on. I've just got to keep going. I've no choice in the matter. I've got to stay alive for the baby's sake. It has got to have its chance to live. I need somebody to look after me and my baby. Just like Mom did. Things are coming full circle, ain't they Pop? This will be another baby who will never know its real father. I know how Mom must have felt.

I'm just going to sit here now and wait for Dale to come and get me, Pop. He will look after me. Good old Dale. I can rely on him and I can even make him believe that he is the father. I don't know if I will ever tell my baby the truth. We'll see in time.

Well, I guess I get to grow older than you after all Pop. Today I am the exact age in years and days that you were when death tore open the roof of your bunker and gobbled you up. Tomorrow I will be older. I wouldn't have bet on it happening a few days ago but here I am, still in the race. I wonder how long I've got left now. None of us knows just exactly how long we've got to live. Maybe it is just as well.

Peaches signed the letter and straightened all the pages. She read it through carefully, reliving once more all the intense memories of her brief affair with MacDonald. Then she slowly tore the pages into small pieces. She could not hold all the pieces in one clenched fist and had to divide the pile between both hands. She squeezed them as tightly as she could, 'Good-bye Joe,' she whispered softly. 'Be seeing you.'

She looked up and caught a glimpse of Dale standing beside the newspaper kiosk, anxiously scanning the crowds for her. She scrambled to her feet and emptied the handfuls of torn paper into a rubbish bin, scraping the last bits from her sticky palms, then picked up her rucksack and went to get him. It was time to go home.